When I Fall in Love

Center Point
Large Print

Also by Susan May Warren and available from
Center Point Large Print:

The Shadow of Your Smile
My Foolish Heart
You Don't Know Me
Take a Chance on Me

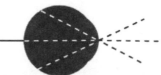

**This Large Print Book carries the
Seal of Approval of N.A.V.H.**

When I Fall in Love

— A Christiansen Family Novel —

Susan May Warren

CENTER POINT LARGE PRINT
THORNDIKE, MAINE

This Center Point Large Print edition is published
in the year 2014 by arrangement with
Tyndale House Publishers, Inc.

Scripture taken or paraphrased from the Holy Bible,
New International Version,® *NIV.*® Copyright © 1973,
1978, 1984, 2011 by Biblica, Inc.® Used by permission
of Zondervan. All rights reserved worldwide.
www.zondervan.com.

When I Fall in Love is a work of fiction. Where real people,
events, establishments, organizations, or locales appear, they
are used fictitiously. All other elements of the novel are
drawn from the author's imagination.

The text of this Large Print edition is unabridged.
In other aspects, this book may vary from the original edition.
Printed in the United States of America on permanent paper.
Set in 16-point Times New Roman type.

ISBN: 978-1-62899-174-1

Library of Congress Cataloging-in-Publication Data

Warren, Susan May, 1966–
When I fall in love : a Christiansen family novel / Susan May Warren.
— Center Point Large Print edition.
pages ; cm
Summary: "Grace must choose between her heart and her head when
she is paired with a pro hockey player at a cooking retreat in Hawaii"—
Provided by publisher.
ISBN 978-1-62899-174-1 (library binding : alk. paper)
1. Women cooks—Fiction. 2. Hockey players—Fiction.
    3. Brothers and sisters—Fiction. 4. Large type books. I. Title.
PS3623.A865W47 2014b
813´.6—dc23
                                                      2014015605

For Your glory, Lord. Every day.

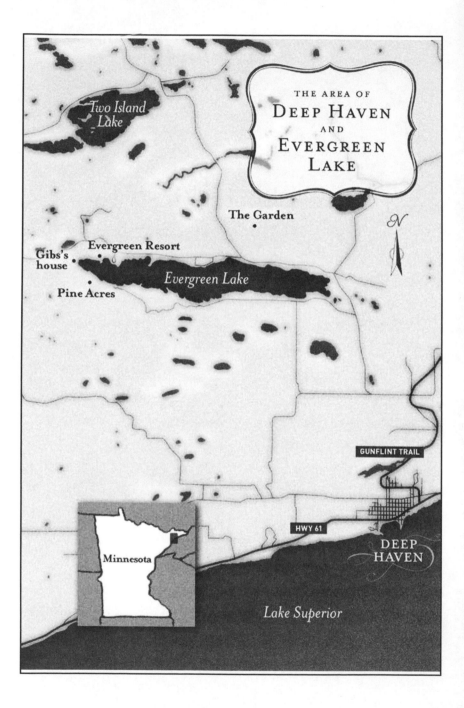

Acknowledgments

Every story has a number of "chefs," and while I might be head chef, I have a crew of talented sous-chefs and assistants in the kitchen, dedicated to the creation of a great story.

My deepest gratitude goes out to the following people:

Aliya Rose Marxen—amazing chef and the brains behind all of Max's and Grace's culinary creations for the Honolulu Chop competition. Her ability to take ingredients and make them into something tasty will win her awards someday. Thank you for making me hungry and for showing me what it looks like to love food and create culinary masterpieces. You are the inspiration behind Grace Christiansen.

Sarah Warren—our family wedding enthusiast and inspiration for Eden's wedding colors and venue. I'm so looking forward to watching you walk down the aisle for your own Memorial Day wedding!

David Warren—my in-house book doctor. Thank you for asking me the hard questions that help me put a plot together.

Noah and Peter Warren—my athletes and inspiration for Max the fun guy in Hawaii. "No, Peter—don't touch that turtle. No, Pete, stop,

stop!" Thank you for giving me the most terrifying moment of my life. At least I could use it in a book.

Andrew Warren—for cooking. You are Max, the master chef.

I'm terribly spoiled.

Rachel Hauck—my brilliant writing partner. Oh, thank you for walking through every scene with me and making me think through every motivation, every action. Our daily conversations inspire me!

The My Book Therapy core team—Beth Vogt, Lisa Jordan, Reba J. Hoffman, Edie Melson, Melissa Tagg, Alena Tauriainen, Michelle Lim. Your daily prayers fueled me and kept me moving all the way to the end. I'm so blessed to have you in my life!

Steve Laube—my awesome agent, who always knows just what to say. I'm so thankful you're on my team.

Karen Watson—for knowing just how to help me craft an amazing story. I'm so thankful for your partnership!

Sarah Mason—for the polish and craft you bring to the editing process. Your talent is fabulous.

My dearest Grace,

All parents, if they look closely at their children, see pieces of themselves. Their eyes, their smile, the shape of their nose. As a child grows older, parents see personality quirks, traces of the same humor, even evidence of similar decision making.

But you, Grace, are my clone. Not just seasoned with my personality traits or even saddled with my nose—you are as if God reached out of heaven and made a copy of myself to put in my arms.

Because of this, I know you probably better than my other children. I understand your fierce loyalty to your family, your so-called "simple" desire to settle in our small town, be a wife, a mother, a homemaker. You were the child who made a party out of everything—from the cookouts you would have with your Barbies and Kens, to our Sunday afternoon football parties, to serving us cookies and hot cocoa in cold arenas as we watched your brothers play hockey. For you, every moment is cause for celebration of the ones you love.

But often I see you eating alone in the kitchen after you have served the event. As if afraid to step into the party.

Afraid to reach for all life has for you.

It is not that you are not courageous. Rather, it is the fear of reaching out to the unknown, unsure if, in doing so, you will fail. You are paralyzed by the knowledge that your regrets would overwhelm you. This, too, I understand, because it also comes from me. I dreamed of a life in Deep Haven, and I feared letting go of it, believing that if I didn't hold tight, I would never have what I'd longed for. But God knows our hearts better than this. He knows our longings, as they are from Him, and He desires to satisfy us with more than we can ask for or imagine.

Oh, Grace, there is so much more waiting for you. Yes, it may be in Deep Haven, but you will never find it by holding on. The amazing, whole, overwhelming, abundant life is found, oddly, by letting go. By living a dangerous faith—the kind of faith that believes in a God who knows our hearts and loves us enough to take our breath away.

The urge, Daughter, to hold on to what you have, to allow fears to hold you captive and keep you from reaching for something else, is not easily overcome. In fact, the nudge to let go may feel like a rending, a tearing from yourself. But it must be done if you are to fall into the arms of your heavenly Father. And this is my prayer for you—that you will leap and fall in this safe place. That you will discover how much more awaits you, just beyond the boundaries of your life.

Reach out, Grace, and discover what you've been longing for.

Lovingly,
Your mother

Chapter 1

It would be the most perfect day of her brother Darek's life. Even if Grace Christiansen had to personally hand-dip two hundred strawberries.

"If you don't leave now, you're going to miss the entire wedding." Her assistant, Raina Beaumont, reached around Grace and moved the bowl of strawberries away from her. "I might not be going to culinary school in a month like you, but I swear I can dip these without making a mess."

But—the word touched her lips a moment before Grace nodded and stepped away from the island in the middle of the industrial kitchen.

The afternoon sun creased the red tile floor and stewed the smells of the kitchen—wild mushrooms simmering in garlic-and-wine sauce, focaccia bread baking in the oven.

She could stand here, close her eyes, drink in the scents, and die happy. Something about seeing her brother—her wounded, broken oldest brother—smile at his beautiful bride-to-be last night at the rehearsal dinner had filled her soul right to the brim. Yes, of course she would dip strawberries and hang twinkly lights from the rafters of the folk school building. Because that's what family did—they shared in dreams, even helped make them come true.

Raina pushed her toward the door. "Seriously, I'll get Ty to chase you out of here or, better yet, throw you over his shoulder and—oh, for pete's sake, you have chocolate on your dress."

"What? Shoot, where's a rag?"

But Raina had already grabbed a wet cloth and was dabbing at the dark stain on the collar of Grace's purple dress.

Grace checked her reflection in the microwave door over Raina's shoulder. Her hair had withstood the test of the kitchen, still caught up in netting. Eden's spectacular idea of having her hair done before she set foot in the kitchen to oversee the final preparations might not have deserved the battle they'd waged. But she shouldn't have worn the dress. Unfortunately, she'd managed that brilliant thought with no help from her big sister, and now she'd have a stained gown for the pictures. . . .

Pictures!

"Oh no."

"I know. It's leaving a greasy spot," Raina said.

"I was supposed to be there an hour early for pictures." Grace pushed Raina's hands away. "Eden is going to murder me."

"I thought this was Ivy and Darek's wedding." Ty looked up from where he stood at the stove, stirring the mushroom sauce. His hairnet looked silly over his dark, nearly shaved head, but no one took his job more seriously than Ty Teague, youngest offspring of the Teague clan. At seventeen, he could outcook any of the Pierre's Pizza line cooks. And he was a starter on the Deep Haven Huskies football team, not unlike his legendary older brother, DJ.

"Ty, eyes on the sauce. And it is; it's just . . . Eden is a little exacting. She has us all scheduled to the minute."

Raina, while listening, had pushed End on the microwave panel, where she'd paused the timer.

Grace stared at the digital clock. "Oh . . . no. What time is it?"

Raina checked her watch. "About 3:20."

"I thought it was 2:07. I'm an idiot—I thought it was weird the clock didn't change. No, no—" She pulled off her apron, heading for the door.

"What?"

"The ceremony started at 3:00!" Grace banged through the door, then spun around and poked her head back into the kitchen. "Listen, fire up the grills at 3:30. Don't turn them on high or they'll smoke—just keep them on low. That way the chicken won't burn. And cook the ravioli al dente. Otherwise it will sit in the sauce and—"

"Go!" Raina glanced at Ty, shaking her head.

"Don't forget the cupcakes! They're in the freezer—"

"Ty, we have a situation—"

"Fine." Grace let the door close behind her and

13

stood for a moment in the most perfect vision of a wedding reception she could imagine.

Her vision. Okay, Ivy's too, but the elegantly rustic room had romance draped all over it. Grace and the rest of the Christiansen women had spent all day yesterday wrapping the timber beams with twinkle lights, covering the long picnic tables with white linens and birch bark–wrapped candles, surrounding the dance floor with potted cedars, also laden with white lights. They'd hung sheer drapes across the length of the room and dropped them behind the serving tables, which, in an hour, would be filled with Grace's creations.

She'd spent a month putting together tonight's menu of grilled lemon-rosemary chicken, wild-mushroom ravioli, parmesan-and-rosemary focaccia, wild-greens salad with buttermilk-Romano dressing, and chocolate-dipped strawberries. Thank-fully, the local donut/cupcake shop, World's Best Donuts, had provided the wedding cupcakes.

But the magic of the night would happen when Darek picked up his bride, Ivy Madison, and carried her into their celebration. No one could be happier for Darek and his new life than Grace. If he could find happily ever after without leaving Deep Haven, then so could she.

First, she had to get to the wedding.

Grace climbed into the family truck and gunned it out of the dirt parking lot of the folk school grounds. The building's sliding-glass doors overlooked the gold-splashed harbor of Deep Haven. With otters frolicking around the docks and seagulls perched to watch the festivities, a sun-soaked breeze blowing off the lake, and the scent of summer in the air, this Sunday evening of Memorial Day weekend held the promise of a beautiful celebration.

She glanced at her phone where she'd left it on the seat of the truck. Five missed calls.

Shoot.

Grace shifted her gaze back to the road in time to slam on her brakes for a couple of tourists, one wearing a baby in a back carrier, crossing the main drag and waving the orange flag provided to alert drivers to pedestrians as they came over the hill.

Easing forward, she made the light, then turned left up the hill to the church. The parking lot was full, music playing as she parked and hustled in.

The sanctuary doors hung closed, an usher standing just inside as she cracked one open. One of Darek's firefighter buddies from the National Forest Service. She gave him a sheepish look as he quirked an eyebrow.

The overhead fans stirred the hushed air and she realized the music had ended and the pastor was praying. Good, maybe she'd arrived just after the processional. She ducked her head but shot a glance at the front, where Ivy and Darek held hands. Beside Ivy stood her matron of honor,

Claire, petite and cute in her turquoise dress, holding Ivy's bouquet of orange gerbera daisies.

Her heart could melt at the sight of Darek in his tuxedo, tall and handsome and healed and giving his heart away. Again. Or maybe fully, for the first time.

"Amen." Pastor Dan lifted his eyes to the crowd, smiled at the couple. Grace looked for a place to scoot down the aisle and slip in at the end of her parents' pew in front. Sure, a few people might notice, but it wasn't as if she'd missed—

"I'd like to present, for the first time, Mr. and Mrs. Darek Christiansen."

Darek looked up, smiled for the crowd, and met her eyes.

Oops.

She stepped out of the way as Ivy and Darek marched up the aisle. Then, before the ushers could open the sanctuary doors again to release the guests, she ducked out.

And caught the bride and groom in an after-ceremony smooch.

"Grace!" Darek said, releasing his bride. He had a grin in his eyes, and she credited Ivy for tempering his anger. "Where were you? We called and called. We finally had to rearrange our pictures—"

"I'm so sorry." She grabbed Ivy's hand, caught for a moment in the radiance of her new sister-in-law. Ivy wore a simple diamond necklace, a strapless taffeta gown, and with her red hair tucked up on her head, she looked like a fairy tale. "You're gorgeous."

"I know," Darek said.

Ivy blushed. "We were worried. Are you okay?"

"I was dipping strawberries and lost track of time—I'm so sorry!"

"That's okay." Ivy leaned in and kissed Grace on the cheek. "I knew I could trust you with an amazing dinner."

The guests had started to spill out of the sanctuary.

"I'm so sorry I missed the wedding—"

But Ivy wasn't listening.

"I'll see you at the reception," Grace said and headed back to the parking lot before Eden could track her down.

Yeah, that wouldn't be pretty.

But soon she'd wow them with her ravioli, impress them with the grilled chicken, stun them with the beautiful dipped strawberries—

I knew I could trust you with an amazing dinner. The Minneapolis Institute of Culinary Arts didn't know what they were missing. Tonight Grace had prepared a dinner that would make everyone forget she never had any formal training. She didn't need cooking school to go places.

And up here, one great party led to word of mouth across the county. She didn't even have to make up business cards.

Grace spied the curl of smoke as she turned onto Main Street. Stomped the gas as she tracked its source.

The folk school.

No.

But her timing was finally perfect as she skidded into the parking lot, right behind the Deep Haven volunteer fire department.

Maxwell Sharpe wasn't going down without a fight.

"Okay, listen, Evan. Your sister isn't doing a good job of blocking around the end, so when I hand the ball off to you, I want you to run straight toward the big oak. Jenness and I will block for you. You just have to outrun a *girl*."

"But, Uncle Max, Lola is older than me, and she's faster. And she hits. And trips. And bites." Evan stared up at him, his blue eyes huge in his head.

Max curled an arm around his seven-year-old second cousin, once removed, although everyone under the age of eighteen was referred to as a nephew or niece, regardless of the official tree ranking. "You don't want to let Uncle Brendon win again, do you? He wins every year. Isn't it time to take him down?" He glanced over to where his older brother huddled with his own cadre of extended relatives, ages six to twelve, ready to draw blood.

Two of Max's linemen had gone in to use the bathroom; only one had emerged. The five-year-old had found a frog and was busy terrorizing one of the toddlers. And his defensive end, nine-year-old Jenness, his secret weapon, lay on the ground staring at the sky, having already whined through the last huddle about her skinned knee.

Where was the fight in the Sharpe family line?

"I'm hungry," Evan started.

"One touchdown, pal. We just need one. Then we'll get lunch."

This put a fire in his nephew's eye, and as his meager team lined up, Max pointed at Brendon. "You're going down."

A moment later, he lay on his back, Lola and three of her cousins on top of him, Brendon laughing. The football Max had lost in the sack. He pushed up, grabbed Lola, and tickled her into the grass, reaching for Daniel and Evan, sandwiching them along with their sister as he gave them wet willies.

"Uncle Max, cut it out!" Jenness jumped on his back, apparently switching sides to protect her generation.

Max heard Brendon laughing behind him, no help at all.

Well, he could pin all his nephews and nieces with the joy swilling through him today. A perfect, blue-skied family picnic; the storm clouds had bumpered their way around the Sharpes'

Wisconsin homestead, hanging just over the horizon but holding back the deluge and allowing the extended family a jolly day of reunion.

He'd spent hours towing one relative after another behind the wakeboarding ski boat that he kept moored at his grandfather's lake place, then took a turn on skis himself, letting Brendon pull him around Diamond Lake.

So he'd shown off, just a little. Max had victory sluicing through his veins after the last two months. Even though the Blue Ox hadn't made it all the way to the Stanley Cup, he'd earned himself a slew of impressive stats as their right wing, and *Hockey Today* magazine planned on running a glossy centerfold feature including him in the "Hot Shots of the Season." They'd even hinted at the cover.

He'd wrapped up the photo shoot in St. Paul yesterday before heading out to the family cabin, where he planned to spend three glorious days before he took off for his annual vacation.

"Max, get your nose out of the grass and fire up the grill. We're starving," Lizzy, Brendon's wife, shouted from the deck, where she held court with Ava, their cute baby daughter, now almost a year old. Their first. And hopefully only.

Max could only take so much dread. They'd all held their breath during Lizzy's pregnancy, waiting for Ava's birth and the test results that would reveal her fate.

Brendon had gotten lucky. Or maybe God had decided Brendon had earned a pass. This time.

In Max's estimation, their family should only push God's providence so far. As for Max, his faith drew the line at putting people he loved in danger. Sure, he believed God could carry him— but he didn't wish that journey on anyone else if he could help it.

He pushed himself off the grass and jogged toward the house, where the older relatives sat at the fire ring. Uncle Ed, who'd lost his wife young, and Aunt Rosie, widowed over twenty years, nursed sweaty lemonades. Rumor was she had a boyfriend, but she hadn't brought him to the family reunion. Too much explaining to do, maybe.

He heard his mother's laughter drifting over the deck above. Probably playing with the baby. And helping with Dad's only remaining sister, Audrey, now confined to a wheelchair, her body gnarled, her brain drifting in and out of the past.

He'd helped his mom pick up Audrey at the nursing home, despite his better judgment. Why bring that reminder to the party? Although maybe that was part of the price of being a Sharpe— dealing with the ugly instead of ignoring it.

"Whatcha got on the menu tonight, son?" Norman, Dad's brother, the only one who'd escaped the curse, gestured him over.

"Shish kebabs. Pork, chicken, and beef.

Marinated them for a day in olive oil, fresh rosemary, oregano, and basil." Max opened the cooler and pulled out sheets of wrapped kebabs, already skewered.

"What's that with 'em?" Ed said, leaning over to survey the offering.

"Squash, zucchini, red onions, basil leaves, green pepper, and mushrooms. But don't worry, Uncle Ed; I have a few burgers tucked away, as well as brats and hot dogs for the less culinary."

"Just because you fly all over the world every summer, cooking in exotic places, don't make you highbrow, son."

"No, but the fact that he helped his team get into the division finals does," Aunt Rosie said. "Your dad would have been so proud of you, Maxie."

He grinned at her, only a little twinge in his chest.

"Where you going this time, kiddo?" Norm asked.

"Hawaii. It's my third year. I can't seem to get the beaches and blue ocean out of my blood."

"Learning to roast a pig?" Ed said. "Now that's my kind of meal."

"I don't think a luau is on the menu. More like sushi and fresh fish, Uncle Ed."

"Shame. Nothin' better than roast pig."

Max tried not to grimace. "If I see any grass skirts and leis, I'll bring them home with me. But I'm mostly going for the education."

"Right," Ed said.

"Leave the boy alone, Edmund." Rosie swatted him. "How long, Max?"

"Three no-stress, sun-filled weeks."

"Well, bring sunscreen with you. A burn is only going to hurt when you put on your hockey pads." She smiled at him, her eyes twinkling.

"Yes, ma'am." He winked, then went over to fire up the grill. He lowered the lid to let it heat up and began setting out the skewers on a tray.

"Hey, Max, remember me?"

He turned at the voice and found it connected to a blonde, all tan legs and mini shorts and a tank top that made him avert his eyes. "Um . . . remind me how we met?"

"Lauren. I'm Lizzy's sister." She switched her Coke to her left hand and extended her right, finding his and holding on longer than she needed to. "I watched some of your games this year. You're amazing on the ice."

He managed a smile and glanced at the grill, untangling his hand to lower the heat. The last thing he needed was to ignite a fire. Out of the corner of his eye, he saw Uncle Ed spying on him. Max turned his back to him. "Thanks. Unfortunately we were shut out against Denver, but hopefully next year we'll bring home the Cup."

"The Cup?"

He noticed the blank look. Probably a football

fan. "The Stanley Cup. It's like the Super Bowl of hockey."

"Right. Lizzy says you have a convertible. Is that yours?" She pointed past him toward the lot, where his Audi sat in the drive.

"Mmm-hmm." He opened the grill and began to lay the skewers on. The grill spit as grease from the meat dripped into the pan. "You might want to stand back."

She giggled.

He glanced up at Lizzy, who was watching him through her sunglasses. If he could, he'd take a skewer and aim it her direction. She knew how he felt about relationships. He wasn't Brendon, wasn't naive, wasn't about to entangle himself with someone he'd only eventually hurt.

He'd seen what his mother went through after his dad died, after all. Thanks, but he couldn't inflict that on anyone.

Even if Lauren did have an overly eager, even pretty, smile. He closed the lid on the grill.

"Maybe you can give me a ride later?"

"Maybe." He saw Brendon heading his direction. "So what do you do for a living?"

"I'm a nurse."

A nurse. Swell. He wanted to ask what Lizzy had told her about him, but he bit it back. No need to start a conversation that would only end in her pity, awkward silences, and maybe some sort of declaration of nonchalance. As if it didn't matter that he would someday die from choking on his own food or even be tempted to take his own life.

"I think your meat is burning," Lauren said.

Smoke billowed from the grill, and he opened the lid. Nice. But so far, dinner survived.

"Max, can I talk to you?" This from Brendon, who appeared behind Lauren, all fun and games vanished from his expression. Now what?

Max had the terrible, unsportsmanlike urge to say no but swallowed it. "Sure."

"Lauren, can you watch the grill?"

"Dude—" Max protested.

But Brendon clamped him on the shoulder and drew him toward the side of the house. Max kept one eye on dinner.

Lauren reached in to turn the skewers.

"Leave them be! They need to char on one side!" Max turned to Brendon. "What?"

"You know what. It's time, Bro. I need you."

It took a second for Max to catch up, and when he did, everything inside him tightened, his breath lodging in his chest. "No—seriously? Look, I know what I said, but I've been thinking and I don't think I can . . ." He blew out a breath. "When did you start having symptoms?"

Brendon stared at him, blank-faced, then, "Wait, no. I'm fine. I promise. Symptom-free."

Max noticed his hands shaking and shoved them into the pockets of his cargo shorts, trying to hide the panic that had crawled up his throat. He wasn't ready. Maybe would never be.

But a promise was a promise, especially between brothers.

"The charity is finally starting to get some traction," Brendon said, motoring right over Max. Over the way his words had rattled him. "We have a number of big donors, and we need a spokesperson. We need you."

Max closed his eyes. "No."

"Bro, you told me that you would help out—be our spokesman, the face, you know?"

"No." Max shook his head, just in case Brendon needed help. "I'm not doing it."

Brendon stared at him, sucker punched. "Why on earth not? You said you would. The Sharpe brothers, changing the face of Huntington's disease. It's what you always wanted."

"Again, *no*." Max glanced at the congregation of family clumped on the deck or around the fire pit and cut his voice low. Not that any of this would be a surprise to them, but if anything could darken this day, it was a reminder of the Sharpe family curse. "It's what *you* always wanted. I wanted to play hockey."

Max turned, but Brendon caught his arm. "I cannot believe you are being this selfish. This disease has claimed too many of our family members. It's going to claim me. And *you*, someday."

"Then maybe we should stop procreating!"

Max wasn't sure where all the volume had come from, but the chatter on the deck above quieted.

His voice turned to a hiss. "I don't want to be known for this disease. I don't want my face to be on your ads. Pretty soon I'll be pitied, not praised. I can't let it define my life."

Brendon looked as if Max had checked him into the boards. "Are you kidding me? It already does! In every important way, it defines you. Tell me the last time you had a girlfriend."

Max looked away, his jaw tight. He glanced at pretty Lauren, at the kebabs. No doubt they were charred, but he couldn't move.

"I'll tell you when—*never*. You live in the here and now, playing hard, living hard, and, buddy, you're going to die alone and sad."

Max set his face, his words harsh. "And you're going to leave behind a wife and a beautiful daughter."

Brendon's shoulders rose and fell. "Yes, I will. But for the precious years I have with them, I'm going to love them with everything inside me. Just like Dad did."

Max's eyes burned, and he hated Brendon a little for that as he turned away. "Yeah, well, you remember him a lot better than I do."

"You remember him just fine. And you know he'd want you to do this. This is his dream for you."

Max rounded on Brendon then, heat in his veins,

his voice. "You're right. I do remember him. I remember that he loved to watch me play hockey. He'd sit in the stands even when his body betrayed him and he couldn't bear to go out in public. When he forgot where he was, and when he couldn't even remember my name. Still, he believed in me. Cheered for me. Wanted life for me, not death."

Now emotion had wrecked his voice, turning it ragged, his eyes burning. "Dad wanted me to play hockey, not be the front man for your useless charity organization." He wiped his hand across his chin and accidently glanced toward the grill.

Lauren was watching him, something pitying and stricken in her expression.

Nice. "I don't need this." He pushed past Brendon, out to the driveway, where he rooted around in his shorts for his keys.

"Max!"

He heard his mother's voice as he reached his Audi. The edge of anger softened at the sight of his petite, generous mother running up to stand next to Brendon, hurt in her eyes.

"I think I'm going to take off, Mom," Max said, not sure she even heard him. But his mom gave him a soft, almost-broken smile. The same one she'd given when Max left home at age sixteen to play in the juniors. The same one she'd offered when Max packed for North Dakota State, and the same expression she'd left him with when

Max moved to St. Paul. "I can't . . . I can't be here."

A knowing, sad smile that understood that Max could never truly face the future. She crossed the distance between them and drew him into her arms. He hung on, just for a moment, and closed his eyes.

"I'm praying for you, Maxie," she whispered.

He nodded, let her go. "I love you, Mom."

Brendon stood at the edge of the yard, hands in his pockets, a hard resolve on his face as Max fired up the car and pulled out of the driveway.

Max looked away. He hadn't reached the end of the road before the clouds finally broke open and poured out tears over the Sharpe family reunion.

If Grace was lucky, no one would miss her. Especially since she'd stolen the cutest bachelor from the dance floor, luring him out under the sprinkle of starlight to tuck him into her embrace. The wind twined through the trees, fragrancing the night with the scent of evergreen. It all conspired to . . . lull him to sleep.

Figured. But six-year-old Tiger, Grace's favorite and only nephew, had endured the long day with the toughness of his breeding. After all, he was a Christiansen, and as ring bearer, Theo "Tiger" Christiansen had important duties. He'd managed to not only hand off the ring to his father, Darek, but also stay clean and even smiling through the entire wedding.

Trouper.

Only at the reception did he start to fade, whining his way through dinner and then stealing one of the cupcakes from the dessert table.

Grace pressed a kiss to his curly blond hair. His lips open against her dress, he'd even left a puddle of drool, dampening the fabric. She loosened his bow tie, drew it off his neck.

If she could, she'd never leave. Everything she wanted, everything she needed, was right here, right now. Even with tonight's near disaster.

Whoever had last used the folk school grill let a hamburger sit on the bottom, charred, yet ready to flame with the next user. Calling in the fire department seemed overkill, but Raina had panicked. They'd doused the grill, saturating Grace's marinated chicken with hose water.

Thankfully, they still had the ravioli, which Ty cooked to perfection. No one seemed to notice the missing chicken after she'd served the strawberries. She hoped.

Music from the local blues band, the Blue Monkeys, drifted out across the dock and the glistening water, mysterious and romantic.

If Grace simply stayed out here, swaddled in the night, babysitting, no one would notice that she hadn't danced once and managed to eat dinner in the kitchen. It seemed a better option than sticking around for small talk.

She had no doubt someone would eventually

ask her about her plans. Inadvertently surface her failures.

Yes, I'd planned to go to culinary school in July, but no, I didn't get in. Which is okay because I like working at Pierre's Pizza.

Really.

Most likely, they'd get stuck on the question "What kind of person gets rejected from cooking school?"

The kind that nearly burned down the folk school building.

She wanted to believe that in His kindness, God had looked down from heaven, seen disaster looming, and saved her from herself. From the dreams of others that said she had to leave Deep Haven to find happiness.

She'd looked around and discovered enough of it right here.

Even with her catering hopes in flames.

"Grace, honey, what are you doing out here? They're getting ready for the toasts."

Grace looked up into the worried face of her mother, Ingrid. She wore a long, flowing lilac sundress and a pair of sandals, her blonde hair short and caught back with a flowered headband. Sometimes Grace could still spot the seventies girl lurking inside her mother.

Ingrid slipped off her sandals and sat on the end of the dock with Grace. "He's so cute when he's sleeping. It's the only time I see him still."

31

"He reminds you of Darek."

"So much. And Casper and Owen. All my boys seemed to charge full speed through life." Ingrid brushed back Tiger's hair. "You did a great job on dinner, honey. Absolutely delicious. You're going to be a magnificent chef."

Grace didn't look at her, opting instead for the canopy of velvet above. "Tonight the stars seem so close you could pluck them from the sky. The vastness of the universe is breathtaking. Even scary."

"And yet, God placed each one of them with purpose."

Grace said nothing. Tiger stirred in her arms, shifting his position.

"Have you thought about when you might be leaving? You need to find a place to live in the Cities, maybe get a part-time job. The summer session starts in a month, doesn't it?"

Shoot. Even her mother.

Across the inky water, the lights from the Coast Guard station dappled the surface of the waves and gleamed against the anchored sailboats. She often wondered how many truly left the harbor to explore the big lake.

A cool wind brushed over the water, raised gooseflesh on her skin.

She took a breath. "I didn't get in."

There. The words didn't sting as much as she'd imagined. In fact, she could taste an odd swirl of relief inside. "I never heard back, so I guess that's a no from them."

Her mother stared at her, frowning. "Are you sure? Have you called them?"

"I'm not calling them, Mom. I'll just sound pitiful. Or desperate." She hitched Tiger up, relieving the pressure from her arm. "The truth is, maybe I don't want to leave Deep Haven."

Ingrid's mouth had pinched to a tight line. Oh no. Grace knew that look.

"Mom, please—I belong here. You and Dad are here, and Tiger." She twirled one of his curly locks around her finger. "I've never been like all my other siblings. I like Deep Haven. I *want* to be here."

"I know, Grace. And a mother never really wants her children to leave home. But she lets them go because she sees how much more is waiting for them. There is more for you than Deep Haven. You need to let yourself discover it."

"Can't you trust me when I say I don't need more?"

Ingrid considered her a long moment, then said, "Let me take Tiger. You're missing the toasts."

She couldn't care less about the toasts. Jensen, Darek's best man, would say something about how their friendship had somehow survived tragedy; then Claire would mention the miracle of Ivy, a former foster child, finally finding a family.

Casper would probably tell some joke about Darek as a child and hint at stealing the bride. Thankfully, they could all count on Eden, the journalist, to say something profound. Amelia, the youngest, would capture each moment with her camera.

And if they all got lucky, her youngest brother, Owen, former hotshot hockey player turned renegade, would put on a smile and try to make them all forget he'd shown up yesterday on a motorcycle, sporting an eye patch for the wedding photos, and informed the clan he was fighting fires with Darek's old outfit, the Jude County Hotshots.

Just in case Mom didn't have enough to worry about.

No, Grace had done her part, and now she just wanted to sit back and watch. Soak in the joy.

But her mother was reaching for Tiger, and what could she do? She surrendered his sleeping body to her mother's embrace and got up, grabbing her flip-flops as she headed down the dock.

She heard her mother behind her, singing to her grandson.

Inside, the Blue Monkeys played a rendition of "Can't Help Falling in Love," and nearly all the guests had emptied onto the dance floor. Darek held Ivy in his arms, caught in her gaze, her smile. Ivy nearly floated in her simple strapless gown with the tiered layers of taffeta. She wore an orange gerbera daisy in her hair, matching her bouquet.

Grace spied Eden and her fiancé, Jace—how could she miss him, really, with his six-foot-four hockey-star frame?—taking up a corner of the floor. Eden twined her arms around Jace's neck, holding on. Casper was making a spectacle in the corner with Amelia, who was laughing at his cornball swing-dancing efforts.

Owen seemed to be absent, as usual. Maybe he'd already left. She hoped he said good-bye this time instead of just sending a postcard from the road.

Grace turned to a table and began stacking plates. Her parents had hired a cleaning crew, but it didn't hurt to start clearing. In fact, she might just head back into the kitchen, do some supervising.

"Grace! Where've you been?" Ivy came up behind her. "We were looking all over for you." She caught her hand. "Come with me."

Good thing Ivy had a firm grip on her hand, because Grace had broken the school record for the hundred-meter dash. "I don't want to dance . . ."

Darek stepped up to the mic as the music died. The congregation on the dance floor stopped, eyes falling on him.

"A round of applause for my sister Grace, who pulled off tonight's delicious dinner." Darek smiled at her as the guests erupted into applause. "Someday she's going to make an amazing chef.

Who knows, maybe she'll even open her own catering business."

Grace smiled, something sharklike, as she looked at Darek. Stop talking, please—

"Maybe she could even cater Jace and Eden's wedding."

She wanted to wince as Eden caught her eye with a dangerous spark of interest.

"Grace, to thank you for your talents tonight, the family put together a little vacation for you. How would you feel about a culinary trip to . . . Hawaii?" He grinned at Ivy, then at Grace.

Hawaii?

Grace waited for Darek to add more as she did the mental math.

Hawaii was two—maybe even three—airplane rides away. One of them across the ocean.

Alone.

Oh no.

She should smile—she knew it. She even tried, but crazy tears filled her eyes. Maybe she could feign shock.

But Darek's smile dimmed and it was all over. "Grace?"

"I . . ." Suddenly everyone was staring, watching. "No . . . I . . ."

Then she was pushing through the crowd, out of the building, and into the night.

What a basket case. But what if she got lost? Or her plane crashed and she had no one to reach out to as . . . ? Just the thought of leaving prickled sweat across her forehead, sent her heart crashing in her chest. She stalked away from the dock, where Ingrid still sat with Tiger, and into the darkness along the shoreline.

It wasn't fast enough to stop Eden from spotting her or running after her. "Grace!"

"I don't want to talk about it!"

But Eden was nothing if not tenacious. Grace heard the sounds of her sister's footfalls behind her, stones scattering on the shore as she ran. "Stop!"

No.

But Eden caught up, touching her arm to stop her. "Grace, what's the matter?"

Hot tears had licked her cheeks, and she didn't bother to wipe them away as she turned to Eden. "I'm sorry. I don't mean to be ungrateful. Really. It's just . . . so far from home."

Eden stood an inch taller and now looked at her, an older-sister concern in her eyes. "No one said you were ungrateful. But we hardly expected you to cry and run from the room. What's the matter?"

"I know." Grace pressed her hands to her wet cheeks. "I'm just being silly."

"You don't want to go to Hawaii?"

"Who doesn't want to go to Hawaii? I mean, it's a wonderful gift."

Eden slid her hand to her sister's. "We thought it would be fun—and you'll get back in time

37

for your summer session to start, I promise."

From ten feet away, she heard, "Eden, everything okay?" Jace's voice, deep and solid and so kind, drifted through the night. Eden had picked a winner with her hockey champion.

"We're good, Jace."

He wasn't moving away, however, and Grace caught a glimpse of him waiting, hands in his pockets, looking up at the stars.

Just in case Eden needed him.

She stared at that picture and a shadow went over her heart.

Everyone had someone. Or something. A future. Plans. Even broken, angry, bereft Owen had figured out how to land on his feet.

Maybe that was it. She didn't even possess the courage to leap. Didn't want to imagine a life beyond Deep Haven.

Yet she looked at Jace standing under the glimmer of the moon, and something inside her broke open, turned raw. Hungry. She *did* want more. A career of her own. A little boy to hold in her arms. And especially a man who might stand in the shadows, close enough to jump in if she needed him.

She could almost taste it welling up inside. Could almost feel the nudge.

There was more waiting for her.

She just didn't want to travel halfway around the world, alone, to find it.

Chapter 2

The Christiansen family stored up happiness like stones on the rocky Lake Superior shore. They shouldn't miss the tiny bit Raina had stolen for herself.

Not exactly stolen, perhaps. In fact, Owen Christiansen had made all the moves. He'd been the one to find her once she'd cleaned up after the wedding and found a lonely pocket of night away from the festivities. She'd been sitting at the end of the dock, letting the crisp waves of the lake nibble at her feet and nursing a glass of root beer as the last song of the night ribboned out into the air.

A perfect night to fall in love.

Owen had picked that moment to appear, almost as if by magic. He'd sat down next to her, and she was a goner.

Yes, she could fall in love with a guy like Owen Christiansen with that dark-blond curly hair, those blue eyes that lured her out of herself, those hockey muscles under his white tuxedo shirt. He'd taken off the jacket and folded the shirtsleeves up over tanned forearms. His tousled hair beckoned for her to touch it, looking spun from gold under the starlight. He appeared a prince, until he donned his eye patch. Then he turned into a bona fide pirate, ready to steal her heart and sail her away with him.

"Whatcha doing?" he'd asked, his voice slow and lazy as if he'd been eyeing her all night. "Are you new in town?"

"My name's Raina. Raina Beaumont."

"Oh, I know a Beaumont—"

"It's my aunt, Liza."

His mouth lifted up to one side, tease in his expression. "The French are invading."

She giggled. "American by birth. But our family hails from Quebec."

If her heart hadn't taken flight by then, it certainly did when he tapped his beer to her glass and said, "French enough. Welcome to town, Raina Beaumont. Can I show you around?"

"No," she said, even though everything inside screamed yes. She hadn't made a lot of friends since she moved to Deep Haven a month ago. Grace Christiansen, yes, but only because they worked at the same pizza parlor.

"Aw, c'mon. I'm harmless." There went the smile again, and she didn't believe him for a millisecond.

"Grace mentioned that she hoped you'd be coming back to town. Said you used to play hockey for the St. Paul Blue Ox?"

His smile dimmed a little, and she vowed not to mention it again. He took a drink, then lifted a shoulder as if shrugging away memories. "I'm a firefighter now with the Jude County Hotshots out of Montana."

A hotshot. Yep, that seemed right.

"How'd you end up working for Grace?"

"I answered her ad in the employee lounge at Pierre's for catering help." She glanced Grace's direction, up the shore to where she'd bolted after her family presented her with their generous gift. "I don't know her that well, but why is she so upset? If I'd been given a trip to Hawaii, I don't think I would have freaked out and run away."

"Yeah, well, Grace hasn't left Deep Haven alone since . . . hmm. Probably since she went to summer camp when she was a kid. She's a homebody. But she wants to be a chef, so we thought it might be a nice gift. Or they did. No one asked me." He said it without emotion, just fact.

"So you're a caterer?"

"Uh . . . actually, I never really worked as a caterer before, but it just seemed like one of those things I could do. I was raised without a mom, had to cook for my brother . . ." Oh, wait. Too much information. See, she did that. Wanted people—Owen—to like her, so her mouth started spilling, babbling even.

She took another sip of root beer. "Your sister is the brains behind the operation, but I helped her plan and shop, and we worked together. I'm hoping she'll hire me again." In fact, by the time tonight rolled around, Raina had felt like they'd

41

formed a kinship, that they had become partners. She felt at least a tad responsible for this night of romance they'd created.

"Darek and Ivy look so happy." She'd stood for a long time watching the couple as they danced. She wondered what that would feel like —to have a man look at her like that. Delight in his eyes, the future in his smile.

Owen picked at the label of his beer. "Yeah. He got lucky—twice, actually. This is his second marriage. His first wife died, left him with Tiger." He looked up, staring across the lake. "Most people don't get second chances like that."

The words settled over the water, washed to shore in the waves. Nope, most people didn't.

She stared at the sky, at the full moon like a spotlight on the water, nearly skimming her toes.

"Want a ride on my motorcycle?"

Raina nodded and he took her hand.

He tooled her around town a bit, then out of Deep Haven, toward Paradise Beach. He'd taken off his eye patch, and she didn't comment about the scars around his eye.

He pulled up, then parked the bike. But before she could get off, he swung a leg over and met her eyes. Something in them stole her breath—a hunger, maybe, or a longing. Then he slid his hand behind her neck and kissed her.

She'd been kissed—and more—before, but this

time felt different. Like this was the kind of guy she could relax around, be herself with. Not like the guys she'd grown up with, where she had to watch her back. Maybe Grace's brother was different. Trustworthy.

The kind of guy a gal could start over with.

When Owen took her in his arms, it felt like that. A new beginning with someone . . . someone who could truly love her, maybe.

She kissed him back, more heartily than she should have, but it soon became the right thing as the stars fell from the sky. He drove her back to Liza's, and that was when she started to make mistakes, especially when he leaned her up against the porch and kissed her again, more ardor in his touch than she had anticipated.

He tasted good, like hot summer nights. And freedom. And happiness.

So Raina invited him in.

She knew better, of course. After all, her aunt Liza slept right upstairs. But she tiptoed inside, opened her bedroom door, and told Owen to slip in before her.

And then she'd fought the guilt, losing herself in his arms.

Now the sun peeked through the slats in the shutters as she lay quietly, listening. Listening to him breathe . . . or . . .

She turned her head. His side of the bed was mussed. Empty.

Then she heard the shower running. Oh. He hadn't left.

She let that thought sink into her as she pulled the covers up to her head. *He hadn't left.* Which meant that maybe he'd stick around today. Maybe he'd take her for another ride on that motorcycle.

Oh no. What if Liza saw his bike out front? Raina slipped out of bed, the wood floor cool against her bare feet. Liza had given her the guest room on the main floor, with the en suite bathroom and access to the tiny sitting porch on the side of the house. Raina pulled back the eyelet curtains and spied the bike across the street, as if he were visiting the neighbors, and remembered him parking it there.

Thank you, Owen. See? Trustworthy.

She reached for her robe, slipped it on. Spied his clothes scattered around the floor. She picked up his dress shoes and set them beside the wicker chair. His pants lay crumpled in a heap, so she folded them, then found his shirt on the back of the wrought-iron bed frame. She pressed it to her nose, inhaling his fragrance. A touch of last night's cologne, the sense of adventure in the wind-scented cotton.

What if he brought her up to the Christiansens' Evergreen Resort, invited her into today's family plans?

The scents of breakfast slid under the door. Bacon, possibly eggs. Aunt Liza would be in the kitchen, wearing a T-shirt and a pair of capris styled with splatters of paint from her pottery studio, her long dark hair tied back.

Her stomach clenched, but she couldn't exactly join Liza at the counter, could she? Not with a guy in her room. When she moved in, she'd practically had to take a blood oath that she'd attend church with her aunt every week—the one caveat to living here rent-free.

No. She'd feign sleeping in and wait until Liza left. Pray—er, hope—that her aunt didn't know the bike outside belonged to Owen.

It wasn't like Raina was going to behave this way again. She'd simply had a moment of weakness or . . . or love. Yes, love.

At least what could be love, someday.

The shower turned off. She heard humming and nearly rested her hand on the door. Instead she glanced in the mirror over the bureau, ran fingers through her hair.

The bathroom door opened. Owen emerged with a towel hitched low around his hips, the hard planes of his athlete's body glistening with the remnants of water.

Raina felt her face heat and glanced away. So she hadn't exactly come to terms with her behavior last night.

"Did you sleep well?" she said.

He advanced into the room, and for a second she thought he'd stop, take her into his arms. But he scooted past her, leaving the fragrance of freshly showered male in his wake, and headed for his clothes. "I gotta run."

"Oh." She didn't look at him, feeling naked as he climbed into his dress pants. "I thought we could have breakfast together."

"I don't do breakfast."

She startled at his tone, something cool and detached in it. Then she slid her hand to the neck of her robe and closed it. "Okay, could we . . . um . . . ? When am I going to see you again?"

She nearly jumped when his hand touched her shoulder, and she looked up at him. Still bare-chested, his wet hair in dark, tantalizing curls around his face. He hadn't shaved, of course, his whiskers blond and ragged across his chin. •

"I had a good time last night, Raina," he said with a smile. "Thanks." He ran his finger along the base of her jaw, then leaned in and kissed her.

Pitiful her, she wanted to lift her arms, tangle them around his neck, but he made no moves to deepen the kiss. To hold on.

In fact, when he pulled away, he winked. "I'll look you up next time I'm in town."

Look her up . . . ? Oh.

She bit her lip, hating the tremble that began inside as she watched him pull on his shirt, button it, then slip into his shoes. It all reeled in front of her as if in slow motion, and a cold realization slid through her.

Then, as if to add to the surreal, raw truth, Aunt Liza knocked on her door. "Raina, sweetie, I'm not sure if you're up, but I left you some eggs and bacon on the stove. I'm heading into work."

Raina froze. Swallowed. "Okay! Thanks! See you tonight."

Owen waited, his eyes hard, saying nothing until the front door closed. Then, "You live with your aunt Liza?"

She nodded, but not before he shook his head, running his fingers through his hair, turning away but not quite stifling a blue word. As Liza pulled out of the driveway in her VW Bug, he moved away from the window.

Hmm. Not quite as cocky as he had been.

But it didn't erase the hurt when he rounded on her. "Sheesh, Raina, you might have mentioned that."

"What?"

"We live in a small town. She knows my parents. If she'd caught us—"

"That's what you're worried about?" She stood there a moment, shaking. "I thought . . . I thought we had something . . ."

"We did." He glanced at the bed, found a smile. "Boy, did we."

If he thanked her again—

"Thanks."

She found his suit jacket, her hands shaking. "Get out."

He frowned. "Why are *you* so upset? I thought you wanted this—"

"Get out!"

"Wow. Okay, fine. Way to turn a good time into something creepy."

Her eyes burned even as she opened her door to him.

Owen strode past her. "Welcome to Deep Haven. I hope you enjoy your stay."

She followed him to the front door, nearly slammed it, and locked it behind him.

Clearly she'd read Owen—and his family— completely wrong. If she never saw another Christiansen man again, it would be too soon.

The thought of sandy beaches should not produce a panic attack. Nor should it make a gal tangle herself in her quilt, staring at the ceiling fan all night.

As if she were slated for execution in the morning.

Now Grace could hear them—the voices of her family drifting up the stairs to the second-floor bedroom she shared with Eden and Amelia—but the thought of turning down their gift kept her glued to her bed.

She was ten again, on the eve of summer camp.

She would simply tell them . . . no. No, she couldn't go, didn't want to go. Thank you, but no.

Grace listened to the shower in the bathroom at

the end of the hall turn off, waited until the door whined open, then propelled herself out of bed.

When all the Christiansens decided to return home, the lineup could take hours. And she had to get this over with.

By the time she grabbed her bathrobe, however, someone else had commandeered the room. She sat in the hallway until the door opened again. Casper walked out, looking freshly shaved, his dark hair in wet curls, wearing a gray *Go Fishing or Go Home* T-shirt over cargo shorts. "All yours."

Grace grabbed a clean towel and emerged twenty minutes later from the small upstairs bathroom. She should get her own apartment, but her parents hadn't exactly kicked her out. And she'd appreciated the opportunity to save for culinary school.

Ha.

She pulled on yoga pants and a T-shirt and padded downstairs. Her mother stood at the granite island counter dressed in a pretty yellow shirt, chopping up an apple, orange slices, and fresh pineapple. She'd shoved almond milk, spinach, and kale into a blender.

"What are you doing?" Grace asked, going around her in search of coffee. She found dregs, still warm, in the bottom of the twelve-cup pot. Glanced at the clock. Apparently the frenzied week before the wedding had finally crept up on her.

"Making a green smoothie. I read about it online."

Grace watched as Ingrid dumped the fruit in on top of the vegetables. "A green smoothie?"

Ingrid slid the lid on, held it, turned the blender on high. Raised her voice. "Yep. I think it's time for us to expand our palates. And eat more whole foods."

Grace pulled out the coffee filters, lifted out the old, and inserted a new one, then measured a new batch of coffee grounds. She spotted Amelia and Eden on the deck. Took a breath. She had to tell them now, before everyone dispersed for the day.

Her mother poured a glass of horrid-looking lime-green froth.

"Mom, no," Grace said as Ingrid handed it to her. "Absolutely not."

"Just try it. Live dangerously."

"I like safe." She turned back to the counter. "Where's the toaster?"

"I put it away to make room for my Vitamix."

"But I like my morning toast."

Ingrid threw more fruit in with a couple handfuls of spinach. "No more toast. We're going green."

"I miss my donuts," Grace said.

"You'll thank me someday."

She followed her mother outside, where the wind meandered through the trees, adding a pine scent to the morning. The promise of blue skies suggested a triumphant Memorial Day. A year ago, the resort would've been full—or maybe Grace should think back further, to the days of her childhood when the parking lot would start filling up every Friday night, to the big bonfires down at the lake, to her mother's chocolate chip cookies and s'mores by the fire.

Now the place seemed almost barren, dormant as new plants struggled for life after last summer's fire. Darek and Casper had managed to construct seven new cabins over the course of this year, and the redolence of sawdust hung in the air. Thankfully, the forest fire had spared the lodge; she wasn't sure where she might have landed if God had taken that from her.

At the picnic table on the deck, Eden paged through a bridal magazine, Amelia looking over her shoulder.

"I like this one—look at that train," Amelia said.

Grace slid onto the bench beside them, glanced at the picture. "Too much tulle."

Butterscotch ran over and shoved her muzzle into Grace's lap. She rubbed the golden retriever mix behind the ears.

Ingrid was pouring out more green smoothie. "Drink up, ladies. It will make you strong and beautiful."

Eden lifted her glass, making the same face Grace had probably made. "Mom—"

Ingrid held up her hand. "Zip it. It's good for you. Time to try new things."

Grace smelled her smoothie. Wrinkled her nose. "No."

"That's the lovely smell of nutrients."

"Not bad," Amelia said, licking her lips. "Tastes like . . . um . . . hmm. What is that taste?"

"Green?" Grace put down the cup. "Listen, I need to talk to you—"

"Not until you have your spinach." Ingrid gave her a strange smile.

"Fine," Grace said, swallowing down the concoction. Not sweet, a little . . . acidic. But not especially bitter. "I might be able to live with this if I get my donut too."

Ingrid rolled her eyes. "Seriously, you need to try new things. Eat more vegetables."

"And go to Hawaii," Eden said quietly.

Oh, shoot. "About that—"

"Make yourself useful." Eden slid another magazine her way. "Find a venue."

Grace opened the magazine—a Minnesota edition of *The Knot*—and started paging through the index. Okay, maybe she'd needed some coffee fortification. "What's this? Finally decided to set a date?"

Eden closed her magazine, something in her grin making Grace nervous. "What?"

"I figured it out. Last night." She touched Grace's arm. "You're going to cater our wedding."

Grace froze. Glanced at Amelia, who apparently agreed because she added a hearty nod.

"No—listen. Ivy's wedding was a small gathering of friends and family. You're marrying Jace Jacobsen, former enforcer for the St. Paul Blue Ox. Future hockey Hall of Famer. You'll have the entire team, not to mention press, there—"

"Shh." Eden leaned in. "Breathe, Grace." She had captured her blonde hair into a messy ponytail and wore a lime-green shirt, capris, her toenails painted a bright . . . green? Grace nearly didn't recognize her uptight sister since Jace popped the question. As if his words had birthed a new, vibrant Eden.

An Eden who'd moved on from Deep Haven. And although Darek had stayed behind to run the resort, he'd certainly turned a page in his life.

Time to try new things. Her mother seemed to be sending her thoughts directly into Grace's brain.

Grace ignored her. "I don't think you want me catering your wedding, Eden. Didn't you see how I nearly set the folk school on fire?"

"Please, Grace. That wasn't your fault. You're an amazing chef—"

"No, I'm not. I know how to follow a recipe, sure, but I'm not a chef."

"But you will be! After your three weeks in Hawaii—"

"A culinary vacation hardly qualifies me to be a caterer."

"It does if we want to have a Hawaiian theme! Isn't that brilliant?"

Uh-oh. But there was no stopping Eden when she had a great idea. Or what she *thought* might be a great idea. Which included meddling in her siblings' lives.

"You can cook us a menu based on what you learn on your Hawaiian vacation."

"Eden—"

"I love that idea," Ingrid said. "A Hawaiian theme."

"Seriously? Hula skirts and leis? That's what you want for your wedding?" Grace said. Amelia grimaced, agreeing with her.

"No, of course not. But tropical, maybe. With passionflowers and orchids? Right?" Eden flipped to a page in the magazine. "Like this. See—it's pretty."

Grace studied a picture of an outdoor venue draped with red, white, and teal curtains, tall orchids arching from milk-glass vases on the seafood-laden tables. And in the middle of it all, a bride and groom clasped hands on a deck, tying the knot in bare feet.

"Did you really set a date?"

"October 21."

"You want to get married in October, barefoot?"

Eden snatched back the magazine. "Hey, you were the one who said you wanted to open a catering company. C'mon, Grace, you could do this. You could cater our wedding, and just think of the contacts you'd have. It's not going to be huge, but you're right; there will be some important people there. This is a chance of a lifetime."

Grace almost reached for it. The *I'm going to culinary school* line she'd been throwing down for the past three years since finishing her online degree. The line that gave her rent-free living, an excuse for extra hours down at Pierre's Pizza, and even kept her friends from setting her up with every stranger who happened through Deep Haven.

I don't have time. I'm leaving. I'm going to culinary school.

But for her mother, she would have brandished it. However, Ingrid just looked at her, one eyebrow up, and Grace said nothing.

Except, wait—"No. Who wants to go on vacation alone? Especially Hawaii." She gave Eden a small, almost-sad grin as if to say, *Oh, what a great idea . . . but even you wouldn't travel alone.*

Well, Eden probably would.

"You won't be going alone. We booked the trip through the Blue Ox travel agency. If you go this summer, you can go with Max Sharpe, Owen's old teammate."

Grace stared at her, a fist in her gut. "You set me up? It's a vacation *date?*"

"What? No. Of course not." Eden frowned at her. "I didn't set you up—"

"It sounds like a setup."

"Well, Max isn't exactly painful to look at. C'mon, you remember him, right?"

"Eden, you're the one who loved hockey. I showed up with cookies. I haven't the faintest idea who may or may not have been on Owen's team."

"He's got short dark hair and pretty brown eyes and—"

"Who has pretty brown eyes?"

Jace had come up on the deck, dressed in faded jeans and a white T-shirt that evidenced he hadn't lost any of his hockey brawn, despite his retirement from professional hockey earlier this year. He set a folded paper on the table. "Hey, a green smoothie." He reached for Eden's glass and Ingrid beamed.

"Max. I was talking about Max Sharpe," Eden said. "Grace thinks we set her up."

Jace put down the cup, swallowed. "No worries there, Grace. Max isn't . . . Well, he's a lot of fun, but he doesn't date. Ever. I'm not sure why, but it feels like he might be one of those guys who prefer to be single." He lifted a shoulder, raising the cup again. "I think he's more committed to his career."

Grace didn't know one hockey player who didn't like a pretty girl on his arm. She searched

Jace's face for guile, but he seemed to be telling the truth. He finished off Eden's smoothie. "Yum."

"You would say that, Popeye." Grace eyed the smoothie, however.

"Grace, go to Hawaii," Ingrid said. "You'll make friends. It'll be fun, I promise."

Grace felt heat flushing her face. "I'm not a kid, Mom. I know how to make friends. It's not that. It's just . . ."

And then her words stopped as everyone looked at her. Waited.

There it was again, the flimsy excuse, on the tip of her tongue. She couldn't look at her mother. "It's a busy time at the restaurant."

"You're staying because you need to make pizza?" Amelia's tone wheedled inside, stung.

Grace's mouth dried, her voice sticking deep in her chest. She wanted to nod or something but couldn't move.

Then—hallelujah—Owen drove up. His motorcycle battered the silence. Everyone turned as he parked his bike just beyond the deck and got off, still wearing his tuxedo from last night.

He lifted two fingers, as in "Peace out," and headed to the house.

It was her mother's expression that unglued Grace's words. The way her worried gaze followed Owen's exit, the cheer draining from her face. The vivid, raw realization that her youngest son just might be destroying his life.

Grace, go to Hawaii. She even felt her mother's eyes on her.

Oh, why not? She glanced at heaven, shot up a tiny prayer. She had no desire to get into this by herself.

"Yeah, okay. I'll go. Why not, right? Live dangerously." Grace reached for her glass.

She could survive three weeks in Hawaii. It wasn't like she was going to prison, after all. It might even be fun.

Grace stared at the smoothie, then lifted it to her mouth and drank it down.

Max just wanted to get the fight with his brother, the game of hockey, and even the pressure of too many fans out of his head and be anonymous for three weeks. Was that so much to ask?

And he might actually succeed if his sister-in-law would let him off the phone. "Won't you come to Ava's first birthday party? Please? I know you and Brendon aren't talking, and it's just killing him."

"Yeah, well, he shouldn't have ambushed me." Max wrapped the towel around his neck, sweat dripping between his shoulder blades, his body still trembling. She'd called him between sets, and he hadn't looked at the caller ID before answering. The Blue Ox training room swam with the smells of off-season conditioning—

sweaty towels, the odor of hard work. Across the room, his goalie, Kalen, lay on the bench press, spotted by a couple trainers.

"He's really sorry, Max. You have to know that. You're so busy, and he didn't want to ask over the phone."

"I called. I left a message. It's on him."

Silence. Then, "He just wants to find a cure."

"Don't we all? But there is no cure for HD, and I'm not going to be the poster boy for pity. Listen, I'll try to make the party, okay?"

"Max—"

He hung up, put the phone on a bench, then went to the pull-up bar and grabbed ahold. Twenty-five pull-ups and he'd call it quits. He didn't want to be sore for culinary school.

Max poured it all out on the ice eleven months of the year, from the Blue Ox summer camp, to training camp, to preseason games and PR events, to photo shoots, to the grueling weekly schedule all the way through play-offs and into the championship. He smiled and gave interviews and conditioned and showed up early for practice and lived and breathed and dreamed hockey.

For one measly month—no, three weeks—he just wanted to cook. Just wanted to enjoy slowing down, creating culinary delicacies, expanding his palate. . . .

Max Sharpe, chef.

He was on twelve when his phone vibrated

again. He let it go until he hit fifteen, then dropped and scooped it up. "Lizzy, listen—"

"Lizzy?"

Oh, Jace. He blew out a breath, testing the impatience roiling through him. Normal or overly sensitive? He schooled his voice into something flat, easy. "Hey, dude. Sorry. I thought you were someone else. You back in town?"

He imagined Jace in his penthouse apartment overlooking the dome of the Minnesota capitol building. Someday he hoped to have his own fancy digs, with views of someplace beautiful. Jace had arrived. It only took him fifteen years.

Max didn't have that long. Ten years, tops, to make the Hall of Fame. To leave a legacy.

"Yep, got back last night. Hey, remember that lead you gave me for the culinary vacation packages?"

"Yep. Great deals. Why?" Max propped the phone against his shoulder, held out his hands. Were they shaking? He couldn't tell. He reached for a bottle of water and unscrewed the lid. No, not shaking, and his grip felt solid.

"I hope you don't mind, but I hooked up Eden's sister Grace with a trip."

"Cool. She'll have a great time. Where is she going?" He lifted the bottle to his mouth, drank.

A pause. "Hawaii. I thought—wait. Aren't you going to Hawaii?"

Max nearly choked. Spitting water out, he coughed.

"You okay, Max?"

"Yeah." He cleared his throat. "Yeah, sure. Uh, Hawaii. Right, I'm going."

"Swell. I told her you'd meet her at the airport—"

"What? Jace, c'mon, dude. I'm on vacation. I don't want to have some fan hanging around me. I'm tired of fans. I'm going there to escape."

"Did I mention she's Eden's sister? She's been around hockey players her whole life. Trust me, the fascination died long ago."

Max sat on the bench, pressing his finger to his pulse to take his heart rate.

"Again, hear me. She's Eden's—and Owen's— sister."

A jump in his pulse there, and Max had no doubt it was due to the flash of memory. Owen, bleeding on the ice. Max, holding the stick that had just crushed his eye. The chaos of the fight still echoing in the frigid night air. Then Owen writhing, screaming.

Owen, whose position Max had filled—some might say stolen—after Owen had to quit hockey. Max, earning accolades meant for the star player from the Christiansen family.

Jace must have read his thoughts, his silence. "She doesn't know, of course."

Because Jace, the only one who really knew, hadn't told her?

Jace read that thought too. "It's between us,

Max. But I'm pulling rank on you here. Grace is . . . well, she's a homebody. According to Eden, she doesn't like to travel by herself. She even got her degree in home ec. Online, believe it or not. So traveling to Hawaii is sort of a big deal."

Nice. A clingy fan afraid of traveling. That would be oh-so-fun.

"She's an amazing cook. She catered a wedding this weekend, and you would have died at the food."

"Awesome." He got up, grabbed his shirt, and headed to the locker room. "This is my *vacation,* Jace. For three weeks I get to be a bum—surf and cook and hang out in the sun. I need this to get my head right, enjoy life a little."

"Enjoy it with Grace. Listen, she's a lot of fun. You'll like her."

"No, *you* listen. I don't care how much fun she is. I have plans. A lot of them."

"Take her with you."

"Parasailing? Cliff-diving?"

Silence.

"I thought so."

"Dude, you owe Owen."

"Now you're just playing dirty."

"If that's what it takes. But I promised Eden you'd keep her safe, make sure she has a good time, and I need you, Max. I'm using my nice voice and I'll even add in *please,* but I'm not really asking."

Max wanted to throw the phone. "Fine. I'll pick her up at the airport. And make sure she gets to the resort. But that's it. After that, she's on her own. That's the best I can do."

Jace went quiet and Max braced himself. Then heard, "Okay. Deal."

"When is she arriving?"

"She's on an early flight tomorrow to LAX, then to Hawaii."

"Okay. Tell her I'll meet her in baggage claim in Honolulu."

"That would be great. I think she's a little queasy about flying, so she'll be glad to know there is someone waiting for her. I'll send you her flight information."

Perfect.

"And, Max? No hanky-panky."

Max hung up on him.

Chapter 3

By the time Max touched down in LAX on his first leg to Hawaii, he'd formed a game plan: find Grace Christiansen and set some ground rules. Like, he'd be glad to make sure she got to class the first day, but he wasn't her tour guide. Wasn't her entertainment. Wasn't her date.

No hanky-panky. Jace's words still burned in his ears. As if he'd fool around with Owen Christiansen's sister. Or anyone.

He wasn't that stupid, wasn't that heartless.

He liked having fun, but not at the expense of everyone's future.

Max hitched his carry-on messenger bag over his shoulder. He'd packed it full of culinary magazines and a political thriller. Just in case the movie on the next flight was something lame, like a Marvel Comics remake. Better to nose into his reading material and set his playlist on a loop for the hop over the ocean.

Vacation started now, regardless of the ball and chain Jace had hooked him up with. Which he planned to shake off as soon as his guilt would allow.

After all, he did owe Owen. The thought never drifted far from his mind, not once over the past five months, so Jace really didn't need to throw it in his face. Still, it didn't mean Max had to saddle himself with some needy tourist for three weeks. The only three weeks where he forgot his life, escaped his tomorrows.

Max stopped at a Starbucks and picked up a latte, then headed to the gate.

He found the waiting area jammed with travelers. People rested their feet on their carry-on bags, some chowing down McChickens, a few standbys checking their flight status. He leaned against a pole and surveyed the group, looking for someone who might resemble Eden, Jace's pretty fiancée. It might have been helpful if Jace had texted a picture along with the flight number—conveniently the same as Max's.

Eden had blonde hair and knew how to carry herself. In fact, in a way, she scared him. It had taken all his courage to call her from the hospital the night of Owen's accident. So if Grace was anything like Eden, she'd be uptight and a little scary. The perfect travel companion.

Or maybe she was the opposite—easygoing, almost reckless. Irresponsible.

That might be worse.

Well, he wasn't going to let Grace Christiansen destroy his vacation, regardless of her persona. He wouldn't be a jerk; he'd just introduce himself and remind her that, although they might be cooking together, the camaraderie ended there. He had a full agenda of surfing, parasailing, snorkeling, hiking, and beach bumming scheduled.

Alone. It was just better that way.

He spied a girl leaning against the wall. Short blonde hair, pretty, wearing green cargo pants, hiking sandals, a tie-dyed scarf around her hair. Maybe in her midtwenties. She seemed put together, in a crunchy-granola kind of way. He knew Grace was a couple years younger than Eden and worked as a chef . . .

Could be her.

He walked closer, just to do a drive-by, glancing at her out of the corner of his eye.

She looked up, away from him, but he caught the glint of something silver. He risked it and waited for her to look back.

A lip ring protruded from her bottom lip. It seemed unlikely for Grace, of the conservative Christiansen family.

He kept moving, glancing at the passengers, his gaze lingering on anyone who might look his age. His eyes fell on a woman sitting at the end of the row, her mouth tight, her blonde hair in a neat ponytail, bangs tucked behind her ears. She wore a jean jacket, a pink shirt underneath, and a pair of white jeans with fancy strappy heels. He guessed her to be an LA girl, maybe heading to Hawaii for a summer break. She crossed her legs, her arms folded, and watched foot traffic as if annoyed.

Apparently sitting with the masses was beneath her. Imagine sitting next to *that* for six hours.

"Excuse me, but are you sitting there?" A woman with brown hair pulled up in a messy bun, wearing low-cut jeans, a red-striped T-shirt, and a pair of Converse tennis shoes, smiled at him. She held an iPod, the buds connected to her ears.

Max looked behind him and realized he had stopped in front of one of the only vacant seats in the area. "No."

"Do you mind?"

He moved, and she sat down. Dropped her

carry-on on the floor with a thud. He'd bet the bank this was Grace. Pretty, put together, even surprisingly friendly. Jace had mentioned she was fun.

"That looks heavy."

"It is. Books. I hate flying, so I like to distract myself." She glanced up at him. Smiled. She didn't look so terrible. Even seemed to be the kind of person who might be just fine on her own, once he settled her in.

Please, please—"I know this sounds strange, but is your name Grace?"

She shook her head. "Sorry."

Too bad. "Okay, thanks."

Max checked his watch and moved to the check-in line the moment they called the flight. Oh, well—the flight was full, and who knew but she'd latch on to him right away. He should probably delay any meeting or suggestion he wanted to hang out.

Better yet, what if she didn't even need him? What if Jace was overreacting?

He'd put money on that last supposition. Jace did have an overactive protector gene. It was what had made him good at his position as team captain. And enforcer.

Max pulled up the boarding pass on his phone and waved it over the scanner at the flight check-in, then headed down the Jetway, greeting the flight attendant before climbing into his seat.

Shoot, he'd wanted an exit row. Or better yct, first class, but he'd opted out of an upgraded ticket in hopes that his flight would bump him up.

He took the window seat, then pulled out a culinary magazine and shoved his bag beneath the seat in front of him.

One by one, passengers filed in past him. He watched them out of the corner of his eye, wondering, calculating. Lip ring girl bumped past, headed toward the back. He spied the brunette a couple rows ahead, climbing into her middle seat.

He plugged in his earbuds and turned on his music. Rascal Flatts came on and he closed his eyes, leaning his head back.

Movement in the seat next to him made him open one eye. Super. Preppy LA girl landed next to him. She'd shoved her bag, a canvas backpack, under the seat in front of her and now folded her hands on her lap, looking straight ahead.

By the set of her jaw, he'd guess she had no intention of making polite seat conversation.

Perfect. No, really, *perfect*. He could escape into his personal entertainment without guilt.

It was the movement of her hands that caught his attention just as he closed his eyes. They shook.

He glanced at her posture out of his peripheral vision. Stiff. Even . . . holding herself together. This wasn't the relaxed annoyance of a frequent traveler.

And her lips were moving. He turned off his music and pulled out one earbud.

Yes, talking. Quietly, as if only to herself. "This is a bad idea. This is a bad idea."

He might agree. "Um, are you okay?"

She startled and looked at him. She had blue eyes, so blue that for a moment, he had the sense of falling. In fact, up close she didn't look quite as snooty. Maybe it was the way her lipstick smudged, just a little, around her mouth, or the coffee stain on her shirt as if she'd stirred the creamer in too vigorously.

She looked away. "Yeah. I'm fine." But her hands continued to shake on her lap.

He had the weird urge to clasp her grip in his. Instead he said, "You don't look okay."

That came out wrong, because she looked at him again, a sort of horror on her face. "Really?"

"I mean, of course, you look fine. But . . . nervous, maybe."

"Oh." She nodded, started a smile, but it vanished before it took root. "Yeah. I . . . don't fly very much. And this is a long flight—over the ocean, no less. I hate flying. Did I mention that? I hate flying. I mean, it's not like I've flown so much as to create a severe aversion to it, but just the concept, you know? Big metal plane in the sky, water below, nothing in between? I'm thinking the entire thing doesn't make sense."

"Not if you put it like that. But it's pure physics and—"

"Don't tell me. I'm going with magic and a lot of prayer to keep us in the sky here."

"Okay." Again, he had the strangest urge to hold her hand. Or distract her. "While you're praying, maybe you could pray that guy up there doesn't take his shoes off." He gestured to the man across the aisle in front of them, who had already leaned his seat back against regulations and pulled out an eye mask and a pair of noise-canceling headphones.

She looked at Max again, this time with quiet fear in her expression. "Why?"

"Because he looks the type to get that comfortable, and my guess is that he's been on a business trip for a few days and hasn't washed those socks."

This produced a tiny smile. "Really?"

"I hope not, but . . . And count your blessings because you could be sitting back there."

She turned her head.

"Don't look!"

She jumped. But cut her voice low. "Why not?"

"Because that poor mother will have everyone staring at her in about twenty minutes when we take off and the baby in her arms erupts into screaming."

"Screaming."

"And wailing. But here's the good news. As

long as you behave yourself, I promise not to take off my shoes or burst into tears. So I'd say, as far as flights go, you're pretty blessed already."

A second smile and this time it stuck. "You're sort of funny, Mr. 9A."

"Thank you, 9B. Now please tell me you brought some reading material because it's a long flight to the beautiful islands of Hawaii."

She winced.

"Okay, how about I let you do my crossword if you promise to leave me at least three blanks at the end?" He handed her his culinary magazine.

"Seriously?"

"I'm just that chivalrous."

"Agreed." She took the magazine and his proffered pen. "You don't mind?"

"Well, I was going to offer to hold your hand, but it might get awkward and a little sweaty, so maybe the crossword is the right fit."

She laughed then, something sweet, like the sound of a puck swishing into a goal, fast and bright and clean.

Again, Max had the sensation of falling, and he actually wrapped his hand around the arm of his chair.

"I'll go with the crossword puzzle," she said, still smiling.

"Good selection, ma'am." He put his earbuds back in. Turned on his music to drown out the pounding of his heart. Good grief, he acted like he'd never spoken to a woman before.

Or maybe just not a woman he didn't, deep down, want to get rid of.

And he'd handed her his crossword puzzle, effectively shutting off more conversation as she bent over and tried to fill in the blanks. He rolled a couple one-liners through his head, trying to figure out how to retrieve the moment.

Or maybe not. Because then what? He'd enjoy her company, maybe share some laughs, and they'd part ways.

Although, wasn't that exactly what he needed? A no-strings, easy, six-hour friendship where he got to be the guy on a plane and nothing else?

He pulled out his earbuds. "Let's start with one down."

Grace just might make it all the way to Hawaii without getting sick. Thankfully, her Dramamine seemed to be holding because so far she'd only experienced one rush of heat, one thickening of her throat and urge to grab the vomit bag in her seat pocket. And that had been on the first flight, before she touched down at LAX.

She'd only *nearly* turned around and bought a ticket for home. Only *sort of* considered it.

Only played the painful conversation of defeat through her head five or six times before she finally found her gate.

If she never flew again, it would be too soon.

Until.

Until the man in the seat next to her turned out to be a gentleman. She'd seen him touring the gate area like a stalker and sized him up then. A big guy, with wide, sculpted shoulders, dark hair trimmed short—military style—and brown eyes that matched the hard-edged look. With his coral necklace, the casual black-and-white jersey shirt, and a pair of faded jeans, she pegged him as a soldier on leave, maybe even Special Forces, a man escaping his high-stress world. He walked with a cool, detached swagger that suggested he knew just how the girls looked at him.

Or maybe he reminded her of a cowboy, minus the boots because he wore flip-flops, appropriate for their destination.

She ignored him after that, trying to keep an eye out for Max Sharpe in case he might be taking the same flight she was across the ocean. She imagined he might have long hair, sport a beard like Owen did during hockey season. Although the season had ended for the Blue Ox a month ago.

She didn't know whether to anticipate annoyance or expectation from Max. Didn't want to consider it. The first thing she'd do when she arrived was let the poor guy off the hook. She didn't need a babysitter. A tour guide.

She was twenty-five years old. She could travel to Hawaii and back by herself. Really.

"One down, c'mon."

She looked over at 9A. He'd surprised her when he leaned forward, leaving behind the brooding soldier and joking with her about the passengers.

" 'Stop, at sea.' Five letters."

He stared at it, frowning. Up close, she noticed that while he might have shaved this morning, he wore an end-of-the-day stubble, something that turned him a little dangerous. And he smelled good. A sort of clean cotton–meets–cologne freshness despite the trapped airplane air.

"Avast!"

She glanced up at him, startled.

"Ahoy, matey. Avast!" He grinned at her, nodded at the crossword.

"Oh, right," she said and tried not to giggle as she wrote it in. But see, she was making friends already. Maybe she'd make more at the culinary school. She didn't need Max Sharpe. Not at all.

"Two down is 'General on Chinese menus,' " she read.

"That's easy—*Tso*."

"Sow?"

"T-S-O."

"Right. I should have thought of that. We don't have Chinese takeout where I live."

"Seriously?"

"It's a small town. We don't even have pizza delivery."

He put his hand over his heart as if in pain. "I'm so very sorry."

"It's okay. I work at a pizza place, so I bring it home."

"Your family must love you."

She lifted a shoulder. "One across. 'Water ring, not gold.'"

He counted the letters. *"Atoll."*

"A what?"

"Atoll. It's a ring-shaped coral reef that encircles a lagoon."

"Wow. You're a fount of crossword information."

He had beautiful eyes. She noticed that, too, when he looked at her and grinned. Crystalline brown, with green at the center, and just staring at them turned her insides all warm.

Or maybe that was the plane jerking through turbulence.

"Oh no." She pressed a hand to her stomach.

"Don't worry; it'll pass."

Grace hoped so.

"Are you okay?"

"I don't travel well. On planes or boats or—I get terribly sick." When she reached for the airsickness bag, he pulled back, his face white. "Sorry."

"No, that's okay." He reached up to hit his call button, but she stopped him.

"Please, don't. I'll be okay. I just need to hold the bag."

"Right." He gave her a smile, but it didn't touch his eyes.

"This is a disaster. I knew it would be. I

shouldn't have come on this stupid trip." She handed him the crossword puzzle. "Thank you, but I think I'm just going to sit here and try not to regret my life."

"Ah, c'mon. It's Hawaii. You'll be fine when you get there."

"No, trust me on this. It's only going to get worse. Like I said, I don't travel well—I never have. When I go someplace by myself, it's always a disaster. I have a terrible time, or I get sick . . . I think I'm just one of those people who should never leave home."

He gave a chuckle and she glanced at him.

"It's not funny. I'm serious. Last time I left home, I got snowed in on the side of the highway. And before that, I visited my sister and got food poisoning from this little Thai place she took me to."

"I love Thai food."

"Me too! That's what made it worse. The fact is, I can't leave home without it turning into a fiasco, and I hate it. I like my small-town life; I don't need more." She should have figured that out instead of letting an impulse lead her down dark—and turbulent—roads.

She closed her eyes, leaned back into the seat, breathing. And now she'd made a fool of herself in front of this nice soldier who probably traveled all over the world.

"Here, drink this."

She opened her eyes to find him cracking open a bottle of water. She took it and noticed her hands shaking.

He twisted the air nozzle, let the air blow over her. She gulped it in, then took a sip of water.

"I'm so sorry. It's . . . I guess I'm nervous. It's not just the flying. Or the fact that I know I'm going to have a terrible time. I'm supposed to meet someone in Hawaii. My sister set me up, and the more I think about it, the worse I feel."

"You have a blind date in Hawaii?"

"No. Yes. I don't know." She pressed the bottle to her forehead and wished it were cold. "I should have said no to the entire thing. But I can't seem to say the word. It's like it's right there on my lips, and yet—nope, it doesn't come out." She shook her head. "And then there's my mom, with her green smoothies and 'live outside the box' encouragement. What if I like the box? She can't accept that. I mean, from the time I was a little kid, I was telling her, 'Mom, I like living at home.' But she couldn't believe me. There I am, ten years old, and she's signing me up for camp, hoping I might love it."

"Camp?"

"Oh yeah. My brother and sister attended, so it must be great, right? I spent the entire week with a stomachache, without a swim buddy, crying myself to sleep."

"I take it you just went the one time."

"No. She made me go again. And again. Until finally they refused to take me. I think the camp director must have called my mother, told her what a fiasco I was."

"I doubt—"

"Trust me on this."

He wore a look of concern that suddenly stilled the whirring in her stomach and cooled the hot flush against her skin. Something about him . . . maybe it was just the freedom of talking to a stranger on a plane . . . but he had a calm, decidedly easy aura about him that allowed her to breathe.

Thank You, Lord, for not putting me next to a jerk.

"The problem is, I'm not sure if my mom is right or if it's just my inability to say no, to stand up for myself. See, I've lived at home my entire life, and everyone seems to think there is more for me, but . . . I don't know. Maybe." She looked at him. "Have you ever felt like there was something more for you, but it seemed just out of reach? Like, you know you want it, but somehow, you're also scared to reach for it? What if, after all this effort, it turns out to be a joke? Or worse— horrible? What if you take the big leap and—?"

"And you fall. And get hurt." His voice emerged small, even tremulous, as if yes, he understood.

"Then you're back where you started, only worse because now you know it's not worth it."

He had stopped smiling, now considered her. "Yeah," he said softly.

"That's what this trip is. Reaching out against my better judgment. And I have this awful feeling I'm going to fall, hard. I'm going to regret getting on this plane."

"Please don't say that so loud."

"Sorry."

He stared at her a long moment, those magical brown eyes holding hers, and she had the uncanny feeling that he might do something crazy like take her hand. But he didn't, just finally took a long breath and smiled. It had the effect of yanking her out of the abyss she seemed to be hurtling toward, his voice kind and even enthusiastic.

"Listen, Hawaii is a blast. There's so much to do. Surfing and snorkeling, parasailing and cliff-diving and turtle watching and beaches . . . not to mention Pearl Harbor and the history of Hawaii. You're going to have a great time. If you didn't already have a travel companion, I'd show you around myself."

"Really?" Oh, she sounded eager. Too eager. It was on the tip of her tongue to say, *Travel companion? What travel companion?*

"Yeah. I'd take you to this restaurant overlooking Waikiki Beach, and we'd watch the bodysurfers as we ate fish tacos. We'd climb Diamond Head and see the crater, take pictures of the view of Honolulu. Watch the surf break.

We'd drive up to the shrimp shacks on the North Shore of the island and then go watch the real surfers on the big waves. On the way home, we'd see if the turtles were still basking on the beaches, maybe take in a sunset."

She rested a hand on her stomach, but the roil inside had started to subside.

"I'd take you to Pearl Harbor—and to the monument, tour the submarine parked there— and then we'd hit a fresh sushi place for some tuna rolls."

"I've never had sushi."

"Oh, you'll love it. It's . . . Well, you have to promise me to have sushi at least once during your stay."

"I . . . Yeah. Maybe."

"That's not a promise."

She tried to give him a smile. "You're very sweet, 9A. But I don't know how much free time I'll have."

He sighed. "I get it. This guy might want you all to himself."

She laughed. "No . . . it's not that kind of . . . meeting. He's just doing my sister a favor. And I'm absolutely mortified. It's like they recruited him to babysit me. I don't need babysitting. In fact, I'm not actually there for a vacation. It's more of a . . . Well, my sister set it up. She wants me to cater her wedding, and she thinks that somehow I'll be inspired."

His smile had vanished, and he seemed to go all stiff, a frown creasing his face. "Um . . . why are you going to Hawaii?"

"I'm attending a culinary school. Three weeks of learning to cook. It was a gift from my family."

Her eyes fell on the magazine in his grip. On the cover, a picture of succulent pasta with summer squash and mushrooms. Then her gaze moved to the bag at his feet, bearing the familiar blue logo of the St. Paul Blue Ox.

Oh no. She saw him then, in her mind's eye, with long brown hair, a beard. A helmet.

Please—"Um . . ."

But he beat her to it. "Is your name Grace Christiansen?"

It was then her stomach decided to clench, roll, and expel the tuna sandwich she'd eaten between flights at LAX.

Oh, how she wanted to say no.

Casper Christiansen had never been the jealous type. He experienced not a hint of envy when big brother, Darek, motored off to Montana to fight fires. Or when Eden moved to the big city of Minneapolis to attend college. He didn't even begrudge Grace her trip to Hawaii.

But seeing Owen pack his motorcycle lit an unfamiliar, searing burn inside Casper. It had grown from an ember to a full-out blaze by the time he'd set down his drill, climbed off the half-finished deck of cabin eight, and stalked up the sawdust path to the parking lot.

"Seriously?"

He couldn't quite manage more than that as Owen looked up with what appeared to be sincere surprise on his face.

"What?"

Now Casper found his voice. "You're leaving? Do you see how much work we have to get done this summer?" He gestured to the twelve cabins, some finished, others with only a frame outlining their future. "You're going to leave Darek and me to finish this alone?"

Owen had the audacity to lift a shoulder. "I'm not a builder."

"Oh, but you're a firefighter?"

Owen shoved a canvas bag into one of his saddlebags. "I guess so."

Casper couldn't quite get his head around this new, dark version of his younger brother that had appeared a week ago for Darek and Ivy's wedding. Owen, it seemed, hadn't shaved since the wedding, his beard sparse with reddish highlights. He wore a blue bandanna on his head, his blond hair curling from the back. That, added to his leather jacket, and Casper suspected he might be going for a tough-guy aura.

He knew the truth. "Bro, I know losing hockey's been rough on you, but consider Mom and Dad. They're trying to get this place put back together—"

"It's a lost cause." Owen turned to him, his eyes cool.

Nope, Casper didn't recognize him in the least.

"Who's going to want to vacation in this moon-scape? Mom and Dad are fooling themselves to think they can rescue this place. Throw it in, Casp. You're only feeding the lie."

Owen turned back, finished strapping the saddlebag. "You should leave too, before this place sucks you in and you can't break free."

"It's not about breaking free, Owen. I have things I want to do too. But it's about responsibility and helping Mom and Dad rebuild."

"Listen, Mom and Dad understand—"

"You think they understand why you came home plastered a couple days ago? And let's not even speculate where you were the night Ivy and Darek got married because I'm pretty sure we won't like where it lands us."

Owen's jaw tightened. "That's my business."

"Not when you live in this town. Not when you're a Christiansen. People are watching, Owen, and guess what, Mom is too. You really hurt her—"

"Leave Mom out of it."

"No, I won't. Because they built something here, and you're walking away from it and humiliating her in the process."

Owen rounded on him. "Yeah, well, I want my own destiny. My own identity. I don't want this." He gestured past Casper to what remained of Evergreen Resort, the still-charred framing of the garage, the cracked and ashy picnic shelter foundation. "I'm leaving, and I'm sorry if Mom gets hurt in the process, but I have to live my own life." He turned his back to Casper.

Casper just barely stopped himself from reaching out, from grabbing Owen back.

Stay calm.

He put as much older and wiser brother into his tone as he could muster. "I promised Darek I'd stick around this summer, help him keep Evergreen on the map. I was counting on you to help us. It's not just rebuilding—it's helping people remember we're not licked. It's about PR, like the annual dragon boat races. We still have a boat in this year's race, and we need you."

Owen let out a laugh, something almost angry. "What, did Darek tell you that?"

In fact, he had. Casper turned his hat around, let the brim shade his eyes. "He asked me to organize it this year. I was counting on you to paddle. We didn't even enter last year, with the fire consuming the county, and we have a comeback story waiting for us. Have you totally forgotten our three years as champions? C'mon— it'll be the Christiansen brothers, paddling home to victory."

He tried to interject memory in his voice, the golden snapshot of him and Darek and Owen crossing the finish line so many years ago, paddles held high.

Yeah, that day he'd felt invincible.

Owen stared at him a long time. Then he laughed. "What happened to you, Casper? You were the one most likely to strike it rich. I used to think you were so cool—a pirate searching for lost treasure. Now you're just . . . Yeah, I'm not sure what you are. A handyman?"

A fist closed around Casper's heart, the memory vanishing.

Owen threw his leg over his bike, grabbed his helmet. "Tell Darek that his pals on the Jude County Hotshots say hi." He started the bike, revved it, then put down his visor.

He raised two fingers a second before he took off out of the driveway.

Casper stood there in the cloud of gravel dust, hating the grit of Owen's words, how it settled deep.

And did nothing to douse the burning inside.

He blew out a breath and turned to head back to the cabin, then opted for the long dock that led to the water. With his mother in town with Tiger, Dad painting inside one of the cabins, and Amelia gone photographing a wedding, the place seemed so lonely.

As if in confirmation, the wind hushed through

the trees and a loon called, mourning across the lake. He sat on the end of the dock, unlacing his work boots. He dipped his feet into the cool, sun-dappled water. The refreshment eased the hot spots, the calluses.

You were the one most likely to strike it rich.

What was he doing here? Casper leaned back on his hands, lifted his face to the sun. He knew the answer—at least why he'd come home. And why he'd stayed.

But . . .

He worked out the square of paper from his back pocket. Unfolded it and smoothed it. Reread it in the sunlight.

Footsteps on the dock, and he didn't have a chance to put the printed e-mail away before a shadow crossed over him.

"I saw Owen leaving as I drove in." Amelia sat down next to him, cross-legged. "I wanted to show him the family shots I got at the wedding. I had them printed." She handed him an envelope. He opened it. Pulled out an eight-by-ten of the entire family, all grouped around Darek and Ivy. Yeah, they looked happy, grinning as they assembled on the boulders along Lake Superior. His parents clasped hands, so much love in their pose.

Not a hint of the struggles of the past year, with the resort, with Owen.

And within himself. He gave the picture back to Amelia.

"What are you reading?"

"Nothing."

She took the paper from his hand. He didn't look at her, didn't want to invite comment.

"Cool. You should do it." She handed the paper back to him. "But where is Roatán?"

Casper wasn't sure why, but his stomach tightened at her encouragement. "It's a little island off Honduras. The lore is that pirates used to bury their treasures there."

"Which is why your buddy Duncan invited you on the dig. Underwater exploration? Isn't that your specialty in your major? Are you going to go?"

"I don't know. It's . . . There's a lot to do here."

"The dig doesn't start until August. You should go. Are you kidding me—five months in the Caribbean? And you'll probably earn credits for your degree."

Like that mattered. He schooled his voice. "I don't know. We have more cabins to build, and I promised Darek I'd run this year's dragon boat for him. We gotta keep the Evergreen spirit alive until we reopen."

"I love the dragon boat festival, but do we have enough for a team?" She flipped through the photos.

"We lost Owen, but we gain Ivy. And there's Dad and Mom, and Nathan Decker and his family, and some others who said they might be up for it."

"You'll figure it out. You always find a way." She got up, shaded her eyes. "By the way, Darek didn't rope you into anything. We both know you're his secret weapon."

"Why's that?" He couldn't help it—he raised his arm and flexed. "It's the guns, isn't it?"

Amelia rolled her eyes. "No, silly. It's because he can count on you to show up. We all can. Think about it. Darek and Owen are bookends—dark and unpredictable. But you're the poster boy for the Christiansen family."

Oh, what she didn't know. He sighed but pasted on a smile.

"I gotta get ready to go. I'm meeting a potential client in town."

He waved his hand as she headed down the dock.

The poster boy.

He stared at the e-mail invitation. Folded it. Threw it into the water.

Chapter 4

Max could stand here forever on his private balcony of the Hokeo Resort, mesmerized by the aqua-blue water, dappled by mysterious coral shadows and shades of rippling sand, and watch as the ocean sent cascade after cascade of frothy white waves to shore in quiet applause.

The sky above stretched to the horizon, so deliciously blue he could taste it, drink in eternity in a quenchless gulp of joy. From here, four stories up, he overlooked the entire rim of Waikiki Beach and the long pier that jutted from shore, where sunbaked ten-year-olds dove from the end for tourist tips and beachcombers pressed divots in the sand, only to be *tsk*ed by the vigilant sea. Catamarans, their tall masts like church spires, moored on the sand, a lure for snorkelers longing to explore the reefs offshore.

Beyond the curve of the beach jutted the dark magnificence of Diamond Head, the dormant volcano. From the jagged rim, a man might too easily mistake himself for an albatross and take flight, to soar over the expanse of blue ocean, the lush rainforest to the northeast, the cobble of skyscrapers of Honolulu, the snorkeling cove of Hanauma Bay, and the bodysurfing beaches on the southeastern shore of Oahu.

The delicate fragrance of plumeria, tuberose, and jasmine, the flowers of the lei that he'd received yesterday upon arrival and that bedecked the lush resort landscaping, sweetened the sultry morning air, but behind the aroma lurked the salty lure of the ocean, the scent of adventure, danger, and mystery.

In truth, the taste of peace rather than the culinary delights lured Max to Hawaii every year. Here, his life quieted, and his inevitable future felt tenable. Hawaii vanquished the bitterness that too easily coated the back of his throat. Freed him to breathe.

It distracted him with the sense that maybe his tomorrows could be rich.

He needed the distraction because Grace's words as he'd dropped her off at her room had chased him into his sleep, all four jet-lagged hours.

You don't have to take care of me, Max. I'll be fine.

She probably would be. Which meant he should be relieved and not gnawed by the fear that she'd miss today's culinary tour. He'd never seen such a vicious case of airsickness, and somehow, over the course of the six-hour flight, his annoyance turned to admiration for her tenacity. For the way she joked through her bouts of nausea. For her determination to finish the crossword puzzle even after her fifth trip to the bathroom. To play through the pain.

Yeah, she had Owen's stubborn athlete genes, and that only made it easier to help her. After all, he owed Owen.

Clearly, however, she didn't know about Max's part in Owen's injury, because when they finally got around to talking hockey and Owen, she seemed less than abreast of the details.

And he certainly wouldn't be the one to reveal how they'd gotten into an after-game, on-ice brawl with a few players from an opposing team. How, in the middle of the fight, he'd accidentally slammed the butt of his stick into Owen's eye socket.

Accidentally. But the fact that he'd filled Owen's position on the first line and ended the season with a personal scoring record stirred the guilt in his gut.

Which was why Max had helped Grace retrieve her luggage and given her a ride in his rental car to the resort. Why he'd helped her to her room and even fetched a bucket of ice, just in case the nausea continued.

He'd done his part, and she was probably right. She could take care of herself. She didn't need a babysitter.

But Jace had failed to mention that his future sister-in-law had eyes that could make a man forget why he was flying to Hawaii in the first place.

Max leaned over the rail, searching for her in the breakfast crowd eating on the veranda. He spied a woman in a floppy beach hat that gave him pause, then decided to scan the crowd in person. He stepped off the balcony into the cool trapped air of his room, his skin prickling against the sudden change, grabbed his sunglasses and a hat, and headed downstairs.

He could live incognito in Hawaii, with his cargo shorts and printed floral shirt. A regular beach bum, although by tomorrow, he'd add a chef's cap and apron.

Today's activities on the school's schedule included a morning tour of the open markets and a tasting of some of the island's best specialties. Kālua pork stands, fresh poke from the seafood market, sweet pineapple, malasadas, baked manapua, and maybe they'd end with a late lunch at one of the many cafés that served loco moco, another island specialty.

Max took the elevator to the open-air lobby, then headed outside to the terrace, where diners ate at teakwood tables. A long buffet of mangos, papaya, passion fruit, kiwi, Hawaiian breads, and fresh and smoked seafood gave guests a taste of Hawaiian breakfast. An omelet chef, however, stood ready at the far end, for those with a more traditional palate.

Max wandered around the terrace, searching for Grace.

"Max! I thought I saw your name on the class list."

Max turned at the voice, smiled. "Keoni. Dude, great to see you." He extended his hand and caught the grip of his favorite Hawaiian chef. "Are you guest teaching this week?"

Keoni wore his hair in a long black ponytail, more surfer than chef with his dark, sea-salted skin. He had probably hit the waves this morning, already found his aloha spirit. He wore his shirt open, his doggers low, and resembled nothing of his accolades as one of the island's most decorated chefs. But only two years ago, Chef Keoni had dived headfirst into a season of *Iron Chef Hawaii* and emerged the winner.

"Absolutely. And scouting talent for this year's Honolulu Chop competition. We're doing a four day cook-off at Honolulu Days. You'd be perfect for it. We want more than locals—we want people who love Hawaii, even if they are haoles."

"Hey, give me three weeks, I'll be as local as you. How's the surf?"

"Junk. All slop. But tomorrow the waves are supposed to be bombin'. Maybe we can catch some after class."

Max's gaze roved around the diners as Keoni talked.

"You'd better land yourself some vittles before the tour leaves." Keoni glanced at his dive watch. "You have about fifteen minutes before we pull out."

"No problem." He clamped Keoni on the shoulder. "Catch ya."

Max stood for a moment on the veranda, watching the breakers offshore, soaking in the heat of the morning. He'd spent too long on the ice, needed the sun to sink some vitamin D into his bones, shore up his body for the next season.

Before he could stop himself, he headed back to

the lobby and hit the up button for the elevator.

He'd just check on Grace, make sure she'd woken up. After all, jet lag could play tricks on a body, especially one as wrung out as Grace's. He wasn't babysitting, just . . . caring. Because of Owen.

He found her room at the end of the hall and knocked. Waited. Knocked again.

He finally heard her shuffling to the door. The bolt clicked and she eased the door open, blinking against the sunlight in the hallway. "Hello?"

"Aloha," he said, probably brighter than he needed to. He schooled his voice. "Uh, you know we leave in fifteen—or maybe ten—minutes, right?"

She opened the door wider, rubbed her eyes. She wore a white T-shirt, and blue-painted toenails poked from the too-long hem of her yoga pants. A black eye mask mashed her hair on top of her head. If he didn't know better, he'd peg her as hungover.

She shook her head and pressed a hand to her stomach. "Uh-oh."

"Do you need to sit down?"

"Maybe." She slid to the floor, bracing the door open with her foot.

He crouched on the other side of the threshold. "Are you still sick?"

"I can't tell." She pulled off the mask. "I don't think so."

"If I say the words *exotic food tour,* how does that make you feel?"

She made a face.

"Right. Okay."

"But—don't worry about me. I'll stay here, lay out in the sun, try to figure out why I said yes to this trip." She closed her eyes, leaned her head against the door.

"You're not going to leave before the fun starts, right?"

"Isn't this the fun?" she said and chased it with a grin. Yeah, Jace had also neglected to mention the smile.

Max answered it with a smile of his own. "I've been on this tour a couple times before, so what do you say we opt out and I take you on your own tour? We'll head up to the North Shore, watch the surfers, then visit the turtles on our way home. And along the way, if you're feeling up to it, we'll stop in at the shrimp trucks."

Her smile dimmed. "No, Max. You're so sweet, but . . . I'm not stupid. On the plane, when you didn't know who I was, you offered to show me around. I realized from your offer to a stranger that you were hoping to *not* have to spend time with me, the girl waiting in Hawaii. I know this is your vacation. And I know how hard you work. So really, I'll just sit this one out and read a book. Be free."

Max couldn't pinpoint why her words stuck a

needle in his chest, why suddenly it seemed as if the buoyant joy of the morning evaporated. Wasn't this what he wanted?

Clearly his mouth wasn't listening to his brain. "Are you sure? It's a gorgeous day."

"Which is why you should be out enjoying it. Go on your tour, Max. Enjoy yourself. I'll be fine."

Absolutely. Of course she would be. And this was exactly what he'd hoped for. "Right. Okay, then. Get well."

"I will. You have fun."

She stood, closed the door.

Have fun. That's why he was here, right?

He took the elevator down, walked outside, and found the group waiting for the Hawaiian Culinary Adventures shuttle near a towering palm tree. Two women in long sundresses, their hair pulled up to expose necks the color of cream, huddled together taking vanity shots, giggling. A couple in their midfifties—him with a baseball cap, her in a pair of khaki shorts and a pink T-shirt—sat on the cement wall. He glanced at their name tags: Chuck and Marnee Miller.

Oops, he'd forgotten his own name tag. He looked around for Keoni. Instead he spotted the registration area, where the hostess stood behind a small table with a rack of bags, leis, and folders filled with the course schedule. She wore a sarong and a tank top with an orange lei strung around her neck. Her silky dark hair and creamy mocha skin suggested a native heritage. "Aloha," she said, smiling.

"Hi. I'm Max—"

"Sharpe. I know." She smiled at him. "Welcome back."

"Yeah. And . . ." He wasn't sure why, but he leaned over to view her sheet. "Can I pick up Grace Christiansen's registration packet too?"

"Sure." She gave him his bag and added another lei around his neck. Then she handed him Grace's supplies.

Maybe he'd simply take them to her quickly, before they left, so she knew what to expect.

Max took the stairs to the second floor, then jogged to her room. Paused.

What was he doing? She'd made it abundantly clear that she didn't need him—maybe even didn't want him. His heart as well as his mouth had decided to check out of the commonsense conversation he'd been trying to have with himself.

Go on your tour, Max. Enjoy yourself. I'll be fine.

He'd simply leave her registration information at the desk and ask them to call her room. Later. After she'd had more sleep—

Wait. Through the door, he could hear something. Ragged breathing, even . . . crying?

"Grace?" He knocked on the door quietly, gently.

The noise stopped with a quick gasp of breath. Oh no. "Grace, let me in."

"No. I'm a mess and I don't want to wreck your vacation."

"You won't wreck my vacation. How am I supposed to have fun when you're back here crying? Why are you crying?"

"Because I'm so disgusted with myself. I'm—"

Suddenly the door yanked open. Indeed, her eyes were red, her face chapped. Sheesh, she was *really* crying.

"Because I hate that I'm such a disaster. I don't want to be the girl who gets so sick on the plane that she grosses out the entire cabin."

"No one was grossed—"

"Or the girl who is afraid to eat shrimp fried on a stick."

"Actually, they grill it—"

"I mean, I'm a foodie, for pete's sake. Or I'm supposed to be, right? I love cooking and this trip is all about food adventuring. It's just . . ." She took a long breath. "I don't know what's wrong with me."

He braced his hand against the doorframe, leaned down, and met her eyes. "Let me show you around Hawaii. Just for today. If you hate it, you can go home—I'll drive you to the airport myself."

"I hate that you are missing your food tour. That

you are here babysitting me. I want you to have fun."

"Who says I'm not having fun?"

She cocked her head at him, shook it. "You might be the nicest person I've ever met, Max. No wonder Owen liked you."

Clearly she didn't know him that well. And that made her the one person he could hang around with safely. The one person he could relax with, without fear of giving her the wrong impression. And just in case they both needed that definition . . . "Yep. Owen was like a brother to me."

In fact, that could be his secret weapon. Because if she started thinking they might have more, he could always tell her exactly how he'd wrecked Owen's life. Or if he got really desperate, how he had only now, and nothing of a future, to give her. Just these three weeks of fun and relaxation and adventure.

But maybe that was enough.

Grace was going to fall in love with Hawaii if it killed her.

Thankfully, so far the prognosis was a slow, even delicious, demise. Overhead, the sky hung a canopy of brilliance, the clouds thick and spongy, the smell of summer, freedom, and the sea scenting the air as they drove along the shore, lazy and carefree. She wore a sundress, flip-flops, and a pink baseball hat.

Like she might be this kind of girl, a woman who shucked off life in trade for adventure.

Max had taken down the top on his convertible Mustang rental and now tapped his fingers on the steering wheel to some country music station. " 'I wish you'd stay,' " he half hummed, half sang, his baseball hat backward on his head. He glanced at her from behind his mirrored aviators. "Stomach feeling better?"

She nodded, although she could admit to a small curl of something amiss inside.

Had Max not happened by, her entire vacation might have been spent staring at Hawaii from her balcony. In fact, if not for Max, she might have taken a flight home this morning. Or a ship, although that might not have been any better.

If not for Max . . . Well, she didn't deserve his kindness, and she knew it. But maybe it had more to do with her brother than her. She got that.

He turned down the radio. "Think you could handle an early lunch?"

Grace nodded. "Although I read in my packet that tonight we are having a luau."

"Yeah, it's pretty tame. They do that the first night so that you get accustomed to Hawaiian food. We'll spend the rest of the three weeks learning to make some of the specialties."

"I saw the recipes. What is poke?"

"Pronounced *pokay,* like *okay*. It's fabulous. A

raw seafood salad—they usually make it with fresh ahi."

"Raw?"

"You know, a lot of cultures eat raw fish. Especially Asian. But even in Minnesota we eat raw fish."

"We eat *smoked* fish caught out of Lake Superior. My father buys smoked herring and trout down at the fish house for our guests."

"Your family runs a resort, right?"

She leaned back, let the sun bake her face, her arms. The traffic had slowed as the road narrowed. The ocean combed the shore just beyond a rim of palm trees and sea grasses. She could drink in the view for hours. Hawaii. Wow.

"Our place is called Evergreen Lodge Outfitter and Cabin Rentals. But it burned down last summer, so we're rebuilding."

"I'm so sorry."

"Yeah, it was terrible. But my older brother, Darek, has a lot of plans to upgrade, so it'll probably work out for the good. Give us a few years and the place will be incredible."

"And you work at the resort?"

"No, I work at a pizza joint."

"That's right." He glanced at her again. "No delivery."

He remembered? After six hours of conversation, a crossword, and calling the flight attendant for another cool cloth for her forehead? "I make a mean spinach pizza."

"I'll bet you do," he said, flashing her a grin.

Maybe, no, she couldn't eat.

"So what else is on the menu at the cooking school?"

"Poi, of course. Which is sort of a Hawaiian pudding. And lomi-lomi salmon, another staple on the luau table. We'll probably learn to roll sushi too."

"So a gal has to learn to like raw fish."

"Might be helpful. We'll make manapua also. It's a sort of breaded pork dumpling. And the finale will be laulau. It's . . . hard to explain. It's made with pork, or sometimes chicken, and butterfish and wrapped in taro leaves, and then in ti leaves and steamed. It's amazing but can be tricky to make."

"Max . . . how many times have you attended this cooking school?"

"Well, this would be my third time."

His third time?

"Why do you keep coming back to the same school?"

He drummed his fingers on the steering wheel. Shrugged but didn't look at her. "I like Hawaii. And . . . cooking. And here . . . well, it's relaxing."

She could almost grab it, the sense of something more, lingering outside their conversation. As if, past his carefree demeanor, Max might be hiding something. "Why don't you buy a house here?"

He laughed. "No. I don't own property. That would get complicated."

"You could get a little vacation house, invite your teammates after the season, cook for them, show them the island. You could let your family use it, and then someday, if you get married, you could honeymoon here, teach the kids how to cook, maybe even surf. Pass it down through the generations, make a real family place."

When he tightened his mouth, she had the strange feeling she'd said something wrong.

Max pulled off the highway into a dirt parking lot. A white food truck marked with graffiti like a modern-day guest book was parked next to a grouping of tables shaded by red, green, or blue canopies. A line of tourists snaked from the walk-up window.

"Wow, it's packed."

"That's because it's world famous. C'mon, it's delicious." He got out and just like that seemed to revert back to himself, the casual cowboy swagger taking on a surfer aura as he moved toward the menu board posted at the edge of the property.

He looked so easy, casual, like he belonged here, belonged anywhere. Could conquer anything.

She wanted that—the confidence to do anything, be anything, go anywhere.

The ability to reach out and grab life.

Grace stepped up beside him and studied the

board. "The garlic shrimp scampi looks good."

"Hot and spicy for me," he said. "I'll order while you find us a table."

Grace looked around the crowded eating area. Not a space in sight. In fact, at least two couples were eating on the hoods of their cars.

But she hadn't worked as a waitress without cultivating a few skills. She zeroed in on a woman sitting with two towheaded boys playing with their prawns, ketchup slathering their cheeks. Next to them, a small pile of used napkins signaled defeat. Grace swung by the condiment table, grabbed a handful of supplies, and headed their way.

Walking by, she feigned nonchalance, then said, "Oh, my, you look fresh out of napkins." She held out the offering.

The mother looked up at her. "Thank you, that's so kind."

"Not at all. I'm just waiting for my—" she glanced at Max—"friend to get us some lunch. I'll get more napkins."

"We're nearly finished. Would you like our seats?"

Score. Grace retrieved more napkins, then helped the mother gather the debris. "Are you tourists?"

"Oh no. The kids and I just love the shrimp. It's worth the drive. We live in Pearl City. My husband is stationed here. I'm from Iowa."

"Minnesota."

"I should have recognized the accent. It's nice to meet a fellow Midwesterner." She propped one of the boys on her hip. He reached for her shell necklace and played with it.

"How long have you lived here?"

"About six months."

"And . . ." Grace checked on Max's progress. "How was it? Moving to Hawaii?"

The woman caught her other youngster before he could run away. "You can do anything as long as you are with the one you love."

Right.

The woman had followed her gaze to Max. "He's very handsome."

Grace stood, flummoxed for a moment. "We're . . . just friends."

"Well, Hawaii is an easy place to fall in love," the woman teased. "Have a great time."

Uh-huh.

Grace slid onto the bench and set the napkins across from her to save Max's place as she watched the woman walk away.

Fall in love. Right. It was enough that she was here in Hawaii, so far out of her comfort zone that she couldn't even see it on the horizon. She wasn't going to be so stupid as to let her heart fall for a guy who lived for adventure only when he wasn't traveling all over America playing hockey. Max, with his big life, was exactly the wrong kind of guy for a small-town girl.

But it didn't mean they couldn't be friends. Just like he and Owen were friends.

"What are you thinking about?"

She looked up as Max set a basket in front of her. Then stared down at the fresh shrimp bathed in garlic and lemon butter, the two scoops of rice and a wedge of lemon, and answered, "Lunch."

"Indeed." He sat across from her, setting yet more napkins on the pile between them. "Enjoy."

If it killed her, yes, she planned to. She picked up a shrimp, refusing to wrinkle her nose.

"I usually peel off the shell, then pinch the shrimp at the tail, and pull. That way you get all the meat." He demonstrated, shooting hot sauce across the table. "Oops."

When she tried it, garlic splattered on her hands. "So it's messy."

"But oh, so good." Max finished off his first shrimp, licking his fingers. "Now, tell me, what was so scary about summer camp?"

She didn't expect that. Just like she didn't expect to like the shrimp, especially with the flavors of garlic and lemon, the butter that dripped from her fingers. "Wow. That's delicious."

He nodded, a silly grin on his face. The fact that he'd managed not to get hot sauce on his chin seemed unfair. She felt bathed in butter.

"There's more food adventuring in your future, if you're ready."

No, she wasn't ready, not at all.

But maybe that was the point. If she waited until she was ready to taste life, it might pass her by.

"It all started with the fact that I didn't have a swim buddy."

He peeled and ate another shrimp. Frowned.

"See, we had a cabin of odd numbers. I think one girl didn't show up, so when it came time to choose swim buddies, I was left out. Which meant that they had to double me up with another pair. Unfortunately, the girls came from the same church, and I swear they made a pact to destroy my camping experience. From the first day, they hated me. They threw my shoes in the lake, put sand in my sleeping bag, and banged my bunk from below in the middle of the night. The last straw was when they put my swimsuit in the chimney and covered it with soot. I couldn't swim after that—it was filthy."

He had stopped eating. "I have this insane urge to track down those two girls and hurt them. Please tell me that you didn't let them get away with it."

"What could I do? I called myself a coward and vowed to never go back. But it set the mood for camp for me, and even though the next year I had a swim buddy, I had already decided I would hate it. And then I discovered the kitchen staff."

"You went to camp to cook?"

"No, but after dinner, when the rest of the campers were playing games, I found the staff singing in the kitchen. It reminded me of home, of my family working together after dinner, so I sat on the stoop and listened, and one of the girls, Kiley, found me. She and the other girls took me under their wing. They would let me help make the late-night snack, and they'd talk about boys and high school, and I felt like they let me into their world."

"So food isn't really about food for you," Max said, finishing his shrimp. "It's about camaraderie."

"Sometimes I don't even eat what I make. But I always watch people eat it. I love it when they make those little sounds of joy." She closed her mouth. "*Mmm . . . yum . . .* those sounds."

"Like these?" He slurped, then licked his lips.

She laughed. "I like watching people be happy. Unfortunately, I sometimes think that food will fix things. After Owen's accident, I kept making muffins and trying to feed everyone into feeling better. But no one could fix it; no one could stop his life from unraveling." She shook her head. "Sorry."

"It's okay. We all hate what happened to Owen." He sighed, and on the tail edge, she felt again that strange, painful sense that she'd treaded into something dark. And why not? Owen was his friend. He reached for a napkin, wiped his fingers. She probably needed a bath.

"Ready to see the turtles?" he asked.

"Really?" She went to work on her fingers, her chin, with a napkin. Yep, a bath.

"Yeah, big sea turtles lying on the shore."

"Every day?"

"Almost. Just basking in the sun."

"Do they bite?"

"No. They're turtles. They lie there. Sometimes they stick their tongues out like this." He opened his mouth to demonstrate.

She laughed. "And then what, cruise director?"

He got up, gathering her plate. "I think tomorrow after class we'll climb Diamond Head, and I'll show you a gorgeous view of the island. And maybe the day after that, Hanauma Bay, for snorkeling."

"Snorkeling?"

"By the end of the week, I'll have you up on a surfboard."

She couldn't help but laugh. "Wow, you have big plans for little me."

"It's time to live a little." He winked. She expected him to move away, but he stood there as the wind shifted, rippled his Hawaiian shirt, revealing those hockey biceps. She noticed a hint of the sun's lipstick on his nose. Those beautiful brown eyes with emerald centers held a twinkle of mischief.

Hawaii is an easy place to fall in love.

And then he sank the hook. "C'mon, 9B, haven't you figured it out yet? For this trip, I'm your swim buddy."

Chapter 5

Max Sharpe had a split personality.

The carefree surfer who tooled Grace around Hawaii, who dared her to touch a sea turtle and showed up barefoot, in black linen pants and yet another Hawaiian shirt, for the first night's luau, turned into Maximoto, ninja chef, when he got near a kitchen.

She almost hadn't recognized him in his chef's whites the next morning—a floppy hat, pants, apron, and a full double-breasted chef's jacket, the sleeves rolled up past his elbows as if girded for battle. He had the demeanor of a samurai—all business, no games.

Apparently Max considered the kitchen a serious, even dangerous, place, one he needed to conquer. Although he saved her a seat on one of the stainless steel stools, he shushed her the second class started. She tried cracking a joke about their instructor, Keoni, who looked like he should be saying, "Let's hang ten, dude!" instead of giving them a talk on the history of Hawaiian cuisine. Max had once more shut her down with a harsh "Shh!"

Admittedly, she hadn't quite expected this level of teaching on a culinary vacation. She thought it might be a cadre of Hawaiian-shirted tourists standing around tasting wine as a chef prepared lunch, allowing them to chop a vegetable or two.

No. Hawaiian Culinary Adventures turned out top-notch chefs. She'd never seen such an expertly equipped kitchen, from the commercial-grade prep counters, each with its own range, and the six large ovens, one for each two-person group, to the expansive dry storage pantry, the racks and racks of equipment, and even a bakery and patisserie area.

Yes, she might learn to cook. Really cook, not just throw together fridge leftovers. For the first time since Eden proposed it, Grace considered that she might be able to pull off catering their wedding.

Maybe she should adopt Max's posture.

They'd spent most of the first day of class reviewing culinary fundamentals: safety and sanitation in the kitchen, proper storage of foods, care and use of equipment. Max had listened with the attention of a soldier learning his AK-47. They'd ended the morning with a quick lesson on poi, which he executed perfectly.

Grace's resembled the texture of wallpaper paste, but she choked it down, chewing on a few gummy chunks, wishing for something—salt or honey or brown sugar or even pineapple—to add to the water-and-taro-plant porridge. She'd quietly made the suggestion to Max, who looked at her as if she'd suggested taking crayon to the *Mona Lisa*.

When the class let out at noon, 9A had appeared.

Max had arrived in the lobby attired in shorts and a crisp white T-shirt, wearing hiking sandals, his aviators clipped to his neck, grinning, not a hint of samurai chef in his demeanor. He kept his promise to take her to the top of Diamond Head and held her hand as she walked out onto one of the platforms overlooking the crater below. Grace stood there for nearly an hour, just drinking in the vast beauty of the island.

Yesterday, after their second day of class, they'd walked barefoot down the shoreline, all the way to Waikiki Beach, where he took her to a restaurant and ordered fish tacos with mango. Her taste buds were living dangerously.

But this morning she felt sure they weren't quite adventurous enough to gulp down the bright-orange lomi-lomi salmon Keoni had them preparing.

"The color has a ritual significance to luaus. The ancient Hawaiians offered kumu, another type of reddish-colored fish, to their god, so the salmon is our modern-day substitute. Be sure to get in there with your fingers and massage the tomatoes, ice, and green onions together. After all, that's what *lomi* means in Hawaiian. 'Massage.' " Keoni demonstrated by kneading his mixture together in a glass bowl on the counter.

Next to Grace, Max massaged his fish mixture with the care of a professional therapist, working the flavors together.

Where was a wooden spoon when she needed one?

"What's the matter?" Max said quietly, glancing at her.

"It's . . . cold. Really cold."

"That's the crushed ice."

"And did I mention slimy? I mean—I get it, but I'm not a fan."

He stared at her. "You're a chef. This is gourmet fish, not gopher guts. Stick your fingers in there and start massaging."

"You know, Samurai Jack, just ease up there. It's food, not a nuclear bomb. The world won't end if I use a spoon."

His mouth opened, and for a second she had the sense of being in second grade, her classmate threatening to tell on her for writing in her textbook.

"Fine. Chill. I'm massaging; I'm massaging." Except her massage spilled salmon onto the counter, froze her fingertips, and left her hands dripping.

She glanced behind her. Marnee Miller had the

masseuse techniques of a master, while her husband mangled his fish. He looked as if he might have taken this adventure for the tasting portion of the class.

Over at table three, the two socialites with perfect hair were giggling; Grace didn't want to surmise what they might be saying. Especially as they kept shooting looks Max's direction. Yeah, well, she didn't blame them. The man could make even a floppy chef's hat look dangerously adorable.

She picked her spilled lomi off the counter and threw it back into her bowl. "I hope this is served with crackers or toasted bread."

"Seriously, Grace. This is sacred food."

She affected a monkish hum as she massaged.

"I can't take you anywhere."

She glanced at him again and caught the hint of a smirk. So maybe, deep inside, Mr. Adventure still lurked. She'd just have to figure out how to lure him out, past the indomitable samurai chef.

"Well done, Max," Keoni said as he walked by their table. He eyed Grace's lomi.

"I think my lomi is going to leave me a big tip." She smiled at Keoni.

He pursed his lips and walked by.

"I did mention that he's one of the top chefs in the world, right?" Max said quietly. "We usually just say, 'Yes, chef.' "

"Oh." She cut her voice low. "But can he fry fish

on the side of a lake? Or make flapjacks that can make a grown man cry?"

Again the smile. It was enough to make her at least try the lomi.

She refused to admit to Max that maybe she wouldn't die. It was better than the poi.

Once again, after class he emerged without a trace of the *Iron Chef* persona, dressed in swim trunks and a T-shirt. "Ready to snorkel?"

She'd changed, per his suggestion, into a one-piece swimsuit and pulled a long T-shirt over as a cover-up. "I should warn you. Underneath this shirt I resemble the underside of a whale."

He tossed her a bottle. "SPF 80. Layer it."

They climbed into the convertible and headed east out of Honolulu, along the Kalanianaole Highway. "Where are we going?"

"Hanauma Bay. It's the top of a volcanic cone, and it's one of the most beautiful places to snorkel on the island, at least for beginners. You'll love it."

"What if I get water in my snorkeling tube?"

"Then you blow it out. I promise—I'll be right there. I won't let you drown."

Swim buddy, right. "I am a good swimmer, by the way. I grew up on a lake."

"I'm sure you are."

"And I'm a good cook too. I just . . . Okay, I don't follow the rules. If it tastes good, that's enough for me."

He said nothing.

"You, however, approach cooking like it's a competition."

"I just want to get it right," he said quietly. "I don't have time for mistakes."

He offered nothing more and she stared at the scenery, puzzling out his words.

The bay stretched out below them in a perfect arc, the water so blue it belonged on a postcard. They parked in the lot and stopped by the rental center for equipment. Max bought an extra sanitizer packet and sat on the bench, cleaning his gear.

Ho-kay.

They watched a short film about the ecology and sea life of the bay, then headed down the hill, towels tucked under their arms.

"Why is the color so patchy—dark in some areas, turquoise in others?"

"That's the coral depth. See, to the left, it's dark because the coral is near the surface. But in the middle, the sea is sandy. Over to the right, it's patchy. That's where we'll find our sea turtles." He looked at her, stuck out his tongue. "Remember, they don't bite."

They picked a spot on the shore, dropped their gear, and Grace donned her flippers, mask, and snorkel. She kicked up sand as she walked to the ocean and nearly tripped on the edge of the flipper.

Max had walked into the cool water, then sat to fit his flippers on. His mask he'd strapped onto his head, pushing it up to his forehead. "Let's get into the water. I'll show you how to clean your mask, and we'll practice breathing."

He'd stripped off his shirt, revealing his wide, sculpted shoulders, still a little on the pale side thanks to his indoor profession. He had a toned chest, probably from his hours in the gym, and a tight six-pack stomach.

Yeah, she—and the rest of the female beach population—might need to practice breathing.

"Right," Grace said and duckwalked into the water. Cool, refreshing. She sank into it, floated out until she was chest-deep.

Max joined her, taking off his mask. "You want to make sure you have a nice snug seal on your mask and that the snorkel fits easily into your mouth." He demonstrated, then came over to adjust her mask.

The world became pinched, and she had the sense of looking through a window. She fitted the tube into her mouth and stuck her head in the water.

Magic. She didn't know how else to describe the abruptness of peeking under the surface and seeing the sea vibrant and bright, suddenly alive. She spotted an orange sea urchin nestled into the rocky sand and a small school of black-and white-striped tangs swimming by.

"Wow," she said and managed to gulp in water. She popped up, coughing.

Max lifted his face from the water and removed his snorkel. "You can't talk. I know that's going to be a bit of a challenge, but if you need to say something, just tap me. We'll surface. Now, blow out your snorkel."

She blew hard and found it cleared. "I think I can do this."

"Of course you can. Here's a hint—keep your face straight down, and let yourself glide on the water." He pointed toward the reef. "Let's head out there."

She nodded, fitted in her snorkel, and followed him as he paddled out. Keeping her face down, she watched the sea world scuttle beneath her. They floated over formations of coral, hard cones and divots of rock in which fish rooted for food. She spotted a few from the ecology movie—triggerfish, with their long orange mouths; a blue bullethead parrot fish; a school of yellow butterfly fish. Even a sinister-eyed moray eel slid by.

Grace didn't even yelp.

In fact, she experienced a surreal sense of power as if she were flying, fearless. She looked around, saw Max swimming nearby, and watched as he inspected hiding places, studied fish. She met his eyes once and saw the smile in them.

I just want to get it right. . . . I don't have time for mistakes.

She didn't understand the reason for his words, but yeah, she could embrace them. Even send up a prayer. *Please, God, don't let me be making a mistake here. Don't let me dive in only to have me land hard.*

Except what exactly might she be diving into?

She felt a tap on her shoulder and saw Max pointing down a crevice in the rocks. She moved closer for a better view. Her hand found Max's shoulder.

A sea turtle slept deep in the mottled shadows of the coral, its shell sparkling with gold in a shaft of sunlight.

She treaded water, watching. Suddenly the turtle began to move. It swam away from her, out of the coral enclave and toward deeper water.

Grace couldn't help it—she began to swim after it, just to see the ballet of its motion in water. It swam farther and she followed, the water becoming cooler; below her, the coral dropped away. Still, like the hypnotic lure of a mermaid, the turtle coaxed her deeper.

She could feel Max behind her now and again, tapping her as if trying to keep up.

Then the turtle shot off and disappeared. She rose to the surface to talk to Max.

Max surfaced five feet away. Something about his expression set a fist in her stomach. "Come back!" he shouted.

She treaded water but had the sense of moving,

and that's when she saw the sign, the buoys. She'd swum beyond the boundaries, into the channel of the riptide.

"Swim back!"

Grace dug down into the water, but even as she kicked, she felt a grab, a tug at her body as the tide yanked her into the dark channel of the sea.

Max was going to get her killed. After all his talk of adventure, he'd pushed her into this, and now Grace would drown, somewhere miles away from home, in the ocean.

He'd tried to grab her as she swam with the turtle, tried to warn her that the ocean could turn on her, that she had to respect it, heed the dangers. But she'd swum past the barrier without even seeing it, and now the riptide sucked her away from him.

"Swim to me!" He launched out after her, every single warning against following a victim into a riptide blaring in his brain. But she hadn't quite lost herself to the pull yet and—

She touched his hand. Briefly, but she was kicking hard, fighting, and yeah, she could swim. He lunged for her again and caught her, pulling against the fingers of the cold current.

"Kick!"

It seemed they'd alerted the lifeguards from shore—a cadre of rescuers on surfboards paddled their direction. He tried to remember his safety training on how to escape a riptide. It seemed he had to swim perpendicular to it, maybe.

Or maybe he should surrender to it, let it take them both to sea.

"Don't let go!" Grace screamed.

Never. He tightened his iron grip on her hand, and they seemed to be breaking free. Or maybe the buoy had simply moved with the wind. His leg began to tighten, a cramp working up the length of it. He groaned.

Then suddenly they popped free, surging forward in a giant stroke. Grace came abreast of him, paddling hard, while Max kicked, fighting the burn in his calf to keep up.

A lifeguard on a paddleboard shot out of the boundary area. "What are you doing?"

Like he couldn't figure that out? Max took the proffered paddle so the guard could drag him closer to the safe zone. Another guard pulled up, letting Grace rest on his board as he paddled her back in.

Max let the guard tow him into the swimming area. "Thanks."

"We should kick you out. Don't you know it's forbidden to go out of the buoy area?"

"It was an accident," he said, glancing at Grace, who now stood shoulder-deep on the sandy bottom. "Believe me—she didn't realize how far she'd gone."

"You were lucky," the guard said and paddled away.

Grace had her arms wrapped around herself, shaking despite the bathtub-warm water.

Max moved over to her, feeling the same dark chill deep inside. He lifted his mask, then hers. His hands cupped her shoulders. "Are you okay?"

She shivered even as she nodded. But her big eyes held his as if needing confirmation, and he didn't know what to do.

Mostly because he wasn't sure of the answer either. No, he wasn't okay.

For a moment there, he'd felt as if a hand reached in, closed around his heart, and threatened to rip it from its moorings.

And because that scared him nearly as much as watching her rocket out to sea, he wrapped his arms around Grace and pulled her to himself. Tight. Breathing in her salty, wet skin, pressing his head against her hair.

Feeling her wrap her arms around his waist and hold on.

Bad idea, because she fit into his embrace like she belonged there, the way her head landed just below his chin, the curve of her body so perfect against his that it only added to the cold tremble inside. His heartbeat probably betrayed him, thundering against her ear even as it filled his head.

What if she'd died?

Max blew out a breath, then another, and finally released his hold. He thought she might be crying, and he felt the same way. Grace folded her arms in front of her and looked at him, her heart in her beautiful eyes . . . and that's when he realized he'd made a terrible, terrible mistake.

He should have seen it coming. After all, each day he'd looked forward a little more to seeing her. And despite her antics in Chef Keoni's class —who suggested crackers with lomi-lomi?—he couldn't deny he longed for her under-the-breath quips.

No, he didn't love poi either, but he wasn't letting her know that. Still, he nearly responded to her words today.

You, however, approach cooking like it's a competition.

Of course he did. Because he didn't have time for second chances. In hockey, in life . . . in love.

And that declaration would lead to an exploration of why. He could just imagine her horror when he told her he never knew when his disease might kick in, what vacation might be his last.

Yeah, he'd ventured way too close to the edge with Grace today, and this was his wake-up call. Any farther and someone was going to get hurt.

"I think we should go."

She bit her lip, then nodded. "I'm so sorry."

He headed toward shore, not able to look at

her. "You didn't know. It's my fault. I forgot to tell you about the riptide."

"But I should have never followed the turtle. I wasn't really chasing it—it was just . . . almost magical—"

"I get it. Really. Let's just get our gear. It's late."

She said nothing, splashing to shore behind him. He took off his flippers in the water, then walked to shore, the sand coating his wet feet. He scooped up his towel, dried his head, draped the towel around his neck.

Grace was drying off, not looking at him. She wrapped the towel around her waist before finally turning to him. The expression on her face felt like a dagger to his chest.

"I'm so sorry I wrecked our trip."

"You didn't wreck our trip," he said softly and turned away before he crumbled.

Mistake. The word roared in his head. He blew out a breath and headed up the shore without looking back.

They dropped off her gear, and she remained quiet as they washed their feet and walked to the car. She laid her towel on the seat, then donned her shirt and slid in.

He should say something. But this crazy, dark pain had bottled in his chest, and he didn't know how to make it better, how to pull them back to safety.

How to make her understand that he hadn't meant to let it get this far.

"Wait until Owen hears that you nearly killed me."

Huh?

She was looking at him, tease on her face. "Yep. You're a dead man."

"I—"

"I mean, here you go, assigning yourself as my babysitter, and you practically drown me. He's going to come back from Montana and take you out."

And just like that, the tension in his chest snapped. Gone. Free. "I think he's smart enough to know that you're trouble."

"Me? Trouble? I'm not the one who . . . fed me shrimp. Or showed me Diamond Head. Or introduced me to turtles."

"Oh, right. Well, I'm not the one who tried to *race* a turtle."

"I would have won had you not distracted me." She grinned, and he wanted to kiss her.

No, not kiss her. Maybe give her a high five or a knuckle bump. Because somehow, the darkness had receded and the prospect of having to drop her off and spend the evening avoiding her died in the wake of her easy laughter.

Maybe she'd pulled them both back from the cliff, back to just friends.

"Now, if you're a cruise director worth his salt,

you'll find me a decent hamburger and some fries. I'm in serious need of comfort food." She leaned back and propped her bare feet on the dash, her blue toenail polish like sapphires in the sunlight.

"As you wish." He put the car in gear, turned on the radio, and considered his demise.

A guy like him had to be on his game, because any more time with Grace Christiansen could take them into dangerous waters, and he was the one who just might find himself the goner.

Of course Pierre's Pizza had to start delivery services with Grace in Hawaii. Because, no, they weren't shorthanded in the kitchen, requiring Raina to arrive early for prep and stay late to clean up. And should someone call in with a rare delivery order, who had to drop everything and run it out to them? Not Ty, who knew Deep Haven better in his sleep than Raina did with a full GPS system, or Stuart, the owner, who'd raised three children in Deep Haven and probably even knew the clandestine hangouts.

No, it had to be Raina who carried the pizza box out to her gray Impala, rain or shine, and drove like an idiot around town, trying to locate the address.

Why? Because it turned out Ty didn't own a car. And Stuart was too busy at the counter greeting guests, friends, residents of Deep Haven who came in not just for pizza but for camaraderie.

Besides, the truth was, Raina had no friends. No camaraderie. No reason for sticking around Deep Haven. Nothing but a car that apparently needed new tires.

"Not again!" She slammed her hand against the steering wheel as the car came to rest in the soggy swamp that had once been County Road 53.

The pizza box lay on the floor, having arrowed forward with her slam of the brakes.

The DOT might consider putting the "road washed out" flags *before* the curve.

Now her Impala lurched to the right as the wheel sank lower into the muck. She opened the door. Thankfully, her driver's side still sat on semidry ground, and she got out, slopping to the center of the road.

Overhead, the sky hovered low and menacing, the late hour of the day hanging through the shadow-shrouded trees.

Raina pulled out her cell phone, held it up, praying for a signal. Nothing. Of course. She could say that about this entire stupid town. There was nothing here. No nightlife, no fun, no friends, no—

She leaned against the car, scrubbing a hand down her face. Okay, so the humiliation of Owen's full-out run from her place over a week ago seemed to sour her outlook on everything. Why couldn't she get his rejection—and her own stupidity—out of her head?

She stood, went around the front of the car, and stared at the mess. She'd simply driven off the hard pack of the dirt road, now smaller after the rain this week. She'd bet Seattle was a drier place than Deep Haven in June.

Maybe . . . Raina put the car in neutral and went around to the front again. Threw her weight against the hood.

Nothing.

She couldn't push and gun it at the same time. Folding her arms, she tucked her head into them on the hood.

The trees shivered off rain, and the silence, the stillness of the forest, wheedled through her.

She lifted her head. Stared into the woods on one side, then the other. She might be one, even two, miles from the highway, back in the hills.

And not a house in sight. In fact . . . She got in the car and pulled up the GPS. It showed her destination as off the main road—this muddy "main road."

Who knew where 1290 County Road 53 might truly be located?

Hadn't she read a story about wolves attacking a woman in her yard in a recent edition of the *Deep Haven Herald*?

Just in case she'd loosened it, she put the car in reverse. Stepped on the gas. Slowly, and then as the tires kicked up mud, she floored it.

Mud splattered into the air, landing on the

windshield, the side windows, as she dug in deeper.

Raina let off the gas, smelled the engine burning. Nice. Maybe she should simply leave the thing and start hiking back to the road. She still had an hour of daylight, right?

She glanced at the pizza, then dove for it, pulling it up on the seat. The smell of pepperoni had tormented her all the way from town. The red padded covering radiated heat. She opened the Velcro, found the pizza still hot. She pulled it out and set it on top of the insulated envelope. Then slowly pried open the box.

A layer of gooey cheese dripped from the lid where it had glued in place as it hurtled from the front seat. Only red sauce, pepperoni, mushrooms, and onions remained in the sauce on the crust.

At least it didn't have olives. She hated them, and if she was going to have to survive on this lonely pizza until help arrived, she didn't want to have to choke down olives.

She scraped cheese off the box with her fingers, then dropped it onto a slice. Considered her actions. She worked the piece free. Maybe she needed a little nourishment now, to help her figure out what to do next. Maneuvering the piece into her mouth, she took a bite. Not too bad, even with the cardboard-flavored cheese.

As she moved to take another bite, a buzzing behind her made her nearly drop the piece. She turned, flicking the automatic locks. Like, what, it might be Bigfoot approaching?

No, worse.

She recognized him on that black motorcycle, in a black helmet, motoring toward her like he'd forgotten something. Maybe one last flicker of her pride to stomp out.

Raina determined to ignore him. Even if— shoot. She could be here forever if she didn't—

He slowed as he drove past her, and then, of course, he stopped. Because he just couldn't help himself. A damsel in distress, another woman whose heart he might take captive.

She just wouldn't look at him. She pulled her Pierre's Pizza visor down, stared straight ahead. Maybe he wouldn't realize it was her. . . .

He knocked on the window. "Are you okay in there?"

Through the glass, she recognized his voice. "Yep."

"Are you sure you don't need a hand? You look pretty stuck—"

"Oh, for pete's sake, I know, okay? Go away, Owen!" Raina looked up then and stilled.

Not Owen.

The man, however, had Owen's features—the same arrogant chin, the same blue eyes. With the exception of his dark curly hair, a layer of dark whiskers, and the concern in his expression, it might be Owen.

Raina glanced at the motorcycle, back at the man, just to be sure.

She rolled down the window as he straightened as if to heed her words. "No—I was—uh . . . I'm sorry!" She opened her door, and he moved back as she got out. "I'm stuck. And . . . yes, sorry. I need help."

"Okay." He gave her a funny look and she realized she still held the pizza slice.

She turned and put it back in the box. Wiped her hands on her jeans. "Um, I didn't know how long I was going to be out here."

"I see." He walked around to examine the car. She thought she recognized him, something about his saunter, the way he crouched down, studying the mess—

Oh, wait. He had to be one of the brothers. She'd seen a guy with his dark looks, handsome with a brilliant-white smile, at the wedding. "Casper Christiansen?"

He glanced up at her. "At your service."

She couldn't escape them.

"I don't think I can get you out of there. You're dug in pretty deep." He stood. "But I'm headed over to a buddy's house for a meeting. He's got a truck that I think can yank this out for you. If you want a ride, we'll see if we can't help you out."

He smiled, and oh, she had issues. Because for a second there, her heart stopped on yet another Christiansen man's smile.

No. She needed help, but she wasn't going to fall for the charm of another north shore scoundrel.

"Yes. That would be very helpful," she said, not smiling back. "Thank you."

He quirked an eyebrow. "You're welcome." He started toward his bike. "And please bring our pizza—or what's left of our pepperoni, mushroom, and onion deep-dish."

Oh. Raina closed the box, put it back into the insulated cover, and locked her car.

"What, you think a bear might steal your satellite radio?" Casper asked as she got on the back of his motorcycle.

"Maybe," she said. She slid her hand through the strap of the pizza carrier.

"Mmm-hmm." He turned on the seat, plunked a helmet on her head. "Hold on now. There's a bar behind the seat, or you can wrap your arm around my waist."

Right. She'd fallen for that once before. She reached behind her as he took off.

Not the wild, romantic ride from last Sunday night. This ride was quiet and slow, the road soupy. When the bike jerked, sliding a little in the mud, she yelped and let go of the bar. Without thinking, she wrapped her arm around Casper's waist.

He too had an athlete's build, a flat stomach, shoulders that evidenced hard work. She gave herself permission to hang on as he drove them farther into the tangle of north shore woods, finally cutting onto a driveway. The gravel drive wove back through the trees to a modern-day log cabin. Cozy and looking freshly built, it sat on the edge of a small cliff, and she guessed the other side overlooked Lake Superior.

A wide porch led to the front door, a wooden bear near the entry with the word *Welcome!* carved into its belly.

She spied another mud-splattered car in the drive, along with a truck parked inside the open garage.

Casper parked the bike, held the pizza as she slid off, then handed it to her and climbed off.

"Thanks," she said as he unbuckled the helmet.

He set it on the seat and took the pizza back from her. Then, strangely, he smiled. "Trust me."

Huh?

She followed him up the stairs, and he opened the door without knocking. "Pizza man!"

Raina peeked out from behind him, saw a couple guys lounging on high-top counter chairs, a pretty, petite brunette on another. Beyond them, two picture windows opened to an expansive view of the lake.

"Hi," Raina said.

"And you found the pizza girl, too?" one of the guys said as Casper parked the pizza on the counter. Oh, wait until they saw the cheese.

Casper had opened a drawer, pulled out a knife. He eased the pizza from the carrier and brought it to the counter. She grimaced at the crushed top, but Casper turned his back to them as he opened it, and she took it as her cue to distract. "Yeah, uh, my car slid into the mud back there, and Casper rescued me."

"He *rescued* you," one of the men said. He had dark-blond hair, deep-blue eyes, and wore jeans with an Evergreen Resort sweatshirt. "I'm Jensen Atwood. Are you new in town?"

"Raina. And, yeah." He looked so familiar; she tried to place him. "My aunt Liza lives here, though—"

"Liza Beaumont is your aunt?" This from the other man—bronze hair, hazel eyes, wearing a black T-shirt with a pair of dark jeans, and from his belt hung a deputy badge.

"This is Kyle Hueston, local law," Jensen said. "He's married to Emma, but she's not here right now. She'll be back in a bit."

"And I'm Claire—Jensen's wife," said the brunette, sliding off the stool. She too looked familiar. "I'll bet Stuart is getting worried about you. Maybe we should call him."

"You know Stuart?"

Claire picked up the phone. "I used to work at Pierre's. Stuart's like a dad to me. I was the one who talked him into delivery service." She grimaced. "Sorry."

"I blamed Grace."

"You should." She laughed, and finally Raina placed them. Darek's best man, Jensen, and Ivy's friend Claire.

Her mistakes surrounded her on all sides.

She toed off her shoes, left them by Casper's at the entrance, then padded across the wood floor to the double windows to stare out at the view.

"Dinner is served," Casper said. "Raina, you want some?"

She turned and found Casper smiling at her, nothing of mockery in his expression. She glanced at the pizza. Not a perfect cheese recovery, but he'd managed to cover the slices sufficiently.

He handed her a plate and winked.

"No, I shouldn't—"

"Yeah, you should." Claire had hung up. "Stuart said to take the rest of the night off. And he asked if you needed help getting out. I told him we could handle it."

They could?

Deputy Kyle nudged a stool from the counter.

Okay. Raina slid onto the stool, accepted the pizza.

Casper set a glass of soda in front of her. Then he lifted his own. "Welcome to the first meeting of the Evergreen dragon boat team."

The what? But even as Casper looked at her, an eyebrow raised, a grin on his face she might call teasing, she found herself reaching for her glass.

Lifting it. Tapping it to Claire's, Jensen's, Kyle's, and Casper's.

"To teamwork and the championship," Casper exclaimed. "Huzzah!"

"Huzzah!" she echoed as one with her new compatriots.

Chapter 6

Clearly her trek out to sea had scared Max more than he wanted to admit. Aloud, at least, because Grace wouldn't soon forget the panic in his eyes or the way he crushed her to himself when they'd returned to shore.

His heart nearly pounded through his rib cage, right into her ear. Right into her heart.

But then he'd released her from his embrace, and for a long while there, the big chill had settled between them. As if . . . as if . . .

As if all her neediness had disgusted him.

See, she knew it would only be a matter of time. The chivalry would wear off and in its wake would be a sort of sad shake of his head and a disentanglement from the girl who took too much effort.

A part of her wanted to offer to return the swim buddy pass. In fact, in a way, she felt sorry for him. Saddled with Owen's sister. She could admit that might have added to his sudden cold front.

And maybe he'd saved her from the awkward moment when he realized she wanted more.

Or that she had wanted more. Sort of. Maybe entertained the idea.

What was a gal supposed to do when a muscled, tall, and devastatingly handsome hockey player pulled her into his arms?

She liked him. Way, way too much because she'd obviously read into things. Into his attention, his laughter. Read into the twinkle in his eyes.

So she'd taken a step back, reined in that messy neediness, and remembered her boundaries. They would be swim buddies. Culinary vacation teammates.

Max, it seemed, got the message. Somehow, she'd brought him back, and although flirty Max was gone, chivalrous Max managed to hang on. He hadn't quite kept his promise about surfing, but he'd taken her for a drive into the mountains in the center of the island, and yesterday he'd wandered Honolulu with her and helped her purchase a Hawaiian dress.

Today, however, rain pinged on the roof of the kitchen, and she guessed she might have to pick up a book from the resort bookstore. She swallowed down the taste of disappointment. Really, the poor man should have *one* day away from her.

Because he seemed almost miserable.

Worse, he'd turned into a bit of a wreck in the

kitchen. Yesterday, while she diligently massaged her ahi tuna, he'd nearly cut his finger off.

And today . . . "Argh, I have lumps!" he said as if he had just missed a goal.

Grace glanced over from where she was making haupia, a sort of coconut pudding, on the stove. From outside, the cool breezes of the rain tempered the steam of the kitchen. Still, she longed for her swimsuit instead of her chef's armor.

Even Max appeared hot, sweat beading across his hairline.

"Did you pour in your arrowroot too fast?"

"I don't know—ah!" He took his pudding off the heat, turned away from it.

The look on his face said that he hovered on the verge of walking out of the kitchen, never to return.

"Max, calm down," Grace said. "Listen, it's just like your mother's banana pudding. You have to keep whisking it like this." She put his pan back on the heat, turned it way down to a simmer, and began to whisk it against the side of the pan.

"I've made haupia before," he growled. "I'm just off my game."

"Then get back in the game. C'mon, you try it." She'd already worked out a couple lumps and now took his hand, guided it with hers.

He took the whisk, blew out a breath.

"See, it's evening out."

"Yeah, okay."

"It's just pudding, Max."

She got pinched, tight lips in answer.

"No time for mistakes. Right." She glanced at Keoni, who was headed their way. "I don't suppose there is some cinnamon contraband in the back . . ."

"Grace."

She smiled.

Keoni walked by, glanced at her haupia. Nodded. Kept walking.

"I got a nod. A nod!"

Max's mouth lifted up on one side. "Calm down, Chef Christiansen."

"You just wish you could make haupia like the master."

"It's my life goal."

The smile stayed as he poured his cream into a rectangular pan and brought hers with his to the refrigerator to chill.

She was cleaning her work area when Keoni returned. "You're doing well, Grace. I have to admit, for a mainlander, you can keep it cool under pressure."

She bit back a quip. Keoni scared her a little, with the seriousness in his dark eyes, the way his gaze seemed to study her.

Max returned to the counter. "Chef?"

"Max, I'd like you and Grace to consider entering this year's Honolulu Chop. It's a four-day competition for amateurs, in teams, and I think you two would do well. I've been watching your partner here, and Grace seems to know how to think on her feet. And you . . ." He lifted a shoulder. "You know Hawaiian food."

Grace glanced at Max, back at Keoni. "You're not serious."

"Why not? You two are a good team."

A good team. She couldn't read Max's face. He wore almost a baffled expression.

"I, uh—"

"Max, we don't have to do this. I know you're just here on vacation."

"The prize is ten thousand dollars," Keoni said. Oh.

"Think about it," Keoni said. "You can tell me Monday, when class resumes." He strode off to inspect more haupia.

Grace stood there, for the first time thankful for the rain that would keep her away from Max's company for the rest of the day.

Poor man didn't know how to tell her no.

Imagine, the Iron Chef meets . . . Well, she wasn't quite Julia Child. Maybe more like the Galloping Gourmet. "Max, we're not going to do this. We're here to learn and have fun."

"Absolutely. Which is why it's Pearl Harbor day," Max said, shedding his apron and chef's uniform.

"What?" She followed him out of the kitchen,

dropping her coat in a hamper and shucking off the chef's pants as she went. Underneath, she wore shorts and a T-shirt. She followed him through the covered shelters that connected the kitchen to the rest of the resort.

He was ten strides away from her.

"Max!"

He stopped next to a pond where water cascaded from the thatched roof of the walkway. Koi swam in the pond, and a white cockatoo clung to a piece of bamboo under the cover of a pair of tall palms. "What?"

"You can stop babysitting me now. Really." She caught up to him, fighting the urge to press her hand to his chest. He wore a black T-shirt, a pair of cargo shorts. "And that includes this competition. I know I've been a burden to you—you haven't even gone surfing yet."

His mouth tightened, and he looked at her with such fierceness that she could almost see the battle waging inside.

"Listen, I'm going back to my room. I'm going to read a book. I like books. I like to read. And I can do that alone. All weekend, if I have to." She smiled at him. "The answer is no. No Pearl Harbor and no competition."

Then she walked past him, straight to the lobby, and got on the elevator.

There. See? That was easy. Just . . . easy. She could let out her breath now.

The doors were nearly closed when Max stuck his hand in and muscled his way onto the elevator.

As the doors closed behind him, he stared at her, a muscle pulling in his jaw, his eyes almost on fire.

She swallowed. "Two, please?"

He didn't move. Then, "Yes. The answer is yes."

Huh? "No, it's not. The answer is no. No competition. And no more babysitting. I can take care of myself."

"Well, I don't want you to."

He hadn't moved, his brown eyes magnetic, still holding hers.

She swallowed again, her throat tightening, a band around her chest. When she opened her mouth, nothing came out.

His gaze roved to her mouth, then back to her eyes. He wore a terrible, almost-raw expression on his face. A tremble touched her, something deep she couldn't place.

Or didn't want to.

Abruptly, he blew out a breath and turned. Punched the button for the second floor. "I . . . I like spending time with you."

His words slid over her, through her. "I like spending time with you too."

His shoulders were rising and falling, and she watched them until they got to her floor. The doors opened.

Max didn't move.

So Grace didn't either.

The doors closed again.

"Why did you come to Hawaii?" he said quietly, the fierceness not quite vanished from his tone.

"I came because my . . . sister . . . bought me a ticket?"

"Why?" He folded his arms over his chest.

"So I could cater her wedding."

"Why?"

She tasted the finest prick of irritation in her throat. "So I could . . . get noticed, I guess."

"Why?"

"Because I want to start a catering company. I think."

"You think?"

"What is this, a pep talk?"

"I want you to care. I want you to see that you could do this. You could enter this contest and win." He tapped his hand to his chest, then gestured to her. "*We* could enter this contest and win. And then you'd have ten grand to start that company with. Maybe even get a little recognition. Don't you want that? To finally reach your dreams?"

His eyes had reddened just a little, and she had the sense that he might be saying more with his challenge. Especially when he pinned her with a long look, something so unraveled, so desperate in it that it stripped words from her.

His voice lowered to almost a whisper. "You were the one who said you wanted more. What if this is it? What if it's right here? Right now? Don't you want to take it?"

Yes. The word wanted to leak out of her. Yes, she wanted more.

But it had nothing to do with cooking. So she nodded. Hoped her eyes, her face, hadn't betrayed the truth.

"Then I'm going to help you get it." He punched one. "We're working all weekend."

"No reading?"

"Not unless it's ingredients."

She wanted to smile, wanted to give in to the giddy rush of joy, but—"Max. Why are you doing this?"

The floor pinged and the door opened, but she didn't move. As Max started to step out, she grabbed his hand. He turned, frowned.

Now he stood blocking the door, in case anyone dared enter. He met her eyes. "Because I come to Hawaii every year and hang out in the same class, and I've never met someone who wants to add cinnamon to haupia. That's crazy, right? Crazy, and yet it sounds good." He sort of smiled, shaking his head. "I almost want to be mad at you, but I can't. How could I? So I'm going to help you. We're going to win this thing, and you're going to go home and start that company." His voice softened. "Besides, I think everyone who gets to have dreams should reach for them. I want to help you reach."

Oh. That was so much better than what she'd thought he was going to say. She'd thought he'd keep it simple, even light, nothing close to the heart—

"Besides, I'm your swim buddy."

Yes. Yes, he was.

Just like that, Max had fixed it. Figured out a way to spend time with Grace without having to justify his reasons. Without having to admit to himself that yes, he enjoyed spending time with her—more than he had a right to.

In fact, he'd let that leak out and wanted to bang his head against the elevator when he heard the words emerge.

But the rest—the rest was all truth. Or at least most of it—right up to the part where he said he thought they could win. But . . . maybe they could. He did want to help her reach for her dreams. Did want her to feel the win, to create something that might endure.

In that way, maybe he, too, could own a small piece of a happy ending.

"So what are we making today?" Grace asked. She'd become all ears, no improv yesterday, as suddenly she took her own future seriously.

"Manapua. It's a sort of pork dumpling. Bread filled with everything from sausage to carrots and mushrooms, even bean sprouts. You make the pastry; I'll make the filling."

He handed her a recipe.

"Not unlike donuts."

"Please don't glaze these."

She waggled her eyebrows at him and went to the dry pantry to retrieve the ingredients while he gathered sausage, onions, carrots, shiitake mushrooms, soy sauce, sherry, oyster sauce, and garlic.

He laid his ingredients on the chopping board and started peeling. The sun was already high—he'd slept in until seven this morning, at first opting out of a beach run for the luxury of lying in bed, opening his sliding door and listening to the waves.

In the wan morning light, with the furnace outside tempering the chilled hotel room air, for the first time since he'd arrived in Hawaii, the darkness had found him, burrowed inside.

Yes, he liked Grace way too much. So much that he found himself wishing for more. For a life beyond these three weeks. He'd like to look up in the stands and see her cheering as he stole the puck, made the score. Wanted to know she waited for him after a game, maybe with something homemade simmering on the stove.

He could even imagine a little girl with Grace's blonde hair, her pretty blue eyes . . . and that's when he got out of bed and changed into his running shorts.

He fought the images with a cruel workout, then showered and found Grace already on the breakfast terrace reading. He wanted to throw her book in the ocean. Instead, he sat down with her and outlined the game plan for the day.

"We'll start with some Hawaiian basics—you already learned lomi-lomi and poke, poi and haupia. I'll teach you manapua and loco moco, and then we'll start mixing it up. The Honolulu Chop competition is all about using Hawaiian ingredients—some everyday, like Spam—"

"Spam?"

"They love it here. The Hormel company actually produced a limited-edition Hawaii can of Spam once."

"Ew."

"Also, I'll teach you about alaea sea salt and saimin—a sort of Chinese noodle. They're very thin and quick cooking. There's bound to be fresh pineapple and coconut on the menu, and any number of the exotic fruits, so we'll go over those."

"Wow, Max, I just have to ask one more time—are you sure?"

He smiled because his voice was too eager and nodded.

Now, with manapua on the menu, she brought back her ingredients, started her yeast fermenting. "So do the guys on your team know you cook?"

He slid crushed garlic into a pan. "Uh. I don't know."

"You don't have them over to cook for them?"

He reached for a carrot, began to peel it. "No. I

mean, I've always been pretty serious about hockey on the ice, but after Owen left, I took it off the ice also. Started upping my workouts, my practice, and that meant no time for friends."

"No time for friends?" She looked at him with what appeared to be real horror. "Then who will you eat with?"

You? He didn't say it, though, just julienned the carrots.

"Well, when we get back, you need to have at least one party. Invite your friends . . . or better yet, your family. I'm curious—do your mean cooking skills run in the family? Was your dad a chef?"

He knew she hadn't meant to walk into that one, so he kept his voice soft. "My mom was the chef. My dad passed away when I was thirteen." He glanced up, giving her a smile that he hoped made it all right.

But she had an expression that could break a man's heart if he let it. "Oh, Max, I'm so sorry. Please tell me he got to see you play hockey."

Funny, she always knew just what to say to take off the sharp edge of his grief. Or regret. Or fear.

"He did. He was my biggest fan, I think."

"Did he have cancer?"

He cut some green onion, added it to the pan. "No, he died of pneumonia." A truth that helped him hide the real cause.

"Oh, that's terrible."

"I remember him coming to my game that last time. All bundled up in a blanket, sitting in a wheelchair. My uncle Norm rolled him right up to the glass, and every time I looked over, I saw him. I had a hat trick that game."

"Wow. I'll bet he was so proud." She sifted in the rest of her ingredients.

"Told me that he expected me to be in the Hall of Fame someday."

She began to stir. "You know, the US Hockey Hall of Fame Museum is in Minnesota, in Eveleth. Only three hours from my house."

"Then someday you'll be able to visit my monument," he said, only half-kidding.

She laughed. "What is it about men that they have to have monuments built to them?"

Was she kidding? "It means you left your mark on something. Then people know you were there."

She looked up at him, her hands coated in dough as she kneaded. "Silly man, people know you were there because of the people you've loved."

He looked away. "Of course. But it would be nice to be in the Hall of Fame."

She kneaded the bread into a golden ball. Set it to rest. "I am sure, Max, that you will be remembered by a host of people beyond your fans."

"I just want to be strong, like my dad. Have his kind of faith. It wasn't until he died that I really thought about eternity, but that moment told me I needed help. On earth and in heaven."

"I think we all need that moment in our lives, right? I figured out I needed Jesus when I was pretty little, and I've been following Him since. It helped to hold on to my faith when Owen got hurt. What about your family? Do you have siblings?"

"I have a brother, fourteen years older than me. He's a big fan. Has a wife and a baby girl."

"Sweet."

"Mix together the wine, oyster sauce, soy, water, sugar, and cornstarch with your favorite whisk."

"On it, boss." She found another bowl. "So . . . what will you do with your half of the ten thousand dollars?"

"My half? It's all going to you, Grace." He poured oil into a pan and added the vegetables.

She set down the blended liquid. "No, it's not. You get equal share of our win."

He shook his head.

"Hey, I know. You could use it to come back here and teach. Or better, put a down payment on that vacation house."

He added the mushrooms, kept frying. Didn't look at her.

"What did you mean by 'everyone who gets to have dreams should reach for them'? Don't you get to have dreams, Max?"

He reached for her sauce and poured it in, stirring as it thickened.

"Every time you talk about the future, you act

as if all you have is hockey. But there is more to life than that."

He turned off the heat, removed the pan from the burner. "This has to cool while the bread rises."

But she wasn't moving. She stood so close, her eyes holding a sort of hypnotic power over him. "Max, did someone hurt you once? Jace said that you never date. Why?"

He opened his mouth. Closed it. Swallowed. "Let's get some lunch." He turned, but she put a hand on his arm.

"Max—"

Fine. "I just don't date, okay? I'm not interested in dating—ever. It gets in the way of hockey and my goals—"

"The Hall of Fame."

"Yes, if you must know. This is all I am, all I have. And I'm not going to waste it falling in love, having a family—it would only make me weak."

She stared at him just as he knew she would, with the half-pitying, half-horrified expression that every woman projected when a man said he didn't want a family.

He sort of felt it too. But he couldn't go there, so he softened his tone. "I'm not heartbroken, Grace. I'm just focused. God gave me one job to do on this planet, and that is to play hockey. And I'm doing that to the very best of my ability. I don't have time for a serious relationship, and I don't want anyone to get hurt or get the wrong impres-sion. So . . . I don't date. And I'm perfectly fine with that."

She nodded, the sadness still in her eyes. "I get it, Max. I really get it." She slipped her arm through his. "I'm your swim buddy, after all."

He wanted to wince but instead took her hand on his arm. "Yeah."

See, this competition was exactly what he needed to help him draw the lines around their relationship. Keep it inside the boundaries.

They walked out of the kitchen, and he unknotted his apron, threw it in the bin. He turned just as she was unknotting hers. She lifted it over her head, but it tangled in her hair bun.

"Let me help," he said and reached for the mess. As his hands worked the apron over her head, the bun fell out, her hair silky and soft. She pulled it the rest of the way free and turned as he tossed the apron into the bin.

He couldn't breathe. Not when she was looking at him with those beautiful blue eyes, when he could still feel her hair cascading through his fingers.

Oh, she was pretty—the kind of pretty that made a man just stop and drink it in. Want to spend every day with it. The sun had only darkened those adorable freckles.

Again, like on the plane, he had the strangest sense of falling.

"Ready? I'm dying for some ceviche," she said,

breaking the magic and heading for the door. Saving them both from disaster.

"I have to admit, I never thought I'd hear those words from your mouth."

Amazingly, he sounded unfazed. Maybe he could pull off his words: *I don't date. And I'm perfectly fine with that.*

She turned at the door. "Oh, I'm full of surprises. And I'm just getting started, 9A."

Then she winked. And Max was very afraid.

Chapter 7

Raina needed medical attention, maybe a therapist to help her figure out this annoying attraction to the Christiansen men.

It wasn't like she went looking for them. They motored right up to the door of her heart and knocked. But what was her problem that she kept letting them in? A girl who'd been burned, who'd watched her pride walk out the door in arrogant Owen Christiansen's back pocket, should be a little more savvy. Should actually pay attention to the warning signs when her heart gave an extra thump at the sound of a motorcycle.

She shouldn't even give Casper a second look after her behavior with Owen. In fact, she'd tried to put it out of her mind, tried not to think about the humiliation, the fact that she'd so completely stepped over her own rules, the ones she'd recently set in her desire to start over. But could she help it if Casper could charm an audience with his laughter, his rousing anthem to victory over this upcoming oversize canoe race?

She hadn't a clue what a dragon boat was, or why it might be so important to win the annual Deep Haven dragon boat race, but she felt the battle cry form deep in her chest. So when Casper had turned to her and said, "You'll paddle for us, right?" she couldn't help but nod. Really, what else could she say?

I've never touched a paddle? I can barely swim? No, those words hadn't breached her lips. Just a swift, enthusiastic nod.

Yep, she needed medication, or perhaps a quick, rousing slap to wake her up to her own terrible addiction to men with curly hair and mesmerizing blue eyes who rode motorcycles.

She refused to walk back into her too-vivid mistakes. But something about Casper's chivalry, getting her out of the mud, not betraying her pizza thievery, had spoken to her. She could give him a chance not to break her heart.

A small, tentative chance.

Raina looked in the mirror at her outfit. The last time he'd seen her, she'd been wearing a pizza uniform, so certainly anything would be an improvement. She wore a yellow athletic shirt and a short black workout skirt. She'd pilfered

Liza's closet for swim shoes and a white tennis visor.

Yes, she appeared a bona fide athlete, a picture of paddling perfection.

Grabbing an over-the-shoulder bag, she shoved a towel in—he did mention water, right?—and headed toward the door.

Maybe she didn't have to steer clear of the Christiansens just because she'd made one mistake. A mistake no one would ever have to know about. Sure, she'd mentioned Owen once when she'd mistaken Casper for his brother, but she'd kept quiet after that. Maybe the Owen mistake could leave town with Owen.

"Hey, Raina, are you leaving?"

Her name from Liza's mouth stopped her on the stoop, and she went back inside, where she found her aunt sketching at the kitchen table.

"Working on some new designs?" Raina said, leaning over her shoulder. Liza had built a tidy business and now shipped her one-of-a-kind pottery around the nation. She'd set up a kiln and throwing bench in the garage of her former home, an apartment above the Footstep of Heaven Bookstore and Coffee Shop. Now she displayed her work at the local gallery and art fairs and held occasional open houses in her quaint, story-and-a-half bungalow just off Main Street.

"Yes. How do you like this?" She showed Raina a rainbow of colors against a red clay background, the word *Abundance* etched into the rainbow.

"Beautiful."

"I'm basing everything on John 10:10, the idea that Jesus came to give us life and to give it in abundance."

Raina smiled. Liza had this way of working God into everyday conversation. As if she actually believed God cared about her. Raina didn't have the heart to tell her the truth. Although if God really existed, maybe He did care about somebody like Liza, a good person who spent her time investing in other people. A person without Raina's mistakes, her past. Yeah, maybe that verse worked for people like Liza who had earned the right to ask. To live abundantly.

A girl like Raina had to make her own future.

"I'm headed out to . . . uh, dragon boat practice, and I'll be back—"

Liza put the sketchpad down. "Since when do you dragon boat?"

"Since I got invited to be on the Evergreen Resort team."

Liza nodded, a smile in her eyes. "The Christiansen team. Is Darek leading it this year?"

"Darek? No, it's Casper."

Liza went back to her drawing. "He's a charmer, that one."

Oh? Raina sat at the table, the smile in her day dimming.

"It's not that he's a womanizer. It's just that,

out of all the Christiansens, Casper inherited the Casanova gene. He's dated a small population of Deep Haven girls, and although none of them would speak a word against him, I fear he's left too many pining."

Raina swallowed down the darkness pitching her throat.

Liza got up, went to the fridge, and opened it. "Not that he does it on purpose. I've seen that smile. Oh, boy, right?"

She gave a small nod as Liza pulled out a bag of baby carrots.

"Casper is a great guy, raised by this wonderful Deep Haven legacy family. I'm just saying . . . guard your heart, honey."

Raina stared down at those silly swim shoes, wishing she wasn't so needy, so terribly gullible. Wasn't the girl who gave her heart away with the slightest hint of attention.

"But you'll love dragon boating. It's a blast." Liza had put some carrots in a baggie and now handed them to her. "Just don't go in the drink. It's still pretty cold."

Cold. Yes, well, she probably needed to put her emotions in deep freeze anyway. Just until they could find a cure for her addiction to heartbreak.

"Who else is on the team?" Liza sat down again.

"Um. This deputy guy, Kyle, and a cute girl named Claire—"

"Ah, I'll bet Jensen is paddling also. And Emma?"

Raina lifted a shoulder. "I don't know."

Liza leaned forward, her eyes gleaming. "But you will, Raina. You'll make friends, and you'll see—you belong in Deep Haven. We're a family here, and it won't be long before you're one of us."

Raina tried to answer with a smile.

But she hadn't belonged anywhere, hadn't had a family for so long, that she'd forgotten what it felt like.

And frankly, she wasn't getting her hopes up.

Today he reclaimed the helm of his life.

Casper stood along the long, low pier that anchored his dragon boat in the Deep Haven harbor and imagined himself crossing the finish line, leading his boat of twenty paddlers to victory.

The sun sparkled on the deep-indigo water of Lake Superior, droplets turning to diamonds, the air cool and tangy with the scent of fresh-cut lawn. Seagulls cried greeting, and a hint of campfire smoke from the harbor campground tinged the air.

He wasn't sure why winning this year's race had surfaced such an inexpressible need in him, but he could almost taste the success.

Finally.

He went down to the boat, checking the seats, the drum. He'd already tested the rudder and repainted the head and tail last week, after he transferred the boat to the cement slab that had once held the resort's garage. Thankfully, they'd stored the Evergreen vessel with other local dragon boats in community storage or they would have lost it to last year's fire.

But it emerged, fierce and bold, armed with a fresh coat of paint and ready for victory.

Just like Casper.

He climbed out of the boat, gathered up the life jackets and paddles, and set them on the grassy shoreline, then looked up at the sound of a couple car doors slamming.

Kyle and his wife, Emma, walked across the parking lot, dressed in shorts and T-shirts, water shoes. Behind them were Kyle's parents, Eli and Noelle, similarly attired.

He'd dug deep for this year's team—it wasn't easy to cajole twenty people into giving up their time to practice, especially on a Saturday. He'd cast the net wide, starting with his own family, then out to his father's best pal, Nathan, and his family, and then to Jensen, Darek's best man, and his wife. Then wider to Emma and Kyle, who played in Claire's band. Finally, he'd roped in Pastor Dan and Joe Michaels and their wives.

Nineteen. He was short one paddler.

And then he'd come upon pizza girl Raina Beaumont. Eating *his* pizza, no less, and he had to smile at that.

She'd mustered up with them, joining in their plans to paddle to victory. He'd invited her to practice today, and a big part of him hoped she showed up.

And not just because he needed people. Yes, it might have something to do with her long, raven hair and golden-brown eyes, but also the way she seemed to adopt his enthusiasm for the race.

If he could inspire a stranger, maybe he could inspire the team.

Although she didn't seem like a stranger. He'd seen her around town, and she'd looked familiar —and then it came to him. The wedding.

He couldn't dig out of his mind the memory of her words as he'd walked up to the car: *Oh, for pete's sake, I know, okay? Go away, Owen!*

Clearly Owen had done something stupid. Maybe even hit on her.

What Casper did know, however, was that he wasn't Owen. And he would erase whatever bad impression Owen had left.

Casper heard more car doors slamming and saw more of his team arriving. Claire and Jensen, his parents with Amelia, Nathan and his wife and oldest two kids. Even Tucker Newman had shown up, taking a break from his snowboarding training.

He sat on the edge of a picnic table as they gathered round, found paddles and life jackets. No Raina. He tried not to let that bother him.

"Okay, gang. I know Darek isn't here yet—he'll be back once he and Ivy return from their honeymoon. But he's put me in charge of practice, and we need to get the hang of paddling together, so we'll start without him. I know that many of you have done this before, but for some of you, it's new." He picked up a paddle. "Just a few paddling basics. You start with the reach. You'll be extending your paddle as far as you can—ideally ahead of the bench of the paddler in front of you. By doing this, you'll maximize the amount of time you pull through the water, and thereby increase your force. The farther our reach, the stronger our pull."

He demonstrated, reaching out. It was then that he saw Raina walk up, quietly, in the back. She had her pretty black hair in a ponytail, wore a cheerful yellow shirt. For a second, the sun broke through the clouds.

He cleared his throat. "Then you want to catch the water. This is done by digging in, like you would with a shovel, all the way to the top of the blade."

Raina had picked up a paddle, was mimicking him.

"Now you pull back through the water. Keep your stroke as straight as possible."

Again, he demonstrated, glancing back at her. She met his eyes but didn't smile.

He offered one anyway.

"Keep the stroke short. This isn't a canoe paddle action, but rather a quick stroke in front of the body. The power of your stroke is through the trunk action of your body, moving it from the reach, through your knee and thigh, and then a quick exit out of the water."

He demonstrated again from his seated position on the table. "It'll be easier to understand when we get into the boat. The key is to stay together, and that means we need to listen to our drummer." He gestured to Emma, who held up a mallet.

"Let's jump in the boat and see if we can get this."

As his crew dispersed, he caught up to Raina. "Hey. I'm glad you made it."

She gave him a cool smile. "Sounds fun." But then she moved away, and he couldn't quite ignore the unsettling stab of disappointment.

He put Noelle Hueston and Annalise Decker, his parents' friends, at the bow, the first row. "You'll set the pace. Listen to Emma's call."

"You just want us here because you think we're the weakest," Annalise said. She wore her blonde hair in a braid, under a hat that said *Decker Real Estate*.

"You won't say that after five minutes of paddling at top speed," he promised, but yes, he prayed they didn't quit on him.

Emma sat at the bow, facing the crew, a barrel tom-tom between her knees, keeping rhythm with a long mallet, not unlike the coxswain of a crew team. Although Casper would be the one to steer the boat from his position at the stern.

He directed people into position, trying to balance the narrow boat for weight, then climbed into the back to man the rudder. The two empty places in the vessel would be filled when Darek and Ivy returned.

He held out his hand for Raina, but she managed to get into the boat without his help, not looking at him. Again, he couldn't shake the odd feeling he'd done something to offend her.

"Push us off, Dad."

After John shoved them away from the dock, Emma began to beat on the drum slowly as the two pacesetters, or strokers, led them out into the harbor.

Casper loved gliding over the water, the keen sense of flying. The quiet hush of eighteen people working as one as their paddles dipped. He steered them away from the dock, parallel with the shore, then around to the future starting line.

"When the gun goes off, we'll start with twenty strong, fast strokes, then get into our rhythm. I'll start us with a whistle. Paddles up—"

He blew the whistle, and as one, they dug in, surging ahead. At the bow, Emma hit her drum swiftly, then at twenty, began to slow, establishing a beat.

Except his mother, on the port side, had gotten

off rhythm a half beat, and now her entire side, in order to keep from hitting her paddle, slowed, readjusting their rhythm. Instead of rowing as one unit, half his paddlers dipped down into the water while the other half lifted their paddles in the reach.

The boat began to sway in the water.

Casper glanced at Emma as the rocking lurched the boat, and panic lit across her face one second before she shouted, "Stop!"

But the starboard side, led by Annalise, injected too much power into their strokes to stop, and they dug in hard.

The boat rocked low, and then, just as Casper thought it might right itself, Claire lost her balance. Jensen, her husband, grabbed for her as she tipped over, and the action surged the boat farther to the side.

They took on water, and with *Titanic*-style certainty, the boat swamped.

The temperature of Lake Superior, even in June, could scrape the breath from a polar bear; it slicked all thought from Casper as the boat overturned, trapping him underneath. On instinct, he pushed away, surfaced fast, and searched for heads.

He spotted his father treading water. "Dad!"

"I'm fine! I have your mother!"

Casper ducked back under the boat, checking for trapped paddlers. Please—

He came up again, the cold like daggers against his skin.

Jensen was pushing the boat toward shore while Kyle grabbed paddles. Casper put his feet down and realized he could touch bottom.

He did a quick count and came up with the right numbers. Ahead of him Raina carried two paddles, wading in. Beside her, Nathan held Annalise's arm. She fell, got back up.

Casper came around behind the back of the boat. "Jensen—let's tip it over."

Jensen stood at the head, and Kyle manned the middle as they flipped the boat. Jensen towed it in to shore.

The cold had numbed Casper's legs and he fell, too, as he waded in. His crew sat on the shore, some of them in towels. They eyed him with a look that might make him turn around and head back out to sea.

"I gotta get out of these clothes," Nathan said, holding a shivering Annalise in his arms. "Sorry, Casper. I'm not sure we're quite cut out for this."

"Mr. Decker—"

"I'm with Nathan," Eli Hueston said. "I think I'm too old for the polar bear plunge." He took Noelle's hand and headed toward their car.

In a moment, Casper's crew had dispersed. Even Jensen abandoned him in favor of hot cocoa with his wife.

Casper, his hands shaking, stood on the shore,

staring at the dragon boat, the seats soggy, paddles and wet life preservers in a heap.

"Now what?"

He looked over at the voice. Found Raina, a towel wrapped around her, shivering.

"Are you just going to let them give up?"

"I don't know. I mean—we were a disaster. Darek always organized the team. We won two years ago."

"And we will this year too." She said it through chattering teeth, but something about the fire in her eyes found the few still-lukewarm spots inside Casper.

"We will?"

"Listen. You got me all excited about this dragon boat thing, and now I'm wet and cold, and you're telling me you're going to give up?" She turned and began to walk away. "I should have guessed."

"What's that mean?" He ran to catch up with her.

She just kept stalking across the shore.

"Raina. What did I do? I thought we were getting along the other night."

She pursed her lips, sighed, looked away. Then finally back at him. "We were."

He raised an eyebrow, hoping for more.

"It's just that I've had an epidemic of people—guys—letting me down lately, and I'm kicking myself for believing this might be different."

Oh. Wow. She knew how to hit a man in the throat.

You're the poster boy for the Christiansen family. He didn't know why Amelia's words latched on to him at that moment or why his body moved almost without thought. But he darted after Raina, catching up, then standing in front of her.

She stopped, frowning. "Hey—"

"I'm not giving up. You're right. I started this, and I'm not going to let one mistake shoot me down." He glanced at their wounded dragon boat, moored like a Viking ship on the rocky shore. "We can win this if we learn to paddle in sync."

She made a sound that resembled laughter, or maybe disbelief, but her face was solemn.

So maybe the sound had come from him, something deep inside he'd been trying to escape.

Would escape, someday, once he figured out how.

He looked at her, at the way she held her towel nearly over her head, gripping it at the base. "Can I buy you a coffee?"

She narrowed her eyes at him.

"Please?"

She sighed again, seemed to consider him, and then said, "Okay. But if you offer me a ride on your motorcycle, I'm outta here."

Huh?

But she was already stalking toward the coffee shop.

Chapter 8

"We send you to Hawaii and you drop off the planet!" Eden's voice came through the phone without a hello.

Grace pushed the speaker button and put the phone on the bureau in her hotel room. "You're just in time to help me pick out a dress for tonight's reception."

"Reception? What reception? I have to admit, Grace, I feared I'd find you curled in the fetal position in your room, nose in a good book."

A book. Yes, she'd been meaning to read one, but, well . . .

What woman in her right mind would pick reading over cooking with Maxwell Sharpe?

Outside, the sun dipped into the inky ocean, streams of fire tinging the waves, igniting the horizon. She'd opened the sliding-glass door of her suite to hear the roll of waves on the shore, to smell the fragrance of plumeria outside her window.

"No reading. Just cooking—isn't that why you sent me here?"

Grace stood in front of the mirror in her towel, lifting her wet hair from her neck, trying to decide if she liked it up or down for tonight. Despite her hours in the kitchen this week—the delicious fun of teasing Max, enjoying his patient attempts to teach her Hawaiian cuisine—she'd managed to deepen her tan. She could thank his desire to keep to their schedule of required fun.

Fun, like expanding her palate into the world of raw fish at a local sushi bar. And strolling down Waikiki Beach under a shower of stars. He'd even talked her into parasailing, the boat arching her high over the water to steal her breath as she surveyed the ocean, the beaches, the mountains of the glorious island.

The perspective made her realize that yes, with this trip, God had invited her into a bigger life, a world of tastes and experiences and . . . friendships.

That's what she was calling it, because Max hadn't, not once since the snorkeling fiasco, hinted at more. And he hadn't really even hinted then, just reacted to his fear, something she'd finally accepted after their walk along Waikiki Beach—the one void of any romance.

Oh, sure, the palm trees had danced under a golden moon, the ocean whispering along the shore and the fragrance of romance hanging in the freshness of the salty air. Max bore every resemblance to a full-fledged storybook hero, walking beside her barefoot, leaving toe prints in the creamy sand. His tan showed through his gauzy white shirt, open three buttons down and teased by the wind. When he looked at her with those brown eyes, a sizzle tremored through her, something that turned into a full-out ache when he dropped her off at the elevator.

"Just cooking? Nothing else?" Eden's voice held a hint of tease.

Grace picked up the phone and sat on the bed. "Nope."

Silence. Grace made a face. Uh-oh—she sensed Eden, the journalist, on the hunt.

"Okay, what's going on? I expected you to call me every day wanting to come home. So props to you for that. But you're spending every day with Max Sharpe, one of the Blue Ox's most eligible bachelors, and you're telling me that you are *just cooking?*"

"Yep. Just cooking." Day after day of grueling hours in the kitchen with a man who knew his way around a saucepan. She just might be in heaven.

"You aren't even remotely attracted to him?"

Grace lay back on the bed, staring at the ceiling fan stirring the balmy air. She could imagine her sister, dressed in jeans and a T-shirt, sitting on her tiny deck in downtown Minneapolis, or better, on Jace's patio in St. Paul, the stars glimmering off the dome of the state capitol building. "I didn't say that."

"I knew it!"

"But nothing is going to happen between us." Grace sat up, running her fingers through her wet hair. "He made that perfectly clear the first day.

He thinks of me as his sister. Or at least off-limits because I'm Owen's sister."

More silence.

Grace got up and put the phone back on the bureau. "It's better this way. We're entered in this cooking contest and we need to be able to work together without distraction if we want to win—"

"Hold up. A cooking contest? And since when doesn't Max distract someone? Hello?"

Grace laughed. "We're going to compete in a local culinary contest called Honolulu Chop. Or at least I hope so. If we get in, then we'll compete for four days. One team drops out with each round. But get this—the prize is ten thousand dollars."

"Ten thousand—wow." Eden's voice changed tone, and Grace could hear the latent cheerleader rising. "You can so do this. No one can open a fridge and throw together ingredients like you can."

"I don't know. I think Max is the superhero chef here. I'm still trying to figure out how to make poi."

"Make what?"

"Nothing. There's a meet and greet tonight, and they finalize the contestants based on a casual, social interview, so you're just in time to help me pick out a dress." She went to her closet, opened it. "Green sundress or white floral Hawaiian dress?"

"How about the black cocktail dress I put in your suitcase for exactly this occasion?"

"Ah, that was you. I didn't know whether to blame Amelia—"

"I have much better taste than Amelia."

"And much skimpier. Seriously, Eden, did you really expect me to wear this?" Grace pulled the dress off the hanger. A halter-style cocktail dress, with a low back and above-the-knee skirt, it seemed like she might show less flesh in her swimsuit. "Where did you get this anyway?"

"I bought it for a cocktail party Jace invited me to a few weeks ago, but I didn't have a magnificent tan . . ."

Grace's skin *had* darkened to a beautiful penny shade. She looped the halter behind her neck, let the dress drape in front of her as she stood before the mirror.

"You want to get Max's attention, wear *that*."

"Eden!"

"I'm serious, Grace. From what Jace tells me, Max is a great guy. And very single. Do you like him?"

Oh, it went way, way beyond like. But she kept her voice small, bored, easy. "Sure. He's nice enough."

"Mmm-hmm."

Grace sat on the bed. "Like I said, he's not interested—"

"Then make him interested."

"No. I don't—I don't chase after—"

"Something you want?"

Grace swallowed, sighed.

"Isn't this what the trip is about? Doing something out of your comfort zone?"

"I'm so far outside my comfort zone I've lost sight of it." She got up and unzipped the dress. "I've done everything short of surfing here. I even went parasailing."

"What?"

"Yes." She climbed into the dress and zipped up the back. "And this competition is me living way outside my boundaries." She smoothed the dress over her hips and saw that it didn't dip too low in front, just enough to show off her tan, accentuate her hourglass shape, and reveal her legs. Who knew she could clean up with such class?

In fact, for a second she took her own breath away.

Silence. Then, "You put on the dress, didn't you?"

Grace sighed. "It's too . . . much."

"You look fabulous in it, don't you?"

She shook her head, reached for the zipper.

"Stop!"

What, could her sister see through the phone?

"I can't—"

"Okay, let's go back to the competition. You want to get in, right?"

"Of course. We've worked so hard. I've spent all

week in the kitchen practicing and learned how to make every native Hawaiian dish Max knows. I can chop up a coconut and even core a pineapple. I'm so ready for this. If it wasn't for tonight's interview—"

"That's why you have to wear the dress. In this dress, you know you're amazing. A winner."

Grace again picked up her hair, held it away from her neck. Tugged a few tendrils around her face. Smiled. Whoops, too much teeth.

"You got this, Sis," Eden said. "You want it, go get it."

Go get it.

She did want it, and if this dress helped . . . "I'll call you if we win."

"You will," Eden said. "Love you!"

The call ended, but Grace let her sister's words linger and find her heart. *You want it, go get it.*

Yes, tonight she planned on winning.

The twilight had curled in like a mist by the time Grace finished tying up her hair, adding a few floral bobby pins and a silver and faux—she assumed it was faux—diamond necklace that Eden had also shoved into her bag. She'd even found a pair of strappy black sandals about two inches taller than she'd ever worn before. She dearly hoped she didn't topple over in them.

But she had to admit, next time she left town, she'd require Eden to do all her packing.

Next time . . . ?

Okay, this vacation had sunk deeper into her skin than she imagined. Making her leave her hotel room looking like a woman who'd never known a life of cutoff shorts, pizza stains, and old Deep Haven Huskies hockey T-shirts.

She looked . . . elegant. Refined. Even sexy, although that word seemed unfamiliar and a little uncomfortable as it touched down in her mind.

Confident. Yes, she'd settle on that description. She wrapped a scarf around her shoulders and hit the button for the elevator.

A low whistle filtered down the hall. She turned and startled at the sight of her teacher, Keoni, walking toward her. He wore a white linen suit, his long dark hair pulled back in a neat ponytail, looking exotic and painfully handsome.

"I didn't know you were staying here," she said as the elevator door opened and he held it for her.

"I live on the Big Island, not Oahu, so the school provides lodging." He stepped in after her, letting his gaze travel over her. "I think someone wants to win this competition."

She grinned. "I do. It's more than just the money—and the fun—though. It's about Max and how much he's believed in me."

Oh, maybe that was too much information. She stared straight ahead and tried to keep her face from heating.

Then the elevator doors opened to the lobby and there stood Max.

So much for trying to keep cool. He'd also brought his A game to tonight's reception. He wore a black suit, tailored to accentuate his wide shoulders and trim waist, and a pink dress shirt, a matching plumeria blossom tucked into the lapel buttonhole. He'd shaved, and the smell of his cologne tugged her out of the elevator. But the expression in his eyes stalled her just a few feet away.

He appeared almost . . . angry?

She wanted to flee the lobby for her room, forget this stupid interview and the fact that she had longed, just a little—or more than a little— for Max to be wowed. Longed to take his breath away.

Grace licked her lips, found her voice. "Too much? I can change—"

"We'll be late. You look . . . you look . . ." He shook his head. "Let's just go."

He held out his arm, but his words cut through her, cold and sharp. She ignored them, bit her lip, and let him lead the way to his car, parked by the entrance. She climbed in, tucking the scarf around her shoulders, tying it in front. Blinking to keep the bite from her eyes.

He got in beside her. "You look real nice." His tone sounded like he might be congratulating the other team on their victory.

But she did look nice—better than nice—and for a moment she hated him for stealing that from her.

He pulled away from the curb and said nothing during the drive to the reception. She glanced at him once and noticed his hand, whitened on the stick shift. Maybe he was as tense as she was about tonight. She dared a look at his face and found his jaw tight.

He noticed her gaze on him and met it. Offered the smallest smile.

Grace turned away, completely confused.

Music drifted from the glassed-in reception hall tucked into the arching, lush mountains and overlooking the Pacific Ocean. A valet took the car, and Grace conceded to taking Max's too-muscular arm as he led them up the stairs and into the party.

Inside the hall, the open doors spilled out to the beach, where tiki lights illuminated a path to the ocean. A band played on the lanai, luring people to the outdoor seating.

Tucked surreptitiously around the room, cameramen captured every nuance of the evening —from the flickering candlelight to the excited hum of guests holding champagne glasses, all dressed in high summer fashion. Most of the men wore linen suits, the women in cocktail dresses. She saw Keoni greet a tall, sun-kissed blonde woman in a sarong, her hair loose and cascading down her back.

"That's Tonie, one of the judges this year. She has a food blog and a show on a local cable network," Max said.

As if sensing Max's words, the woman looked over at them, smiling when her gaze fell on Max. Hungry. Interested.

A tiny knot tightened in Grace's stomach. Good grief, she wasn't jealous, was she?

"Uh, Max, I thought this was just a local competition. It's not going to be on any cable shows, right?"

"I don't know. I think they'll broadcast it locally, but no, I don't think anyone outside Hawaii will see it."

She couldn't place the feeling inside her—relief? Or maybe disappointment?

Well, they probably wouldn't even be chosen.

"Let's eat," Max said, guiding her toward the food, his hand warm on the small of her back.

A lavish buffet of appetizers spread out as if hinting at the competition awaiting them. Grace left Max and perused the delicacies, reading the cards. Chicken yakitori, spanakopita, assorted dim sum, shrimp tempura, oysters Rockefeller, salmon roulade, ahi poke, sashimi, and grilled garlic shrimp skewers.

Behind her, Max had picked up a plate, started to fill it. Grace, however, had lost her appetite, strangling a bit on the taste of her own imminent failure. The knots in her stomach multiplied.

"I need some air," she said and headed away from the table, out toward one of the smaller lanais. She stepped into the balmy heat and drank in the cool ocean breeze.

"Are you okay?"

The man, dressed in a black suit, black shirt open at the neck, was nursing a glass of red wine on the next lanai. His words left the tinge of an English accent in the air.

"I'm fine. I'm just . . . nervous, I guess. I didn't expect to be here. I only came to Hawaii to learn to cook for my sister's wedding, and suddenly I'm in this crazy contest." She turned away from him and stared out at the ocean. "Don't get me wrong—I want to win. I think we can win. Or . . . thought so until now. My cooking partner is so talented. It's just . . ." She closed her eyes, breathed in more air.

"Just?" he said quietly.

"Lots of pressure. All those cameras watching our every move. And . . ." She looked out toward the ocean, the darkness, the mystery. "I don't want to let him down."

"I see."

She glanced over her shoulder at the man as he took a sip of his drink. He considered his wine, then her, his blue eyes latching on to hers. "Be yourself, keep an open mind, and do your best. I have no doubt you'll blow everyone away."

What kind words, and being delivered with

that British accent didn't hurt either. "Thank you."

He nodded, lifted his glass to her, then turned to go inside.

"They're introducing the contestants," Max said behind her.

She followed him inside and stood next to him. From the podium in front, Keoni was introducing the contest and this year's field of entrants. Six teams all vying for entry, with five slots. Keoni singled out a brother-sister team of native Hawaiian descent, a hippie husband-wife team who ran a café on the North Shore, and a father-son pair from the base at Pearl Harbor. The sight reminded Grace of her father pairing with Owen.

That might be fun to watch.

She recognized the two ladies from their class, gussied up in Hawaiian dresses and leis. They waved to the crowd, giggling, as they were introduced.

When Keoni called their names, Max took her hand and raised it with his above their heads. Nodded to the crowd with a "bring it" athlete's expression.

Super. She'd forgotten his other persona, the hockey player, the guy who didn't know how to lose. Aka ninja chef on overdrive.

Grace let go of his hand as soon as he lowered hers and wrapped her arms around her waist. She barely heard the names of the last contenders, muscle-built brothers from California who'd flown over for the competition and waved from their perch by the appetizer table.

"When do the interviews start?" she asked.

"I don't know," Max said, looking over her head around the room, anywhere but at her.

"Max! I didn't know you were going to compete!"

Grace could have predicted the voice came from Tonie, the blonde. She watched as the woman wrapped an arm around Max's neck.

Max kissed her on the cheek, his smile warm. "You look gorgeous, as usual," he said, so much charm in his voice that the dark burn in Grace's chest could turn her to cinders.

Tonie smiled, lifted a shoulder. "I would have gladly been on your team if you'd called me."

Uh, I'm standing right here. Grace shook her head and made to move away, but Max caught her with a hand to her back. "Have you met my teammate? Tonie Addison, this is Grace Christiansen."

Grace held out her hand, found Tonie's slim and cool in hers. The woman's eyes held a glint of challenge even as she smiled. "Nice to meet you. Are you a chef?"

Grace couldn't help it. "Yes. I'm the kitchen manager for a restaurant in northern Minnesota." She didn't have to mention it was a pizzeria, right?

"Lovely." Tonie's gaze flicked over Grace, her expression hooded. "I wish you the best of luck." She smiled at Max, then moved away.

"I want to go home," Grace said quietly, not necessarily to Max, but he caught it.

"What?"

She glanced at beautiful Tonie, with her shimmery skin, the way she could glide through a room. *Tonie* looked like the perfect partner for Max, the one who could help him win any competition.

Grace just looked like a girl trying way too hard. She rubbed her arms. "I don't know what I'm doing here. This was a terrible idea. We're going to get destroyed, knocked out in the first round." She shook her head. "I don't want to do this. I feel stupid."

"Well, you don't look stupid," he said gruffly. She probably wore too much hurt in her eyes because suddenly his expression changed. He took her by the elbow and walked her toward the door.

Keoni intercepted them. "Are you leaving?"

Max nodded, and Grace couldn't look at either of them. Somehow she'd wrecked this entire evening.

"Grace isn't feeling well," Max said quietly.

Keoni nodded, something enigmatic in his eyes. "I see."

"Sorry, dude."

Keoni said nothing as Max led her outside, handed his ticket to the valet.

"Max, you should stay. I'll get a cab—"

"No."

She didn't know how it was possible to shiver in Hawaii, but she felt as if she were standing in the middle of a Minnesota snowstorm at the height of January.

In fact, in that moment, she longed for it.

Grace just *had* to wear that dress.

Just when Max had all his feelings tightly in check and somehow managed to keep himself safe from her effect on him, she had to appear in a dress that could make him forget his own name.

It skimmed over her body like a glove, flaring out just above her knees, the V-neck tempting his eyes to travel where he could get into big trouble. She wore heels, accentuating her beautiful legs, and with her hair piled on top of her head, blonde curls dripping down around her face, she looked nothing like the woman he'd spent the last two weeks with, covered head to toe in her white chef's apparel.

The moment the elevator doors opened, his breath had squeezed from his lungs, the band around his chest cutting off even his heartbeat. Images from their practice sessions over the past week flashed before him—flour on her chin that he longed to nudge off with his thumb, the way she laughed at his hockey stories while perfecting her poke, even her teasing towel whips as she shooed him away from her manapua dough.

He could nearly hear the walls crumbling, a gritty, brutal crash that left him weak as she floated off the elevator, turning his world to Technicolor. He hadn't realized he'd been living in black and white and muted grays until that moment.

He smiled . . . or thought he did—he couldn't remember. And he'd tried to compliment her but had only a vague recollection of something terse emerging from his mouth.

However, whatever he'd offered wasn't enough because he'd hurt her—he got that when she looked at him in the car, her blue eyes holding back pain.

Right then he'd wanted to pull off to the side of the road, turn to her, and . . .

And . . .

And this was why he agreed to escape the reception. Because if Keoni looked at her again like he'd seen a wave at Mavericks, Max just might toss the surfer chef into the drink. He hadn't missed her conversation with Chef Michael Rogers on the lanai either. The man had stepped inside the door and gulped the rest of his wine like a shooter of tequila.

Well, Grace did that to a guy. Appeared in his life and knocked the wind right out of him. Max could use his own stiff drink. Or maybe a run down the sand into the cool breeze, the darkness, to clear his head instead of thinking about . . .

"Are you mad at me?"

Grace sat beside him in the convertible, clasping her scarf in front of her. The wind played with her hair, tugging at it, twining long golden strands into the breeze.

"No," he said but conceded that yes, he sounded angry. Or maybe just focused, although she might not know the difference. He schooled his voice. "No, I'm not angry. I'm . . . I wanted to get into the competition."

Actually, that wasn't remotely the truth. He couldn't care less about this competition, other than its giving poor, desperate him a reason to spend more time with her. As if he could truly teach her something.

Grace could cook circles around him—he'd figured that out on day three when she'd rescued his haupia. He might have taught her how to make a few Hawaiian dishes, but she knew exactly what to add to enhance flavor. She'd even suggested a few substitutions, thinking on her feet. Two days ago she'd created a mouthwatering chicken curry variation to manapua. Yesterday she made mahimahi tacos with fresh cilantro slaw that could make a man follow her to the mainland.

Not that he would, because they were only vacation friends. Just here for another week.

He couldn't think about that either. Because in a week, it would all be over, every glorious minute where he'd duped himself into believing this would be enough.

Except if she dropped out of the competition, she might also drop out of class. Even get on an airplane.

He couldn't move, his hands white-gripped on the steering wheel.

"I'm sorry. I wanted to be in it also," she said quietly. "I don't know what came over me. I just . . ."

He glanced at her, and—oh no, was she crying? Max grimaced and pulled into the nearest parking lot, one stretching along Waikiki Beach, and turned off the car.

For a long moment, he said nothing, only listened to the waves wash to shore, back out again. How had he turned into such a jerk? "I'm sorry. I know I sounded mad and probably even overly competitive—"

"It's my fault. I saw those cameras and . . . and your friend Tonie and . . ." She looked away, wiped her cheek.

His friend Tonie? "C'mon. Let's take a walk." He leaned over, locked his cell phone in the glove compartment, then got out, circled the car, and caught up to her as she opened her door.

"Wait." He knelt before her, took her slim ankle in his hand, and silently unbuckled her shoe. He did the same with the other, then picked up her spiky heels. In them, she'd stood nearly to his nose, her beautiful eyes so accessible, her lips only—

Yes, this was much better. Now she stood to his shoulder, her power over him diluted.

Until she reached up and pulled her hair out of its twist. When it trickled into the wind, he turned away, letting her shoes dangle from two fingers. He toed off his own shoes as they reached the sand, shoved his socks in them, and took them in his other hand.

His feet sank into the cool, creamy mortar as he led them along the shoreline. A full moon hung over them, turning the waves to an icy shimmer, the water frothy as the surf thundered to shore. He could make out a group of night surfers hot-dogging.

Grace walked beside him wordlessly.

He dug deep, hoping for the right words. "After my dad died, I quit hockey."

She glanced at him, frowned.

"I couldn't play anymore. All the joy had gone out of it for me, and it seemed pointless. After all, if he wasn't there watching my games, why bother?"

They passed the beach area of one resort, moving toward the light of the next. "And then about halfway through the season, my uncle Norm woke me up early one morning, and he and my mom all but wrestled me into the car and drove me to the arena. My old team had a tournament, and they forced me to sit in the stands, watching."

She had turned to watch him speak—he saw it out of his peripheral vision. But he continued to stare ahead at the glimmering darkness of the ocean, the memory an ache so ripe he could feel it tightening his throat.

"I longed to be on the ice. To hear the roar of the crowd, but also to feel my own power as I skated toward the goal, juking out the goaltender, slapping in the puck. I love the ice. I love playing. I knew that if I gave it up, I wouldn't be honoring my dad. I'd be turning my back on what he wanted for me. What I wanted for myself."

She had caught her lip between her teeth and now stared at the ocean too.

"I couldn't stay in the stands, so at the end of the first period, I went into the locker room and talked to Coach. He let me sit on the bench with the team, and the next day at 5 a.m. I showed up for practice. I haven't walked off the ice since."

Grace seemed to be watching her feet kick through the sand. They had passed the second resort. He recognized the boardwalk, the deck, and the palm-edged walkways of their lodgings ahead.

"I don't know why you're abandoning the ice, but after these two weeks, I see more in you, Grace, than someone who sits in the stands. You are an amazing chef. You can do this if you want it."

She looked at him then, and her mouth twitched as if trying to smile. Her eyes glistened, shiny in the moonlight.

He wanted to stop. To take her face in his hands, to run his thumb down her cheek, maybe chase away a tear. Instead he put it all into his voice, softening it, adding the urgency that churned inside him. "And you're not alone. We make a great team, and I'm in it to win it if you are."

Something in her eyes shifted as if his words had filtered through the layers of fear or frustration or even disappointment to latch on and pull her out of herself.

"I do want to do it. It's just . . . I'm in way over my head here."

Yeah, well, him too, but . . . "I have an idea. C'mon." He angled across the boardwalk toward the lobby of their hotel.

She trotted after him to keep up. "What are we doing?"

He punched the elevator button and got on with her. At her floor, he handed over her shoes. "Change into your swimsuit and meet me here in ten minutes."

She frowned, but he answered with a grin, something birthed from the idea swirling inside. "Trust me."

When she nodded, it was all he needed to head

upstairs, change into his doggers and surf shirt, and race back down, towel around his neck. He slipped a tip to the concierge, who let him into the surf shack. He picked out a board and a long-sleeved rash guard and returned to find Grace in the lobby.

She wore a pair of swim shorts and a tankini top, her towel draped around her neck.

He handed her the rash guard as she eyed the board. "Put this on."

"Max . . ." She glanced beyond him at the board leaning against the arched door. "You do know it's night."

"Yep." Grabbing the board, he jogged off the deck, down the boardwalk, toward the beach. He glanced over his shoulder, just to confirm that she'd followed him.

"Max?"

"Trust me!"

He headed down to the water, stopping where the waves creased the shore, the sand thick and swampy. Foam lapped at his feet, tugging at him, urging him into the cool mystery of the dark Pacific.

Grace caught up. He turned, grabbed her towel and his, and tossed them back onshore.

She was staring at him not unlike that first day, when she realized he meant it when he said he'd take her sightseeing. The words came easily. "I'm your swim buddy, remember?"

She nodded, not a hint of confidence in her face. "It's time for you to swim."

He held out his hand and imagined it took everything inside her to grab it. But she did, and he walked her out into the surf. He reached waist level and stopped. "Get on the board."

"Really?"

"I want you to feel the water under you, to catch the rhythm of the wave."

She climbed aboard and he affixed the surf leash to her ankle.

"Stretch out on it, your chest in the middle, and start paddling. I'm right here with you."

She began to dog-paddle, and he kept one hand on the board as they ventured out. The beach sloped slowly, shallow long into the ocean, so he touched bottom even as they paddled out past the break zone to deeper water. He finally started treading but kept the board in reach with Grace angled out toward the ocean.

"Sit up and balance. Feel the water move under you."

She sat up, dangling her feet. The moon trailed an iridescent finger along the water, and she sat in a puddle of brilliance, her skin glistening. She had the power of a mermaid, the ability to bewitch him, pull him under.

He shook free and turned, one hand on the board, as he watched the waves. "Look for lumps on the horizon. Those are called sets, and in them are the waves that you might catch. If you ride over the swell, they'll surge by you, then peak and break. Beginning surfers have to learn how to read a wave and find the right one. Sure, you'll choose the wrong wave, but you just paddle back out and try again."

She was watching the horizon, her hands circling in the water.

"Now, when you find the right wave, you're going to turn around and paddle hard to get under it. You'll have to start paddling before it gets to you, and if it goes past you, then you've lost it."

"And I have to try again."

"Right. But tonight I'll get you in position."

"You want me to actually surf?"

More challenge than panic in her voice, and that's why he loved her.

No . . . liked. Enjoyed.

"Once I catch the wave, what do I do?"

"You have to get up. You get your knees under you, then push with your arms and pop up, balancing with one foot in front, the other in back. But tonight, I just want you to ride the wave in. We'll work on getting up later—"

"I wanna try."

He looked at her.

"I'm going to try." She'd set her jaw, tight, almost angry.

Okay, then. Max stared out into the horizon. The

night cast an eerie quietness over the dark waters, and for a second he feared what might be below, unseen. Strange because he'd always loved the bite of danger, the sense of skirting death, the adrenaline of living recklessly.

Now, the fear came quickly, settled in his gut, tingled through him. As if for the first time it might actually take root.

"Now?"

A set of swells came toward them, but he shook his head. "Not yet."

They bobbed in the water, letting them ride by. Then another set. Finally, "Okay, I think these are the ones. Let's get you turned around, and when I tell you to, paddle hard. When you feel the wave begin to take you, get your knees under you and pop up on the board. Or . . . you can just stay on your knees."

"Just tell me when."

He turned her around as she stretched out on the board. Read the sets and—"Now. Paddle hard." He pushed her out at an angle, then paddled with her, just to get her going.

But she was windmilling hard in the water and he could see the wave lift her. "Stand up!"

Grace pushed up to her knees and stayed there for a second—so long that he thought she might just . . . Suddenly she popped to her feet. She balanced there, a perfect silhouette against the light of the moon, the sparkling water.

The wave carried her in. It wasn't pretty, or even remotely correct, but she stayed on, almost all the way to shore before the board slowed. Then she paddled air, losing her balance, splashing into the water.

Max swam hard toward her.

Ten feet from him, Grace sprang up, laughing, water streaming from her mane of gold hair. "Wow—I did it! I did it!"

Before he knew it, she'd launched herself at him, diving into his arms, hers curling around his neck.

The warmth of her body jolted him, but he reacted fast. He caught her at the waist, stood in the water and swung her around, feeling how small and perfect and—

Oh, boy. He wanted to stay right here, holding her, molding her to himself in the darkness, the vastness of the ocean around them.

Safe from time and life and especially incurable diseases that would steal the magic away.

How he hated his life sometimes, the part that stole his tomorrows.

She leaned back, met his eyes. "I did it."

His gaze caught on the shimmer of water on her eyelashes. If he angled his head down, he could just brush her lips—

Max found a smile, praying that his heart didn't actually explode from his chest. "Yeah, you did. You're a regular surfing Betty!" He heard his own too-exuberant enthusiasm. But maybe it would hide the tightening of his throat, the desire that thrummed through him.

"A what?"

"Nothing. You were fabulous." Yeah, that sounded nearly normal. He put her down, let her back away. Cleared his throat. "Wanna go again?"

"No." She stood in the water, hands on her hips. "I shouldn't have let a few fancy appetizers, wandering cameras, and a hot blonde scare me away from the goal line."

"Is that a football reference? Because I don't do football—"

"But you do cook. *We* cook. And we'll be an amazing team if we can just get a chance to compete. I wanna call Keoni and tell him that we want our interview. I'll beg him if I have to."

"What are you talking about? We *had* our interview. You talked with Chef Rogers on the lanai, and Tonie already knows I can cook. Not to mention Keoni was the one who pushed us into this in the first place."

She stared at him. "What are you saying?"

"Those are the judges, Grace. And if they like us, we're in."

Her eyes went big. "I hope they like us."

"They will," he said. "They'll love us."

She smiled, something soft and perfect and brilliant in the moonlight, and he wished for a wave to knock him over and sweep him out to sea.

Or maybe he'd already been swept away.

Chapter 9

For the first time in her life, Raina had found a place she might actually belong.

Or at least be needed.

Since Casper had bought her coffee in an attempt to warm her after her dip in the cool Lake Superior water, Raina had learned four things.

One. Casper might be pegged as the town Casanova, but he'd turned into a gentleman around her. Which made her wonder if Liza had him confused with Owen.

Two. Raina possessed latent dragon boat paddling skills.

Three. Casper desperately needed help garnering his team's confidence if he wanted to win back the Evergreen Resort dragon boat trophy.

Four. She, despite her past with Christiansen men, wanted to help him earn said confidence. Especially after his enthusiasm at her idea to have paddle training onshore.

No more live-water practices until they learned to work together, in rhythm. She'd followed with a suggestion that he have a team barbecue after their first in-water practice.

The team had invested in the cookout idea and eagerly assembled by the lake after Saturday's practice, more interested in eating than paddling, perhaps. The Huestons brought a pasta salad; Claire and Jensen provided soda; the Deckers furnished fresh chocolate chip cookies.

It felt like a family reunion. Especially with the campfire crackling on the shore, mingling with the laughter and hum of conversation among the team members seated in camp chairs and Adirondack chairs around the flames.

If only Raina didn't feel like the cousin no one knew. But maybe with her decisive action to help save the team spirit, she might be grafted in.

Unless, that was, she let the hamburgers burn.

"Turn the flame down!" She rushed over to the grill, where Casper manned the spatula, reached around him, and turned down the heat. A char had already formed on the meat, the scent of the garlic powder turning acrid.

"Sorry. I thought they weren't cooking fast enough," Casper said.

Raina put the lid down. "Trust me. Trap the heat, and in a minute or so, flip them." She handed him her special recipe barbecue sauce—a tangy concoction she'd experimented with for days before getting right. "Then brush this on them. I'll be back to check your work." She smiled, winked.

Shoot, what was wrong with her, adding that wink?

She'd clearly lost her head. The last thing she needed was Casper flirting with her.

Except, why *hadn't* he hit on her once in the past week? Was she that repulsive?

Casper grinned in response. "Thanks, Raina. You're a lifesaver."

Yeah, whatever. But his words wouldn't leave her as she returned to laying out the buffet in the picnic shelter. The large Tupperware container held Noelle's salad, with corkscrew pasta and green olives, and Raina uncovered a plate of Annalise's cookies under cellophane. Oh, someone had added caramel bars—she guessed that was Ingrid's contribution.

John and Ingrid had shown up today with Tiger—Darek and Ivy still on their honeymoon. They'd put a life jacket on the six-year-old and set him between them in the boat, an extra incentive for everyone to work together. It worked—the kid possessed a sort of magic charm because the team not only paddled in unison, but on the last run, crossed the bay in record time.

Team Evergreen might just win this crazy event.

Raina returned to the grill, opened the lid. The rich scent of the garlic-and-seasoned-salt marinade on the burgers could call a dead man to the table for supper. "You can turn them now."

"Aye, aye," Casper said.

"Funny." But she watched as he flipped them. "Yum."

He closed the top. Turned to her. "No, I'm serious. I think we're finally getting it. I might be

198

the captain, but you're definitely first mate. Thanks for not letting me give up."

Like she would give up on this man. His very eyes held her captive. Blue like the lake and with the power to take her under, too. He'd grown his dark hair a little long, covered today by a red bandanna tied at the corners like a candy wrapper. The ends curled out the back. He wore swim trunks and flip-flops and over everything an apron that added an odd domestic appeal to his rugged exterior, the one accentuated by the lime-green team T-shirt with the sleeves ripped off. His arms evidenced all his hard work rebuilding the family resort, a farmer's tan now fading after a day on the lake . . . It all had the power to stun her a little.

And yes, conspired to make her want to help him.

So much for her swearing off Christiansen men.

"Should I add the sauce?" he asked.

"Yes, just dab some on each burger, close the lid for another minute or so, and they'll be ready. I'll grab a serving platter."

She found a plate and was returning when she saw Colleen Decker sidle up to Casper. A pretty girl, athletic. Raina had overheard talk about her attending St. Scholastica in Duluth in the fall on a volleyball scholarship. She wore athletic shorts and a dragon boat T-shirt rolled up at the sleeves and cropped to show off her toned midsection.

Colleen stared at Casper as if he might be the

man of her dreams. She held out a plate. "Are the burgers ready?"

"Nope. Not yet," Raina said, speaking past the strange bite in her throat. "I'll dish them up and put them on the buffet."

Colleen frowned at her, then refocused on Casper, her expression about as transparent as cellophane. "So are you going to the dragon boat street dance? I hear the Blue Monkeys are playing."

"Probably. You'll have to save me a dance." He smiled, and Colleen cast a look at Raina, ownership in it.

Of course, everyone in Deep Haven belonged to each other in a way.

"Platter?" Casper said as he opened the lid to the grill. Colleen stepped back and Raina held out the plate for the burgers.

"Can you tell everyone dinner is ready?" she asked Colleen.

Colleen narrowed her eyes but returned to the congregation by the fire.

"She likes you," Raina said, not sure why she'd mentioned that.

"I know," Casper said. He finished plating the last burger. "I heard she and her longtime boyfriend, Tucker, are on the outs. I sort of thought he joined the team to get her attention, but it doesn't seem to be working. Or maybe she's trying to make him jealous; I don't know. Trust me—she'll get over it." He smiled again, and well, Raina could hardly blame the girl, really.

She liked him too.

The crowd gathered around the banquet, and just as Raina was about to take a plate and start self-serving, Casper announced prayer.

Prayer. Okay, right. She'd seen him in church, a few rows behind Liza's pew. She hadn't really expected him to bring God outside Sunday, however.

Still, she bowed her head, prayed with them, surprised at how many echoed his *amen*.

She served herself, then brought her plate over to the campfire, finding a perch on a log. One by one, her team joined her.

Claire sat on the folding camp chair she and Jensen had retrieved from their truck. "These are amazing burgers, Raina. I love the sauce. Did you work as a chef in Minneapolis? That's where you're from, right?"

Across from her, Eli and Noelle Hueston took chairs, and beside them, their son Kyle and his wife, Emma, their drummer. "I used to live in Minneapolis," Emma said. She forked pasta into her mouth. "Yum."

"Yeah. I grew up in Minneapolis," Raina said, hoping they'd move on. "I worked here and there as a chef. But it's an easy recipe. Just some brown sugar, molasses, honey, Worcestershire sauce, mustard, liquid smoke—stir it together, add salt and pepper."

"Oh, I have to have a recipe. I could never throw anything together like that," Annalise Decker said, sitting on a bench across the fire. "To just guess? That takes special talent." She smiled at Raina. "This was a great idea, by the way. Thanks."

The water lapped the shore, a family of seagulls landing nearby, hungry, watching for dropped tidbits. The smell of campfire smoke tinged the misty evening air, the coals crackling as the sunlight flamed across the lake.

The conversation turned to past dragon boat races, other teams, then a rating of the annual fish burger stand and an opinion on the new cupcakes at the donut shop. Raina listened, quiet, soaking in the sense of family, even laughing at the inside jokes.

Casper stood just outside the ring, eating his burger and looking on, a strange smile on his face.

She glanced at him now and again, and he met her eyes once. She heard them then, his words from before.

I might be the captain, but you're definitely first mate.

First mate.

She finished her burger, collected a few empty plates, and found the trash. She overheard Casper talking about the next practice, then saw Jensen and Claire, Kyle and Emma packing up their folding chairs. Noelle retrieved her bowl of pasta, and Annalise distributed the remainder of the cookies to the crowd. Raina didn't realize how focused she was on cleaning until she looked up again and realized the majority of the team had left.

Including, it seemed, Casper.

Without saying good-bye. At least not to her.

Only John and Ingrid remained. Tiger stood on the shore, throwing rocks into the lake.

She tried not to let Casper's escape bother her as she bundled up the garbage.

John retrieved the bag from her. "Great dinner," he said.

She managed a smile.

Ingrid found her empty container of caramel bars. Her blonde hair pulled back with a headband, she wore a pair of capris, the oversize lime-green team T-shirt like a tunic. In a way, Ingrid reminded Raina of so many of the PTA mothers who had lined up in their minivans, picking up kids after school.

Raina had walked home after school, her key dangling from a string around her neck. She'd never had a PTA mother.

But she'd wanted one.

"Raina, you are turning out to be the Christiansen family's secret weapon! First you help Grace pull together a delicious wedding dinner, and now you're helping Casper build team spirit. We just might have to adopt you." Ingrid gave her a one-armed hug before following John out to their

Caravan, leaving Raina alone with the now-doused fire, the empty picnic shell.

The seagulls moved in, picking up the picnic scraps, the sun falling behind the clouds, the sky a mottled, bloody red.

Raina shooed away the gulls, sat down at the fire, picked up a stick to poke at it. John had doused it with water, so the embers swam in an ashy-gray stew.

Heat pressed her eyes. One minute she'd been in the middle of the conversation—okay, on the edge listening, but here, on the team. The next . . . Despite Ingrid's words, it felt like the story of her life. She got up to check the area for any more garbage, threw out a couple runaway napkins, then headed toward the beach to walk home.

Behind her, tires crunched on gravel. "Raina!"

She looked up. Casper got out of his truck, closing the door. He jogged over to her. "Where are you going?"

She blinked, fast, hard, not wanting him to see the moisture in her eyes. "Home?"

"On such a beautiful night? Don't you want to see the best place in all of Deep Haven to watch the sunset?"

He stood there, twirling his key chain, grinning as if they'd planned this, a friendly sunset date. Or maybe they had—she had a faint recollection of him mentioning the sunset today at practice. He'd been serious?

She frowned. "But . . . you left."

"Sorry. I had to run to the office and pay for our use of the picnic shelter. I forgot and I didn't want them to think we were running off, leaving the bill behind."

She stared at him.

"What?"

"It's just . . . you aren't at all the guy I thought you were."

"Who did you think I was?"

She shook her head. "It doesn't matter now." She glanced toward the setting sun, not sure if she should give him an out. "I think people had a good time—"

"Are you kidding? They had a great time. Now c'mon . . ."

Before she could stop him, he'd reached out, taken her hand. And then they were walking along the beach, like a couple.

It took her a second to catch up. He had strong hands, the kind used to hard work, and she was just about to tighten her grip when he let hers go.

Oh.

"Most people don't know about this secret sunset-watching getaway. They come down to the harbor and sit on the beach. But there's this little path here . . ."

He led her down the rocky shoreline, past a boat launch to a tiny trail through the woods. He held back a branch and she followed the path.

It emerged only thirty feet later onto another beach.

"See, the land sort of juts out to the south, and most people walk out on the rocks there. But trust me—this is the view you want." He took her hand again—this time she didn't read anything into it—and led her to a grouping of boulders, a shelf of rock that slid out into the lake, the water caught in pockets and crannies. He stopped at a couple tall rocks and lifted her easily on top of one, then climbed up beside her.

Casper leaned back on his hands as if they were old friends catching the sunset every day.

It felt comfortable. Easy.

"In a second, the sun is going to go down, and the sky is going to turn this amazing mix of red and orange. The lake becomes a sort of deep purple, and the clouds will be streaked with color as if they're on fire."

"You sound like you've seen this before." She didn't want to add the sudden thought that he'd brought other girls out to this very spot.

"My dad and I used to come here. He would fish on the big lake sometimes, and after we pulled in the boat, we'd sneak back here, take in the magic."

"It's beautiful."

"It's just one of the many treasures of Deep Haven. One of the reasons I love living here." He sighed. "And one of the reasons I hate the thought of leaving."

"You're leaving?" Of course he was. She should have seen this coming.

"I don't know. I've been offered this internship in Roatán. It's an island off Honduras where there's a number of shipwrecks and pirate treasures."

She couldn't help but laugh, then stopped when she saw his expression dim. "Sorry. I'm sorry. I thought . . . You're serious."

"Yeah, I think so." He wrinkled his nose at her. "Or I thought so. Until just a second ago. It does sound a little hokey, doesn't it? But I'm an archaeology major, so—"

"So it's not hokey at all." She glanced at the sunset, and indeed, it had turned magical, the colors revealing the artistry of God.

Funny, she never would have had that thought before moving here. Maybe Liza's religious thinking had infected her. The thought sank in and didn't hurt.

"Is that what you want? To be a treasure hunter?"

"I'd like to find something precious, yes. Maybe Blackbeard's treasure. Or a lost artifact from the Crusades."

"So you're like what's his name—Indiana Jones?"

He laughed and it sweetened the air. "I guess so. Mostly I just want to find the things hidden, the treasure that no one sees or doesn't think to look for." He picked up a rock, tossed it into a puddle of flame. "What do you want?"

A home. A family. This moment with a man who wouldn't jump on his motorcycle and drive away.

"I want to be safe," she said quietly, before she could stop herself.

His expression drained. She tried to lighten her words with a smile but then looked away. "I came here because I had nowhere else to go, and Liza offered me a home."

He was still looking at her, and she blinked, fighting another rush of tears to her eyes. Why had she said that?

"You came to the right place," he said finally. Then he wove his hand into hers.

He didn't take it away, even after the sun had disappeared, even after the sky turned from fire to soft indigo velvet.

And as he drove her home under the glow of a fresh moon, she conceded that maybe, yes, she had.

I want to be safe.

The words dug into Casper, had turned him in his sleep. Who could have hurt Raina, made her feel unsafe?

That thought had plagued him deep into the night, until finally he'd gotten up, found himself a stale cup of coffee, heated it, and sat outside, watching the stars.

With her words, her behavior this week started to make sense. It had taken him an entire cup of coffee and small talk, even some teasing to get her to look him in the eye after their accidental dunking in the lake. As if she were angry . . . or afraid of him.

Then, after their first team paddle, onshore at her suggestion, he'd glanced around to offer her a ride home and found her halfway to Liza's house. Not that it was a far jog from the harbor, but . . .

But he'd hoped to ask her out for another cup of coffee.

Instead, he'd caught up and walked her home, then sat on her front porch, telling her about Darek and the rebuilding of the resort.

She listened, her golden-brown eyes on his. As if she liked hearing him talk.

As if he might be interesting.

And then during practice, she'd started calling him Captain, my Captain. He had no doubt she meant it as a joke, but the moment she piped up, so did Emma, and finally the entire team started calling him by the nickname.

He could admit he liked it.

So clearly she'd started to mean more to him this week than he'd realized. And tonight at dinner—what was that wink? It nearly took his heart from his chest with one swift motion.

Raina had this serious, almost-bossy way about her, with the way she organized the buffet table.

Then, the next moment, she turned quiet, a servant, like she had with her silent but thorough cleaning up after the campfire.

He couldn't believe everyone left her there alone.

Or that she had thought he wasn't serious about watching the sunset. He'd only mentioned it twice during practice.

His coffee had gone cold, the wind off the lake carrying a briskness that tempered the humidity of the night. He sat and wondered again why a girl might wish to be safe.

Whatever her reason, Deep Haven was the perfect place to hide while a person figured out their next move. He knew that better than anyone.

When the sliding door squealed open behind him, he turned to catch his father walking out, wearing jeans and a paint-stained sweatshirt, his fishing hat. He smiled at Casper. "Wanna see if the walleye are hungry?"

Casper dumped his coffee out on the grass and headed down the dock, following his father to the tied-up canoe.

He got in at the stern, let his father take the bow, and paddled them along the shore. He'd fished Evergreen Lake for so many years that he didn't need directions across the smooth plane of water, glassy and gray in the fading darkness. He held the canoe steady as his dad landed his cast just outside the marshy area, where the walleye would be waking from their slumber.

His father said nothing as he reeled in. Cast again.

Casper lay back on the stern, arms under his head, feet on the gunwales, watching the sky turn to pewter.

"She's lost, Casper."

He frowned, glancing at his father.

John didn't look at him as he continued. "She's searching, and she looks at you like you could be her world. Be careful."

Casper sat up. "Dad. Are you talking about Raina?"

His dad reeled in again, checked his jig, recast. "I like her. Your mom and I both do, but I see the way you look at her—"

He did? How did Casper look at her?

"I'm just saying, I think there is more to her than you know. She's been hurt and I don't want you to think you can fix her." He gave a soft flash of a smile. "That's Jesus' job."

Casper nodded. But maybe Jesus could use him to help.

The thought settled inside him, and he carried it with him all the way past his father's early morning catch of three walleyes, into breakfast with his family, and to church, where he slipped into a pew beside his parents.

But not without noticing Raina, dressed in jeans and a yellow T-shirt, sitting next to her aunt Liza. Third row from the front, on the right-hand side.

I want to be safe.

The words dogged him through the praise and worship, through the sermon, and pressed a hand against his back after the service ended, pushing him through the crowd until he found her.

His heart gave a little jump when Raina's eyes lit up. "Casper!"

"Hey." His hands suddenly decided to turn sweaty. As if he had never asked a girl out before. Good grief, his voice had even turned tail on him.

He smiled until he could round it up, then said, "So . . . every Sunday night my family has a campfire . . . and . . . well, would you like to join us tonight?" He could have hung the moon on her smile, her nod. "I'll pick you up around five, then."

For the rest of the afternoon, Casper buried himself in the finishing work of cabin seven, hanging a door, installing baseboard in the bedroom, and measuring for the decking.

He came in at four, showered, changed into fresh jeans and a T-shirt, and headed into town on his motorcycle.

It wasn't until he'd pulled up to Liza's house that he remembered her words: *But if you offer me a ride on your motorcycle, I'm outta here.*

He saw them echoing on her face as she came out of the house. Maybe she'd had an accident on a motorcycle once. His stomach clenched as he swung his leg over his bike and walked up to her with an extra helmet.

She looked so pretty standing there, wearing a

floral top with jeans and flip-flops. She had a shade of pastel pink on her toes, her hair in a messy ponytail.

"I totally forgot about your fear of motorcycles," he said with a grimace.

"My fear . . . I . . . *Oh*. Yeah, my *fear*." Her eyes widened but she took the helmet. "I'll be fine. Just don't go too fast. Or flip the bike. Or . . . park. No parking."

Parking?

She smiled at him and put on the helmet. "I'm ready, Captain, my Captain."

And just like that, the tension in his chest eased. She climbed onto the bike, settled her hands on his hips.

He would have preferred she wrap her arms around his waist, but this would do. For now.

Casper followed her rules—not too fast, no wheelies. He did, however, have to park the bike in the dirt lot of the family's lodge.

Raina got off and handed him the helmet. She stared at the lodge house like she had at last night's sunset. "It's beautiful."

It was? He saw the roof still needing repair from the fire and the ash-pocked cedar boards, graying and warped with age. He saw tall, angry weeds along the walkway, two stones that had cracked with age, and the ugly paint job he'd done on the red door so many years ago, an adolescent reaction to having to work on a Saturday.

He saw the forest burned and dismal behind them despite the wall of evergreens they'd planted along the far edge of the property. He remembered too well the lick of the fire, charring their resort, a memory only barely blotted out by the handful of framed-in, half-built cabins now dotting the property.

The place looked sickly, feeble. Wanting.

But it had given him a good reason to stick around this spring, this summer, without having to answer any probing questions.

"Have you lived here all your life?" she asked, now taking down her hair, running her fingers through it.

Don't put it back up, he silently asked, but she wound it against her head, secured it.

"Yeah," he said. "Evergreen Resort has been in the family for four generations." He gestured to the pathway that led to the fire pit.

He didn't know when the family campfires had started, just that he'd spent every Sunday he could remember gathered with his parents and any family members in town, roasting marshmallows, trading highs and lows of the week.

His father had already started a blaze, his mother unloading her basket of graham crackers, chocolate, and marshmallows. Tiger waved his stick in the air like a weapon, and Casper caught it with one hand. "Whoa there, kiddo."

Tiger giggled, especially as Casper pulled him

into his arms like a football and tickled him. Tiger screamed with laughter, fighting him. Casper finally let him down and glanced at Raina. She was grinning, her eyes glistening.

Huh.

Ingrid looked up. "Raina, honey. So glad to see you. Grab a stick. We're a little ways from roasting, but it's always good to be armed."

John smiled at Raina, then glanced at Casper, question in his eyes.

Casper ignored him. "We're short family members tonight. Amelia is on her way, I think, but Grace is still in Hawaii, and I'm not sure when Darek and Ivy are getting back." He didn't mention Owen, mostly for his mother's sake.

Raina claimed a stick and found a spot on one of the long rough-hewn logs.

He wiped his hands on his pants, his stomach suddenly churning. Okay, this felt weird—her here, as if it were a date.

With his parents sitting across from them. Oh, boy.

Tiger had grabbed a handful of marshmallows. He came over and offered Raina one from his grubby mitt.

"Tiger, Raina doesn't want that—"

"What are you talking about? Of course I do. Thank you, Tiger."

Tiger grinned. Casper stuck out his tongue at his nephew.

"Hey, we'll have none of that, Casper," Ingrid said, laughing. She brought a plate with chocolate and a cracker over to Raina. "Have you ever made s'mores before?"

"No," Raina said, taking the offering. "I'm a city girl. This is my first s'more experience."

Tiger took it upon himself to show her how to spear the marshmallow with the stick, watching her progress while Casper retrieved his own supplies and sat next to her.

"Not one camping trip as a child?" he asked.

"Nope. My dad was a trucker. It was just me and my brother most of the time, and he didn't have time to take us anywhere. We sometimes went to day camp at a local church, summer school, but never camping."

John slapped a mosquito. "Welcome to the woods."

Casper wanted to ask about her mother but didn't know how. He imagined her alone for long stretches of time, her dad on the road. Imagined her coming home to a cold, dark house, afraid in the middle of the night, caring for her brother.

No wonder she longed for people, the team, community.

"Casper says that you are living with your aunt Liza," Ingrid said, finding warm coals.

"She's my dad's sister. He wrote to her and asked if I could move in after . . ." She shook her head. "My dad was dying, and he was worried about me."

Her dad was gone too?

"What about your brother? Is he in the Cities?"

She held her marshmallow over the fire. "He died a few years ago."

Oh. Casper glanced at his mother, who was watching Raina with a look of concern. His dad wore a grim expression.

"I'm so sorry, Raina." He hadn't meant to stir up all this pain.

She sat there, roasting her marshmallow, watching as the skin rose dark and caramelly, puffy. "Thank you. I'm trying to put it behind me."

"Do you plan on staying in Deep Haven long?" John asked.

Casper frowned at him.

"I like it here. So far."

"Dad?"

"I was just wondering if we could count on her next year. For our dragon boat."

Oh.

Raina laughed. "Only if Casper is captain again."

He let himself smile at that.

"But if I could, I'd stay here forever—oh!" Her marshmallow flamed and she yanked it from the fire, shook it. It flew off her stick, landing in the dirt.

"That's okay. I did that one of the first times I roasted a marshmallow too." The voice came from behind them, light and cheerful. Casper turned to see Ivy and Darek walking down the path.

"Daddy!" Tiger launched himself at them and Darek caught his son, twirling him around.

"I didn't expect you back until later this week," Ingrid said, wrapping Ivy in a hug. Ivy wore the sunshine of Cancún on her skin.

Darek came up behind her, Tiger over his shoulder. "Tropical storm," he said. "They evacuated us three days early." He set Tiger down. "But maybe I'm back in time to check on Casper's progress with this year's dragon boat."

John had finished roasting his marshmallow and now made it into a s'more, crushing it between two graham crackers and a piece of chocolate. "We finally learned how to paddle without upsetting the boat."

"You swamped a dragon boat?"

"It's not that hard to do," Casper muttered. "They got out of rhythm." He wanted to glare at his dad. Whose side was the guy on?

"Maybe I should take over. Ready to declare mutiny, Dad?"

"What? Are you kidding me?" All eyes turned to Raina. She had found her feet. "You can't just come back here and take over. Casper's been working hard, and he deserves your respect."

Darek stared at her. "Who are you?"

"I'm . . . I'm his first mate."

"His . . ." Darek looked at Casper, then suddenly

218

started to laugh. Casper didn't know how to respond.

Raina did. "What is it with you arrogant Christiansen men who think you can just use people? Casper has been working to get this team going, and you can't trample over him as if his feelings don't matter!" She stormed past Darek, up the path, toward the driveway.

Casper scampered after her, seeing Darek's smile dim as he passed. "Raina!"

He caught up with her next to his truck.

"I . . . I don't want to be here right now." Her eyes were red as if—

"Are you crying?"

"Can you take me home?"

He nodded and reached for his helmet. What exactly had just happened?

"No. Not on the bike." She went around the truck and got into the passenger side.

Oh. Okay. He got into the truck, pulled out.

Casper drove in silence as Raina folded her hands on her lap. Were they shaking? Finally he asked, "What happened back there?"

"He just made me so angry, to mock you like that. Especially after you've worked so hard. It's not like you tried to swamp the boat. You put your faith in us and *we* swamped it."

He frowned, not quite seeing it that way.

She sighed. "Okay . . . I guess I overreacted."

"I've never had anyone overreact for me

before." He reached for her hand. "I kind of like it."

She glanced at him. "You do?"

Enough to wish they'd brought the motorcycle. He ran his thumb over her hand. "Yes. Would you like to see the sunset again?"

She nodded, her right hand wiping her cheeks. "Very much."

Safe. The word reverberated through him. As he held her hand, feeling it warm in his, his father's words came back to him about Jesus fixing her broken places.

Please, Lord. Use me for good in this woman's life.

Chapter 10

Max might be right. They could win this.

The sky arched blue above Grace, the day shiny and brilliant. When the announcer introduced Max, the crowd went wild.

Grace stood behind Max, raising her hand when the announcer—a local newscaster by the name of Palani—introduced her as Max's sous-chef for round one, appetizers. Every team had to have a head chef and a sous-chef, and she'd volunteered Max for head chef before he could make the mistake of pushing her to the front.

Now he stood fully inhabiting his Maximoto,

ninja chef, persona, a warrior in the kitchen, his short military cut giving him a steely demeanor.

Of course the crowd loved him. She loved him.

Loved, at least, the hero he'd turned into over the past two days. He'd made her believe she could fly—on water, anyway. More, he'd made her believe that if she reached beyond herself, she might find something amazing.

She might not have won his heart, but she'd won his admiration when she had called Keoni and asked him to give them another chance.

Keoni had already chosen them for the competition.

They spent yesterday in their interviews, and she'd managed to sit in a chair, stare at the camera, and somehow communicate her desire to start a catering company.

She had no idea what Max said after he kicked her out of the studio.

Now she sorted through what Max had taught her as she stared down the competition—the hippie couple from North Beach, the Pearl Harbor father-and-son soldiers, the Hawaiian sister-and-brother team, and the two women from their cooking class. Max had dubbed them the Twinkies.

She didn't want him calling her anything but the best sous-chef he'd ever seen.

Last night, he'd spoken the magic words. "You're ready."

He said it over a dinner of shrimp tacos from

Lola's, across the street from the Waikiki pier, just before he took her back out in the water.

She'd gotten up on her board a total of ten times. One of these days she might even learn how to read the waves, catch one without Max's help. Until then, she let him push her out with the wave, trusting him and paddling hard to find her groove, get her balance. Ride the swell to shore.

"Chefs, are you ready?" Palani said.

Max, standing beside her, nodded, and Grace mimicked him.

"Then take your stations."

They would cook live at outdoor kitchen stations before a grandstand audience—a discovery that had nearly turned Grace around at the edge of the stage. But Max kept his hand on the small of her back, nearly pushing her forward, and what could she do?

Now he took her hand, probably fearing she might bolt. But she hung on, letting the strength of his grip sweep through her.

We make a great team. Yes, those words, too, had been said last night as he looked into her eyes, so much in his that it shucked her voice from her.

He felt something for her; she just had to believe it.

Please, God, help me not be a fool.

She followed Max to their station. The hippies were next to them, the military team on the other side.

Palani stated the rules, the time limit, and then introduced the ingredients. "Today, chefs, you'll make us an appetizer out of ahi, ramen noodles, black poppy seeds, and . . . oranges."

Grace stared at the basket of ingredients as everything hollowed out inside her. Seriously?

But a glance at Max's game face shored her up. "Go!"

She ran for her basket, scooped it up, returned to Max. He had already pulled out two knives.

"What are we going to do?"

His mouth tightened to a grim line. "I don't know."

"You don't know—but you looked so confident!"

"Never let them see you sweat, baby. Okay, listen, we've got ahi, so we could make a sort of sushi—"

"Oh, that's it. What if we boiled the noodles al dente and made a shell out of them, like spaghetti pie. Then you'll do your ahi massage in a little vinaigrette, something sweet that goes with poppy seeds."

"Right." A spark lit his eyes. "How about shoyu sauce and oil? We can add some mirin . . ."

"What?"

"It's, uh . . . Japanese sweet rice wine. Just trust me."

"I do." She had already found a pot, was filling it with water.

He grinned at her and began to clean the tuna.

Grace set the water to boil and grabbed the

oranges. One in each hand, she looked at Max. "What if we supremed these, then blackened them a little?"

"Nice work, swim buddy. Way to use your mad culinary skills."

She found a cutting board, then cut off the ends of each orange. Setting one on the cut end, she worked her knife between the inner edge of the skin and the meat of the fruit, ever so gently removing the pith and skin and leaving behind the juicy fullness of the fruit. She cleaned the extra pith off with a paring knife. Then, holding the orange in her hand, she cut along the membrane of each section, slicing on the inside to separate the fruit meat from the membrane wall. She removed each segment of meat from the shell.

Finally she squeezed the juice from the membrane into a bowl and handed it to Max. "Use this in the vinaigrette."

He had cleaned the tuna and now cut it into pieces. She glanced at the clock, discovered that fifteen minutes had passed and she hadn't yet dropped the ramen noodles into the now-boiling water.

Max seemed to read her mind. "I'm on it," he said, grabbing the noodles.

Meanwhile Grace spread out the oranges on the cutting board and found the blowtorch.

"Please, let's not catch anything on fire," Max said, standing guard over the boiling pot.

"Stand back, 9A. You don't want to mess with a girl and her brûlée."

He laughed, and so did the crowd.

They were miked. How could she forget that?

Max must have seen her expression because he touched her arm, met her eyes. "It's just us," he said softly. "Focus."

She nodded quickly and reached for the sugar. Focus. Forget the crowd. She sprinkled sugar on the oranges, then ran the torch over each one to melt it. She added a touch of sea salt across the brown, crispy surface as Max pulled the noodles from the water. He ran them through a cold rinse, then arranged them in custard cups.

"How long under the broiler?"

"One minute? Maybe two? I don't know." She stood back, glancing at the hippies. They'd concocted a sort of ceviche, it seemed, leaving the noodles uncooked and crunchy. Max had his arms folded now, willing the noodles to harden. Behind her, she saw the military boys sautéing their ahi, creating a soup with green onions, cilantro, and noodles. The oranges they'd hollowed out, as if to house the soup. What they'd done with the fruit meat, she couldn't guess.

"It's coming out." Max reached in with his towel to grab the tray. "Hot! Hot!" He slid it onto the counter and jerked his hand back. "The towel's wet."

Grace cast a look at the clock. Six minutes left.

Max ran his hand under water while she poured Max's vinaigrette over the ahi, added salt, and massaged it. "Did you add the orange—?"

"Yes!" He turned off the water, grabbed a fresh towel, and transferred the custard cups to a plate. Carefully, he turned each dish over, catching the shells in his hand, then plating them.

They'd turned out perfectly, a nest to cradle the ahi. Grace placed a spoonful in each nest as Max added two slices of oranges to each cup. She garnished the three cups with black poppy seeds and stepped back just as Palani called time.

Max slipped his hand into hers, and Grace just about cried with relief.

But she'd never had so much fun in all her life.

One course down, three to go. Max still didn't know how they'd hung on. Not against the hippies' tropical ceviche or the military team's ahi bisque in an orange cup or even the aloha siblings' orange poi sauce over ahi. He'd clearly underestimated the competition.

He had to admit, however, that Grace might have saved the day with her brûléed orange supreme. She'd even named their dish, the words rolling off her tongue as she presented it to the judges: "Ahi tartar in a rice noodle cup, garnished with char orange supreme."

It sounded like something out of a gourmet

magazine. With their appetizer course, Max had stepped into a surreal world of culinary dominance, especially with the elimination of the military team.

In a crazy way, it felt as if he were in the Cup play-offs, only . . . better. Max wanted to shout or pump his fist in the air or . . .

Maybe just sweep Grace into an embrace, although that didn't seem appropriate for the competition.

And definitely not safe for his heart.

But oh, she'd done something to him—he felt it, and it was more than just wanting to weave his fingers into her hair, take her in his arms. The feeling exploding inside went way beyond wanting to kiss Grace Christiansen.

He had changed clothes, perched himself on the Mustang, waiting for her as she emerged from the changing rooms. She wore shorts, a tank top, and carried a string backpack over her shoulders.

She high-fived him. "Way to go, master chef."

Oh yeah, he was in trouble. He found his voice. "You're in the driver's seat tomorrow."

She climbed into the passenger side. "I don't know. We made a great team today, but I can't plate like you can."

"So I'll plate, but you—" he got behind the wheel, grabbed his aviators—"you're in charge of amazing."

"Huh?"

He grinned. "I think you know what I mean."

She smiled and slid down in her seat. "So where to today, cruise director?"

"Pearl Harbor. It's time for some history."

He found a country station on the radio and headed out of Honolulu, north toward Pearl Harbor. The endless blue sky arched over him, the sun kissing his skin as he sang along to Jake Owen. " 'I'll go anywhere, anywhere with you.' "

Grace hummed with him.

They cut off the highway, followed the signs to Pearl Harbor, found a parking spot, and headed toward the monument.

"One of my favorite movies is *Pearl Harbor*," she said, and he had the urge to hold her hand again.

He fished out his wallet, paid for their tickets despite her protest, and rented a couple headsets for the tour.

He'd visited Pearl Harbor before, during his first year in Hawaii, and the depth of the soldiers' sacrifice had taken more from him than he'd expected. Too many young lives cut down. Destroyed. It skirted too close, so the next year, he'd avoided the monument.

Now he listened to a minute-by-minute account of the attack on the naval base, imagining the boys stationed here, fighting for their lives. He stood at the wall, studied the map that outlined the Japanese attack, and imagined a blue-skied

Sunday morning, the sun glorious, no hint of disaster on the horizon.

It felt too close again. The sense that death, or at least pain, lay anchored just out of sight, waiting to attack.

Max stared across the water of the bay to the white monument built over the battleship *Arizona*, and that's when he felt Grace's hand slip into his.

He held on and didn't care.

They took the ferry to the monument in silence, hands clasped, watching the oil still rising from the massive ship–turned–tomb.

He couldn't speak with the immensity of it all.

When they finally took the ferry back, he deliberately hung on to her hand, wishing.

After they turned in their headsets, Grace went to sit in the garden overlooking the harbor.

He slid onto the bench next to her and leaned forward, elbows on his knees. Took off his sunglasses. Glancing at Grace, he saw her eyes reddened, watched as she whisked a tear from her face.

"Sorry. I thought this would be inspirational," Max said.

"It is. The bravery. The sacrifice. These men had no idea they'd give up their lives when they joined the military. We were in a time of peace, despite the turmoil in Europe, and these boys were in the prime of their lives, stationed in beautiful Hawaii. What could go wrong?" Another tear rolled down her cheek. "It just makes you think about life, stepping out and not knowing what is out there and—"

"And the tragedy that could happen."

"Or the glory." She let a smile tug up one side of her mouth. "Not that any mother or sister or wife might see it like that, but still, these men are heroes. Their legacy is one of honor. That's what their courage to step out earned them."

He clasped his hands together, staring out at the water. "Do you think any of those wives or girlfriends regretted loving their soldier?"

She frowned. "Because of the grief? Are you saying they might've been sorry they loved? Of course not. You don't know what's going to happen when you fall in love. You don't think the man you give your heart to is going to die."

"It's a possibility. Especially in war."

"Yes. But he could also come home, and no woman is going to not fall in love because her man *might* go to war and *might* not come home."

"But what if you *knew* someone you loved wouldn't come home? What if you knew your . . . let's say boyfriend or husband . . . would die? Would you still love him? Marry him?"

Max wasn't sure how he got here, to this moment, to these words, but he couldn't take them back. He found himself holding his breath, waiting for her answer.

She shook her head. "How could anyone know that?"

"Let's just say that you had a crystal ball and could see the future."

"What kind of crystal ball? Where do you get this crystal ball?"

"I don't know! It's just a crystal ball, okay?"

"Like the witch's in *The Wizard of Oz*?"

"Oh, for crying out loud. Forget the crystal ball. Let's say you could travel forward in time . . ."

"In a time machine? Like a DeLorean?"

"Yes. You can travel forward in a DeLorean—"

"Or maybe it's like a portal, a rip in the space-time continuum—"

He closed his eyes, shook his head. "Please, Grace. Let's just say you could. However you see the future, you know with *certainty* that the man you love will die. *Would you marry him?*"

She leaned back, giving him a hard look. "Tell me about this man I'm in love with. Is he good-looking?"

He opened his mouth. Closed it. "Huh?"

"I just want to know about this man you've hooked me up with. Is he cute or not?"

"Yeah, sure."

"Muscles?" She raised an eyebrow. "Because I like muscles."

"Fine. He's built. Spends hours every day in the weight room."

"Well, not too much. Because I don't want him to neglect me."

He sighed. "No. Never."

"So he's reliable."

"Absolutely."

"And built."

"We established that."

"Great. But is he kind? Does he buy me flowers? Does he sing me love songs? How about cooking? Can he cook?"

He stared at her. "I . . . I don't know what to say to that. I guess I thought we were having a serious conversation here."

"We are." She smiled. "So here's the really important question. Does this man love Jesus? Does he know that God has an amazing plan for his life, and is he willing to hold my hand through the good and the bad?"

Her words silenced him. He felt them in his chest, burning.

"Yes, this man loves Jesus," he finally said. "And he wants to believe that."

"Well then, if that's the case, yes. I would still marry this everything-I-hoped-for man. In fact, I would marry him if he wasn't perfect—if he didn't know how to cook and he occasionally forgot flowers." Her smile dimmed, and she looked away. "I would marry him and love him for as long as we had because I don't really care about anything on that list but a man who loves Jesus and loves me."

She met his eyes then, and oh, Max wanted to

reach out. To take her hand. To pull her into his arms.

But he couldn't breathe. So he put his sunglasses back on and got up, headed for the exit before he could break into tears.

Chapter 11

Raina could hardly believe Casper hailed from the same stock as Owen. Instead of dropping her off and driving away Sunday evening, he'd picked up dinner—a basket of fried chicken from a local diner—and spread out a picnic as they watched another glorious sunset.

Raina had managed to forget her anger at his brother—his family—as she settled into his arms. He hadn't tried to kiss her, but he had leaned her back against him to watch the sky light on fire, the world turning to gold, then crimson as the horizon surrendered to the night.

But now, two days later, her words dogged her, winding into her brain, churning her stomach. *What is it with you arrogant Christiansen men who think you can just use people?*

She shouldn't have erupted, shouldn't have let her past sour the perfect evening she could have had with his family. Maybe she'd overstepped there a little. Even if Darek, who seemed cut from the same cloth as his kid brother, Owen, deserved it.

But if she hoped to keep things civil, even encourage team unity before the next practice, she had to smooth things over with Casper's family.

"You want this on your tab, Raina, or do you want to pay for it now?" Ty asked as he boxed the pizza.

She picked up the large pepperoni that she'd made after she'd gotten off shift. "Put it on my tab," she said and headed out the door.

She slid the pizza onto the front seat of the car, leaving one hand on the box to steady it as she drove to Evergreen Resort. She couldn't decide if she hoped Casper was there or not.

Her insides had coiled into a knot by the time she turned onto the drive for the resort. The temperature rose ten degrees up here in the woods, and she could still smell the faintest hint of ash in the air, despite the greening pines across the lake.

How long might it take for the woods to come to life again?

Raina pulled in next to a blue-and-white-striped work truck, the hood open. She grabbed the pizza and got out.

John Christiansen looked out from where he hunkered under the hood. "Hello there."

She didn't wait for the courage, just blurted out

what she had to say. "I came to apologize." She held out the pizza. "I shouldn't have responded to your hospitality like that. I'm so sorry. I'm way too dramatic, I know it, and I should have kept my feelings to myself."

When she first met John, he'd intimidated her with his large, almost-imposing presence, his barrel chest and bald head, those dark-blue eyes that could see right through her to her secrets. Now he considered her a long moment, and the power of it could take her apart.

Especially combined with his next words. "Raina, did one of my boys hurt you?"

The strength went out of her knees. She managed a quick shake of her head.

"Hmm." He narrowed his eyes. "You know, if they did, I'd want to know about it."

She wanted to run. But growing up without a father around, having to stand her ground to teachers, social workers, and finally her brother, she didn't possess a huge amount of flinch. "No." She cleared her throat. "Why?"

That sounded mousy. She added a smile but knew it was off-kilter.

He considered her another long moment as if weighing her words. Then, "Pizza, huh?"

She nodded, too vigorously. "Pepperoni."

John came around the truck, wiping his hands on a rag. He wore a pair of grimy, oil-slicked jeans, a stained shirt, a gimme cap with a worn, cupped brim. "Ingrid's in town. I think Casper and Darek are working on a cabin."

She glanced past him toward the cabins and heard the faint scream of a Skilsaw. "Then we'll save them some." She put the box on the hood of her car and opened it, retrieved a napkin and handed him a slice.

He set his wrench on the side of the engine compartment and took the pizza. "Thanks."

"Is this a Chevy?"

"Yep."

"A 1980s model?"

"Yeah, a 1984. I got it not long after Ingrid and I were married."

"My dad had one of these. Diesel. He used to work on it when he was off the road." She peered into the engine compartment, the smells of oil and grease luring her closer. "I'd come home from school, and I'd know whether Dad had an overnight turnaround or a few days off by whether the hood was up on the truck. He was always tinkering with it." She leaned in, noticing cables to the battery, a new radiator. "What's wrong with it?"

"Won't start." He'd folded the pizza like a sandwich to eat it.

"You tested the battery, right?"

He raised an eyebrow.

"It's the first thing Dad would do. Are you getting fuel?"

236

He stepped up to the truck, wiping his fingers. "Yep. I just changed the fuel filter too."

"So maybe it's a spark?"

"Nope." John indicated a spark plug kit on the ground. "I was just ready to take off the distributor cap and test the timing." He leaned over the engine. "Hand me that screwdriver down there. The one with the star-shaped head."

She found the toolbox. "The Torx driver?"

He raised another eyebrow, accompanied it with a hint of smile.

She leaned over, watching him. "I helped my dad rebuild the entire engine one summer. We had parts all over the garage, but we got the truck running. I remember him piling me and Joey into the cab and driving us to Dairy Queen in celebration. I hadn't seen him smile since my mom left, but he ordered us both large cones and got one for himself. He put ice cream on my nose and dared me to lick it off."

She didn't know why she'd decided to tell him that, but he didn't react, didn't suddenly look at her like she'd taken out a piece of her heart. He simply removed the cap and handed it to her. Raina put it on the ground next to the toolbox.

"Get in and give her a crank," he said.

She climbed into the driver's seat, the smell of age and grime embedded in the cab. "Ready?"

John stuck his hand out from beyond the hood to give her a thumbs-up. She cranked. The engine didn't turn over, but she could hear it working.

"Okay!"

Raina turned the truck off and got out. "So?"

"Timing is good, and the belt looks okay." He stepped back, scratching his head at the base of his cap. He'd already left a black smudge there. "I'm going to have to remove the spark plugs, see if we have enough compression."

She grabbed a piece of pizza and leaned against the truck, catching up with her memories. "What I didn't know was that Dad was planning a trip to see my great-aunt in South Dakota. We were about thirty miles from her house out in the middle of nowhere when the truck died again on the side of the road. We pulled into this grassy truck stop, and my dad climbed under the hood. He tested everything and decided that we had to replace the cylinder gaskets."

She watched as John pulled out the spark plugs, then disabled the ignition coil. "He called my great-aunt and asked her to come get my brother and me while he fixed the truck. She lived in this tiny house on the edge of this Podunk town, but it had a swimming pool and every day, while we waited for my father to show up, we'd go swimming. The pool had a slide and a diving board, and I made friends with all the kids in town. An entire week went by before I caught on that he hadn't shown up yet."

She put her pizza back in the box. She hadn't

realized she would end up here—the day when she stood on the stoop of Aunt Rae's house, her hands on the screen door, refusing to go to the pool until her father arrived.

"Why don't you climb in; we'll give it another go," John said, breaking through the quiet, sketchy past.

Raina climbed in.

"Keep your foot off the gas!"

She cranked the engine while he tested each of the spark plug holes.

"Okay, you can stop." He leaned out from under the hood. "Just stay there. I'll need you to crank again."

She sat in the cab, the familiarity of the truck casting her back to sitting on a cracked, weedy stoop for another week—hot, hungry, her stomach all gnarled and angry as she waited.

"Raina?"

She looked up to see John staring at her, something of worry in his eyes.

"Sorry."

"Give it another go."

She cranked while he tested the spark plug holes again. Then he held up his hand to stop.

She got out. "So?"

"There are holes in a couple of the cylinders. I'll need to replace gaskets." He was wiping his hands with a rag.

Cicadas buzzed in the afternoon heat.

"So did he ever show up?"

Huh? She looked at John.

"Your father. He sent you to your aunt's house. Did he ever show up to get you?"

"Yeah. He'd had some trouble with the engine, had to catch a ride to Sioux Falls for parts." But she kept her eyes away, haunted by her own words.

Deep inside, she'd feared he'd wanted to leave her there. It would have been easier than trying to figure out what to do with two hungry, unruly kids.

"Got any more of that pizza?" John asked.

She nodded and gestured to the box. He helped himself, again folding the pizza like a sandwich. "You're pretty good at this. Fixing cars. Catering. Paddling boats."

"I try to help. To fit in."

He finished the slice. "You fit in just fine, Raina, without trying."

Her throat swelled. "I guess Casper didn't need my defending."

He gave a low chuckle. "Oh, Darek and Casper have plenty of war wounds. I think we could all use a little defending sometimes." His eyes found her, too much warmth in them for her to bear. "But Casper is not the one I'm worried about."

Oh. She couldn't breathe. It felt like that moment when her father had shown up, opened the truck door, and said, *Climb in, I'm taking you home.*

"Apology accepted," he finally said softly.

"Hey! What's going on?" She looked up to see Casper approaching. He wore a black T-shirt, the sleeves stretched around his biceps, a tool belt hanging low over a pair of nearly white faded jeans. Sawdust littered his dark hair.

"Just hanging out, eating pizza with your first mate," John said. He winked at Raina fast, and she turned away before she did something else strangely dramatic, like cry.

Max couldn't dislodge the spur of anger Grace's words had ground into him. Crazy, he knew, but he had stared at her walking away at the Pearl Harbor monument, and even over dinner at the resort, and a burning fury began to move through him.

What kind of woman said she'd marry a man she knew would die? That was . . . wrong. Nuts.

Infuriating.

Because it sparked a thousand impossible dreams. Like a desire to get married. To have a home. Even children, although he'd never have his own. Suddenly he completely understood why Brendon couldn't hold himself back any longer, despite his fatal prognosis, and had married the woman who made him, for the first time, feel alive.

Who gave him something to live for.

That only made Max's anger sharper because he

already had something to live for. Hockey. Or at least that's what he thought before he'd gotten on a plane to Hawaii and sat next to a woman afraid to fly. Afraid to reach out and live.

Funny how helping her leap into life had ignited the same desire in himself.

Grace had the power to tug him out of his dark places, drive him to his last nerve, and stir in him such a longing that he found himself . . . making soup.

"Seriously? Soup?" Max said, looking at their basket of ingredients. Day two of the Honolulu Chop competition, and he desperately needed to get his head back in the game.

"Yes," Grace said as she sorted through their ingredients. Today, the morning had started with a downpour, and gray clouds hovered over the island. They'd break free by afternoon, but for now, a cool, clinging mist hung in the soggy air. Grace wore her hair back, her sleeves rolled up, so much verve on her face, he thought they might have a chance at making it through this round.

But soup?

"Listen, Mr. Grumpy Pants. Not only is this the soup-and-salad phase, but soup is good for the soul. More importantly, it's actually hard to do well, so you can bet the others won't go near it. The good news is that you happen to have a gourmet soup chef in your midst."

She was miked, and he heard the audience,

thinner than yesterday's, twitter. "Okay, soup girl, what are we making with our . . . plantain, tofu, and pineapple?" He pulled the ingredients out of the basket.

"The plantain is a starch, so we're going to treat it like a potato. Get out the pressure cooker."

"Are you sure—?"

"Have you never eaten mashed potato soup?"

"Not with bananas."

"Trust me."

He guessed he deserved that. But how could he trust crazy?

He found the pressure cooker, added chicken broth, then peeled the plantains, cut them, and added them to the cooker. Grace was already sautéing a chopped onion, garlic, and ginger on the stove, and she threw those into the pot. He set it on high, clamped the lid on. "Let's hope that cooks in ten minutes."

She handed him the tofu. "Chop this up." Meanwhile, she went to work on the pineapple, trimming and skinning it, cutting it into quarters, and removing the core with a paring knife. Finally she sliced it into long spears.

He'd taught her that, and he smiled at her skills.

Max glanced over at the hippies. They were chopping the plantain, making a salad with it and the pineapple.

That sounded like a winning combination, and

he nearly mentioned this when he saw Grace fire up the grill.

"What are you doing?"

"I'm grilling the pineapple."

"What is with you and fire?"

"I keep thinking about yesterday's brûlée, and how the char brings out all the flavor. Quick, make me a glaze of honey, lime juice, and black pepper."

He ran to the pantry, found the ingredients, and whisked them together. She'd arranged the pineapple spears on a plate, and he ran the glaze over them with a brush.

Grace picked them up with her fingers and plopped them on the grill. "Give these about four minutes per side. Wait until they start to dry out on the surface, but don't overcook them or they will turn mushy. Or burn."

"Yes, chef," he said, and she stuck out her tongue at him.

The crowd laughed.

And then so did he because it felt so natural and even easy to be in the kitchen with her, watching her work, seeing her mad skills at throwing together dinner.

He could do this every night. Forever.

That thought sparked another flame of frustration.

She opened the pressure cooker and steam billowed out. Fishing out one of the plantains, she tested it on the counter, squishing it. "I think it's ready." She ladled out the pieces and dropped them into a blender. Then, scooping up the chopped tofu, she dropped that in also.

She set the blender on puree, the sound a buzz saw across the kitchen. The other contestants' heads gophered up, checking on their progress.

Max glanced at the clock. Thirteen minutes left. He turned the pineapple.

"Almost done?" Grace ran to the pantry and returned in a minute with turmeric, coriander, cumin, and a bunch of fresh cilantro. She added the spices to the soup, chopped up half the cilantro. "Give me four of those spears."

He handed her four on a plate, and she dropped them into the blender, sped it through, and turned it creamy. Then she dumped it all back into the cooker and popped the cover back on, turning it up.

He pulled the rest of the pineapple off the grill. "Now what?"

She stared at him a long moment before saying, "We need some cream."

Cream. He headed for the refrigerator as she pulled out soup cups. She plated the pineapple, then opened the lid of the pot and ladled the soup into the cups.

Max returned, and Grace used a spoon to design a creamy flower in each bowl, like someone might with a cup of coffee. Then she garnished each soup with cilantro.

It kind of resembled pumpkin soup, with a hint of yellow, a sprig of green, and the charred pineapple so fragrant, it just about made Max reach for one.

"Don't you dare," she said.

He wondered if she could read his mind. Probably.

She stepped back, took his hand, held it up with hers as Palani called time.

The hippies had built their salad on a slab of tofu. The aloha siblings had created a grilled tofu and plantain dish with onions, lime, garlic, and ginger. The Twinkie girls had made a tofu salad with pineapple and plantain chips.

Palani walked by each of them, surveying their dishes with the crowd and the camera. Then they loaded them on trays to present to the judges.

Yesterday Tonie had made a point of mentioning Max's use of Hawaiian condiments—the mirin and shoyu sauce. It just sounded good, really. Tonie could have called it vinegar or soy sauce. But if she wanted to help him win, he wouldn't fault her.

He hoped today she wouldn't mock Grace for her simple ingredients.

And that the soup would taste good.

He stood with Grace, fighting the urge to take her hand again and then angry that he longed for her touch. He watched the hippies present their dish while trying to rewrite yesterday's conversation to something that made sense and sorting through what they might do today after the competition that would help him find his footing again and—

"We're up." Grace nudged him and gestured to the tray.

Already? He'd missed the hippies' feedback and the Twinkies', so he hadn't a clue how they'd fared. He presented the soup to each of the judges.

Keoni made no sign of recognition and Chef Rogers had his gaze on Grace. Tonie raised an eyebrow and he smiled as he stepped back.

"We made a tofu and plantain yellow curry bisque, garnished with cilantro and served with charred pineapple," Max said.

He found Grace's hand in his as the judges dug in.

He was never good at reading faces. Body stance, skate direction—yes, he got that. Could read a player's forecasted moves better than his own sometimes. But he had nothing as the panel tasted the soup.

The crowd seemed to hold their collective breath.

Then Keoni smiled. "Delicious."

Palani handed him the mic.

"Smooth, creamy. The curry is perfect, with the slightest hint of sweetness from the pineapple."

Grace squeezed Max's hand.

"I agree," Rogers said. "Some of the pineapple is just a little mushy, but that's hard to get right."

Max kept his smile.

"But the texture is perfect, and the caramel char on the pineapple is an interesting blend with the curry." Rogers looked at Grace, warmth in his smile.

Max tightened his hold on her hand.

Tonie set down her spoon. Licked her lips. Sighed. "I have to admit, I didn't think you could pull it off. Soup is . . . well, it's easy to step over the line from a hint of curry to overpowering. But this . . . yes, I agree with the panel. Although I might have added a smidge more ginger and a little less pineapple." She looked at Max. "And I didn't find the pineapple overdone."

Not a glance at Grace, but he didn't care. They moved away and listened to the judges evaluate the aloha siblings. Who apparently hadn't followed the instructions at all and, according to the judges, created a main dish instead of a delectable side.

Max had to stop and orient himself a moment when the results came in, let it sink in that he and Grace had made it to the main course round.

He had to admit, deep inside, he hadn't expected them to advance past the first round. Then again, nothing with Grace Christiansen seemed predictable.

Grace was jubilant and nearly hugged him onstage. However, she waited until they'd exited, until the cameras shut off, before flinging herself into his arms. "You were fabulous!"

He held her as long as he dared, then put her down. Smiled into her eyes. "No, you were. Who would have thought . . . soup?"

"Curried potato soup is one of my mom's favorites. Only she makes it with coconut milk. The swirl of cream—all Mom. And the pineapple we had a few years ago during a cookout. So I wasn't completely original."

"You were fantastic," he said, meaning it.

"But you're wearing the hat tomorrow, Chef Maximoto. I can't handle all this pressure. It's just so . . . Wow." She pulled off her hat. "I could use some surfing."

Surfing.

With that, the last of his anger worked free. Because despite knowing that he had to leave her in five short days, he would still choose every wonderful, infuriating, frustrating, glorious moment of being near her.

"Let's catch some waves."

Chapter 12

Okay. Fine. She could admit it.

Grace was in love with Maxwell Sharpe. She'd probably fallen for him on the airplane ride over the ocean, when he'd practically helped hold her barf bag. Definitely when he shoved his foot into her door and forced her to escape from her hotel room and raised her meager expectations of this trip. But it had only been cemented when he'd helped her believe she was capable of more than she'd ever dreamed.

Like snorkeling. Parasailing. Surfing.

Being a finalist in Honolulu Chop.

When Palani had uncovered the Twinkies' plate during today's main course round, leaving only the hippies and Max and Grace to compete in the dessert finale, Grace simply had no words.

No words except *I love you, Max*.

She wanted to grab his beautiful face with both hands, look him straight in those hypnotizing brown eyes, and blurt it out.

Maybe even kiss him. Oh, she'd thought about it—a lot, in fact. What it might feel like to be in his arms—really be there, not just by chance, but because he wanted her.

Sometimes she thought she saw it in his eyes too. A flicker of desire that broke free from wherever he tamped down his emotions. That was about when he turned away, cracked a joke, or announced they would do something adventurous.

It made her wonder if his words at Pearl Harbor weren't hypothetical, but rather a sort of cryptic message. Which felt weird because what did he mean, if you knew someone was going to die? Max wasn't dying—one look at the man shouted the contrary.

She leaned back on her hands on the cushion of

her towel in the sand, watching as he paddled hard with a wave, caught it, and stood, riding the angle to the shore. Water glistened off his hard-packed body, the ripples in his stomach, his sculpted shoulders. He wore sky-blue trunks, and against the twilight blue of the sky and the ocean, he looked like a man made for the sea.

Hard to believe he spent nine months of the year on ice.

She couldn't think about that—about leaving. Four days until her vacation was over, and how did anyone expect her to return to her mundane, pizza-tossing life after the exhilaration of Hawaii? Of Honolulu Chop? Of Max?

Maybe she didn't have to. Maybe . . . maybe if she told him how she felt, it would unlock whatever trapped him, whatever kept him from unleashing his own feelings. After all, he carried the deep pain of losing his father. Maybe he was simply afraid of losing again.

If she let go of her heart, handed him a piece of it, maybe that would be enough for him to give her a piece back.

Then what? They continued their relationship in Minnesota?

She watched him tumble into the surf, emerge, grab his board, and paddle out again. She'd begged out of today's surfing, wanting to give him time to surf on his own. Not that he'd complained, but after today's competition, Keoni had come up to her while Max was completing his set of interviews for tomorrow's taping and mentioned that Max hadn't joined any of the locals this year.

Oops.

Still, she'd practically had to force Max to leave her on the beach while he joined Keoni and a school of other surfers fighting for waves.

After all, she had that unread book.

Right. Her mind kept wheeling back to the photo session today, the one featuring her and Max dressed in their chef's attire, posing with knives and lobsters and other island treasures. Once he'd picked her up, thrown her over his shoulder. She banged on his back until he released her. He'd been laughing too, the sound of it infectious.

The cameras caught the entire thing, but she didn't care. After all, who would see it? Honolulu Chop didn't exactly garner a national audience.

It was that moment, laughing in his arms, when she'd realized she didn't care if he didn't say the words back. She loved him. And somehow she'd figure out a way to tell him before tomorrow's competition.

In her bag, she heard her cell phone sing, and she reached for it, fumbling to answer, glancing first at the caller ID. "Mom?"

"Grace! I'm so glad to hear your voice. How are you?"

She sank into her mother's welcome voice. Oh, where to start? "I'm great, Mom. Absolutely great. I love . . . Hawaii."

"Wow." Her mother laughed on the other end, and Grace imagined her sitting at the family picnic table, listening to the loons as the sun set—or maybe it was later, with the moon rising over the shaggy pines to the west. "Is this the same woman who looked white as a sheet at the thought of getting on a plane?"

"Nope. That woman is long gone. I'm tan and I'm surfing and I'm . . . I'm not coming home."

Silence.

"I'm kidding, Mom." But she stared into the surf, where Max and Keoni fought for the same wave. Her words contained some truth.

She didn't want to leave this magical place where she'd learned to dive into life and live large.

"You know, I've always wanted to visit Hawaii. If you decided to stay—"

"Seriously, Mom. No." Grace laughed the idea away, despite the lingering tingle of desire. "But I am learning lots about cooking for Eden's wedding. I'm even in a cooking contest!"

"I know."

"How—?"

"Your sister told me, and I looked it up online. There are pictures of you and Maxwell Sharpe, with comments about the food you're making.

Even videos of you two, and I downloaded the last episode. I saw that you made my curry potato soup!"

"Yeah. Except with plantains and tofu. And today—you should have seen it, Mom. Our ingredients were a pig knuckle, mangoes, and arborio rice."

"What kind of rice?"

"It's risotto rice. We made a mock roaster pig knuckle with mango risotto. You should have seen Max. He seared the knuckle in a cast-iron pan, then roasted it in butter and fresh rosemary in the oven. I was worried it wouldn't get done, but it was juicy and just a little rare and absolutely succulent. While he worked on the meat, I made the mango risotto."

"Risotto. I've never even tried to make that."

"It can be tricky. I sautéed some onion with the risotto in coconut oil, then added white wine, coconut milk, and some water and kept stirring until the rice absorbed the liquid. I grated in some fresh nutmeg, and then after the liquid absorbed, I added the mango. We served it on top of the pork with a little rocket arugula, and it was so pretty. The judges loved it."

"You amaze me, Grace."

"It was all Max. He came up with the idea—"

"It sounds like you two are a great team. You seem to be having a lot of fun."

A great team. Grace watched as Max lost his

footing on the board and fell into the surf. "I think I'm in love with him, Mom."

Silence, and Grace quickly followed with, "Oh, I didn't mean to say that out loud. I . . ." But she had to tell someone or she might burst.

"Does he love you?"

"I don't know. I sometimes think so, but he hasn't said anything. Maybe I'm just reading into all this. Wishing for something I can't have. I don't want to do something that I'll regret."

Max popped up from his tumble into the sea and grabbed his board, this time climbing on and riding it to shore.

"You always told me that you were only going to fall in love once. And when you did, you'd give your heart away completely. I'm so glad you like him. But you need to take a breath. Does he love Jesus like you do? Is he going to be the husband who leads you closer to God?"

"I . . . Oh, I hope so, Mom. He says he's a Christian, and I see it in him. He's so kind and patient, and he believes in me, even pushes me to believe in myself. He makes me want to . . . to do the things I've always wanted to do but been too afraid to try."

"Like fall in love."

She dragged her finger through the hot sand, made a heart. "Yeah. Like fall in love. I've never really felt this way about a guy before . . . or even wanted to."

"Are you going to tell him?"

"I don't know. We have one day left of competition and then a couple more days until we fly home Sunday afternoon. I keep wondering . . . or hoping . . ."

"You're hoping to see him when you get back to Minnesota."

"He does play for the Blue Ox. And Eden lives in Minneapolis. What if I moved to Minneapolis and . . . ?"

Again, silence.

"Or not. I don't know. Maybe that's a terrible idea. It could backfire and then what?"

"Then you get back up and you keep following God's open doors. Just like this trip. You trusted God, and see what's happened? More than you could have asked for or expected. Look at you. Surfing. A cooking star—"

"I don't know about that."

"Yes. You're brilliant, Grace. And how would you have known that unless you trusted God to show you what He would do with an open heart?"

She wouldn't really qualify her heart as open when she got on the plane. But maybe . . . maybe God had done something with her fledgling hopes. Her longings for more.

Max came to shore now, glistening under the sun and smiling at her.

"I gotta go, Mom."

"Eden will pick you up from the airport on Monday. You might want to stay with her a couple days, just to talk about the wedding."

Max grabbed his towel, covered his head.

"Go for it, Grace. More than you can ask or imagine. Believe in God's plan for you."

"I love you, Mom," she said and hung up.

Max hunkered down next to her. "Your mom, huh?"

She put the phone away. "I was telling her how spectacular you were today."

"As were you. Want to know a secret?" He leaned close to her. "I've never made risotto well. I was totally at your mercy."

His eyes skimmed her face, his lips so close she could almost taste them. Water hung from his whiskers, dark and rough after a full day. He smelled like the ocean—salty, mysterious—and the scent of his coconut oil sunblock.

She couldn't speak, only managed to bite her lip.

His eyes dipped to her mouth; then abruptly, he sat up. "Maybe we should get back to the resort and clean up before dinner. We have a five thirty reservation."

"Uh-huh," she said, not moving.

Now. She should tell him now. Before the moment ended. Just open her mouth and say it. *I love you, Max. You changed my world.*

But her chest tightened, trapping the words

inside. "We're going to win tomorrow," she said and wrinkled her nose at her cowardice.

He glanced at her and grinned. "Yep."

She laughed and the knot in her chest eased. *Yep.* Maybe she didn't have to say it right now. Maybe she'd wait until tomorrow, after they won.

Then they'd have two full glorious days to savor their victory . . . and figure out how to bring it home to Minnesota.

Tonight Max would have to keep a tight grip on his heart if he had any chance of leaving Hawaii in one piece.

Grace descended the hotel steps and came toward him wearing a green sundress, her hair down, floating like gold around her shoulders. A hint of orchid fragrance lifted from her skin, and he conceded that he hadn't a hope of getting out of this without pain. His only consolation lay in the fact that the four sweet hours he would escape with her tonight on the catamaran dinner cruise might be the most glorious of his life.

The kind that could sustain a guy during the dark, hollow days ahead of him.

So he gave her his arm and determined to keep his wits about him, to not let his affection take them too far, to keep his heart safely in his chest.

"Where are we going?"

"I have a surprise for you." He walked her down the boardwalk toward the catamaran tied up to the long dock. The sun hung low over the sea, fading fast, but twinkly lights wound around the mast of the boat, turning it magical. Their captain, a friend of Keoni's named Lio, sat on the end of the boat, barefoot, his legs dangling down. He wore a Hawaiian-print shirt, a baseball cap over his shaved head.

"Aloha," he said, jumping up and climbing onto the dock.

"Sorry we're late," Max said. He'd retrieved a couple of his messages before hopping in the shower. One from his agent, who called with some interesting celebrity endorsement opportunities. He skipped over the three from Brendon, not willing to let his brother's aspirations sour his vacation.

Sorry, Bro, but he wasn't going to tear open the fabric of his dismal future for the world to pity him. For Grace to pity him.

He wanted her untainted admiration for as long as he could have it.

He held his hand out for Grace as she climbed over the edge onto the sailboat. Her blue eyes landed on him, wide, a smile telling him he'd chosen tonight's dinner correctly.

"This is incredible, Max. Do we have the boat to ourselves?"

"With the exception of our skipper, Lio."

Lio waved to her from where he was casting off, and Max helped her to the front of the boat.

Netting stretched between the two hulls, but he directed her to the deck in front of the cabin. "We're not going out far, just enough to see the lights and get some dinner."

"Dinner?"

"Lio, along with being a talented skipper, runs a private dinner cruise." He hunkered down beside her, watching as the boat slipped away from shore. "On the menu tonight: crab cakes with spicy aioli, tropical fruit salsa over macadamia nut–crusted basa fish, and grilled asparagus."

"Yum." She shook out her golden mane of hair. "I love boats. We have canoes and a fishing boat, and once my parents rented a houseboat for a couple days on Lake Vermilion. But I've always wanted to have my own boat."

For a second it tripped his lips—the notion that maybe next year they rent a yacht, sail around Hawaii. Instead he leaned back on his hands, breathing in the scenery and the sense of her beside him, not letting his tomorrows steal his today.

"What do you think they'll throw at us in the competition tomorrow?"

"I don't know. Maybe star fruit. Or mahimahi. We haven't had a lot of seafood to deal with yet."

"How would we ever make a mahimahi dessert?"

"I don't know. Maybe grind it up and put it in

something with dark chocolate? Make a sea-salt caramel to go with it?"

She stared at him. "You're so brilliant. Where did you learn to cook like this?"

He reached up and caught a strand of her hair when the wind twined it around her face. "I did mention I've been going to culinary school during the off-season for a few years now, right?"

"But . . . you have to have some natural ability. Does anyone else in your family cook?"

He hadn't let her too far into his family, but maybe he could give a little more away, just a couple pieces. "After my dad died, my mom needed a way to provide for us, so she became a private chef. She liked to experiment with cuisine from different cultures, and she'd often try out recipes on us before she made them for her clients. She'd say, 'Boys, what country should we visit this weekend?' and then we'd dig up recipes from Thailand or China or even Russia and attempt to make them." He shook his head, the memories savory. "*Attempt* is the key word there."

"If there is one thing this competition has taught me, it's that you just don't know what will taste good. You have to throw things together and try," she said.

Try. He put the word behind him. "My mom could make anything delicious from what she pulled from the cupboard. Not me. I like to follow recipes."

"I know, Mr. Get It Right the First Time."

That was him, wasn't it? But looking at her, he had the sense that letting go of needing it to be perfect might be okay.

"Yeah, well, we wouldn't be in the final round without you, Grace, and your ability to take a chance."

Take a chance. His own words were lethal tonight, and he looked away at the darkening shoreline of Honolulu, the buildings quickly turning into spires of light jutting into the velvety sky.

He felt Grace's gaze on him. "I wouldn't have entered the contest if it weren't for you, Max. You . . ." She swallowed. "You made me feel like a winner before we even entered. I don't care if we win tomorrow. I'm just happy right now. Happy I met you."

His throat thickened, his chest tight. "What if . . . what if . . . ?" What was he doing? But the words swirled out of him, already beyond his control. "Have you ever seen a Blue Ox game?" Oh, idiot. Of course she had—her brother had played for the Blue Ox. Before Max destroyed his career, before Max *took his place.*

He should just throw himself overboard right now. Because he saw where this would end, yet he seemed unable to stop himself from barreling toward the catastrophic finale.

"Not live," she said. "Amelia and Casper went

last season, but Eden was always the one with the tickets, so . . ."

"Uh . . . well . . . maybe you could come to one of my games." Oh, boy, he sounded like a seventh grader asking a girl to the middle school dance.

"I'd like that. But only if you win. Because I'm not driving all the way down from Deep Haven only to sit there and watch you get creamed. That would be horrible. You'd be all grumpy pants and I'd have to make you soup to cheer you up. And fresh pineapple isn't easy to get in Minneapolis in January."

Her words tugged out a grin, and he glanced at her. She met his eyes with a smile. Oh, he loved the way she could take any situation and make it . . .

Perfect.

Everything dropped away. All the hesitations, all the reasons swirling in his head why he shouldn't take her in his arms. Instead, he saw her sitting across from him in the convertible, feet up, with that silly blue toenail polish. He saw her eating shrimp, her chin smeared with butter, and chasing after a turtle, her eyes wide with fear as the ocean reached out to gulp her.

He heard her laughter as she parasailed with him and her determined voice as she fought to learn to surf. And he saw her in chef's attire, that blonde hair trickling out the back of her hat as she bossed him around in the kitchen, bringing in the win.

He couldn't stop himself. He cupped her face, ran his thumb down her cheekbone. "Grace . . . I . . ."

Her smile had dimmed, leaving behind so much raw emotion in her eyes, it tugged him right in. He let his gaze drift to her lips, then surrendered a small groan and kissed her.

He didn't stop to linger, didn't explore or nudge, just dove in, full-on, tired of holding back, of needing her. He kissed her like he'd dreamed about for a week or longer, with a sort of desperation he could no longer keep locked away.

She tasted of sunshine and sea salt, and he looped his arm around her waist, pulled her against him, his other hand curling behind her neck.

As usual, she fit perfectly into his embrace.

Best part of all, she kissed him back. Surrendering, giving, meeting him with hunger in her own touch.

Finally. Grace.

Oh, Grace.

He could probably devour her whole, but the sound of his own heartbeat thundering against his chest made him break away.

A smile slid up her face. "Took you long enough."

He wanted to sing. "Sheesh, 9B. If I knew you could kiss like that, I would have flirted with you more on the plane."

"You did enough flirting, Maximoto. Let's not talk about the plane." She leaned in and kissed him again, running her hand against his cheek, her touch so sweet, so right, he could die right now a happy man.

The stars had long since started to fall from the sky when Max returned Grace to her room. Lio had dropped them off at the dock, and Max cajoled her, without too much effort, to walk along the beach, finally pulling her into his arms in the soft, cool sand.

They just sat together, wrapped in an embrace, watching the stars, listening to the ocean cheer. He would have suggested they stay until sunrise, but they had a competition to win.

Although, like she said, he already felt like a winner.

A winner in denial, maybe, but even his future felt . . . Well, she had said that for the right man, she'd surrender her heart, even if she couldn't have a lifetime. He couldn't bear the idea that she might be telling the truth.

She simply didn't know how Huntington's disease destroyed lives. And not just the victims'.

But he didn't have to think about that now.

He opened his hotel door to the sound of his cell phone chirruping where he'd left it charging on the nightstand. He crossed the room and picked it up.

Brendon? At this time of night? He answered it, worry sluicing through him. "What's the matter? Is it Ava?"

"Huh? No, everyone's fine."

"Why are you calling me so late?"

"Oh, shoot, right. What time is it there?"

"After midnight."

"Sorry, dude. I'm heading out for a jog and got the time mixed up. I was thinking you were ahead of us, not behind us."

Max dropped his key on the nightstand and began to unbutton his shirt. "So what's so urgent?"

"It's you, Max! You're all over the Internet with this cooking thing."

Max stilled, sank down on the bed. "What?"

"Yeah, I saw you last night on the ESPN around-the-world segment. What's this about a cooking contest in Hawaii?"

He pulled off his shirt, tossed it onto a chair. "It's just a local thing."

"Not anymore. Not when Maxwell Sharpe is involved. It made WGN news in Chicago."

"How did they find out?"

"Seriously?"

Right. If his face was well-known enough to garner celebrity endorsement requests, then probably people would notice him on a local cable show. He hadn't really thought about that.

"So, yeah, I'm in this competition. It's no big deal."

"You're in the finale! You and Owen Christiansen's sister? That's sort of a big deal."

"It's not—I don't think we're going to win."

"Huh? Of course you are. Have you not seen the Facebook page for the contest? You're the favorites. And that Grace Christiansen, she's a cutie."

"Yeah. Are you calling to wish me luck?"

"No. I mean, of course. But if you win, don't you see? This is our perfect opportunity to raise awareness—"

"Oh no."

"Stop being so selfish. And narrow-minded. Has it occurred to you that God made you great at hockey so you could do something with it? Something beyond your Hall of Fame aspirations?"

"Brendon, let me figure out what God wants for my life on my own."

"The world is going to find out someday, Max. Let them see what true courage is."

He swallowed. "Okay, fine. If I win, I'll let you write up something about it." He winced at his words, but the chances of them really emerging the victors . . .

"You've got this competition in the bag, Max. The whole family is rooting for you. Thanks, Bro. You're the champ."

He smiled at that. "Thanks, Brendon." Max hung up, resting the phone on the bed.

And again dreaded his tomorrow.

• • •

If Casper hadn't gone into the drink before and learned how to manage his crew, he certainly would have driven them into a pylon with Darek on board. "Look, dude, if you don't want me helming this, just say so."

Darek raised his hands, letting his paddle rest on his lap. "No. You have a strategy. Just because it happens to be different from mine . . ."

Every eye in the boat looked at Casper, sizing him up against Darek. Even his parents—his dad sitting in the middle of the boat, his mother in the front.

Nice.

The seagulls onshore rose and began to call, as if adding to the mocking, the jeers. Not that anyone had said anything when Darek showed up for practice today, but they didn't have to.

One look at Darek and his build, with years of knowledge under his belt, and the choice was clear. If they wanted to win, Darek should captain the boat.

But no one said it, and Casper's pride wouldn't let the suggestion leak out. He tamped it down and ignored the voices in his head.

This was his boat to captain.

A slight wind bullied the dragon boat and he reached down to grab the dock, lest it slip away from him and out into the harbor.

A rudderless ship. Darek would have a field day with that.

"I trust you, Bro," Darek said, but his smile resembled shark teeth.

Casper couldn't help it—he cast a look at Raina. He needed, for a moment, the confidence she gave him, the belief. Call him a sap, but when she looked at him like that, he became a champion.

She smiled, something soft, kind, and it cut through the clatter inside.

"Let's take her out for one last paddle." The team had already gone through their strategy twice, and now he got in the back, letting Kyle and Jensen push them away from the dock.

In the front, Emma kept time, slowly beating the drum as they paddled out to the imaginary starting line.

Eight rows in front of him, Raina, with her long hair in a braid down her back, paddled in beat. He wanted to run his hand down that thick braid, pull her into his arms, see her smile—

"Casper! Are you planning on hitting that sailboat?" Darek turned in his seat, two places in front of him, his expression a growl.

Casper steered them away from the skiff. "Let's sing a paddling song," he said to Emma.

She started them in a chant. "Hey, Captain, can you hear it? Listen to our dragon spirit!"

He smiled, hearing Raina's voice rise above the shouts.

He wasn't sure how she'd gotten so far into his heart so fast, but he wasn't arguing.

Still, he had to focus on this race if he wanted to win. As they maneuvered toward the starting line, he raised his voice with the rest of his team. "Gonna set a record pace. Gonna paddle to first place!"

He turned the boat so they were heading back to the docks. Emma slowed the drum until they were floating. "Bring us to a stop," Casper said, and a few paddlers slowed them in the water.

"Okay, give me twenty-five hard strokes, as fast as you can; then Emma will set the pace. Ready?"

Paddles came up.

In the race, they'd take off to a gun, but he started the stopwatch around his neck and simply shouted, his voice carrying across the water. "Go!"

The boat lurched forward, nearly knocking him backward. They counted off together. *One, two, three—"*

He could admit that having Darek back on board made for extra power. They motored through the water, a slick, fierce dragon skimming the surface as they dug in. "Twenty-five!"

They'd started to settle into their standard pace, still as one, a motorized team of paddlers with beautiful form, strong strokes. The water peeled back from the keel, cool and dark, and he angled them toward the finish line.

Onshore, he caught sight of Seb Brewster, the

captain of the town team. *You're going down, Mr. Mayor.*

They surged over the halfway point. "Keep it strong, team!" He glanced at the watch—they'd shaved sixteen seconds off their previous time.

In front, he saw Annalise Decker start to slow. "Annalise—take your paddle out of the water if you can't keep up!"

She put it on her lap, and the aft side kept rhythm. He glanced at the clock. Still under their best time.

In the middle of the boat, he heard Nathan, his father, and even his brother groaning.

"Push it!"

They sailed across the imaginary finish line—drawn from the end of the long pier and the corner of the trading post onshore—and he clocked their time. "Fourteen seconds faster than our best time!"

The crew leaned over their paddles, breathing hard, drifting now toward the dock.

"Probably too soon to suggest we go again?"

Kyle Hueston looked back like he might arrest him and Casper grinned. "Just kidding. Great job today. I think we're ready for competition."

They floated to the dock and the crew disembarked. He gathered up the paddles, the life jackets. Then he, Darek, Kyle, and Jensen hoisted the boat from the water, together carrying it to the trailer.

"I'll park it in the shed," Darek said, and Casper

wondered if he just wanted to spend time with his beloved boat.

Casper cast a look at Raina, who was drinking from one of the water bottles Ingrid had passed out. She wore nylon athletic pants and a green sports tunic today, along with her Keens.

He left Darek alone and sidled up to her. "Can I interest you in dinner?"

She looked at him, nodded.

Something had changed for her since he'd caught her talking to his father. She'd seemed to relax. Laugh more easily. Last night she'd even played a game of speed Scrabble with him and his parents. Like it was just another normal Wednesday night at the homestead, one she so easily fit into.

She climbed into the passenger side of his truck. "Do you mind if I run home and change clothes? I'm a little sweaty."

"No problem. I'll drop you off, go home and shower, and pick you back up."

"Where are we going?"

He lifted a shoulder.

"I have an idea," she said, her eyes twinkling. As they neared her aunt's house, she turned to him. "And bring the motorcycle."

The motorcycle? Uh—

But she got out before he had a chance to follow up, and shoot, if he couldn't see them riding off into the sunset.

His parents had beaten him home, so when he arrived, he found his father in the family room, surfing the Internet for car repair manuals.

"Still can't get the Chevy running?"

"I'll figure it out," John said. He turned and stopped Casper with a hand to his arm.

Casper stilled. "I know I can't fix her, Dad."

His dad lowered his hand. "Good. But that's not what I need to talk to you about." He took a breath. "I don't know how to ask you this, but . . . is everything . . . okay with her? And you? I mean, I see you getting closer. You've been a gentleman, right?"

Casper stared at him, not sure—"We haven't even kissed." It felt weird saying that to his father, but having someone keep his emotions, his desires in check might help. "But yeah, of course. Why?"

John shook his head. "It's what she said about all us Christiansen men . . ."

"Arrogant. I assumed she was referring to Darek."

His dad's mouth tightened to a grim line.

Casper clamped a hand on his shoulder. "I promise, Dad, I'll be a gentleman."

But his dad's expression, his words, dogged him into his room, the shower, out again.

Go away, Owen!

The memory of her voice that day on the road reverberated back to him as he pulled on a T-shirt.

He shook his head at the memory. Maybe his ornery kid brother had cut her off on the road or even snuck into the kitchen at the wedding and stolen food.

Or, as he first guessed, hit on her. Which only churned up a strange heat in his chest.

Especially at her word used at the campfire. *Arrogant?*

What did that mean?

He put it out of his mind, picked up an extra helmet, and headed to town.

Raina sat waiting on the front steps, a backpack over her shoulder, wearing capri-style jeans, a white shirt, and a jean jacket.

She took the helmet, slipped it on, and climbed onto his bike as if it were as natural as a sunrise.

Women confused him.

Then she slipped her arms around his waist and leaned in.

They confused him a lot.

"Where to?" Casper said.

"Paradise Beach."

She knew about Paradise Beach? He gunned it out of town, heading up the shoreline, the sun lazy as it sank behind them, casting long, shaggy fingers of shadow across the road. The lake had calmed, turned to a whisper on the shore.

He stopped at one of the many inlets to the lake along a stretch of pebbled beach named for its agates and view.

Raina got off, using his shoulders to steady herself, then led him out to the shore. Sitting, she pulled two turkey wraps, a couple bags of chips, and bottles of soda from her backpack. She opened a Tupperware container filled with cookies.

"You just whipped this up?"

"I made the cookies yesterday. But yeah."

He reached for a wrap. "Impressive."

She grinned at him, peeled the plastic off the other wrap. "We're going to win, you know."

"The other teams are really good."

"But we're awesome! And with you as our captain, we are so going to win."

"Well, I'm no Darek, but we're getting faster."

"Casper! You're an amazing captain, a thousand times better than Darek."

He took a bite of his wrap. "You didn't paddle under him. He has three championships under his belt, is legendary around here."

"You're next."

"I don't know. It's hard to carve out your own legend when you have brothers like Darek and Owen. One is the town hotshot, the other the hockey hero."

"And you—what are you?"

Her question stumped him. He'd never exactly known. "I am the brother in the middle. I was always either following in Darek's shadow or setting up Owen for the win. I guess I'm still trying to figure out where I belong."

Her voice turned low. "You're the best brother, in my opinion."

He didn't know why, but her words found soft soil and burrowed in, sweet and nourishing.

She smiled at him, the wind teasing her black hair around her face. He fought the urge to catch a strand, press it between his fingers.

His voice fell soft, almost a thought more than words. "What is it about you, Raina? Where did you come from? How is it that you simply appear one day in my life as my champion? You're so . . . undefeatable. You make me believe we're going to win."

Her smile dipped a little, and she looked down as if embarrassed.

"Did I say something wrong?"

She shook her head. "I just . . . You make me feel like I'm a part of the team."

He frowned. "You are a part of the team."

"Like you *want* me on the team."

He did want her on the team.

And then he got it. It wasn't about just being a part of a community. It was about being chosen by him. Wanted by him.

His gaze traced from her eyes to her mouth, and his throat suddenly got very dry. He reached for a bottle, uncapped it. Drank a swig of soda.

It ignited his entire body on fire. He looked at her again.

"Can I ask you something . . . silly?" She had caught her lip between her teeth.

Without thinking, he reached up to ease it free, then kept his hand cupped to her face. "Yes, anything."

"My aunt said . . . well, that you had a lot of girlfriends . . ." She looked away. "I'm sorry. That was stupid—"

"No—it was . . ." He could hardly breathe for the pressure in his chest. "No, Raina. I have a lot of girls who are my friends. I find girls easy to be around, but no . . . I haven't dated many girls in Deep Haven or beyond."

He searched for her eyes, and she met his, her bottom lip caught in her teeth once more.

He couldn't help it. Gently he ran his hand behind her neck and drew her close, searching her gaze a moment for permission before he touched her lips with his.

Her mouth tasted sweet, of her soda and the honey mustard on the wraps. Her response was soft and just eager enough to urge him on, even as she put her hand to his chest. For a second, he thought she might push him away, but she grabbed his shirt and pulled him closer.

Casper scooted in and wrapped his arms around her, deepening his kiss.

Raina. Who knew such happiness could be found hiding in Deep Haven?

She fitted herself to his body and seemed to

relax in his embrace. And that's when he heard his father's voice, thrumming deep in his head: *You've been a gentleman, right?*

So far, yeah. But he hardly had gentlemanly thoughts sparking in his brain at the moment. In fact, he had her locked in his arms on the beach as the sun began its descent . . .

Casper ran his hand over her cheek and lifted his head.

Her eyes hung on his, the slightest smile at the corners of her mouth.

Maybe he'd sit right here for a while. He wound his fingers through hers. "How did you know about this place? I thought only locals knew about Paradise Beach."

Just like that, her expression darkened. "Uh . . . I . . . I don't know. Maybe . . . maybe Aunt Liza?"

Oh yeah, Liza, of course. Still, he sensed a funny shift in their moment, in the way her hand loosened and she started to pull away.

He gripped it, holding on. "So did she tell you that this is the perfect beach for finding agates?"

It seemed to work. "What are agates?"

"Tiny, beautiful rocks that look like mini granite stones. Treasures embedded in the shore." He wanted to pull her into his arms again. More, he wanted to reach inside to that dark place and pull out her fear. To make her feel safe, wanted.

Yeah, he wanted to fix her. And maybe, just a little, he could.

"Will you help me find one?"

Casper nodded. "I think I can do that."

Chapter 13

A storm front had rolled in since their beautiful evening, thunderstorms hovering over the island of Oahu, sending a gray pallor over the last day of competition. Waves thundered onto the shore, almost deafening, and the pitter-patter of rain suggested their crowd might be meager today.

Still, nothing could sink Grace's buoyant spirit.

She'd already won. Because last night Max had finally taken her in his arms. She could still feel his embrace around her, taste his lips on hers.

She'd slept a total of two hours, maybe, but this morning everything buzzed with anticipation. She buttoned her chef's jacket, glancing at Max, hoping for a smile.

He wore his game face, freshly shaved, looking dark and intense. She'd guess it was his hockey face. Owen had a similar expression.

He'd met her after breakfast, already in competition mode. She tried to tease him, but he just looked at her with steely, serious eyes.

For a second, she feared that he regretted their romantic, glorious evening, but then he'd taken her hand, holding it in his iron grip as they advanced to the tents and the crew trailers, splashing through puddles, then breaking into a run when it started to rain. He'd nearly shoved her into the trailer.

"I'm not going to melt, Max," she said, laughing, but he didn't smile. As if he might truly be protecting her.

So maybe she'd wait until after the competition to tell him that she loved him. She meant to say it last night, but . . . despite his affection, the words still glued to her chest. She wanted to say it once, forever, to the right man.

To Max.

"Five minutes to set."

Max began to breathe deeply. "Did you know that we're on Facebook? And that videos of our show are on the Internet?"

She nodded. "My mom told me yesterday. Sorry; I would have mentioned it to you—I forgot."

He drew in another breath, blew it out.

"Are you nervous? You seem nervous."

He smiled then, but it was all teeth, nothing of his eyes. "We got this."

For the first time, she didn't believe him.

They stood with the hippies and Palani as he introduced them. A bigger crowd than she expected sat in the stands and their cheers rose for Max, who waved.

She expected him to take her hand as they manned their stations, but instead he walked ahead of her.

Like a man to an execution. Wow, he was really wired. Or maybe tired. Or . . .

What if he regretted kissing her?

She pressed a hand to her roiling stomach. Smiled into the cameras. Game face—she had one too.

Then Palani spoke into the mic. "Today's ingredients for the final round, the dessert course, are . . . kiwi, macadamia nuts, carob chips . . . and our challenge ingredient: Spam!"

Spam? She glanced at Max, who was frowning.

"Ready?" Palani said.

"We can do this," she whispered to Max. He didn't look at her.

"Go!"

Grace ran for her basket, turning over the ingredients. Kiwi and carob chips. They were like chocolate, and Spam was . . . it was soft, right? She picked up the basket, raced back.

Max looked almost white.

"What should we do?" she said.

"Uh . . ."

She wanted to shake him, or maybe slap him hard, but he was just staring at her, like a walleye out of water.

"Okay," she said, "how about . . . chocolate . . . um . . . ?"

"Mousse."

She met his eyes, saw a flicker of the man she knew. "Mousse. That's good. And what if we candy the kiwi? I'll brunoise it, and we'll put it in the mousse."

He nodded, enthusiasm lighting his voice. "Good. And we'll roast the macadamia nuts, use them as garnish."

"Max, you're brilliant!" She wanted to kiss him.

Max grabbed the Spam, opened it, and dropped it in a bowl as she peeled the kiwi. He dumped the carob chips into a double boiler on the stove, stirring for a moment before he added the Spam.

She grabbed the coarse ground sugar and measured a half cup into a pan, added water, started it boiling.

Max took his chocolate mix off the stove. He disappeared into the pantry, returning with eggs and cream and adding them to the mix.

Meanwhile Grace dropped the kiwis into the dissolved sugar mixture, turned it to low, and grabbed the macadamia nuts and some butter.

Behind her, she heard Max begin to whip the mousse. "Don't forget vanilla," she said as she chopped the nuts. "Maybe even some honey."

"Yes. Right."

She threw two tablespoons of butter into a hot pan, tossed in the macadamia nuts, a handful of kosher salt. She put the salt down, then after a minute, rescued the nuts, setting them to cool.

"How's the mousse?"

"Nearly whipped." He took the kiwi off the stove, spooned it out, and set it on a baking tray, then shoved it into a dehydrator. "Thirteen minutes."

Grace grinned at him.

He grinned back, and the memory of holding his face in her hands stirred inside her.

Across the stage in the next kitchen area, they heard a crash, then swearing.

The hippie wife stood holding a blowtorch, her tray of Spam on the floor.

A twitter went through the crowd as the husband and wife scrambled to find a new can of Spam and rescue their dessert.

Grace turned away and headed for the dehydrator as Max added another half cup of sugar to the mousse.

The kiwi seemed sticky yet dry enough to brunoise. She dropped the fruit onto the cutting board, julienned it, then turned it and cut it into tiny sections.

"Six minutes," Palani called.

Max had the mousse in custard cups, chilling in the freezer. Grace grabbed the sugar, the macadamia nuts, and tossed them together.

They were working without comment now, Max grabbing the plates. Grace took the custard cups from the freezer and plated them in the center. Max dabbled the fruit on each one while she dusted them with macadamias.

They stepped back just as Palani called time.

The hippies had barely finished plating, their presentation a mess.

"I think they made a kiwi cobbler with blackened Spam," Max said.

"We got this," Grace whispered. She reached for his hand, but he put it behind his back, chef-like.

Okay.

She held her breath as the hippies presented their dessert. Ten thousand dollars. She hadn't truly given the money any real thought until now. Ten thousand dollars would help her buy equipment, even rent a commercial kitchen. She could be in business by the fall . . .

"Interesting," Rogers said. "I've never had blackened Spam before, but you managed to pull it off, even with the fiasco."

"I like the macadamia crust on the cobbler—I just wish your dish had a bit more pizzazz," Tonie said.

How hard was it to make cobbler, really? Oh yes, they had this.

Grace took their tray forward and set it before the judges. "We have a carob Spam mousse, topped with candied kiwi and roasted macadamia-nut garnish."

Keoni raised an eyebrow, a smile hinting on his face.

Rogers nodded, and Tonie glanced at Max with a smile.

Grace stepped back, bit her lip. Held her breath.

She pinpointed their demise on Keoni's face, the first to finish his spoon of mousse. Disappointment, almost pain, creased across it.

Then Rogers grimaced and lunged for his water.

"Oh, this is terrible!" Tonie actually took her napkin and spit the mousse out.

Beside her, Max hung his head, even as Grace stood there, stunned. "What—? I don't understand."

"Do you know the difference between salt and sugar?" This from Tonie, who had finished her water and asked for more.

"I do—"

"Well, something isn't right. I'm not sure if it's the kiwi or the mousse, but this is inedible."

Grace couldn't move. She mentally retraced her steps. Sugar—she'd put that on the right side of the stove, the salt on the left, but maybe she'd picked up the salt . . . Or what if she'd given Max the salt, and he'd mistaken it for sugar? They'd been working so fast that—

"I think our winner here is clear," Rogers said. He motioned the hippies to the front, even as Palani announced Grace and Max's fate.

Chopped.

She stood stunned for a long moment, until she finally felt Max's hand on her arm. He led her offstage and she watched, still numb, as Palani presented the couple with their check.

They'd lost. How could they have lost? They were so brilliant, so resourceful, such a magnificent team.

Max had turned away, a hand cupped behind his neck.

"This is my fault," she said, realization slowly burning through her. "I gave you the salt—or rather, I set it down, and you probably mistook it for sugar. Or maybe I salted the kiwi—oh, Max, I'm sorry."

He looked at her, his eyes fierce, almost angry. Then he shook his head. "I'm so sorry, Grace," he said quietly and walked away.

She stood there, frozen, rain dripping down the sides of the tent as he walked to his Mustang, got in, and drove away.

Max couldn't look at himself. Couldn't face the person he'd become, especially after seeing Grace's face when the judges tasted the mousse. He'd nearly bolted then, but he'd stayed until the end.

But when she blamed herself . . . he nearly lost his stomach right there.

He felt like he'd put the puck in his own team's net.

He went straight to his hotel room, opened his duffel, and began to pack. He didn't fold anything, just shoved it as fast as he could into the bag.

Grace had already sent him a slew of text

messages, and now he reached for his phone and turned it off, slipping it into the pocket of his shorts. He didn't need a message from Grace to tell him what kind of jerk he'd become. How he'd completely betrayed them. He already knew.

He'd thrown the contest. He knew perfectly well which ingredient he was adding to the mousse when he reached for the container.

For a second there, he thought he wouldn't have to do anything to slide into second place. The hippies always managed to wow the judges, present something creative but local, giving the food a Hawaiian twist.

Then they had to go and drop their Spam. And in a blinding flash, Max knew, just knew, he and Grace would win.

That's when he became a saboteur, a shyster, a betrayer.

He couldn't face her.

He picked up the duffel, threw it over his shoulder. He'd buy a ticket when he got to the airport. He took the stairs down so he wouldn't see her, spied on the lobby for a long moment, then scooted across it to the checkout counter.

"Did you enjoy your stay, Mr. Sharpe?"

He kept his voice low. "Yeah. Sure. It was great." He pulled his baseball cap lower over his eyes. *Please don't let Grace walk in right now.*

The thunderstorms had dried out, a warm sun beginning to bake the pavement, evaporate the puddles. The air hung on to the moldy, thick odor stirred up by the rain. Muggy. On a day like today, the surf should be calling him. He had planned an afternoon of celebration. They'd surf, and then he'd seriously considered telling Grace how much she meant to him. Approaching the idea that maybe they could have more.

Until, of course, Brendon's phone call. The rude awakening to the brutal fact that Max would never escape who he was, even in Hawaii.

When he'd agreed to his brother's plan last night, he hadn't actually thought they might win.

He should have known better—should have known Grace better. He *did* know her better.

"I see you're checking out early. Are you unhappy with your stay?"

"No. Of course not. It was fine, just fine."

"Can I inquire as to the reason you're leaving early?"

"It's personal. Just check me out."

The woman bent her head and he regretted his tone. Apparently he hadn't enough gentleman left in him to be kind even to the hotel staff.

"Would you like to book for next year? We have a special—"

"No." He winced, forced a smile. "But thank you."

"Thank you for visiting with us, Mr. Sharpe." She kept her polite smile as she handed him his receipt.

He shoved it in his pocket, went outside, and gave his keys to a valet. Then he hid next to a palm tree until the valet brought back the Mustang.

Dropping the duffel into the backseat, Max got behind the wheel and gunned it. He'd never felt like such a chump in all his life.

He turned on the radio, trying to drown his thoughts. The country station came up, a song about running out of moonlight.

He should have stayed on the beach with Grace. Should have never answered his phone. But then what? His brother might have appeared with a company of reporters, forcing his hand.

He tightened his grip on the steering wheel, cutting through traffic, driving too fast. He earned a horn and gritted his teeth.

Brendon had called him selfish. It fit. The magnitude of his selfishness could flood his throat and choke him.

In fact, he remembered Grace's words from their day at Pearl Harbor: *I don't really care about anything on that list but a man who loves Jesus and loves me.*

He did love Jesus. But until recently, his belief affected only him. He didn't have to focus on anyone but himself and only had to trust his future—not anyone else's—to Jesus.

But the minute he let Grace into his life . . . Well, he didn't know if he had enough faith for that.

The traffic screamed by.

This was why he shouldn't fall in love, why he shouldn't put his heart out for a woman. Why he should have never, ever shown up on her doorstep in Hawaii. The fact that she was Owen's sister only made it worse because, guess what—now Owen had more reasons to hate him.

He parked his car in the rental area and took a shuttle to the airport. At the airline counter, he put down his card. "I need a first-class ticket, one-way, to Minneapolis."

Ticket in hand, he slung his duffel over his shoulder and headed toward the gate.

Still an hour and a half before his flight. He sat in the corner, pulled his hat down, slouched. He probably needed something to read. Reaching into his bag, he took out the magazine from his trip in.

The magazine naturally opened to the crossword. He traced his finger over the word *atoll*. And then *avast*. Swallowed past the boulder in his throat.

Max closed the magazine and pulled out his phone. Maybe he could find some sports scores, watch ESPN. He turned it on, seeing two more text messages from Grace. He deleted them without reading them.

He was checking the NHL preseason chatter and predictions when his phone rang. Brendon's face appeared.

He grimaced and took the call. "Hi."

"So how'd you do? Did you win? Of course you won."

"No. I didn't win," he growled.

"No . . . really? What happened?"

Even to his brother—maybe especially to his brother—he couldn't come clean. "One of us mixed up the salt and sugar and put salt in the dessert. It wasn't pretty."

"Aw, man, I'm sorry. I suppose that sort of thing happens."

Not in a gourmet kitchen. Not with trained chefs. "Yeah."

"So a couple more days in paradise and then you're coming home, right?"

Max blew out a breath. "I'll call you when I get to Minneapolis."

"Swell. And then we'll figure out when Lizzy and I can taste what you learned."

"Sure."

"Hey, Bro. Thanks anyway for your offer."

Max made a sound, sort of a grunt, and clicked off. He couldn't take any more. He shoved the phone back into his pocket.

A family entered the waiting area. A father, mother, and two little blond boys. The boys pulled their own carry-ons, featuring pictures of the Hulk and Iron Man. The husband, tall, lanky, wore a baseball cap imprinted with the Chicago Cubs logo. The woman sat down and pulled one of the boys onto her lap. Began to tickle him. The little boy's laughter sweetened the air.

Max ground his jaw.

For a second he had the urge to race back to the hotel. Back to the woman he . . . yes, loved. The realization twisted inside him, twined around his heart.

He could go back and apologize. Pretend that it wasn't ending.

It wasn't like she knew what he'd done.

But the lies could suffocate him.

He just couldn't lead her on one more day. And that glued him to his spot, watching passengers fill the gate area, tan and happy from their vacation. Too many wore *I Love Hawaii* T-shirts, leis, floppy hats.

He'd checked and found that he and Grace had been on the same flight back to Minneapolis. Now Grace would have to fly home by herself. No one to hold her barf bag. No one to ensure she switched planes safely. What if she sat next to a jerk?

Or a guy like him, who could recognize her beauty?

He picked up the magazine again, telling himself that would be best. He would have to break it off eventually anyway. He'd known going in that it was just a vacation friendship. It could never be more than that.

Maybe if he'd kept it to friendship . . . But one

look at Grace and deep down, he'd known he couldn't stop there. He'd lied to himself for three weeks, until he'd pulled them both in to drown.

Worst vacation of his life.

The gate attendant announced first class. Max grabbed his bag without a look back at the family, the other passengers. He handed her his boarding document.

"Aloha," the pretty attendant said. "How was Hawaii?"

He ignored her and got on the plane.

Max had left Hawaii. Flown out or taken a ship or even swum. But he'd really left Hawaii. Without an explanation. Without a good-bye.

It took a full day for the truth to sink into Grace's heart.

When he'd walked away from her after the competition, she stood, too stunned to do more than watch him go. Unable, even, to run after him. To stop him.

Keoni had driven her back to the hotel, his own expression grim, as if he was sorting through Max's actions.

She'd changed, texted Max. Waited, texted again. Finally, around dinnertime, she went to his room.

A family dressed in beachwear, fresh from the mainland, answered his door.

Just in case he'd simply moved rooms, she

asked about him at the hotel desk. They gave no information other than that he'd left.

She spent the rest of the evening by the pool, her eyes thick with tears, rereading page 3 in her stupid novel, listening to his words in her head.

He didn't have time for mistakes.

Like the wrong ingredients.

The wrong partner.

Her.

It still seemed so impossible that she'd driven him clear out of Hawaii.

By the next day, the unfairness rooted in her bones, turned her brittle and angry. What kind of person simply abandoned the team? Upset or not, he owed her an explanation. She had stopped texting him, given up after leaving a couple voice mails.

Still, like a lovesick fool, she kept her phone by her side. Hoping. Hating herself for hoping. Running conversations over in her head, none of them satisfactory.

She sat on the beach while the sun burned her, watching the surfers, the lovers strolling hand in hand, trying not to remember Max's arms around her, the way one look from him made her feel strong. Capable. Extraordinary.

By Sunday morning, she simply wanted to endure until her late-afternoon flight. She got up, showered, and packed. Hating that she looked like a swollen crawfish, she donned her sunglasses and went outside for breakfast on the terrace. The Twinkies sat at a table and lifted their hands to her. She waved but made a U-turn and headed toward the beach.

Sunday seemed like any other day at the resort—paddlers on longboards in the lagoon, surfers testing the swells, children digging channels out to sea, women in bikinis on straw mats soaking in their vitamin D.

At home, her family would be returning home from church. They took up an entire row, sometimes two. Surely Darek and Ivy had returned from their honeymoon by now. Tiger would have taken a perch between them, although sometimes he opted for Grace's lap. She too often let him play thumb wars with her when the sermon got long.

They'd all be gathered at home for brunch—something Grace would have prepared—or they'd grill, eating outside on the picnic table. Casper would take volunteers to go fishing. Darek would disappear to work on the framing of his house, now in the rebuilding stage. And in the evening, they'd gather for their ritual Sunday night s'mores around the fire.

What was she doing here in Hawaii alone, when she should be in Deep Haven with her family? Why had she agreed to this trip, this disaster? The entire thing seemed like a trick, as if God had held her dreams out in front of her only to yank them away.

She'd stepped onto the hot sand, heading toward the water, when a sound caught her attention. Music. A hymn.

" 'O, how He loves you and me . . .' " A flute played the melody and lured her closer, toward where a man dressed in a blue Hawaiian-print shirt was singing. A woman in a matching blue floral dress danced a sort of hula to the words. Fifty or so onlookers sat in folding sports chairs or in the sand, some under tents, listening.

Grace leaned against a palm tree.

The man finished the song, then welcomed them to Waikiki Beach Church. "There's no better place to worship the Lord than on the beach in Hawaii."

Grace folded her arms.

"I know that for many of you, this is a dream vacation. Something you've saved for, planned for, hoped for over many years. I hope it has been—or will be—all you wanted." He gestured to the ocean, the beauty. "But I'm here to tell you that you can find paradise without ever leaving your homes."

Grace pursed her lips and started to walk away.

"Paradise is not what you see, but a relationship with the One who made it."

She'd heard this before. And had no interest, really, in sitting through a sermon about how if

296

she just trusted God more, she might find happiness.

She'd reached out—no, flung herself out—on this great adventure, and God had dropped her. Hard.

"The key to finding what God has for you is not reaching out for paradise . . . but letting go. Falling. Losing control."

She stopped.

"But most of us are too afraid to truly let go, to hold open our hands and receive what God has for us."

Maybe just another minute . . .

"Consider the journey of Peter, who left his nets to follow Christ and ended up denying Him. Peter believed in Jesus, followed Him, but hadn't been transformed by Him. He walked with Jesus, obeyed Jesus, and called Him Messiah. But until that dark moment of denial, Peter hadn't come face-to-face with his own heart, selfish and angry and afraid. It wasn't until Peter saw the kind of person he was and regretted his sins that life began to change for him."

Grace tucked herself back under the palm tree.

"John 21 tells the story of a repentant Peter who longs to make things right with his Lord. And when Jesus asks Peter if he loves Him, Peter heartily replies three times that he does. Peter is confronted with grace. Jesus doesn't condemn him for his actions. Rather, He charges Peter with a new command: 'Feed My lambs.' Peter wasn't just to follow his Lord, but to be so close to Jesus that he became Jesus to His people. Love, forgive, serve. Peter would share a relationship with God like Jesus has. This is the transformation Jesus intends for us, a wholeness, a closeness in our relationship with God that is beyond our wildest hopes."

The preacher scanned the crowd. "So many of us come to Hawaii because we long for paradise. For more than our lives give us. That *more* is waiting for you right here." He lifted his Bible. "You may be walking with Jesus, but has truth broken your heart? Have you been undone by the gospel in the face of your own sins? The truth is that you can follow Jesus . . . or you can walk with Him step by step. The Bible calls this abiding with Him. It starts with transformation and ends with the joy, the abundance, you long for."

He gestured to the ocean, where a man and woman dressed in Hawaiian attire stood at the waves' edge. "If you would like to experience more joy, more hope, more peace . . . abundance, I invite you to come forward and be baptized today. Repent—regret your sins and let Jesus forgive you. Fill you with His grace. His love. A new life. More than you could have ever asked for or imagined."

Grace's feet moved.

She looked down, seeing herself shuffle through the sand, her throat thick.

For years she'd been clinging to her own expectations of what God should be giving her. She had come to Hawaii looking for something, and when it hadn't turned out just as she hoped, she let it burn a hole in her faith. But what if God had brought her to Hawaii for this one thing? To face her own selfishness, her own fears, even her anger?

What if He'd heard the silent longing of her heart and answered it, not with Max but with *Himself?*

Here, on the beach, if she understood right, God was inviting her into the *more,* the abundance her heart longed for.

Grace wiped her cheek as she headed toward the edge of the water. The woman standing in the shallows took her hand.

"I am a follower of Jesus already," Grace said, the words like a breath inside her soul. "But I want more. I want to let Him transform me. I want an amazing, abundant life with Jesus."

"Then today you shall have it."

Grace walked fully clothed into the water, the salty freshness cool against her ravaged, burned skin. She waded out to her waist before the woman stopped her.

"What do you want to say to God?"

Grace looked to the scrape of cirrus clouds

white upon the blue canvas. "Lord, I confess that I have clung to my own fears and even recently harbored anger against You in my heart. I want to do more than follow You. I want to be transformed . . . I want the abundant life You promise."

The woman nodded. "With the confession of your sins, you are forgiven and transformed." She held out her hands.

Grace grasped them as the woman dunked her, quickly, into the ocean. She surfaced, blinking into the sunlight, water streaming down her cheeks. She took a breath of the warm, fragrant air, and it filled her lungs, overflowing.

"Do you love Him, sister?" the woman asked.

Grace nodded, her eyes hot despite the cool water. "I do."

"Then feed His sheep."

Grace closed her eyes, the salt sinking into her skin, ocean water dripping down her back.

My heart belongs to You, O God.

With the confession, she could almost taste the sweetness of His grace.

She stayed on the beach, singing with the congregation until her clothes dried. Then she changed, checked out, and caught the hotel shuttle to the airport.

She finished her book on the plane ride home, with not a hint of airsickness. Eden met her at baggage claim at a terribly early hour Monday morning and drove to her Minneapolis apartment.

When Eden mentioned Max, Grace told her simply that it hadn't worked out.

Grace finally entered Eden's apartment, the fuzzy fatigue of too much travel pressing into her bones. She curled up on her sister's couch and prayed that the life she'd found in Hawaii had followed her home.

Chapter 14

Grace could not imagine a more beautiful bride than Eden. Her sister stood on the bridal shop platform, holding up her arms as the gown attendant fitted her. The woman lifted the train. "We'll gather it in a bustle for the dance, of course. But do you like how it flows?"

Eden skimmed her hands down the bodice and over the long layer of white, creamy satin. The dress accentuated all her curves, with an embroidered floral overlay that sculpted her body and dropped to just below her hips. Elegant and simple, with exquisitely lacy cap sleeves and a V-neck frame, the dress would take Jace's breath away.

"What do you think, Grace? Do you like it?"

Grace could hardly speak. After all, her sister was a vision of beauty, and she wanted to smile. In fact, she did smile. She did put warmth in her eyes. She did answer, "Yes, I love it. You're so beautiful." But it seemed that her heart had turned to ash with the question.

Five days since she'd last seen Max, and the pain of it had the power to sour her reawakened relationship with God. She wanted to hold on to the abundant life, the joy that the pastor had talked about, but it all seemed to be slipping like sand from her grip.

"Are you okay?"

"Yes. Yes, I'm fine." Grace got up, walked over to her sister, and turned her around to face the three oversize mirrors. "Look at you. You're absolutely a vision. Jace is going to flip."

"I don't know. I still can't believe this is happening. And so soon."

Grace frowned, meeting her eyes in the mirror. "What do you mean so soon? You have five months before your wedding." She made a face. "On second thought, yeah. Five months and a to-do list as long as one of those novels you're writing—"

"Actually, no . . . I need to talk to you about that. I wanted to call you in Hawaii, but I thought it might be better to talk face-to-face."

Eden handed the attendant the veil she'd tried on, shaking her head. "We moved up the wedding. The Blue Ox have offered Jace a coaching position, and he has to report early for practice. He wants to get married before the season starts."

"That's great . . . but oh, boy. When is practice?"

Grace said, trying to buoy the sinking feeling in her chest.

"It starts in less than two months. So, leaving time for a honeymoon, we'll have the wedding in . . . six weeks?"

"What?" Grace stepped back. "No. You can't possibly pull a wedding together that fast."

Eden looked at the attendant. "Well, actually, we've already talked about it. We have two more fittings, right?"

The woman nodded.

"And we're doing just fine. Look, the dress is perfect, and we have the venue, even the band— the Blue Monkeys are playing. They can't wait."

"Yes . . . ," Grace said, her voice low. She felt as if she were speaking through molasses.

"Well, this is what I need to talk to you about." Eden came off the podium and tugged on Grace's hand to make her follow her back to the dressing room. Eden disappeared behind the curtain with the attendant while Grace stayed on the other side. Probably a ploy to soften the blow because Grace knew what was coming next.

"I'm serious about you catering the wedding."

"No—Eden, I know you said that, but you can't expect me to be the maid of honor and cater your wedding—that's crazy. It was a nice idea, and yeah, I'm glad I went to Hawaii, but if you remember, I missed Darek and Ivy's wedding, and . . . this could very well be a disaster."

"It won't be a disaster. You'll just plan every-thing and get Raina and Ty to do it."

"Eden, really. Let's just whiz past the absurdity of catering a wedding that *I am in* and think. Six weeks. That's so soon. I can't possibly pull it together by then."

The attendant emerged from behind the curtain, carrying the dress. The curtain fell back. Eden's voice came through again. "What do you mean? Of course you can. Just a week ago you pulled together an entire course in thirty minutes using crazy ingredients—and nearly won! If anyone could pull this off, it's you!"

"Oh, Eden." Grace looked at her own visage in the mirror. Tan, lean, looking healthy. Why, then, did she feel so dead inside? "This is way over my head."

"You only think it is." She poked her head around the curtain. "Listen, the venue has a serving staff, and I know you could get people to help you in the kitchen. What about students from the local school? All you have to do is plan and prep. Raina can do the rest."

"Of course Raina could help. Ty too, and yes, that's a great idea about the cooking school, even if they did reject my application, but the real problem is . . . I don't know Hawaiian cooking that well." She sank onto a tufted stool. "I can't put this together on my own."

"Don't be silly. You just spent three weeks

learning how. Use the recipes you learned." Eden smiled. "I trust you." She disappeared again behind the curtain.

Eden shouldn't trust her—not after the salt fiasco. In fact, this plan had the makings of a disaster. "How many people are coming?"

"About a hundred of our closest friends?"

Grace had no words.

"How about if I shorten the list to seventy-five. Keep it intimate."

Seventy-five was intimate?

"C'mon. You just pulled it off for Ivy and Darek."

"Are you kidding me? Seventy-five guests for a sit-down Hawaiian-theme dinner is a far cry from Ivy's and Darek's forty friends and some chicken on the grill."

Eden came out a moment later, back in her jeans, flip-flops, and a T-shirt. She took Grace by the shoulders. Met her eyes. "You can do this. And you will do this because I'm desperate, Grace. I need you."

Grace felt as if she were Owen on the receiving end of one of Eden's legendary pep talks. No wonder Owen turned out to be a star—Eden talked him into it.

She sighed. "I don't know."

Eden looped her arm through Grace's. "Fine. I'll sic Jace on you."

"That's just playing dirty."

Eden grinned. "I knew it. You are a sucker for hockey players."

Grace started to smile, especially since she knew it was so true. She'd do just about anything for Jace—even more for Eden, of course, but yeah, something about hockey players turned her weak.

Even if she hadn't realized it until three weeks ago.

They walked out the door of the bridal salon into the hot summer. Eden clicked the locks on her car—Owen's old car, his Dodge Charger. He'd left Eden the wheels when he ditched Minneapolis.

They pulled out and got on 94, headed east.

"Where are we going?"

"Jace wanted to take us out for dinner tonight. Have a little welcome-home celebration. I hope that's all right."

"That sounds great." Her body buzzed, still set on aloha time. Right now she'd be finishing class, and Max would be getting ready to surprise her with their afternoon activities. Hiking, parasailing, surfing, or maybe just a walk along the beach.

Something fun, even romantic. Something that would change her life.

Something that she should forget.

"You're awfully quiet over there." Eden veered toward St. Paul.

"I'm just tired."

"You haven't said anything about Max."

Grace lifted a shoulder. "Nothing to say. He was my cooking partner."

"What are you talking about, nothing to say? You two stole the show!"

She glanced at her sister. "Don't tell me you saw the videos too."

"I was a fan! I tweeted about you, cheered you on. I was glued to every episode."

Grace sighed.

"Grace . . . last time we talked, you were going to wear a hot dress and get the guy to notice you. Then you land on the show. And now you're all . . . 'nothing to say'?" She put her hand on Grace's. "What happened?"

She didn't know where to begin.

"Did you tell him you had feelings for him?"

"No." Not really.

"Oh. Did he tell you?"

"No." Not really.

"Did . . . did you ride home together on the plane?"

"No."

"Give me something here. Please tell me that at least you're going to see him in Minneapolis."

"Nope."

Eden said nothing else as they drove.

Jace lived in a beautiful high-rise apartment complex in the heart of St. Paul, just blocks from the arena where he used to play his heart out and now would help coach the Blue Ox.

The doorman sent them up, and Jace met them at the door of his apartment, wearing jeans and a Nike T-shirt. "Grace." He swept her up in a hug.

She couldn't help noticing how much it felt, for a second, like being in Max's embrace. Big. Strong. Breathtaking.

Except he wasn't Max. Didn't make her heart race. Didn't make her want to pound her fists on his chest and demand answers.

Eden closed the door behind her and gave Jace a kiss. Grace walked to the tall glass windows that overlooked the skyline. The sun had already begun its descent behind the gleaming buildings to the west.

"I hope you don't mind—I invited Max," Jace said. "I thought we could have a little celebration for your almost win."

Grace whirled around, her mouth open, but didn't have to say anything because Eden had Jace's arm and was shaking her head.

Jace's eyes widened. "What?" He looked at Eden, back to Grace. "What don't I know?"

Eden sighed. "I don't know why, but Max and Grace didn't hit it off like it seemed they did on national television."

"It wasn't national television. It was local cable, and I had no idea the world was watching." Grace moved into the kitchen, leaned against the black granite countertop. Sighed. "Okay, the truth is—you saw the fiasco. The moment when we realized we'd ruined our dessert."

"Yeah. That was . . . wow," Jace said, his expression betraying the horror of the moment.

"Max didn't take it well. He totally freaked out and . . . and then he just left."

"He left you at the competition?"

"No." She took a breath, searing her lungs. Blinked her tears away. "No. He left . . . Hawaii."

Silence thrummed in the room as the couple stared at her. So apparently his behavior was exactly as horrible as she thought. "He hates me."

"Oh, Grace, he doesn't hate you."

"No, you don't understand. He loves cooking. And he hates mistakes. I blew it big. I handed him the salt, and . . . I embarrassed him."

Eden took her hand.

Jace shook his head, a grim look on his face. "I'm going to have to hurt him. I have no choice." He didn't seem like he was kidding.

"No, Jace. It's fine. It's no big deal."

"It is a big deal. Especially after the Owen thing."

Now Eden turned to him, and she nearly chorused with Grace. "What Owen thing?"

Jace stared at them, the blood draining from his face. "Uh . . ." He ran his hand behind his neck. "Oops."

"Jace Jacobsen, tell me what you're talking about."

Oh no, Eden used her scary voice.

He winced, clearly drawn in by her power. "It was an accident, no doubt, but Max came to me shortly after Owen's injury and confessed that he believed he was the one who hit Owen. It was his stick, his movement. His fault."

The room went silent. Grace's heart hammered in her chest.

And then, like a wave crashing in and wiping clean the past, she got it.

Max didn't blame her—he blamed himself. Maybe that was why he'd apologized at the competition. But she hadn't listened, and . . . it was too much for him. Not only had he hurt Owen, but he'd hurt her too. Accidentally, both times.

Max didn't do accidents.

She used the counter to balance herself, to keep herself upright as the phone rang. Oh, Max.

Jace answered the phone. He spoke quietly, then hung up. "He's here."

Trust Me. The words tucked into Grace, and she took a breath. *Trust Me and expect more.*

"Okay. Let him in."

The last place Max wanted to be was riding in Jace's penthouse elevator, about to face his old captain with the news that he'd let him down. Apparently he'd perfected that MO. First Brendon, then Grace, of course, and finally Jace.

And probably himself because of the hundreds of promises he'd broken over and over and over during the three weeks in Hawaii. Like, don't date a girl more than twice. Never date anyone connected to the team. And finally, don't let a girl into your world—hockey, cooking . . . heart.

Yeah, he'd broken that one and he still couldn't look at himself. In fact, he'd arrived home and locked himself in his condo, watching reruns of old hockey games, hoping he might scour from his mind the look on Grace's face when he'd abandoned her at the competition. Or maybe the sound of her voice in the messages she'd left him—shaky, worried.

At least Grace had gotten home okay. He'd called to check on her flight. But he should have at least texted her. Wow, he'd turned into a grade-A, first-class jerk.

Or maybe he'd always been that.

The elevator opened and he took his time dragging himself down the hall to Jace's door. He still couldn't figure out why he'd agreed to come. But Jace's voice in his message, his insistence that Max come over for dinner . . . it sounded less an invitation than a command.

Although, maybe that was just Jace. Bossy. Always the enforcer.

When he leaned on the bell, the door opened almost immediately. Jace stood there, a mountain of darkness as he glared at Max.

Huh? "Hi?"

"Get in here." Jace practically hauled him in by his shirt, and it took everything inside Max not to swing at him.

"What—?"

Then he saw her. Standing in the kitchen, her arms wrapped around herself. Looking fragile and beautiful, she took his breath away just as surely as if Jace had hit him. He closed his mouth and swallowed. "Hi."

"Hi," she said.

He looked at Jace, keeping his voice low. "I didn't realize—I mean, you didn't mention—"

"That Grace was going to be here? Yeah. I was going to surprise you, dude. After what I saw on the Internet, it seemed like you wanted to be together." He held out his hands. "You can imagine my surprise when I heard that you ditched her in Hawaii."

Max ground his jaw and looked at Grace quickly before turning back to Jace. "I . . . I'm sorry." He glanced at Grace again. "I'm sorry."

And he had nothing more than that. He couldn't be here with her. Even as he glanced at her a final time—just one more glimpse of her before he walked out of her life—he was shaking his head, heading toward the door.

Jace blocked him as if he'd spent a decade playing lineman for the Vikings.

"What?"

"That's not a good enough apology, Max."

He agreed with Jace, but he stood there, shoulders rising and falling, trying to find words and failing.

Any more apology might also need an explanation. What would he say? *I abandoned you in Hawaii because I sabotaged our contest so I didn't have to tell you that I'd led you on for three weeks? Because, baby, even though I love you, I can't marry you.*

Even with the thought, his eyes burned and he looked away.

Oh, he wanted to tell her. The thought bubbled up, filled his chest. He wanted to tell her everything, to lean into the wild hope she'd stirred in him, and to believe that yes, they could—

"I don't need an apology."

Grace's soft voice, closer than he could bear, slid over him.

She was smiling, something gentle in her eyes—warmth, even compassion. "I understand why you left."

"You . . ." His face twitched. "You do?"

She touched his arm, slid her hand to grip his, and squeezed, her eyes so kind he might really start to cry. "I know about Owen."

Owen. Owen?

Oh—she knew about *Owen*. His breath nearly left him. "You . . . What . . . ?" He looked at Jace.

Jace's mouth made a tight, grim line. "Sorry. I

told her. It was an accident, but they needed to know."

Max turned to Grace, looked at her hand in his. "I should have told you." As he spoke the words, he felt the cool relief of telling her the story. "I was—am—still horrified at what happened that night. I shouldn't have jumped into the fight. Shouldn't have been out there in the first place. I relive that moment over and over and—"

"And when you thought you'd lost us the competition, it only added to that moment," she said.

Coward that he was, he nodded.

He gave her a soft smile but extricated his hand from hers. See, this was just another reason why he couldn't be with her. Why he didn't deserve her. Because—

"If it helps, I forgive you, Max, for walking out on me. And for . . . well, for Owen, even though it's not my place to forgive."

Because she just might be the kind of woman crazy and loving enough to be with a guy who had no future. He didn't know what to say, so he just met her eyes. "Thanks."

"I forgive you too, Max," Eden said, although he thought he could still see that night in her eyes. Sometimes the phone call he'd placed to Eden to tell her that he and her brother had brawled with another team still played in his mind. He still heard that quick, horrible intake of breath when she realized everything they'd worked for had died.

Max moved toward the door. "I gotta go."

But Jace didn't budge. "Dude. Shake it off. So you made a mistake. You gotta stop living in the past or it's going to eat you alive. Trust me on this." He clamped Max on the shoulder. "In fact, I have a brilliant idea. You and Grace are a great team—everyone watching that competition saw it. And I need help, buddy. Eden and I are getting married before training camp starts, and Grace is catering for us."

"I know. She mentioned that."

Grace looked at him, startled. "You remember?"

He remembered everything. Like how he'd had to practically force her into the competition, using exactly that reason. And how she'd stared at him with those huge, beautiful blue eyes in the elevator, just like she did now, and it nearly made him crazy with wanting to kiss her.

Which only made him think about the curve of her against him as the moonlight settled around them on the beach and the soft sound she made, deep in her throat, when she kissed him.

And that only brought back how amazing she smelled, the ocean wind and the plumeria flowers embedded in her skin, her buttery-smooth skin that tasted like coconut oil and salt and—

He blew out a breath. "Yeah, I remember."

"But the thing is, we had to move the wedding

up, and she's actually in the wedding, so . . ."

"She needs your help," Eden said.

"What—no, I don't!" This from Grace.

Even Max frowned. "Why not?"

"Because . . . uh . . . you've got hockey, right?"

"Not until after the wedding." What was he doing? A voice in the back of his head shouted at him to agree with her.

"Exactly. And Max took the same class you did—learned the same techniques. He can help you with everything. You'll be a team again!" Eden looked at Jace as if this was part of a devious plan coming together.

Grace sank her head into her hand. Her shoulders sagged a little, and Max realized he had to help her. It was only six weeks, and then he'd be training, on the road, and able to break free of this power she seemed to have over him. This way she possessed of making him want more, believe more, hope more.

She was like Hawaii—she caught him up in a world where he forgot about his future and made him live right now.

"Yes." He heard himself say it before his heart caught up. "Yes, of course I'll help. I make a great sous-chef."

He searched for Grace's eyes, longing for the spark, that way she had of making everything all better.

Please.

Grace looked up at him and took a breath, wariness in her expression.

Oh no.

"Fine. But I'm going to clearly mark all the seasonings." Then she winked.

This might be the best six weeks of his life.

Chapter 15

Tonight Raina would purge Owen and her mistakes from her life.

Tonight, under the spray of stars, she would dance with Casper and forget her past.

Raina stood in front of the mirror, fixing her hair into a messy bun for the third time. Maybe she should leave it down. Casper seemed to like it down. He was always playing with her long braid or twining escaping tendrils around his fingers.

She let it fall over her shoulders.

In fact, he seemed to like *her*. He laughed at her pitiful jokes and found her eyes in a crowd, like when he was talking to the team or stopped by Pierre's just when she got off shift.

And he'd kissed her. Sweetly, as if she was someone he cherished.

She'd chosen Paradise Beach last week, suggested the ride on the motorcycle for exactly the reason of erasing Owen from her memories.

She tried not to compare Casper to Owen, but the sense of magic with Owen couldn't touch how Casper made her feel. Not on the edge of herself, falling over into danger, but safe. As if her feelings—not his—mattered.

Sadly, Owen still lodged like a burr in her mind. But today she'd walk in the opening parade of the dragon boat competition with Casper, side by side, his first mate. Like she belonged there.

"Knock, knock." Liza stood at her open door, leaning against the jamb, holding a cup of coffee. "You look adorable."

Raina felt a little silly in her black workout pants and the long, oversize team T-shirt. But she'd added a scarf around her neck and a pair of pink Converse tennis shoes. "We're marching in the parade."

"And then you're going out with Casper, I'd guess."

Raina felt a flush on her skin. "He's really nice. A gentleman. I promise. I don't think he's the love-'em-and-leave-'em type."

"I hope so." Liza lifted her mug. "I'm glad to be wrong. Just keep ahold of your heart, honey. Only one person can give you the love you really want, and it's not Casper."

"Let me guess . . . 'Jesus loves me; this I know.' "

"It's not just a song."

"I know, Aunt Liza. But sometimes Jesus feels

too far away. I'd prefer a human's—a man's—hug." Raina picked up her backpack, hung the strings over her shoulders. Fought a wave of nausea. For the second day in a row, she'd woken with an upset stomach. Maybe she should eat more before going to bed, but she hadn't had an appetite.

Liza stepped away from the door. "That's part of the plan too, Raina. But men will let us down. Only God won't."

She didn't want to argue with Liza, but God had let her down plenty of times. And hello, He'd let Liza down too. After all, wasn't her aunt still single and approaching forty? No thanks.

"I don't know when I'll be back," Raina said, heading for the door.

"I'll be at the parade, cheering you on," Liza said quietly, and Raina had to turn around and go back for a hug.

She felt more of Jesus here with Liza than she ever had at church.

A banner flapped in the wind over Main Street, packed with cars, pickups, motorcycles, and a slew of out-of-town competitors practicing in the bay. The annual dragon boat festival lured teams from Canada, Minneapolis, and as far away as Milwaukee to compete. Thankfully, the Evergreen team only had to win the local division, comprised of maybe seven homegrown teams.

All manner of dragon boats—with intricately

319

carved heads painted green or red, bearing sharp wooden teeth and etched manes, their boat bodies painted to resemble scales—floated in the harbor. It looked like Deep Haven had morphed into a medieval moat of legendary aquatic monsters.

Music drifted from the stage set up in the park, a few kids dancing to the beat of a folksy hometown band. Raina walked down the sidewalk, searching for the lime-green shirts of her teammates. On the way she spotted the downtown team, shop owners and the mayor, in their hot-pink shirts, and another team from the east end of the county, the Moose Valley team, in their denim blues.

"Raina!"

Her name floated on the scant wind, and she turned, found Claire waving to her from a cluster of other members. John and Ingrid, who also waved, and Kyle, Jensen, Emma, Darek—and there, Casper. He sat on a rock, looking at a clipboard.

She picked her way through the crowd. "Hey, everyone."

Casper looked up, met her eyes.

Yeah, her world could come to a screeching halt with his smile.

"Just in time. We're the fourth boat team in the parade. We all have to stop in front of the judges' booth and do our team chant. It's not judged, but it stirs up the competition."

Emma climbed onto a rock. "Let's run through it!"

Raina lifted her voice in one accord with the group, caught up in the camaraderie, the power of the team.

They had the win locked up. Especially when Casper climbed up beside Emma, pumping his fist in the air, raising a spectacle as if they were truly Viking warriors going to sea, to battle.

After the chant, he came off the rocks, grinning. "Hey," he said.

Then he kissed her. Right there in front of everyone and . . .

Yes, this night would be perfect.

She'd never participated in a parade before—especially a small-town parade. They lined up around the block in the parking lot of the senior center. Emma led them out, keeping beat on a drum strapped over her shoulders, rousing team spirit. Raina carried one end of the team banner, opposite Casper, and behind them, each teammate held a dowel affixed to one part of a long Chinese dragon, light green, modeled after their boat.

She glanced over now and again at Casper, who grinned at her. Oh, Captain, my Captain.

They stopped in front of the judges' booth to chant, and by the end of the parade, she never wanted to leave Deep Haven.

She could become a Christiansen, grow old here with Casper. Live happily ever after. She just had to make sure no one ever discovered her mistake with Owen.

Casper found her after they tucked away their parade paraphernalia, the team dispersing into the party. "Ready to dance?"

"Yes." She would just ignore the twinge in her stomach that refused to go away. And the sense that if she didn't get something to eat soon, she might . . .

"Are you okay? You look kind of pale."

"I think it's the heat. And I haven't eaten much today."

He slipped his hand under her elbow and led her to a bench. "Sit here. I'll get you a drink of water."

But she wanted to dance. Still, the sight of Casper running off to the local cheese curd vendor, asking for water on her behalf, seemed enough.

He cared. He really cared.

But her head started to swim all the same, and she lay down on the bench. Just . . . for . . . a . . . moment . . .

"Raina! Wake up . . . Raina . . . Okay, everyone make room."

What? Raina opened her eyes, realized she'd fallen asleep—or passed out? She tried to push herself to a sitting position, but nausea rolled over her.

In front of a crowd of gawkers, she left her meager lunch on the sidewalk.

Gross.

But Casper didn't seem to mind. "Here, drink this," he said, helping her to a sitting position. He crouched in front of her. "An ambulance is on its way."

Ambulance—"No, Casper, I'm fine."

"You're not fine. You passed out. And you're sick." He clasped her hands, his expression a little undone. "You scared me."

Oh.

"Make a path!"

The voice came from beyond her. Her view seemed fuzzy around the edges, so she blinked and then a couple of EMTs appeared. One of them was Pastor Dan from the church where Liza—where she—attended.

"Raina, what's going on?" He knelt beside her, putting a defibrillator and a medical kit on the ground. Next to him stood a taller man in his forties. Sandy, curly hair. It seemed she recognized him too. Wait, yes—Joe somebody, the husband of Liza's friend Mona.

Dan slid a pressure cuff onto her arm, pumped it up.

"I'm fine—really, I'm fine."

"Shh," he said.

Casper had barely scooted over for them. Now he sat on the bench, put his arm around her. "Let them do their thing."

It was so silly. She just hadn't eaten very much

today. She said that to them as Dan took her blood pressure reading.

"Your pressure is a little low. I think we need to bring you in, get some fluids in you, see what's going on."

"No." She moved to take off the cuff, but a wave of nausea hit her again, and she put her hand to her mouth.

"Here." Joe shoved a disposable bag toward her and she lost the fluids Casper had given her.

She wiped her mouth with the napkin Casper handed to her. So maybe she didn't feel stellar.

But this night was supposed to be perfect.

"You're definitely going with us," Dan said. He gestured to the ambulance, and to her horror, they brought over a stretcher.

"Please—"

"Just do it," Casper said. "I'll be right behind you on the bike."

"No, Casper." She let Dan and Joe lead her to the stretcher, help her lie on it. "You have to be here. You have to announce the team from the podium later. You can't come with me."

But he was already dialing his phone. She heard his voice even as they began to wheel her away.

"Darek, yeah, it's me. Can you introduce the team? I need to go to the hospital with Raina; she's not feeling well. Yeah . . . no worries; I'm sure she's just fine."

But at the tail end of his voice, she thought she heard the finest edge of worry.

She *was* just fine. This was so silly. And yet her stomach still roiled.

They put her in the ambulance, shut the doors, and Joe drove toward the ER. Thankfully they didn't turn on the siren. She might have died of embarrassment or begged them to simply keep going straight out of town.

Dan took her temperature. "It'll just take a second to get to the hospital. They'll give you an IV. You'll be feeling better soon."

"I'm fine." It seemed the mantra of the hour.

They parked at the hospital, wheeled her through the double doors into the ER. "We're going to transfer you onto a table," Dan said.

"I can do it myself."

But they didn't listen, just grabbed the edges of the sheets and plopped her onto the exam table.

"I don't feel well again."

A nurse came up to her. "Hi, honey. My name's Denise. We're going to take good care of you."

She put a basin under Raina's chin even as she sat up and leaned forward. Nothing came out. She lay back, her face flushed and hot.

"Let's find out what's going on," Denise said as she got the chart from Dan. "Not much of a temperature. A little elevated, probably from the heat. I see you've been throwing up."

"Could be heatstroke," Dan said.

"We'll wait until the doctor comes in. Let's get some tests done." She hung the chart on a clip at the end of the bed. "I'm going to start an IV." She looked at the guys. "I think we got this."

"All right." Dan patted Raina's arm. "You hang in there. I'm sure we'll see you in church on Sunday."

She gave him a small smile. "Please don't call Liza."

He nodded, frowned. "Sure."

"I don't want to worry her."

He nodded again. "Take care."

As he left, Denise broke out the IV kit, grabbed some gloves. She looked at Raina, her eyes kind. "So you're Liza's niece? You helped cater Darek and Ivy's wedding, with Grace, right?"

"Uh, yeah." She didn't remember seeing the nurse at the wedding, but she didn't know many people. Had only made one friend that night— although she wouldn't necessarily call Owen a friend.

Oh, she hated how he invaded her mind, uninvited, sending regret like spears through her body.

She sighed as she held out her arm for the needle. Denise drew blood, then put in the IV. "When did you start feeling punky?"

"Three or four days ago. I thought I'd picked up a bug, or maybe it was fatigue from the practices for the festival." Except, if she thought about it, she hadn't been feeling well all week and had thrown up yesterday too.

Denise took her pulse. Wrote down notes. "Okay, I'll be back."

Raina lay back and closed her eyes. The IV flooded cool solution into her veins.

"Hey, there you are." She opened her eyes and Casper stood above her. Handsome, worry in his beautiful eyes. "Sorry I'm late—I had to dig my bike out of a thousand cars." He pulled up a stool. "What did they say?"

"I don't know yet." She hated hospitals—the smells, the antiseptic, the surreal sense of loss and tragedy that embedded the walls. Everyone acted so cheerful and happy in hospitals. But they weren't cheerful, happy places. They were places of darkness and fear. Places where ten-year-olds lost their mothers to cancer.

Casper seemed to sense her mood even as he took her hand. "Hey, I can find someone to replace you. It's no—"

"What?"

He pushed her back down when she tried to sit up.

"No, I'm totally paddling. Are you kidding me? I'm your first mate, right?" The question seemed to hang there between them. She wanted him to grab it, to assure her.

Thankfully he smiled, then touched her face, running his thumb down her cheek. "Yeah. Sure.

As long as you get cleared by the doc, you are paddling. And if not, you're going to stand on the dock and wave us in."

That made her feel better, she could admit. "I really wanted to go to the dance tonight. I think we can still make it."

"You know, we could turn on music here. Who needs a band?"

But it wasn't the same as being in his arms under the starlight, the waves applauding as they swayed to the music. "You should go. Colleen Decker really wants you to dance with her."

He laughed. "Right. I don't think I'm going to leave you for Colleen Decker. Besides, there are plenty of guys lining up to dance with her."

Silly her; she shouldn't be jealous of an eighteen-year-old, but his words dispelled any lingering remnant.

Denise came back in. "I need to talk to Raina, Casper, so if you want to step out, we'll call you when we're done."

Casper got up even as Raina wanted to protest, but something about the look in Denise's eyes told her to let him go.

Denise closed the curtain and pulled up the stool. She seemed to be waiting for Casper's footsteps to die before she said, "I'm trying to gather all the information before the doctor comes in . . ." She paused. "You couldn't possibly be pregnant, could you?"

A chill went through Raina. She couldn't move, couldn't breathe as her brain kicked back over the days.

Oh. Oh, my. She was late—two, maybe even three weeks. She put her hand to her forehead. It prickled with sweat. "I . . . I don't know." Her chin began to tremble. How stupid. Of course. She gritted her teeth to keep the tears from forming, but they did anyway, streaking across her cheeks and into her ears. "I don't know. Maybe."

Denise patted her arm. "I'll run a test. In the meantime, just lay here and rest. The doc will talk to you when he comes in."

The quiet descended around Raina like a fog, cold and suffocating. No. Oh, please, no.

Casper returned. Pulled back the curtain. "So are they going to release—? Raina, are you okay?"

His voice had gone so unbearably soft that she winced, pressed both hands over her eyes. No, no, no—pull it together. He couldn't know, couldn't see. How could this have happened?

"Raina? What did the nurse say?"

She shook her head. Then, reaching deep inside, she summoned the strength cultivated from being a girl without a mother, a girl who watched her brother slide into drug abuse, a girl whose father ended up in jail. A girl who spent most of her life alone.

She knew how to survive. She would survive.

Raina ran her fingers under her eyes, forced a smile through the shattering of her hopes. "Oh," she said, her voice only a little shaky. She cleared her throat. "I'm fine. I just feel silly for being so needy. Why don't you go to the dance and tell everyone I'll be there later."

He frowned. "No, I'm staying here until the doctor arrives."

"Uh . . . I'll probably need something to eat then. Would you mind digging me up a sandwich?"

He nodded. "That I can do." He leaned over to press a kiss to her forehead.

When he left, she didn't wait for the doctor. Didn't wait for Casper to return. She simply got up, eased the IV out of her arm, and held a cotton ball against the blood. Then found a Band-Aid and peeled it over the wound. She grabbed her bag and headed out the door just as Denise came down the hall.

"Hey!"

"I'm fine." Raina waved, not looking back. "Really, I'm fine!"

She left the hospital before anyone could stop her.

Grace hadn't recognized the man who sat across the table from her at Sammy's Bar and Grill last night.

Sure, he'd looked like Max, with his tan skin,

those devastating brown eyes that could whisk a girl back to a star-strewn beach and stir up memories of the smell of the ocean on his skin. And his laughter—she'd recognized that, too, deep and breathtaking, a rumble under her skin, almost hypnotic.

Yes, the man across from her had looked like Max, sounded like Max, but in truth, Max hadn't shown up all night. Even though she'd forgiven him.

Not that he needed forgiveness, perhaps, but he appeared undone when Jace revealed his secret about Owen. That's when Grace had heard it. The small voice inside her that said, *Do you love Me?*

You know I do, Lord.

Feed My sheep. Forgive him.

Forgive.

The word had taken root inside, and her heart went out to the man who couldn't escape his mistake so much that it drove him away from their friendship. If that was what they had. She wasn't quite sure, because even after her statement of forgiveness, fun Hawaii Max hadn't appeared.

Instead, she got a prickly version of Iron Chef Max. A Max who recited some of the many dishes they'd made in school, took notes, and promised to e-mail them to her. A Max who picked up the dinner tab and left without even a one-armed hug.

A Max who seemed determined to erase the

three glorious weeks they shared in Hawaii, as if they'd never existed.

Maybe they hadn't. Maybe she'd read into everything.

No. Her memories wouldn't let her believe that.

Which meant that Max wanted to forget everything that happened. That truth had lodged in her throat throughout dinner, over the past three days of helping Eden shop and pull together her wedding details, and even during the drive to Deep Haven this morning.

Poor Max. The last thing he wanted to do was help her with the wedding.

And she wouldn't force him. Thanks, but she could do this on her own. Especially with Raina and Ty by her side.

Best-case scenario, she never talked to Max again, and she filed their vacation in Hawaii away, never to look at it again.

"Sis, when did you get back?" The voice rose over the crowd perched along the beach getting ready to watch today's competition, finding Grace where she sat on a boulder onshore. Darek picked his way around the fold-up athletic chairs, kids eating ice cream, onlookers dressed in dragon boat festival shirts and foam hats, some with bandannas.

Grace stood to greet him, and he swooped her up. "A little while ago," she answered. "You were all gone already, so I thought I'd come to town, watch the race."

He put her down, set her away from him. "You look amazing! Hawaii agrees with you. Look how tan you are!"

Please don't ask me about the vacation. "How was the honeymoon? You're not so pale yourself."

He grinned. "We survived."

Out in the harbor, the first racers streaked across the lake to the roar of the crowd. "How's the team?"

"Casper's at the helm this year."

"Really? What, did he pry the rudder from your hands?"

"Funny. No. I was gone, and we needed a team. Besides, am I the only one who's noticed that he didn't go back to school in January? He's . . . depressed. Or he was, until he started training for this competition."

Grace rose on her tiptoes and kissed Darek's cheek. Patted it. "That's why you're the big brother."

He blushed a little. "Yeah, well, how do you feel about paddling?"

"Why?"

"Raina quit the team, and we need someone."

"Raina was paddling?"

"Yeah. Casper recruited her. But she didn't show up for practice today. Casper went to her house, but she didn't answer the door."

She frowned. "I'll have a chat with her."

"Better hurry. Our race is in an hour. Thanks, Sis."

Grace picked her way through the crowd and out to Main Street, where vendors lined the sidewalks. She walked past the cheese curd stand, the fish burgers, the kettle corn, and spied Ivy standing in line with Tiger, his hand tucked into hers.

Now that he had a new mother, maybe he'd spend more time on Ivy's lap than Grace's. She should have expected that.

She took the shortcut through the parking lot of the realty office, then cut across the street at the light. Liza lived two blocks off the highway that ran through town, in a cute two-bedroom bungalow with dormers and a wraparound porch.

Raina's car sat at the curb.

Grace knocked on the front door. "Raina?" No answer, but because she was a local and she'd been inside Liza's house more than a handful of times, she tried the door.

It opened, and she went inside. "Liza?"

"She's not here!"

The voice came from behind one of the bedroom doors.

"Raina, what's going on?"

"Grace?" Footsteps accompanied the tone of surprise. They stopped at the other side of the closed door. "What are you doing here?"

"I'm here because Darek is in a panic. He wants me to paddle because apparently you've left them with an empty space."

Silence.

"Raina, are you okay?"

More silence.

"Okay, well, um. Do you want me to paddle for you?"

Silence again. Then, "How was your trip?"

It was . . . heartbreaking? Breathtaking? Life changing?

"I learned a lot about Hawaiian food. In fact, my sister wants me to cater her wedding in six weeks."

"Six weeks?" The voice came closer.

"Exactly. I have to pull off a dinner for seventy-five, and I need you. You're my secret weapon."

Silence.

"Raina, what's going on? Can I help?"

Grace nearly put her hand to the doorknob, but the door finally opened.

Raina stood there, wearing a lime-green dragon boat shirt, her eyes red, swollen. At least she had team spirit. "I wish you could but . . . no one can help."

"Why not?"

Raina sat on the bed. "Because God is laughing at me."

Grace sat beside her. "God isn't laughing at you, Raina. What happened? You can tell me."

The look on Raina's face could make Grace weep. "I think I'm pregnant."

Grace tried not to gasp, but the tragedy in Raina's voice only made it worse. "Are you sure?"

Raina pointed to three store-bought tests lined up in a row on the nightstand. Two negatives and a positive.

"Best two out of three?"

"I don't think so," Raina said softly.

"But you don't know for sure." Grace took her hand, holding herself back from asking who the father was. It didn't matter, maybe. "Honey, listen. You're not in this alone. It's going to be okay." The tone in her voice made her believe it too. "I learned a lot in Hawaii—more than cooking. Mostly that once I got past the fear and past holding on to what I thought I wanted, there was more waiting for me." She swallowed, letting the truth rise up. "I know it's difficult to see right now, but if we trust Him, God can bring us through these dark places, through our fears and even what we think is impossible, to give us more. More of Him. Even more of ourselves, through Him. In fact, He can do more than you can ask or imagine if you let Him."

She let her own words sink in to nourish her, too.

Raina looked at their hands. "I highly doubt that God is interested in helping me." She met Grace's eyes. "But thanks for saying that. You're right. I can survive this."

"Well, I'm interested in helping you. We're teammates."

Raina drew in a long breath.

"And I know Casper is counting on you."

That seemed to only make her cringe.

Grace frowned. "What—?"

"Nothing. Yeah, I know."

"Good. Now, let's get you back on that dragon boat team where you belong. Evergreen needs you."

Raina swallowed, looked away. "Okay."

Grace leaned in to embrace her. "You're not alone," she said again.

But when Raina got up, the smile she gave Grace didn't touch her eyes.

Chapter 16

The dragon boat victory should have filled the hole inside Casper, should have buoyed him, given him a reason to believe he could build a future here.

Instead, it pinged around the hollow place inside him. The place where, only days ago, he'd let his affection for Raina find fertile soil.

What had happened between them, he hadn't any idea. One minute she was smiling into his eyes, leaning her face into the pocket of his hand, and the next, she'd left the hospital while he fetched her a vending machine tuna sandwich. He'd driven to her house, found her holed up in

337

her room. She refused to open the door to him, and for a desperate twelve hours, he'd thought she might not even paddle in the competition. Then she'd reappeared, wearing a life jacket, holding a paddle. Except, not the Raina he knew, that he . . . that he'd started to love. He could admit he'd started to harbor hopes that maybe Raina could be the reason he stayed in Deep Haven. So what if he didn't go back to school, didn't pursue his archaeology dreams. Couldn't he be like Darek and build a home here? Certainly *two* brothers could rebuild and run the resort.

But that Raina had vanished, it seemed, leaving only this strange, polite, detached shell behind. Sure, she smiled like Raina, and she laughed at his jokes and urged the team to victory. But she never fully looked at him.

Even after they placed first in their division.

Even at the victory party.

And especially when he offered her a ride home. Which she declined.

He tried not to let that dig a hole in his heart. If he could just get her alone . . . but she refused to open the door to him or answer her phone.

So for the last two weeks, he'd buried himself in finishing cabin seven. And he'd read and reread the e-mail from his buddy in Roatán, contemplating the treasure hunt.

Maybe it was time to leave.

Meanwhile, he hung around, hoping to catch a

moment with Raina when she arrived at the resort to meet with Grace, helping her pull together the catering menu for Eden's hurried wedding. He even devised excuses to be in the same room. Like needing a refill on his water bottle or grabbing a quick sandwich.

As he closed the door behind him, he spied Grace pacing the kitchen, holding the phone like she might throw it. "I'm going to kill her."

Raina sat on one of the stools, dressed in shorts and a T-shirt, her hair pulled back into a long ponytail.

"What's going on?"

His words elicited a grim expression from Grace and a flash of surprise from Raina.

For a moment, a smile seemed to crease her face. Then it vanished, and she looked down, burying her attention in the pile of recipes, menus, and ingredient lists scattered on the granite countertop.

Grace set the phone down, leaned against both hands on the counter. "*Your overeager sister* has agreed to a pre-wedding photo shoot that includes shots of the food for *Hockey Today* magazine."

Huh?

"I know—I can't believe it either. It's less than a month before the wedding and I have to some-how scrounge up a gourmet sampling of the dinner I plan to serve—by Saturday! Is she nuts?"

"What's on the menu?" He walked to the bread box, pulled out a loaf, and retrieved the peanut butter.

"I don't know. I was thinking we'd have poke and maybe ahi and ebi sushi for appetizers, although I'll make some California rolls for those who don't like ahi."

Raina didn't even flinch at the conversation. She probably saw Grace in need and, just like she had with Casper, bellied up to be the first mate.

His throat burned as he reached for the marshmallow creme.

"Hey, don't put that knife in there. You'll get peanut butter all over the marshmallow."

"Seriously? Grace, calm down."

She took the knife from him, went to the sink.

His gaze tracked to Raina. She didn't look at him, but he took the opportunity to wander over and reach for the menu. "Smoked mahimahi tacos? Misoyaki butterfish? Short ribs?" He put the menu down. "Wow, that sounds great."

Grace smiled at him, and he glanced at Raina, hoping for something. She avoided his eyes.

"So has Eden seen the menu?" he asked, taking the clean knife from Grace. He dug into the marshmallow creme.

"I guess so. I sent her some ideas over e-mail, and suddenly I'm cooking for a national magazine."

"Has she ever even eaten mahimahi? Or butterfish?" He closed the sandwich, leaned against the counter.

Maybe he could wait Raina out. She'd have to look at him someday. Or better yet, what if he simply hauled her onto the deck, out of earshot, and made her tell him what he'd done? He'd racked his brain—was still racking his brain—and couldn't come up with anything.

"I don't know. The Hawaiian food was her idea, remember? I'm just trying to throw her the wedding of her dreams," Grace said, retrieving the menu.

He raised an eyebrow at her. Since returning home, Grace seemed changed. More resolute. Always an optimist, she had a way of making people believe that anything was possible. And now she seemed to be living up to her own words.

"You're really going to pull this off, aren't you?"

Grace sighed. "Absolutely."

But it was something in her sigh that made Casper hesitate. "But?"

"But I've got to hire serving staff and go to Minneapolis and check out the venue, not to mention order the fish . . ." She glanced at Raina. "Maybe we should just have fluffernutters."

He laughed, and even Raina's mouth tweaked up.

How about that? It seeded an idea. "What can I do to help?"

Grace glanced at him. "Really?"

"Sure. I'm at your service." He kept one eye on Raina.

"Okay. Uh, I have to work, so you and Raina could track down where I can buy butterfish in Minneapolis. You could give her a ride into town later?"

Yes! "I'm on it."

"I think I'll go back with you, Grace. I have some things to take care of," Raina said.

Oh.

Grace gathered her notes, putting them together in a file folder. "Okay. I have to get changed. I'll be down in a bit." She disappeared upstairs.

Leaving Raina and Casper alone.

He didn't move.

She slid off the seat, headed for the door. No—no—

"Raina, can we talk?"

"I gotta get going."

But he caught up to her, positioned himself in front of the door. "Please."

When she looked up at him, her face mirrored the brittle smile she'd produced in the hospital. "Listen, Casper, I know I've been acting weird—"

"Was it something I said? Or did? Was I a jerk without knowing it?" He didn't know where all this desperation came from, but he had to get behind her broken expression.

Figure out why he couldn't fix her.

She shook her head, and he reached out and lifted her chin. Tears shone in her eyes.

"I don't know what I did, but you have to know, I'm so sorry for it."

"It's not you, Casper. It's me. I . . ." She pressed a hand to her mouth. "I made a terrible mistake." She sighed, her body shuddering.

He couldn't help it. Despite her posture, her chilly, almost-fearful demeanor, he pulled her to himself.

And like a miracle, she surrendered and let him hold her, the icy wall between them shattering. She curled her arms around his shoulders, laid her head against his chest. "I'm sorry," she said. "I'm so sorry."

"Shh," he said, smoothing her hair. "I'm here to help. Let me help."

She said nothing, just took a trembling breath.

He wiped a tear from her cheek and found her eyes.

There she was, the Raina he knew. The one who cheered him on, called him Captain, believed in him. His gaze tracked to her lips.

"Oh! Uh . . ."

The gasp from Grace—he couldn't tell if it was shock or horror—had the effect of a blade, slicing Raina from his arms. She stepped back, her eyes huge as she stared at Grace standing in the foyer, dressed in her Pierre's Pizza outfit.

Something dark, even angry, flushed over

Grace's expression. Casper had the uncanny feeling of being dressed down, like he should run.

Her gaze went to his hand, still at Raina's hip. "Wow," she said. "Out of all my brothers, I didn't expect this from you."

Then, her mouth tight, Grace pushed around them to the door. She stopped on the threshold, looking back at Raina. "You coming?"

Casper's heart broke a little more when Raina nodded.

He wasn't sure why he felt like he should keep apologizing.

A good workout always cleared Max's head, got his heart pumping, helped him focus on the essentials.

Like hockey. Showing the coaches he still ranked among the best wings on the team. And . . .

And like coming to terms with the fact that Grace didn't want his help catering the wedding, despite her words about forgiveness. He didn't blame her—not really. Because he hadn't found the strength to forgive himself, either. Not for what happened with Owen. Certainly not for betraying her at the competition.

Which meant that, without having to help her, he only had to keep Grace tucked safely in the darkest corner of his mind so she couldn't escape, roam around, sending tentacles of pain through him.

Running on the treadmill in the team workout room with the music blaring, the televisions muted on different sports games, he could lose himself and forget the sound of her laughter, the way her words could leach tension out of his day, leaving it bright and sunny.

Rain teared down the giant picture windows, the sky mottled and bleak. Another day of rain—it sent a fog up from the river to linger on the streets of St. Paul, tempering the heat of July. Max had spent the better part of the last three weeks in the gym and had his body in top working order.

Now he slowed the treadmill to a walk, spent a few minutes slowing his heartbeat, and then stopped the machine, stepping off to take his pulse. Perfect.

Conditioning—one of his secret weapons. Learning to live above the pain, to press forward. Endure.

Max could wring out his shirt, his hair sopping with sweat, now longer and shaggy. He shaved it short once a year, and by January it would hang below his ears; by May, be long enough to gather into a ponytail, if he wanted.

He'd stop shaving right before training camp and start a nice growth of beard for the photo shoots in the fall.

Grabbing a bottle of water, he drank it, resting as he contemplated another set of sit-ups.

"Hey, Max. Is Grace still having a meltdown?"

He turned, saw Jace coming toward him. Sweat trickled down his face, a towel around his neck.

Meltdown? His expression probably betrayed his confusion because Jace shook his head.

"And you didn't know because you haven't even bothered to call her." Jace got on the treadmill, started it at a walk.

"That's not true. I . . ." Okay, he'd picked up the phone. Stared at it. Once, listened to a voice mail he hadn't deleted. "I e-mailed her."

Jace kicked it up to a run. "That's teamwork."

"Listen, she doesn't want my help."

"You keep telling yourself that. *Hockey Today* is doing a spot about the wedding, and they want to include a couple shots of the food. They're doing it Saturday afternoon at my place. Apparently Grace is a little freaked out."

A magazine spot? He kept his voice even. "She'd call me if she needed me."

Jace looked at him. "Seriously? How well do you know her?"

Well enough to feel the burn of his lie. "Can we talk about something else?"

"Sure. How about the fact that this wedding is everything to Eden, and while I would have preferred to hire a caterer, it means the world to her to have Grace do this. Which means that I need you, Max. Don't let me down."

"Fine."

Jace frowned, but Max didn't stick around, just headed to the locker room.

But what Jace had said kept dogging him. *Meltdown.*

He'd seen one of Grace's meltdowns, and the memory of it hung on to him like a burr, digging in.

But if she'd needed him, she would have called and—

Oh, he did know her better than that. He stepped into the shower. Tried to figure out what to say.

Hey, Grace, I know we haven't talked, and I said I'd help—

Grace, what's the deal? Why haven't you called me?

Grace . . . I need you. Please forgive me.

Yeah, he hadn't the foggiest idea how to start.

But he got out of the shower, dressed, and sat on the bench, holding his phone in his hand, her number on the screen. Maybe he'd just start with . . .

"Hello?"

Her voice jolted him, sending a thousand currents of heat through his body. He swallowed, dug up his voice. "Grace? It's Max."

Silence.

Then, "Hi." To his surprise, a hint of warmth layered her voice. Wow, he didn't deserve that, but he leaned into it.

"Hi. I was just checking . . . I mean—" He blew

out a breath. "Grace, I'm sorry I haven't called you. I sort of thought that maybe you didn't want to talk to me."

She sighed. "No, Max. It's just . . . I don't want you to feel obligated to help me. You got roped into this, and I'm letting you off the hook."

He tried not to lunge too desperately to refute her words. "No—I want to help. How can I help?" *Please, let me help.*

"I hear you've got a magazine shoot Saturday." He could see her, dressed in a pair of jeans, a T-shirt, her blonde hair in a messy ponytail. The ache filled his chest, turned his voice ragged. "I could . . . We could—"

"Oh, Max, it's just a disaster." Her voice broke a little then, and there she was, his teammate, the woman who, for a while, felt closer than any friend he'd ever had.

"What's going on, 9B?" He took a chance with that but couldn't help the tenderness in his voice.

"I threw around a few different menus and finally settled on poke and manapua, misoyaki butterfish . . . but I couldn't find butterfish anywhere, so Casper ordered it sent in, and we just found out it's on its way to Milwaukee, not Minneapolis. It'll get there and the dry ice will be dissipated and I'll have rotten gourmet fish—"

"There's no butterfish in Minneapolis?"

"I've called every fish market, but they only have the usual—tuna, salmon, some local varieties, and shellfish. One place hadn't even heard of butterfish. I tried to substitute with mahimahi, but even that I have to fly in. And the worst thing is if I don't get it today, I'm sunk. The butterfish has to marinate for *at least* twenty-four hours."

He got up, closed his locker. "Okay, so the butterfish is taking a side trip to Milwaukee. You know, there's not a lot to do in Milwaukee. No surfing, no parasailing—"

He got a giggle and it only urged him on, like the roar of the crowd.

"Listen, I got this. You don't worry about a thing."

"Max, you don't have to—"

"Please don't say that, Grace." He grabbed his stuff and left the locker room. "Because I do."

She sighed and didn't fight him. "Thank you."

"Come to Minneapolis. The butterfish will be waiting for you."

"I'm actually in Minneapolis. I'm staying at my sister's."

She was?

"Um . . . how would you feel about a trip to Milwaukee?"

"Now?"

He could hardly keep himself from shouting. "Uh-huh. I'll pick you up in an hour?"

"Seriously?"

"Grace . . ."

More laughter. "Right. I'll be ready."

He hung up and pushed through the double doors to the parking lot. The rain had stopped, the slightest hint of sunshine breaking through the clouds.

Max had chartered a plane to fly them to Milwaukee and rescue their butterfish from the coastal food market, the mistaken destination of her order.

The sheer generosity of his action took Grace's breath away, and by the time they'd returned from their adventure Thursday night, her determination to keep him off the playing field of her heart had taken serious hits.

She kept clinging to her moment on the beach, when she'd recommitted her heart to Jesus. She hated how fickle it now proved to be, how easily she turned to Max, hoping he might pull her into his arms. Reignite the flames that he'd stirred in Hawaii.

"Ready to flash sear the ahi?" Max stood at his stove, a beautiful stainless steel gourmet appliance that fit perfectly in his condo kitchen. In fact, she could live forever in his made-for-an-Iron-Chef work area. A Sub-Zero fridge, a long black quartz countertop, two sunken sinks, and a bar for guests. It all looked into a living room with an oversize leather sofa, a flat-screen TV. On the screen, a rerun of an old Blue Ox game played on the NHL channel. Max barely looked at it as he cooked.

This Max she recognized, the one dressed in jeans and a black T-shirt, barefoot and wearing an apron.

This was her favorite Max.

Or maybe it was the fact that cold and nervous Max, a man she nearly didn't recognize, had vanished two days ago, somewhere over Eau Claire.

Sports-cover Max had met her at Eden's door, tucked her into his Audi convertible. He slicked up well—she knew that—but to see it in person unnerved her. He'd worn a suit jacket over a printed tee, a pair of fancy shoes with his jeans.

Grace, on the other hand, had destroyed Eden's apartment looking for something that didn't feel like either a Saturday afternoon on the sofa, watching the Lifetime channel, or Sunday at the park. She finally settled on skinny jeans, a sleeveless shirt, and sandals.

She still felt underdressed and silly sitting next to Max Sharpe in his fancy convertible, driving to the airport and being treated like she was royalty.

After they'd climbed aboard the plane, Max shucked off his jacket, sat down across from her, and smiled. It was the smile, the same one he'd given her just before he put a snorkel mask on her face, that hinted at the man behind the polish. The troublemaker who pushed her, even surprised her with what she was capable of.

Oh, her fickle heart had wanted to push her into

his arms at that moment. She stayed planted in her seat, however, listening to him talk about team injury updates and forecasts for the next season—all stuff she'd never heard him mention before, as if he hadn't wanted to broach the hockey topic.

Maybe forgiving him for hurting Owen had freed Max to share this part of his life with her.

He'd then turned to menus and recipes.

"Why don't you flash sear the ahi for the poke, for those who can't manage fully raw fish?"

Then he'd moved on to her dessert problem. Sure, they had a cake ordered, but Eden also wanted something Hawaiian—

"What about a macadamia nut–coconut cake? You could serve it with a warm coconut glaze."

Yeah, she'd wanted to kiss him right then, and it didn't help that the shine in his eyes, the warmth, told her that he'd missed this too.

They made ingredient lists as they flew over Wisconsin's heartland before touching down in Milwaukee. He'd suggested dinner out, but she reminded him of their marinating schedule.

How she loved a man who would fit his life around the seasoning needs of a fish.

They arrived home after dark, but instead of dropping her off at Eden's, he'd brought her back to his place.

No romance on the agenda, he worked with her to whip up the marinade, a mixture of sake, mirin, sugar, and miso. He'd stored it in his refrigerator, turned, and high-fived her.

She would have preferred a hug, but maybe that wouldn't do her any good. Not if she hoped to stay untangled from the disaster looming at the conclusion of Eden's wedding when he walked out of her life for good.

Now Max finished searing the ahi, plated it, and put it in the fridge to chill. Meanwhile, she'd diced the green onions and thinly sliced some Maui onion she'd found at the food market he'd taken her to yesterday. Next she prepared a sauce with a dab of mayonnaise, pickled ginger, masago and shoyu from the Asian market, sesame oil, and Hawaiian salt that he just happened to have in his cupboard.

She'd died and gone to culinary heaven.

"We'll plate it with a swirl of the mixture, then the ahi and some greens and the onions." He held a towel in his hand. "Let's see how the cake is doing."

They'd prepared the cake in individual Bundt pans, and it saturated the kitchen with the aroma of the islands—nutty coconut, fresh vanilla bean. He opened his oven, pulled out the pan. Set the spongy cakes on the baking board. "We'll let these sit for a few minutes, then remove them from the pans and poke holes in them. When we get to Jace's place, we can warm them, then pour the glaze over."

Eden had rightly chosen Jace's place for tonight's photo shoot, although they could have easily taken the shots here in Max's beautiful kitchen overlooking the Mississippi River.

"What's next?" he asked.

Next? Oh. "We'll grill the butterfish at Jace's, and I have a Waimanalo salad with greens, an orange, an avocado, goat cheese, and macadamia nuts."

"Yum." He tossed the towel on the counter. "I think we've got this, 9B."

The name took her breath, just for a moment, and she nodded, hating the sudden rush of tears and her still-tender heart.

She turned away, untying the apron.

"Grace, are you okay?"

She nodded again but didn't look at him, just tossed the apron over a chair and headed for his bathroom.

Grace washed her hands. Stared into the mirror. He hadn't done anything, really, but be kind to her, and if it weren't for that night on the boat, she might dupe herself into believing that they were—could be again—friends.

She closed her eyes. "Lord, You know I gave my heart to You. And that was for keeps. So help me to keep Max in his rightful place. Help me not to start wishing for things I can't have." She spoke the words softly so she could hear them, remind herself. "Help me trust You."

Do you love Me, Grace?

"You know I do, Lord."

Then feed My sheep. Be his friend.

She blew out a breath. Yes, she could be a friend.

"Grace, we gotta go!"

She exited the bathroom and saw that he'd packed all the food in various containers. A real traveling gourmet. A reminder to check on service supplies and the staff at Eden's venue struck her as she picked up the warm cakes and followed him out of the condo.

He put the food in his trunk, stacking it carefully. "It'll be fine for the trip to Jace's."

She trusted him—the man seemed to care more for her photo shoot than she did.

Although, admittedly, the spread would get her the recognition she needed to launch her business. A business that Max had helped her set up yesterday online. A few clicks to a web template and suddenly she felt real.

Grace's Catering, "Distinctive food for distinctive events." She even listed her cell phone number and displayed pictures of their cooking event that he'd grabbed off the Internet.

Yes, he made her feel real.

"Thank you, Max," she said as they drove to Jace's.

"Hey, it was fun."

Fun. Like "Hey, let's shoot some hoops, play

some hockey" fun. Buddy fun. *Okay, Lord. I can be his friend.*

When they pulled up to Jace's, Max let the valet park his car while they brought the food upstairs. Jace met them at the door in a pair of dark dress pants, a gray metallic shirt, a black tie. Inside, Eden had spiffed up too, wearing an emerald-green dress.

The power couple.

A photographer worked to set up the shoot in the dining area. A man about Grace's age—young, hip, wearing jeans and a printed button-down shirt rolled up at the sleeves—adjusted photography umbrellas to even the light. The writer for the piece had commandeered Eden for an interview.

Grace felt a little like the hired help as she entered the kitchen, but Max appeared anything but fazed as he unloaded their supplies. Eden excused herself from the interview and sidled up to Grace. "So . . . how is everything going?"

"Fine," Grace said, almost too cheerfully. But she didn't have time to explain. Especially with Max firing up the oven. "Oh no, I need a broiler pan," she said to Eden, but Max produced one from the drawer under the stove.

Broiler pan, check. It only reminded her that everywhere she turned, Max kept saving her.

"Go out to the deck with Jace. We got this," Grace said, wishing she felt her words.

Max looked at her, winked.

Oh, boy.

She put the butterfish in to bake, then plated the poke. Meanwhile, Max warmed the cakes in the oven, then made the coconut sauce.

"Did I hear correctly that you're Maxwell Sharpe, from the Blue Ox?"

The writer had come in off the deck, nosing around the kitchen. A blonde with curves, wearing black slacks, a white blouse and vest, she leaned over Max, a little too much interest in her posture.

"I have a pretty delicate sauce here," he growled.

Grace shot him a look but didn't say anything. For a second, memory flashed. He'd used that same tone on the last day of competition.

"Are you involved in the catering company or just helping out a teammate?"

"Excuse me; I don't want to burn you," he said, taking the saucepan off the stove. He poured the sugary syrup over the cakes, each on its own dessert plate.

"Oh, that looks good," she said.

Grace pulled the salad fixings from the fridge, began to assemble it.

"What kind of salad is this?"

"It's called Waimanalo salad, from the Koʻolau Range area in Hawaii. It's a mix of romaine, red kale, red oak leaf, arugula, and lollo rosso. There's also some curly cress and tatsoi, an Asian green, along with some island favorites—oranges, avocado, goat cheese, and macadamia nuts. On it, I'm drizzling a dressing made from Maui onion and olive oil."

"Sounds delicious."

"I hope so." Grace went to the oven, pulled out the butterfish, moved it to the broiling rack, and set the heat to broil. "We'll be setting the table in five minutes."

The photographer had moved in, started snapping shots, and she cringed. No one told her she'd be in the shot, and she wore her jeans and pink Evergreen Resort T-shirt.

A real beauty.

But then Max came up next to her. "Ignore them. Smile. You have a pretty smile, 9B."

Oh, Max. He had the terrible ability to knock her off her feet. She never knew when she might get blindsided by his tease, his devastating smile.

She carried the salad to the table, then went after the poke. By the time she returned, Max was plating the butterfish. Perfectly caramelized on the top, the broiler had blackened the edges and turned the fish to a beautiful burned-butter color.

The smell was so good it could roll her eyes back into her head.

Max added the plates to the table and uncorked a bottle of white wine while Grace garnished the cakes with whipped cream, kiwi, shaved coconut, and a dusting of macadamia nuts. She set the cake plates on the table. Max lit a long silver taper candle.

"Wow." Eden had come in off the deck and stared at the meal. "That is beautiful. Isn't it, Jace?"

He stood behind her, his expression looking like a mixture of feigned happiness and dread. "Is that fish?"

"Butterfish. We had it flown in from Hawaii and marinated it for the last two days in misoyaki sauce," Grace said. "The salad is made from local greens, and this is poke. It's seared and served with a spicy Asian mayonnaise sauce."

"Grace, this is amazing," Eden said.

She felt Max slip his hand into hers, and for a moment, she stood again before the judges. She wrapped her fingers around his.

The photographer zeroed in on the food, taking shots from every angle. Finally he suggested a pose of Eden and Jace eating.

They pulled up chairs, lifted their wineglasses. Another shot.

Then, while Eden tried the butterfish, Jace speared the poke. Grace couldn't read his expression. Max's hand tightened on hers.

"This fish is delicious. Try it, Jace," Eden said.

He looked like he might be going in for gallbladder surgery, the way his face twisted. A darkness began to spread through Grace.

He cut the butterfish, forked it. Slid it into his mouth. Swallowed.

"See?"

He nodded. "Delicious."

"Let me get a shot of you eating the fish, Mr. Jacobsen," the photographer said.

Jace took one bite, then another, finally asking, "You need a third?"

"One more."

But to Grace's eye something didn't seem right. Jace's eyes had started to water, his voice turning raspy. She untangled her hand from Max's, ran to the fridge, poured him some water, and returned.

"Jace, are you okay?"

He coughed. "Yeah." Except his voice sounded as if it had been run over a washboard. He drank the water, then got up. "I'll be right back."

Eden put down her napkin and followed him from the room.

Grace stayed for a moment, her eyes on Max, then followed Eden.

She found them in Jace's bathroom, him rooting through his medicine cabinet. "What's wrong?"

"I'm allergic to certain kinds of fish."

"What? How come I don't know this?" Eden said.

"I don't know. We never eat seafood—" He coughed. Tears ran from his eyes.

"But didn't you look at the menu?" Eden said.

"That's your . . . job . . ." Jace slapped his cheek.

"What's going on?" This from Max. Pretty soon they'd have the entire magazine crew in the bathroom with them.

"Jace is allergic to fish!" Grace said.

Max closed the door, trapping them inside. "Well, don't let them know."

Grace turned to Jace, who had sat on the edge of his giant Jacuzzi tub. "The man is going into anaphylactic shock. We're going to have to hospitalize him. How are they not going to know this?"

"I'm not . . . Oh no. Make way—" Jace dove for the toilet.

Max and Grace turned away.

"Whoa. Okay. I'm getting rid of them," Max said.

Grace stood there, stricken, watching Eden press a cold cloth to Jace's forehead.

She'd taken out the former enforcer for the St. Paul Blue Ox with a butterfish. Her hand found the counter, and she leaned against it. "What did you think we were going to serve on your Hawaiian menu, Jace?"

He leaned against the wall, sweat beaded across his forehead. "A roast pig? Maybe some pine-apple?"

Oh, boy. She might be ill right alongside Jace. "I'll go help Max get rid of them."

Eden caught her hand. "I'm so sorry, Grace. For the record, I thought it was delicious."

"It was good . . . just deadly," Jace said.

Yeah, she could pretty much use that description for the last two-plus days. She found Max in the kitchen, cleaning off the plates. "I sent them home with the Bundt cakes," he said.

Grace shook her head. "He wants a pig."

"Huh?"

"You know, dig a hole, light a fire, add a pig, shove an apple in its mouth. Jace thought we were having a luau."

Max appeared appropriately horrified. He put down the dish, met her eyes. "Don't worry, 9B. It'll all work out."

But she couldn't help it. She sank her face into her hands, the frustration and stress leaking out in hiccuped breaths.

Max's arms went around her, his hand running down her hair. He smelled like the kitchen—tangy, sweet—his embrace even stronger than it had been in Hawaii, if that was possible. Her head fell against the hard planes of his chest, and she let herself sink into him.

Jace was right. Good but deadly, because she hadn't a prayer of not falling for Max Sharpe all over again.

Chapter 17

When Jace had called him for a pickup game of hockey, Max assumed the big guy just wanted to work out his pre-wedding restlessness. After all, he had roughly twenty-nine hours before he walked down that aisle and . . .

And that might put any guy in the mood to gather his buddies, slap around a puck, play hard into the boards, even without protective gear.

Marriage. A life with someone you loved. Forever.

Max tamped the sudden, unwelcome spurt of jealousy and slapped the puck to Kalen Boomer, who juked out Sam Newton, one of Jace's old buddies and former Minnesota Wild player, sliding it between his skates and heading for the open net.

The practice arena soared above them, the sound of their sticks on the ice like gunfire. Max loved the way the breath of the ice seeped into his skin, despite the fire of a good sweat.

Kalen took the shot and it bounced off the post. Sam scooped up the rebound and shot it out to Jace. The two had a groove, and with Sam playing the role of Jace's best man, it felt like they had history off the ice, too. Max raced down to fight for the puck, but Jace slapped it into the goal, circling behind the net, his arms raised.

"Had enough there, kiddo?" Sam said, laughing.

"I don't know, old guy." Max fished the puck out. Played with it, kicking it between his feet as Jace came around to steal it.

"Who you calling old?" Jace said, jabbing for the puck. "I feel like I'm seventeen again."

"You play like you're seventeen." Max out-sticked him, headed for the net, and scored, Jace not even giving pursuit. But his laughter filled the arena.

The ebullient joy in the air had the power to lift Max out of the dark place that threatened to pull him in, that sad place of reality reminding him of what he and Grace could never have. The camaraderie of the past two weeks, e-mailing, phone calls . . . the memories—the argument it churned inside him could sink him.

They skated into the box, and Max reached for his water.

Jace had already grabbed a towel. "By the way, I'm trying not to worry, but I do need to know you got this."

Sam grabbed his skate guards. Kalen had taken the puck, begun to work on his stickhandling out by the red line.

Max swallowed his water. Wiped his chin with his sweater. "No worries. We reworked the entire menu. We're roasting a pig just for you, dude. Grace hired serving staff and even prep cooks from a local culinary school, and her friend Raina is helping with the preparations. And if this is an excuse to back out, you'd better tell me right now because that pig is going in the hotbox first thing in the morning." He reached for his towel, seeing Sam disappear to the lockers.

"Fear not; I'm not going to bolt."

"Good. Because Grace and I put too much into this to eat all that pig alone." He thought Jace might laugh and looked up when he didn't.

Jace wore a solemn look. "Don't break her heart, Max."

He stilled.

"I'm not stupid," Jace said. "Okay, I might be, but Eden certainly isn't, and she told me that something happened between you and Grace in Hawaii. And I saw you holding her hand at my condo."

"It's nothing." But he didn't look at Jace when he said it, bending instead to fit on his guards.

"Right. And I suppose it was nothing in Hawaii, too? Because I saw the video of the show. That looked like flirting to me."

Max kept his expression easy, nonchalant. "We were teammates."

"We used to be teammates. I don't remember you calling me nicknames. At least not the kind that sound like names of endearment."

Max narrowed his eyes at Jace. "Okay, fine. There were sparks." Liar. He'd call it a full-out inferno. But . . . "It doesn't matter now. It was just a vacation thing. It's over; I have to focus on my career."

Jace ran a towel over his head. "Huh. I used to say that too. But the fact is, hockey is just a sport. Grace is a life. A future."

Apparently now that Jace had turned into a coach, he thought he had the right to speak into Max's life. Or maybe he always had. "It's none of your business, dude."

"When it comes to Eden's sister, yeah, it's my business. And frankly, Max, you're my business too. We're friends and that means something to me. You gotta get it through your head that someday all this is going to end. Maybe tomorrow, maybe in ten years, but you won't have hockey anymore. And then what? If I'd had Eden in my life earlier, I might not have taken so many risks. I'd have had less to prove, maybe a longer career. I don't know. But I know that having her on the sidelines makes winning that much sweeter. And this next season of my life . . . that was worth the wait."

But see, Max had no next season of his life. "I'm no good for her, Jace. Trust me on this."

Jace frowned. "What are you talking about?"

He hadn't wanted to go there. He blew out a breath, wishing he could escape back to the ice.

But maybe that was the problem—he spent so much time playing hockey, breathing in the icy air of arenas, because it numbed him to the raw, ugly truth.

"I'm gonna die, Jace."

Silence, and then Jace . . . laughed? A short burst of disbelief that made Max frown at him.

"We're all going to die, Max." Jace shook his head. "What kind of lame excuse is that—?"

"I have the faulty Huntington's gene."

Jace closed his mouth. His eyebrow twitched, a tiny frown creasing his forehead. "What?"

"It causes a hereditary disease where your brain starts to deteriorate. Basically, in about five—maybe ten—years, I'm going to stop being able to walk, reason, or even talk. I'll eventually become totally reliant on someone else to take care of me. And I can't let that person be Grace."

Jace sank down onto the bench. "Seriously?"

"My dad died from it, and my brother and I both carry the faulty gene that causes the disease."

"Are you sure—?"

"It's going to happen, Jace. I can't escape it. Unless, you know . . . I jump from a bridge or something."

He was only half-kidding, and Jace must have seen that in his eyes. "And I thought my migraines were a bummer."

Max lifted one side of his mouth. "Yeah, well . . . my brother runs a nonprofit organization for the research of a cure, and he wants me to be the poster boy." He ran his hand across the air, an imaginary headline. " 'Huntington's Doesn't Have to Destroy Your Life.' "

"Does it?"

"You tell me. Don't say you're not feeling sorry for me right now."

Jace swallowed.

"Right. You can imagine my joy when my brother said he was going to put me front and center on his foundation's website if I won the cooking contest."

"He did?"

"I'm not an idiot. I know the difference between salt and sugar."

"You threw the contest."

Max fisted his hands in his towel. "It was just a stupid local contest . . . I never thought . . ." He shook his head. "I let her down, I know. But it would be a thousand times worse if she knew the truth."

"I'm going to have to fight you on that one. Do you seriously believe that Grace is the kind of person to walk away from someone she loves just because he *might* get sick?"

"Will. Full stop. I *will* get this disease. I *will* die a long, horrible death. But you're right. I know she's not that type of person. It's not just about Grace's commitment to me—it's her future. I can't have kids. I didn't want to pass down the disease, so a few years ago, I went under the knife. If Grace is with me, I'd steal her hope of a family. And then she gets to watch me die. Yeah, I'm a real package."

"So you'll break her heart instead."

"I already did—and trust me, it's better left where it is. Now I just have to keep her at arm's length until the wedding."

"How's that working out?"

"Not great, thanks to you." He glanced at Jace, serious.

Jace rubbed his hands together, staring at them. "I'm not sure I should apologize. You're good for each other. Maybe you can't have forever or a family, but you have something rare—someone who loves you. And I can't figure out, for the life of me, why you'd want to stop living just because someday . . . you'll stop living."

His words settled over Max.

"Or maybe you've never started."

Max looked away, the memory of Hawaii rushing through him. Of being caught up in a world where his future didn't touch him, where it might be only Grace, only . . . grace.

Yeah. Maybe he hadn't started living until he'd met the one woman who made him realize that he wanted to.

Sure, he'd figured out how to hold on to his faith while staring at his bleak future. But how could he ask Grace to do the same?

"Tell her, Max. She deserves to know. Let her decide for herself."

"And what if she decides she . . . ?"

"Doesn't want you? That's the problem, isn't it? You want to reject her before she gets a chance to reject you."

"I have nothing to give her. To give anyone. I am living a worthless life." He gritted his teeth, looked away. "At least for anything beyond hockey."

"I know a little about thinking your life is worthless, Max. God made you, and as long as you are on earth, your life is valuable to Him."

Max wanted to shake his head.

And he wanted to lean into Jace's words.

"Your life is also valuable to Grace. It could be that she needs you just as much as you need her."

Max didn't need her—the words nearly crossed his lips, but he bit them back. Because, yes, he did. The thought poured through him. He needed Grace like a thirsty man needed water.

What if he *did* tell her he loved her?

Jace must have read his mind because he clamped him on the shoulder. "I know. Facing death is one thing. But letting a girl know how you feel—that should terrify any man. Maybe we should stay right here and play more hockey."

"Grace, you are absolutely a fairy godmother. You create magic wherever you go." Eden walked through the open space of the warehouse they'd rented for the wedding, nearly floating with the joy on her face.

Grace looked up from where she was directing the delivery boys with their boxes of fresh fruit back to the kitchen. She put down her clipboard. "Blame Raina. She's little Miss Tinker Bell with her twinkle-light obsession."

Indeed, the space glittered. Raina had draped lights from the girders over the expansive eating area, and on each table, in a tall vase filled with pearly marbles, curly twigs dangled tiny pots with votive candles.

The service crew Eden rented with the space had already set the tables, covered them with deep-blue tablecloths and gold-rimmed plates. The florist had stopped by with a sample of the bouquets, a mix of orchids and the exotic birds-of-paradise, a few ginger spires. White plumeria flowers would decorate the serving line, even circle the platter on which Grace would serve . . . the pig.

It had arrived yesterday, an entire 125-pound animal, freshly slaughtered and prepared for roasting, with the ribs split so it could lie flat on the grill that Max had delivered.

Max to the rescue again. He'd breezed in yesterday, checked her ingredients, then stuck around to help her make the dressing for the salad. And tomorrow he'd run the kitchen while she stepped out of her role as chef to play maid of honor.

This just might work.

Especially since, with the overhaul of the dinner, the menu had been simplified. In fact, the entire thing took a turn toward redneck with Jace's allergic reaction to fish.

Scratch sushi. And anything to do with seafood. Or, for that matter, Hawaii. She and Max had reworked the entire menu to suit Jace's palate.

The only thing that remained was the Waimanalo salad. Now the menu featured, along with the roasted pig, a gingered-mango sauce; truffle macaroni and cheese; roasted zucchini, mushrooms, and summer squash; pineapple fruit kebabs; and Hawaiian sweet bread.

Grace could finally sleep through the night.

And Max had been more than she'd expected or imagined. Not only helping her overhaul the menu, order the ingredients, and train the staff, but making her believe, once again, that she could do this. Last night he'd given her another pep talk as they washed the dishes and loaded the sauces into the refrigerator. He even helped her roll the silverware into napkins and tie them with raffia.

And watching him, sitting on the stage rolling napkins, she realized . . .

She loved him. More than her fledgling feelings from Hawaii, the fullness of her emotion took root, embedded her bones. He'd glanced at her as she struggled to swallow the realization away.

How would she possibly say good-bye to him

after the wedding? Especially since he had no more reason to be in her life?

Max seemed to sense her mood because he'd gotten quiet too, and it nearly touched her lips to ask.

He'd driven her home then, pensive in the darkness, and when they pulled up to Eden's apartment and she turned to him, the expression on his face stopped her. As if he might want to say something to her.

She waited in the silence until he looked away and said, "Call me if you need anything. I'll drop by the venue tomorrow."

She'd ached with the frustration of it all when she got out of the car.

"Do you think Jace will like it?" Eden asked, still surveying the room.

"Are you kidding me? He will love it," Grace said.

"He won't even see it. He'll be so entranced with his bride," Raina said, joining them. She wore her hair up, a pair of jeans and her chef's jacket. "Grace, I finished chopping the vegetables and put them back in the cooler."

"Perfect. Where are we with the fruit?"

"I have Ty storing it in the cooler now."

"Sounds like you have everything under control," Eden said. "I knew it. Has anyone seen Mom and Dad?"

"They should be getting to the hotel anytime,"

Grace said. "I should go back and change for the rehearsal. I still think I was crazy to agree to be in the wedding party and the head chef—"

"Listen, that's what you have me for," Raina said. "You did all the hard work. We—me and Ty and the crew from the cooking school—have this."

The smartest thing Grace had ever done was take Eden's idea and offer the local Minneapolis Institute of Culinary Arts class a chance to help cater. Not only did she get their services cheap, but she'd met the director.

A relationship she hoped to cultivate. Maybe someday she could ask for a second chance to apply.

"Besides, if I get in over my head, Max will be here," Raina said.

Right. Max would be here.

Grace picked up her clipboard. "I just want to go over tomorrow's schedule with the team, and then I'll head back to your place, Eden, and get ready for the rehearsal dinner."

"You're a lifesaver, Grace. No one could have pulled this off but you."

And Max—ah, there he was again, ever present. "And Raina," Grace said, winking at her friend.

But Raina had stilled, was looking past her toward the door.

Grace turned and spied Casper standing there, holding his motorcycle helmet. "I just came by to see if I could help," he said, his gaze landing on Raina.

Grace's heart twisted at the hope in his expression. Once Raina had told her that Casper was not the father of her child—and had never been a candidate—the sad fate of his heart had Grace wanting to tell him the truth about Raina's situation.

But it wasn't her news to tell. And Raina clearly didn't have it in her to tell him, not yet, despite Grace's urging that Casper deserved to know. Did Raina plan on waiting until she started showing and Casper had to ask?

It didn't help that he'd pitched in, ordered supplies, helped Grace dig up recipes, offered his suggestions as she experimented with flavors, and generally hung around her planning sessions with Raina for the last three weeks. Despite the fact that Raina barely looked at him, Casper appeared undaunted.

In the darkest part of her heart, Grace could admit that maybe, despite the hurt ahead for Casper, it would be best for him to let her go.

She hated to think that perhaps the same thing applied to her and Max.

Casper entered the room and Raina fled back to the kitchen.

Grace walked over to him, wanting to hug away the dejection on his face. "Hey."

He forced a smile. "Mom and Dad are here. I'm headed to the hotel. Anyone need a lift?"

She knew who that *anyone* meant. "I'm headed back to Eden's in a bit, but Raina might need . . ."

Her voice trailed off as Max came in behind Casper.

He could stun a girl by just the way he walked, a sort of easy swagger, as if he held the world in his hand. Now he wore black jeans, a black-and-gray-striped button-down shirt, a pair of cowboy boots. His hair had grown, and it looked fresh from a shower, spiky on top.

He even smelled good, a spicy aftershave mixed with soap.

"Hey," he said.

Grace probably wore the same pitiful, hopeful expression as Casper. "Hi."

Casper turned. "Hey. You're Maxwell Sharpe. I remember you. Owen's friend, right?"

Poor Max. For a second, he looked wrecked. Then he met Casper's outstretched hand. "Yeah. Uh . . . remind me . . ."

"Casper. I'm the middle brother."

Max pumped his hand. "Nice to meet you. I came to give your sister a ride to the rehearsal dinner."

And although her brain screamed at her to say no . . . "Sure, that sounds great." She glanced at Casper. "Raina can drive my car back to Eden's place." Sorry, Bro.

She gave the room a once-over, then went to the kitchen to drop off her schedule, talk through tomorrow's events with the staff, and retrieve her purse.

When she came back, Max stood in the middle of the room, looking at the grandeur. "It's really pretty, Grace."

"Thanks."

"You know how to take something ugly and turn it beautiful."

"Well, I wouldn't actually call the space ugly—"

"It's a warehouse with brick walls and a cement floor and big metal doors. It was ugly. Now it's breathtaking."

Oh.

"Ready to go?"

She nodded, and to her surprise, he held out his hand.

She took it, lacing her fingers with his, feeling the warmth. His thumb curled over her hand, caressing tiny circles, sending tingles up her arm.

When they got to the car, he walked around to hold the door open. He'd taken the top down, but the heat of the day lingered. The late-afternoon sun spilled gold around the buildings, glinting on the windows of the warehouse across the street.

Grace got in and watched as Max circled the car, climbed in.

He seemed . . . different. Like the Max she'd seen that last night before the competition in Hawaii. He glanced at her, and she thought she saw something sweet, even hopeful, in his eyes.

He drove them out of the warehouse district, down Hiawatha, but kept going past Eden's street, heading southeast.

All the way to Minnehaha Park. He parked in the lot and got out.

"Max?"

"I need to talk to you, Grace. And this seemed to be the prettiest place I could find." He came around to her side, opened the car door. "Will you take a walk with me?"

This was where he told her that they could only be friends. That she needed to get the thoughts about him out of her—

He took her hand again.

They walked along a path lined with towering oaks and elms, cottonwoods that shivered with the wind. Behind it all, the roar of the falls reminded her of Hawaii.

He gripped her hand tighter.

"Are you okay?"

He said nothing, his face suddenly grim.

"You're scaring me, Max."

"Sorry." He took a breath and stopped. The pathway overlooked the falls, the spray rising up to capture the late-afternoon sun. He released her hand.

"What's going on?"

"I need to tell you something and I know that you'll want to make it better, but you can't and it's going to . . . Well, I wouldn't even tell you at all, but you deserve to know."

She rubbed her arms, chilled despite the heat. She should head him off before he made this more awkward for both of them. "Max, if you're going to tell me that we can't have anything past right now, I get that. And it's okay. You always said that you weren't looking for a relationship. I should have believed you. I know what happened in Hawaii was a mistake. And yeah, I was hurt. I was really hurt."

"I'm so sorry, Grace. I didn't mean to hurt you—"

"I know. You had to get back to your real life. It was a fairy tale in Hawaii, and being with you on vacation changed my life. See, when you left me there, something happened."

He looked at her fast, a crease in his brow.

"Nothing bad. In fact, it was all good. I realized that . . . well, I'd gone to Hawaii looking for something. It wasn't until you left that I realized the thing I was looking for wasn't you. It was God. I want more out of life than just . . . just staying where my fears trap me. I want to know all that God has for me—His love, His power, His grace. And it wasn't until I gave up everything I was holding on to and reached out for *Him* that I realized it was right there, waiting for me. I'd just missed it because I thought I could find it in you."

He seemed worried, even hurt, so she touched his cheek. "You are an amazing man, Max. You are brave and patient, and you can cook circles around me. But I am going to be okay without you."

His eyes glistened and his expression broke, something desperate in it. "But I don't think I'll be okay without you." He took her face in his hands. "I love you, Grace. Wow, I want to love you. I want you in my life. I want to grow old with you and have babies with you—"

She kissed him. Just rose up on her toes and pressed her lips to his.

She tasted salt in his touch, and it only whetted her heart for him. She wrapped her hands around his neck, pulled him closer.

And then, with a tiny groan that escaped from deep inside him, he kissed her back. His arms went around her, and he pulled her to himself, into his strong arms, kissing her as if he couldn't get enough of her. He touched his lips to her eyes, her cheeks, returning finally to her mouth.

Max. She slowed his pace, running her thumbs down his cheekbones.

Sweet Max was crying.

He pulled back and tried to smile, but it was lopsided. He opened his mouth, but nothing emerged.

She'd rendered him speechless. *I love you, too.*

The words were bubbling up, ready to burst from her, when his phone rang.

He stared at his pocket as if it might contain a bomb.

Grace laughed. "Get it, Max."

"Uh—"

"Seriously. I'm not going anywhere."

He held her hand, though, as he glanced at the screen, then frowned and answered the phone. "Yeah?"

He listened for a bit, his face growing darker. "I'll have to call you back." He hung up, pocketed the phone.

She asked, "What's the matter?"

"It's probably nothing. I need to get you home so you can change for the rehearsal dinner."

Oh. She couldn't deny the boulder that landed on her chest. He held her hand all the way to the car, tight, as if he couldn't bear to let the moment go either. But they'd have more. At the wedding tomorrow and then . . .

Then . . . ?

It was on her lips to ask, but it felt so vulnerable and raw. Maybe she'd wait until she told him she loved him. Maybe then they could talk about a future.

He glanced at her now and again, squeezing her hand as he drove. But when they pulled up to Eden's house, he didn't get out.

Didn't kiss her good-bye.

He just drove off, and she had the strangest sense, like she did in Hawaii, that she might not see him again.

Silly, right?

At night, it became easier to forget her mistakes. Her appetite returned, her stomach stopped betraying her, and Raina felt normal.

At least as normal as she could muster, given the fact that her life seemed to be unraveling before her eyes. Her plans to stay in Deep Haven, to become a part of Casper's life, his family, were all a gnarled, sad mess.

In a way she *was* a part of the family, except she wasn't going to show up on the Christiansens' doorstep with Owen's child in her arms, like an episode of *All My Children*.

No. Any hope of being a part of that family Owen had stolen from her. Maybe she'd stolen it, too, but regardless, she could never return to Deep Haven. To the Christiansens.

If only her car hadn't quit on her earlier this week, she could leave. But maybe as soon as the reception finished, she'd get on a bus, head west. Maybe to . . .

It didn't matter. Anywhere but where her memories might find her.

Raina stood in front of the sink, letting the steam rise as she finished washing the last of the butcher knives. She'd already prepped the salad and vegetables for tomorrow, already looked over the schedule, already been assured that everything would hum along as planned, the vegetables roasting, the pig on the grill. She'd sent home the kitchen assistants and then taken a final walk through the venue.

The beautifully decorated warehouse did capture the romance of the event, with the lights glittering, reflecting the joy awaiting Jace and Eden. Raina had stared at the dance floor too long, remembering her hopes for dancing under the stars with Casper.

How stupid she'd been to think that there might be a happily ever after waiting for her. That happened to other people, with lives that made sense.

She plunged her hand back into the hot, sudsy water, feeling around for a knife handle. The slick blade ran across the meat of her middle finger, burning even as she pulled back. Blood ran down her arm.

She grabbed a towel, pressed it against her finger.

"Are you okay?"

The voice jerked her around, and she saw Casper advancing into the kitchen.

"Did you hurt yourself?" He wore his leather jacket over a white shirt and tie, a pair of dress pants, but his five o'clock shadow added a rugged appeal.

The kind of appeal that might make a girl forget

her woes and jump on the back of his motorcycle.

Which, frankly, was how she'd gotten into this mess in the first place.

"I know better than to put a knife in the sink. I just got absentminded. It's nothing, though—a small cut." She should have expected him to show up—he'd seemed to be hovering the last few weeks, close enough to hear if she decided to call out, to need him.

Oh, how she needed him. But shame kept her mute. Now she watched, her heart bleeding out even as he came over, took her arm, inspected her wound. "It's not deep—probably doesn't need stitches. Do you have a first aid kit?"

She pointed toward the kit attached to the wall, and he went to retrieve it.

"What are you doing here?"

He found a Band-Aid, a cotton ball, antiseptic, some antibiotic cream, and returned to her, moving her to the table. He patted it, and she slid onto the smooth surface. "The rehearsal dinner's over, and I didn't see you. I thought maybe you needed help with something, so I swung by, saw the lights, decided to make sure you were okay."

Of course he did. Because that was Casper, the guy who showed up. Who stuck around even when she'd done everything she could to push him away. She watched as he cleaned her wound, then doctored it with the ointment and Band-Aid.

He wrapped the wound, then lifted her finger to his lips and sweetly kissed it.

Her face heated. "Casper . . ."

"I don't know what's going on, Raina. But if you let me, maybe I can fix it."

She sighed, pulled her hand away, and slid off the table. "I don't think you can fix this." She returned to the sink, but he moved her aside.

"I'll finish this."

She picked up a towel as he shucked off his jacket, rolled up his sleeves, and plunged his hands into the water, gingerly feeling around for the knife. He found it, washed it with a rag, and handed it to her, handle first.

She dried it as he pulled the plug, letting the water drain. She put the knife away.

Then she stood in the quiet kitchen with him as he wiped his hands on a towel. He was such a handsome man, his eyes so blue it seemed she could fall into them, never surface.

"Casper, I . . ."

But she had no words because he took two steps toward her, caught her face in his hands. She didn't have a bone in her body to resist when he leaned down and kissed her.

It was gentle, like before, but with a firmness, a resolute strength that made her lean into him. He smelled like freedom and tasted sweet and gingery. She pressed her hands to his chest, felt the frame of his work-hardened body.

How was she supposed to say good-bye to a man who kept showing up in her life? *But if you let me, maybe I can fix it.*

What if he could? What if—? No, it was crazy to think he'd still want her after knowing . . . knowing . . .

She pushed him away, her eyes filling. "I'm sorry, Casper."

He stared at her, breathing hard. "Tell me what I did!"

"You didn't do anything! It's not you. I'm . . . I'm leaving Deep Haven."

"What? Why?"

"I . . . I need . . ." Shoot, once upon a time, lies had come so easily. "I can't be with you. I did something I shouldn't have and . . ."

He closed the gap between them, took her hands, his voice earnest. "Whatever it is, it's okay. Listen, sometimes life just . . . it blindsides you. And for a while, you're lost." He leaned into her. "I came home from college because . . . I hated it. And my grades showed it. I'm not cut out for college. But the worst part was, for the first time in my life, I didn't know what to do. I've been hiding in Deep Haven—and then I met you and I realized I was supposed to be there. With you. I thought that coming home was failure, but don't you see? It was victory. *You* are my victory, Raina. You and I—we can be happy there."

Tears burned their way down her cheeks.

Oh, how she wanted to grab ahold of his words.

But it didn't in the least compare to her failures. "What about your trip to Roatán? Your pirate's treasure?"

"I already decided that I am staying in Deep Haven. No more treasure hunting for me—I found my treasure right here." He cupped his hand to her cheek. "I think I'm in love with you, Raina."

She tore her hand away, choking back a sob. Then she pushed past him and headed toward the door.

"Raina!"

"I'm not in love with you, Casper!"

There, she said it, and she didn't slow as the words emptied out of her. Just ran past the tables toward the exit.

"Raina!"

No, no, no! But her eyes were blurry and she couldn't see where she was going and—"I'm sorry; I'm so sorry."

Arms caught her. "Sorry for what, baby?"

She looked up and, with a cry, pushed herself away.

Owen seemed almost the spitting image of Casper, with his dark pants, jean jacket, his blond hair windblown. He looked past her to Casper, concern on his face. "What's going on here? You okay? My brother giving you trouble?"

"Stay away from me, Owen," she said softly.

"Whoa. I guess you're still sore at me."

She wanted to slap him. Instead, she cast a desperate look at Casper.

Casper stared at his brother, stricken. "Raina?"

She had the surreal sense of her world shattering, right there in the middle of the twinkle-lit dance floor.

With a sob, she pushed past Owen, out into the night.

She had no illusions; she'd finally managed to cut Casper out of her life.

Please, Lord, let me not be too late.

The desperation in Max's prayer made him lean forward into his steering wheel, look heavenward.

He hadn't talked to God much in the past ten years, not wanting to bother God too much before he really needed Him, but . . . today, right now, he needed the Almighty to look his direction. To care. To stop Brendon from doing something stupid.

His headlights cut a swath over the dark, twisted highway of northern Wisconsin, illuminating shaggy evergreen, the forest thick with birch, oak, and poplar.

He'd already nearly hit two deer, and now his gaze darted from one side of the road to the other. He glanced at his cell phone, then back to the road, wishing he could pick it up, call again.

But his phone had died an hour ago, and in his

rush to leave, he'd forgotten his charger on the counter.

At least he'd called Jace, left a message, cryptic though it was. *Jace, I think my brother's in trouble. Tell Grace I'm sorry.*

Coward that he was, he couldn't face her.

"Brendon's missing." The two words spoken by Lizzy, her voice trembling, had cut off every word he'd wanted to say to Grace.

Every apology, every stupid admission of emotion—all gone. What was he doing, declaring his love for her, telling her he wanted a future with her? He could bang his head on the steering wheel with the memory of it, the stupidity of his actions.

His conversation with her hadn't in the least gone the direction he'd planned. He'd wanted to sit her down on the rock wall and tell her the truth. *I sabotaged our contest.*

He imagined her expression, raw, hurt, the question emanating from her: *Why?*

He forced himself to see the rest. The part where he told her about his disease, his fear of leaving someone behind, of . . .

Of watching her walk away.

Instead, he'd skipped over the essentials of that conversation to the happy ending. The part where he held her in his arms, kissed her—no, inhaled her—pulling her to himself until he felt whole and loved and healed.

He should be grateful for Lizzy's call, the

reminder in two words of exactly why he needed to walk away.

He kept dancing around the truth, like a moth around a flame, when he should have listened to his head instead of his heart.

But Brendon was different. He had a wife. A child.

A brother who needed him.

Max hit the brakes, slowing as he passed through the tiny resort town on the edge of Diamond Lake. This late at night he didn't expect to see lights on, and he rolled by the darkened gas station, the library, the coffee hut, the bait and tackle shop, the long, low motel flickering a Vacancy light in neon red.

Impatience swilled through his veins as he accelerated back onto the highway toward the family cabin.

Please—

He'd called Lizzy the moment he got back to his apartment and found out that she'd come home to a note on the counter. *Gone fishing.* Lizzy might have believed him except for the prognosis Brendon received from the doctor last week. The one that showed his disease progressing faster than average, as if catching up to Brendon after its years of leniency.

"His cognitive test showed a severe decrease in his memory, and the psychomotor test, where they combine memory and writing, was twice as bad. It's coming on, and fast." The tremble at the end of her voice told Max the truth.

She knew about the pact.

"I'll find him."

His promise now sat like an ember under his skin.

He slowed, looking for the signage to their road, then turned onto the gravel drive. The road threaded through thick forest toward the lake.

He drove up to the house, turned off the car, and got out.

The rush of wind in the trees, the faintest sound of bullfrogs along the shore, the rich fragrance of pine swept over him, an attempt to calm his racing heart.

But there in the driveway sat his brother's economy Nissan. And beside it, his uncle Norm's old truck.

His uncle wouldn't have . . .

But Uncle Norm had experienced the devastation of watching his siblings' disease advance through them, destroying them from the inside out. Dealt with the aftermath, filling in the gaps their deaths left behind.

Yeah, maybe.

Max went in the side door, flicked on the light. It bathed the kitchen and the main room that overlooked the lake.

"Brendon!" His voice boomed through the house and carried the edge of panic cultivated during the five-hour drive. "Where are you?"

He cut through the kitchen, down the hall. "Brendon!"

"Sheesh, you're going to wake all of Wisconsin! What's going on?" Brendon appeared at the door to one of the guest rooms, bare-chested, wearing a pair of pajama pants, his hair askew. "Is Lizzy okay?" He braced his arm on the jamb, blinking into the light.

Max didn't know whether to hug him or deck him. Instead he turned and hit the wall, everything inside him spilling out hard and fast.

"Are *you* okay?"

"No, I'm not okay!" Max rounded on him. "Why aren't you answering your phone?"

Brendon held up a hand. "Chill, Bro. It never rang. You know we get spotty service out here—"

Max let out a blue word, something that brought his uncle Norm to his door. "Max!"

He turned to his uncle, still hot. "Uncle Norm, seriously—Brendon takes off, leaves a note for Lizzy saying he's gone fishing, and—"

"And we're fishing, son. You should see the freezer. Brendon landed an eight-pound walleye."

Max wanted to hit something again as he stared at his uncle, his brother. But he turned away, stalking down the hall, his hand to his head.

He sank into the old recliner, scraping his hands down his face. Fishing. He could still taste his heart in his mouth, despite his efforts to swallow it down.

He heard the floor creak and looked up to find the duo staring at him like he might be the crazy one.

Then the realization clicked on Brendon's face. "Oh . . . wow," he said, sinking onto the tweed sofa. "You thought . . ."

"What was I supposed to think?" Max might never flush the anger from his voice at this decibel. He took a breath, schooled it into something less threatening. Something that contained the horror he felt. "Lizzy told me about the tests."

Brendon flinched one eye and looked away.

His uncle sat next to him on the sofa. "What tests?"

Max shook his head, wishing it all away. Wishing he'd had the courage to stand beside his big brother and raise the money to fight this. Wishing his mom didn't have to go through this again. Wishing . . .

Wishing he were back with Grace, caught in a place where he could forget . . . or at least hang on to someone a little stronger than himself.

And there she was, her words in his head. *I want more out of life than just . . . just staying where my fears trap me. I want to know all that God has for me—His love, His power, His grace.*

Yeah, he wanted it too. More than wanted it—he hungered for it.

Grace. Power. Especially courage.

Uncle Norm turned to Brendon. "How bad is it?"

Brendon's hands shook and he stretched them out, swallowed. "It's bad. It's progressing faster than I'd—we'd hoped. But it's not so bad that you needed to drive here, Max, and stop me from . . ." He shook his head. "I love Lizzy and Ava and I want every second I can have with them. I'm not going to do it."

"Do what?" Uncle Norm asked.

Max took a breath. He couldn't—

"We made a pact after Dad died," Brendon said softly. "It was stupid, my idea. But I was scared and angry and . . ."

"We agreed to help each other end our lives once we started showing symptoms," Max said quietly. "Either by not stopping each other or . . . assisting." Now he couldn't look at his uncle, at the disbelief, the horror on his face. "I'm sorry, Uncle Norm. But you don't know what it's like, looking ahead, knowing—"

"Yeah, I do, son. Your dad came to me when you were born. He told me how, when he married your mother, he told her he had the gene. She knew she'd lose him, and she married him anyway. That took him apart, but he lived with the specter of the disease so far out in front of him, he didn't consider how it might touch him until you were born, Max. See, they planned Brendon. And then they found out he had the faulty gene, and they vowed not to have another child. Suddenly it became real, and your dad started to

394

panic. He started to think like you, and the idea of him suffering and then passing that along to his son undid him. He went through a terrible darkness."

Uncle Norm shook his head. "I feared for his life. And then . . . then you came along. Surprise."

Max knew that, had resigned himself to the fact that he was a mistake. His entire life from beginning to end—worthless.

"But that's when everything changed. Having you is what kept your father sane as long as it did. He was already showing signs of the disease when your mother got pregnant, and then you were born and something changed inside him. You were a gift to him during his darkest moments and a gift that your mother held on to long after he left this earth." He smiled as if caught in memory. "Oh, how he loved to watch you play hockey. He'd call me and we'd go to your games."

"He used to go to my practices. I remember him sitting there in the bleachers, early in the morning, wrapped in a blanket, shivering."

"He wanted to capture every moment with you, just like he had with Brendon. You made his life rich, right up to the end. And it made him realize that any life, no matter how short or long, was worth living."

Now Max's eyes burned. "I don't understand a God who would give life, only to have us suffer. It's not fair."

"Everyone dies. It's a surety. You could die tomorrow, and despite the horror of this disease, the days of health are that much more precious because we know what lies ahead." His uncle's voice thickened. "I miss my brother every single day. Frankly, sometimes I feel like it's unfair that out of all my siblings, I'm the one who escaped. We all suffer with this disease. But suffering can either destroy you or it can save you. Because without suffering, we don't need more; we have enough. But when we suffer, we can't help but reach out. It forces us into God's arms, and that's where we find not only what we need, but more than we can imagine. We find Him."

He clamped a hand on Brendon's shoulder, squeezed. "Your dad discovered this, and you will too, Brendon." His eyes glistened. "And I will too, all over again."

Max couldn't bear it. He looked away, clenched his jaw.

"Your dad loved being married to your mother, Max. She was joy in his life, and she told me at his funeral that it gave her joy to walk her husband into the arms of heaven. It's the greatest privilege a spouse can have."

Brendon cupped his hand over his eyes. His shoulders shook.

"You will make it through this, boys. Your mother raised strong men, knowing you'd have to have the courage of your father. And you will, if you don't let the suffering steal the richness of living. Focus on life."

Max got up, went to the window, stared out at the lake. The sky arched above it, starlight dappling the water's surface like tiny eyes cast into the darkness.

Focus on life. That's what Grace had done for him. Helped him see life, embrace life. Want life.

And maybe if he hung on to that, God just might help him—and Grace—face death.

Brendon came up behind him. "Let's make a new pact."

Max turned.

"Let's end well." Brendon stuck out his hand.

Max ignored it, pulling Brendon into an embrace. "You got it." He blinked, turned away, ran his palm across his cheek.

His uncle rose from the sofa. "Now if it's all right with you, I need some shut-eye if I'm going to face the fish at 5 a.m." He ruffled Max's hair as if he were ten years old. "I think there's a walleye with your name on it."

Max laughed, but . . . wait. "Oh no. I have a wedding to put on." Both Brendon and his uncle stared at him.

"Okay, long story, but I promised Grace that I'd help her cater her sister's wedding, and she's counting on me."

"Grace?" Uncle Norm asked.

"Grace," Brendon said. "You know . . . *Grace.*"

"Right. The salt-in-the-mousse girl."

Oh . . . "Actually, that was me. I sabotaged the competition because I—"

"Didn't want to go public. I wondered about that, but I realized I shouldn't have been pressuring you."

"Except you were right. I shouldn't let fear keep me from doing what's right."

"Only when you're ready, Max," Brendon said. "But more importantly . . . Grace? Are you two together?"

"Not if I don't get back for this wedding."

Chapter 18

Streams of pink and lavender ribboned across a cirrus cloud–streaked sky, the melody of sparrows outside the window lifting in the summer breeze. The sunrise heralded a beautiful wedding day for Eden and Jace.

Except that Grace's assistant had vanished.

With Grace's car. And Eden had left early to eat breakfast with Ingrid.

Which meant Grace had to find a ride to the reception venue.

Max wasn't answering his phone, so she hung up after the third ring, feeling foolish. Needy. He was probably already at the venue putting the pig on the grill.

She called Casper. He sounded ragged around the edges but picked her up on his bike thirty minutes later and ran her over to the warehouse. He hadn't shaved, wore a black T-shirt and jeans, and looked like he'd spent the night staring out the window, his eyes rimmed with red.

"Are you okay?" she asked as she climbed off the back of the bike. She reached out to him, but he forced a smile. Oh, Casper. He just couldn't let anyone see that far inside.

"I'll be back later. You need anything?"

"Maybe a ride to the wedding? I don't see my car anywhere." She frowned. Neither did she see Max's Audi. "You haven't heard from Raina, have you? I thought she'd be here."

"No," he snapped. "Sorry. I have no idea where she might be." He revved his engine. "Try Owen."

Owen? "He's in town? Why didn't he show up at the rehearsal?" And what did that have to do with Raina?

Casper had a grim set to his mouth. "Why does Owen do—or not do—anything? Do you know if Raina and Owen ever . . . ?" He swallowed, his jaw tight.

"Casper?"

"Nothing. I can't even think it. I'll be back later."

She had the urge to run after him, to stop another moment when she saw someone she loved driving away, not returning. She was clearly letting her fears bleed into her imagination.

Grace made her way to the kitchen and found the staff busy with their assigned tasks. One crew brandished knives, cutting the fruit kebabs, while a small cadre of chefs assembled the salads, covering them with cellophane and setting them back in the cooler. She found Ty talking with the cake decorator, a pretty blonde about her mother's age whose team was delivering the cake sections in boxes.

"Where's Raina?" she asked.

"Dunno," Ty said. "I thought she'd be here. We still need to get the pig on the grill."

"Max isn't here either?"

Ty shook his head. She stifled the spear of panic. No problem. He'd be here—he wouldn't let her down, not for this.

"Okay, let's get the pig on the grill." Grace donned her chef's coat, tied her hair into a net, and worked on a pair of rubber gloves while Ty directed the cake lady to the table in the meeting area. She stepped outside and called an assistant over, a girl with long black hair caught up in a net. "Can you get the coals cooking?"

"Yes, chef."

Yes, chef? Okay.

Back inside, she went to the cooler. "Ty, I need your football muscles."

The animal hung from its haunches, and she put

her back into it as she lifted the pig's front. Ty unhooked it from the rack, and together they carried it to the stainless counter.

A few of the student chefs came to admire the animal.

"How many people will this pig feed?"

"About eighty. It's over 125 pounds, so I think it's enough."

Grace had made the injection fluid last night— apple cider, apple juice, and water. Now she took the needle, filled it with juice, and bent over the body. Working in the hindquarter area, she injected the meat just under the skin, then began working her way around the body.

She'd attracted a small crowd. It felt a little awkward to be helming a crew of culinary students—especially since she hadn't actually attended culinary school—but she didn't betray her secret.

Or failure. Although she'd stopped thinking about it.

In fact, she hadn't felt like a failure since Hawaii. Since Max had helped her believe in herself.

She massaged oil into the pig's body, head to toe. "This helps keep the skin color even, will crisp it up."

Weird, now she felt like she might actually be teaching.

She glanced at the clock. Twenty minutes had

passed, and if she didn't get the pig cooking soon, they'd have to stall Eden's wedding.

"Ty, let's get this animal on the grill." She took the front hooves, Ty grabbed the back, and they lifted it onto the portable grate one of the students had brought in from the cooker.

She seasoned the animal with sea salt, granulated garlic, black pepper. "What's the temperature?"

"It's 225," her grill chef answered as she stirred the coals with a shovel, evening them out.

"Add some of that hickory wood," Grace said, gesturing to the bundle by the door. The grill chef replaced the drip pan and set a bucket under the spigot that would collect the runoff grease.

"Ready?" she asked Ty, and he nodded. They carried the dressed pig on the grill grate outside, set it on top of the drip pan. Closed the lid.

She looked at the grill chef. "What's your name?"

"Aliya," she said, her smile eager.

"You're on pig temperature patrol. Every few minutes, I want you to come out and check the temperature of the grill. It should hover between 225 and 250. If the heat is too high, open these dampers here. If it's too low, close them. Got it?"

"Yes, chef."

Surreal.

But even more surreal was the fact that, as she went inside to check on the kitchen progress, neither Max nor Raina had shown up.

Grace stood in the kitchen, ticking off her to-do

list. Cake, check. Fruit kebabs, check. Pig, grilling. Salad, in the cooler. Vegetables . . . "Ty, where are we with the vegetables?"

"I'll get them oiled and on the baking trays."

So maybe she didn't need Max. Still—

She pulled out her phone. Checked for messages. Nothing. She found his number, debated for a second, pressed Send.

It rolled over to voice mail. Like he didn't even have it on.

Without Max and Raina, she still had the Hawaiian bread to make, not to mention the citrus sauce for the pork.

"Grace! What are you doing? We're supposed to be at the hairdresser." Eden came barreling into the kitchen. She wore a yellow T-shirt, a pair of athletic pants. "We gotta go!"

Behind her trailed Amelia and Ingrid. Except both of them had stopped in the main room, caught in the fairyland.

Raina deserved to be here for this.

In truth, Grace was starting to get worried. "You haven't seen Raina, have you?"

"I saw Raina last night." Owen came into the kitchen looking tan and fit, wearing a Jude County Hotshots T-shirt and baggy jeans. He still wore the eye patch, hiding his scars. Probably for confidence more than necessity. "Hey, Sis!" He pulled her into a hug. "It smells great."

"Except I'm missing my kitchen help."

"When I saw her last night, she was upset. Casper was here, so maybe he could tell you what was going on. Maybe she burned something." He lifted a shoulder.

Or maybe she and Casper had finally had the talk. Poor Casper. No wonder Raina vanished. Although not showing up for work felt extreme.

"Hey, where's the party?" Jace's voice echoed through the warehouse.

"Isn't it bad luck for the groom to see the bride before the wedding?" Owen said. He went out to run interference.

"Grace, is everything under control?" Eden was clearly unconcerned about Jace's presence but must have read her face.

"I think so, but . . . well, Max took off last night, and I don't know where he is."

"Max isn't here? Isn't he supposed to be in charge for the day?"

"Yeah, but—"

"But nothing. He should be here! I can't believe he is doing this again. Ditching you when you, when we—" Eden gestured to Grace, back to herself—"need him." She shook her head. "You were right, Grace. Maybe you didn't need him after all. I mean, look at this. You have everything under control."

"I wouldn't have, without Max. But yes, Ty can handle everything, right?"

Ty wore a wide-eyed, pale expression.

Ho-kay.

"We need Max. And Raina. I cannot believe they both abandoned you," Eden said.

To put it like that . . .

"Max didn't abandon you. He had his reasons." Jace appeared in the kitchen doorway.

"Sorry, Sis. He still thinks he can push me around," Owen said, but he wore a smile.

"What reasons?" Eden said. "What possible reason could Max have to take off and leave Grace today of all days?"

Jace's voice cut to low. "Eden, trust me on this—"

"Max? As in Max Sharpe?" Owen's voice sliced through the conversation.

Eden glanced at Grace, who'd stilled at his tone. How much did Owen know about that night he got hurt?

"Yeah, uh . . . he's been helping me with the wedding." Until now.

Owen frowned at her. "Are you two *together?*"

She swallowed.

"They're together, yes," Jace said quietly. "Owen, listen—"

He held up a hand. "No, actually, I don't want to hear it. For his own good, you'd better hope Max doesn't show up." He walked away, and if possible, the kitchen got quieter.

"You know where Max is?" Eden said to Jace.

"Let's not talk here," he growled and glanced at Grace.

What—?

Eden took off after him as Jace stalked into the reception area. Sure—like Grace would let this conversation happen without her. She followed them.

Jace had Eden in a huddle, leaning down to speak into her ear.

Eden's expression as she glanced at Grace stopped her cold. She slowed, winding her way around the tables. "What's going on?"

Jace appeared ill, shook his head.

"Max's brother is in trouble. He . . . Max thinks he might be . . ." Eden sighed, took Grace's hand. "Max's brother has Huntington's disease. And Max went to make sure that he was okay."

"Huntington's disease?" Grace frowned at Jace, who wore such an odd, pained expression that she reached for one of the chairs. "Isn't that a hereditary disease? Something like Lou Gehrig's?"

"Yeah," Jace said softly.

Again, the way he looked at her . . . Her grip tightened on the chair. "Does . . . does Max have . . . ? Is Max sick?"

Jace drew in a breath. "Not yet."

Not. Yet.

"Oh." She pulled out the chair, lowered herself into it. "He's . . . *going* to be sick."

"Someday. Yes."

Eden sat across from her, her own expression stricken, probably mirroring Grace's. "That accounts for a lot. Like his weird behavior, hot, then cold—"

"Then hot." Grace's eyes had started to fill. "He told me he loved me. That he *wanted* to love me. Wanted to grow old with me. Wanted to have a family . . ."

Eden slid her hand over Grace's. "But wanting it is different from actually having it."

Grace pressed a hand to her mouth, her body tight, numb.

No wonder he kept walking out of her life. She kept pulling him in and he kept trying to extricate himself without hurting her.

Oh, Max.

"He doesn't want anyone to know," Jace said, coming over to Eden. "That's why he threw the cooking contest. His brother tried to publicize the event, and Max couldn't—"

"Bear for me to find out." The words settled over her—*he threw the cooking contest*. That made sense, then—his exit from her life, even why a guy like Max might let guilt push him into helping her with this wedding.

She looked at the glittering, beautiful room, the sunlight cascading through the high windows, diamonds in the sunbeams. The sounds of laughter filtered from the kitchen as the students prepared for the most beautiful day of Eden's life.

Grace put her hands over her face, her shoulders shaking.

"Oh, Grace."

She wanted to put up her hand, to say she was fine, but—

No. She'd never be fine. Because suddenly it all made sense . . . from his reckless behavior in Hawaii to their conversation at Pearl Harbor, even his cryptic words that day in the elevator. *I think everyone who gets to have dreams should reach for them.*

He believed he didn't get to have dreams— because his dreams coming true would mean destroying hers . . . like having a family. A home. A husband to grow old with.

I am going to be okay without you.

No. No, she wouldn't.

The truth hung over her, descended into her, wrecked her. *Oh, God* . . . Her prayer stumbled there, stuck inside.

"C'mon, Grace. Let's get out of here," Eden said.

"I—I have . . . to . . . make . . ."

Ingrid entered, carrying place cards, Amelia behind her. Ingrid knelt beside Grace. "Honey, are you okay?"

Owen joined them. "What did he do to her?"

"Owen, stay out of this," Eden started.

"There you are!" Casper's angry voice jerked Grace's head up. Her brother stormed in, still looking as rough-edged as he had this morning.

"Casper, are you all right?" Ingrid said, rising, but Casper was advancing hard, something wild in his eyes.

Still, no one expected him to launch himself at Owen. He tackled his brother to the ground, slammed his fist into his face. "What did you do to her, you jerk?"

He hit him again, but Owen had reflexes born from being the youngest and grabbed Casper's arm, the next blow just grazing his face. "Get off me!" He pushed Casper, and they rolled over in a tangle, wrestling, their fists finding ribs.

"Casper! Owen!" Ingrid ran toward them.

Grace got to her feet, grabbed her mother's hand. "Stay back!"

They banged a table and dishes crashed to the floor. Amelia screamed.

Jace plowed into the battle. "Guys—break it up!"

John, Darek, and Ivy walked in. Tiger ran ahead, but Ivy caught his hand.

Grace's stomach hollowed at the look on her dad's face.

"What on earth—?" He ran over, but Darek beat him to the pair. Jace got hold of Owen while Darek hauled Casper up.

Owen's eye patch had fallen off, the ugliness of his wounds laid bare. Blood ran from his mouth, his nose, his eye plumping. "He started it!"

Casper had shaken Darek off and now leaned

over, clutching his knees, breathing hard. "Get him away from me."

"What is wrong with you, Casper?" Ingrid's voice shook, but Grace heard the fury gathering. "Have you been drinking?"

The look on his face pained Grace. The expression of a broken heart.

"No, Mom. I haven't been *drinking*. There's only one member of this family who drinks and destroys things." He looked pointedly at Owen.

"Hey! What's that supposed to mean?"

"Why don't you tell me why the first time I met Raina, when she thought I was you, she said, 'Go away, Owen!' Why she accused Darek—our family, actually—of using people. And why Dad had to ask me if I'd ever hurt her. It wasn't because of *us,* was it, Owen?"

What—?

Grace looked at Owen, at the disheveled, angry, reckless person her brother had become, and suddenly she saw it. Owen and Raina sitting at the end of the dock the night of Darek and Ivy's wedding. Raina laughing as Owen charmed her.

Oh no.

He didn't. They didn't . . .

"I don't know what you're talking about," Owen snapped. "I never hurt Raina. We . . . So we hooked up." He lifted a shoulder, nonchalant, but Grace could see how he glanced at their mother, couldn't hide the flicker of embarrassment.

It was only going to get worse.

"You . . . hooked up," Casper said softly, and the expression on his face was so terrible, Grace glanced at Darek.

He slid a hand over Casper's shoulder.

It was then that her heart finally shattered because her brother Casper, the one who had never been anything but light and laughter and teasing, put his hand over his eyes and wept.

Silence descended around them.

Finally Ingrid took Grace's hand. Then Eden's. "John, I'll leave you to get our boys to the church. I guess we've all forgotten this is actually Eden and Jace's happy day. I'll expect smiles, even if you fake it, for the next six hours."

She glanced at Amelia, then turned. "Come, girls. We have to put on our pretty faces."

Focus on life.

Max drove right to the warehouse, the words thrumming in his head for the last two hours.

He wanted to throw his cell phone out the window, shout at the top of his lungs, *Grace, I'm on the way!*

No doubt she thought he'd abandoned her. Hopefully Jace had given her the message. *Tell Grace I'm sorry.*

He could almost see her staring at Jace, incredulous. *Sorry? What did that even mean?*

It was Hawaii all over again.

He got out of the car, started for the reception hall. Stopped.

What if Jace had told her the reason Max had to see his brother? What if . . . what if she knew?

Max stood in the lot, the heat of the afternoon on his shoulders, trickling down his back. What if she knew and she looked at him with pity?

Suffering can either destroy you or it can save you. Because without suffering, we don't need more; we have enough. But when we suffer, we can't help but reach out.

Reach out. Past pity, past fear, for Grace.

And for grace.

God, I know You don't hear from me that often, but I'm feeling desperate here. In fact, he felt desperate pretty much all the time.

Maybe he needed God all the time too. He blew out a breath.

Give me courage.

He opened the door to the warehouse.

Out drifted the odor of burning sugar, acrid and sharp. He took off at a run through the reception room, to the kitchen.

Two assistants were fanning smoke where it emanated from the sink. Ty was running water into a pot, causing a hiss from the darkened mess inside.

"What happened?"

Ty looked up at him, his eyes wide. "We had a little kitchen fire."

"A little kitchen fire? The entire venue stinks, and there's smoke everywhere."

"It's my fault. I was stirring the mango sauce and it started to boil up, and pretty soon I couldn't stop it, and then it spilled over and began to burn . . ." This from a skinny, long-haired student who held a rag to his hand.

"Did you hurt yourself?"

"It's just a burn—"

"Run some water over it, then go find a couple fans, see if you can get them going in the hall. Ty, let's get more made." Max glanced around the kitchen. "Where's Raina?"

"She never made it in." Ty opened the fridge. "And then they had a big fight."

"Who had a big fight?" Max reached for his chef's jacket. "Raina and Grace?"

"No. I think it was Jace and . . . maybe Owen?"

Oh no. Owen was here? He'd forgotten that.

"I think it was the other brother. The one with dark hair. He came in and beat up the other one," said a girl with short blonde hair.

He stared at them. "The Christiansen family had a fistfight?"

"Yeah," Ty said. "Sort of. I just know that Grace and her mom and sisters took off, and then Mr. Christiansen made all the guys reset the tables. We helped, but the sauces got started late and—"

"Has anyone made the bread?"

"I did," the blonde said. "It's cooling, about ready to slice."

"And the pig?"

"Nearly roasted, sir," said a girl with dark hair pulled up in a net.

"Ty, let's get started on that sauce."

But Ty just stood at the open cooler door. "We're out of mangoes."

"What else do we have?"

"I don't know. Some ginger. Carrots. Red onions." Ty looked at Max. "Four oranges and two limes and a coconut."

"C'mon, chefs. Think outside the box." Max went to the cooler, pulled out the ingredients. "If there's one thing hanging with Grace Christiansen taught me, it's that you have to reach out and try. You never know what is going to taste good."

The words left his mouth, and he let them hang in the room.

Reach out and try.

He grabbed the bag of red onions and handed them to the blonde kitchen assistant. "Julienne these." Then he shoved the carrots into the arms of the brunette. "Clean these and grate them."

"Yes, sir."

"Someone find me a bottle of white wine." He picked up the tray of oranges. "And a knife, please."

Ty handed him a knife and he sliced the fruit in half. "I need these juiced."

Max returned to the cooler, found garlic and the coconut. After he crushed and minced the garlic, he pulled out a pan and went to the stove. He retrieved the olive oil, added it to the pot, began to heat it.

"Onions!" The cutting board slid next to him, and he began to add them to the pot, stirring. He glanced at the clock.

The ceremony would be starting soon. Shoot, he should have left earlier, should have made his uncle wake him. He didn't realize he'd overslept until they returned with a stringer of walleye and were frying them up for breakfast. The sweet camaraderie of his brother and his uncle had mended the wounds from the panic of the night before. Helped foster the courage to drive home and face Grace.

Max tossed the garlic in, and the tangy redolence curled around him. The onions turned translucent. "Carrots!"

Ty brought them over. "What are you making?"

"I don't know yet."

"Really?"

"It's going to be great, though."

"What if you make a mistake?"

"Then we figure out something else, right? C'mon, buddy. Just because it's not perfect doesn't mean it won't be delicious." The carrots sautéed to a beautiful, rich orange. "Get me the orange juice."

He poured it into the pot, turned the heat down. Grabbed the white wine and added it. Added more. Put the top on. Okay, please let this work.

Please, *please* let this work.

Because his words to Ty sank in and suddenly seemed right—he and Grace might not have the right ingredients for happily ever after, but maybe they could make their own version of it.

Maybe the recipe wasn't always worth following.

Maybe, in fact, it was time to improvise.

Chapter 19

Eden would take Jace's breath away. Grace stood behind her sister, pulling out her train, layers and layers of fluffy chiffon. "You are gorgeous."

Eden seemed stunned herself, staring into the floor-length mirror. Her dress outlined her slim figure—a V-neck, cap sleeves, princess-style, with a cluster of fabric flowers at the bustle. Not overly beaded, just enough to catch the light. And in her hair, loosely twisted into a chignon at the nape of her neck, a simple veil that fanned out to her waist.

"He won't be able to speak," Grace said as she handed Eden her bouquet of orange-and-white roses, blue plumeria.

Eden met her eyes, then turned to Grace, catching her hand. "Are you okay?"

Grace tightened her jaw against a well of heat in

her throat. She just had to keep breathing, keep focusing on Eden and her perfect day and everything she had in front of her and—

She pressed a hand to her mouth, looked away. "I don't think so." She wiped her hand across her cheek. "I'm so silly. It's not like Max and I—" She shook her head. "We probably didn't have a future anyway."

"Why would you say that? Of course you did— you do. He loves you—even Jace can see that." Eden touched her cheek. "But the bigger question is, do you love him?"

Grace drew in a trembling breath. "Yes. I do. He makes me feel as if I could do anything. Go anywhere. He makes me a better version of myself."

"So . . ."

"So—for how long, Eden? Ten years? Less? And then I get to watch the man I love die an excruciating early death. And what about kids? He'd leave them behind—"

"Shh." Eden pulled her into her arms.

Grace held on. "I don't know if I'm strong enough to walk toward Max, knowing I'm going to have to let him go. Maybe he was right to push me away."

"Grace. You're one of the strongest people I know."

"But I'm not. I'm . . . scared a lot of the time. And I'm trying to be the woman who trusts in Jesus, but I just feel like I'm going to . . . well, that

I won't be strong. Not at all. And the worst part is . . ." She stepped out of Eden's embrace. "I haven't told him I love him. I wanted to but . . . I think I was scared. Maybe he was right to believe that I would run away. Maybe—"

A knock, and then the door burst open. Tiger ran into the room, dressed in his mini tuxedo, Ingrid on his tail. Her mother wore her game face, the one reserved for those moments when she hid her emotions for the good of the family. Whether those emotions were about Casper and Owen's fight or her oldest daughter walking down the aisle, Grace didn't know.

She wouldn't easily purge Casper's fight with Owen from her own mind either. The event cast a wretched pallor on the day. Watching her brothers tangle on the floor—well, she'd seen it in jest for years. Never in hatred. They all needed their game faces today.

Her mother came up to Eden with a genuine smile, however. "You are a sight to behold." She took Eden's hand, surveyed the dress. "Wow."

"Mom, they're almost ready." Amelia had followed her in, wearing the same blue bridesmaid dress as Grace. She wore her auburn hair in a similar chignon, and for a second, the sight of her stunned Grace into the realization that her little sister had turned into a grown woman.

Who was headed to Europe for her first year of college.

Oh, if only Grace possessed that kind of courage. To leap out in faith, to trust and believe—

"Aunt Eden, you're so pretty!" Tiger said.

"Are you ready to carry the ring, big man?" Eden asked.

He nodded. And the sight of him, his blond hair all slicked into place, dressed like a miniature version of her brother, so adorable she could gobble him up, made Grace want to weep.

She'd never have one of these. A miniature version of Max. Or if she did, how could she protect him from the fate of his father?

Yes, Max had been right to push her out of his arms.

"Ready?" Ingrid said to Eden.

Eden nodded.

Grace picked up Eden's train and followed her out. At least one of the sisters would marry her prince.

"Eden Joy Christiansen, do you take this man, Jace Maynard Jacobsen, to be your lawfully wedded husband . . . ?"

Grace listened to Eden say her *I do,* captured by the expression on Jace's face.

Max had looked at her that way. In the park, before his phone call.

He could look at her that way again.

Oh, she loved him. Standing here beside Eden, the sense of it could send her to her knees, make her weep.

She took a breath, kept her smile. *Oh, God, I love him. But I'm afraid.*

Do you love Me?

The voice rumbled through her, the question filling her so she could almost taste it. *You know I do.*

Then feed My sheep.

"Jace Maynard Jacobsen, do you take Eden Joy Christiansen to be your lawfully wedded wife?"

Give him your heart.

She stilled, hearing the voice twine through her like a whisper.

"I do," Jace said.

Grace couldn't help her tears. *I will, Lord. But how—?*

Walk with Me. Trust Me.

The words settled over her like a breath, a fragrance. Walk with Jesus. Trust Him. Yes. It would be, in truth, the only way. But perhaps that was the point. The more she needed, the more she would lean into Him. The more of God she'd discover.

More.

Could it be that Max was part of God's *more* for her?

She glanced at her mother, sitting in the pew just a few feet away. Oddly, Ingrid's smile was not on Eden, but on Grace.

Live dangerously.

Maybe living dangerously had more to do with

faith in a big, unpredictable God than it did doing something foolish. And maybe she didn't have to do this alone on earth, either.

"You may kiss the bride."

Jace leaned down and sweetly kissed his wife, catching her face in his hands. "I love you," he said, loud enough for Grace to hear.

More.

Yes, being with Max, loving Max, would fill her life with more, not less, even when their days turned dark and difficult.

Grace handed Eden her bouquet, casting a look toward the back of the church, where Casper and Owen stood sentry on either side of the door, both looking like they'd rumbled for the Sharks and Jets.

Eden and Jace walked up the aisle, Grace following with Jace's friend Sam. Amelia came out of the pew and followed behind.

Grace nearly broke into a run when she reached the narthex, handing Amelia her flowers. "I gotta get to the reception." She turned to Casper. "Give me a ride?"

"With pleasure. Let me grab my stuff." He took off down the hall, clearly as anxious as she to escape.

She did notice, however, that he stopped and kissed Eden on the cheek, shook Jace's hand as he dashed by.

"You're still wearing your dress," Amelia said.

Thankfully, Eden was a smart bride and had let Grace pick out her own attire. She could easily hike up her short blue dress for the motorcycle ride. Sure, it might not be ladylike, but at least she'd get to the reception hall before anyone burned the place down.

Casper reappeared, holding a backpack and his helmet.

Grace hooked his arm. "Let's go."

He didn't look back as he headed outside. Nor did he say a word as he retrieved an extra helmet from his seat. He turned to fasten it on her head. "I'm leaving, Grace."

She caught his hands. "Wait—what?"

"I gotta go."

But—

"I was asked to be part of a treasure diving crew in Central America this fall, and I kept putting it off because . . . well . . ." His jaw tightened. "I thought I might be sticking around. But I can't."

"Casper," she said softly, "don't run away."

His expression bore more pain, more truth in it than she could bear. "No. I'm just . . . changing scenery for a while. I'll be back. I promise."

"Mom and Dad?"

"They know." He kissed her on the cheek, then fitted on the helmet.

She blinked back the bite in her eyes.

He got on the bike, held out his arm for her.

Grace climbed on, wrapping her arms around his waist. "Be safe, Casper. And come back to us."

She felt him sigh, his rib cage rising and falling hard as he gunned the bike.

She hung on to him, her eyes closed as they drove through Minneapolis toward the warehouse. It pulsed inside her to tell him that Raina needed him, but they weren't her words to say. And who knew where Raina had vanished to?

Keep him safe, Lord. Heal his heart.

Casper dropped her off at the warehouse. Flipped open his visor. "Don't burn anything."

"I love you, Bro."

He smiled, but it didn't touch his eyes.

And then he was gone.

She stood on the sidewalk, watching him go. Oh, Casper.

Just before she turned away, she caught sight of her car, parked down the street away from the warehouse. Or at least, what looked like her car.

Raina? Grace ventured toward the car, peered into the window.

Raina stared straight ahead, hands cupped to her mouth, tears running over them. She stared in the direction Casper had driven.

When Grace knocked on the passenger window, Raina nearly jumped through her skin. Her bloodshot eyes widened.

"Can I come in?"

Raina wiped her cheeks. When she leaned over to unlock the door, Grace saw that her hair looked greasy. Had she slept in the car?

Grace slid into the front seat. "Hey."

"I'm sorry I stole your car."

Grace gave her a smile. "In the scope of things that happened today, trust me—you can have this old clunker."

One side of Raina's mouth tweaked up. Then it vanished and she looked again in the direction of Casper's exit. "Where did he go?"

"I don't know. Central America, he said."

"Roatán. There's some sort of pirate dig there."

"He was always a treasure hunter."

"He said that." She closed her eyes. "I hurt him. I really hurt him."

"Yeah, you did," Grace said. "But . . . that's the risk we take when we love someone. He'll be okay." She touched Raina's arm. "What about you? Are you . . . ? Did . . . ? I need to know, for my parents' sake. Did Owen do something to hurt you? Should we know about anything?"

"Just that I'm stupid and fall hard for Christiansen men. Although Owen was just a weak, stupid mistake. Maybe it was the wedding and I was lonely, and you were going to Hawaii and I felt sorry for myself and . . ."

"And Owen is dark and troubled and needed someone too."

She nodded. "I never meant to fall in love with

Casper—I especially never meant to hurt him."

"I know," Grace said. She took her hand. "So the baby is Owen's?"

Raina nodded.

Oh, boy. "You should have told me. I would have listened."

"How could I tell you that? I was so ashamed, and you love your family so much. You'd do anything for them." She glanced at her. "Even agree to be a maid of honor *and* cater your sister's wedding."

"Agreed; that was a bad idea. But . . . I am not ignorant of my brother's mistakes, believe me. I am on your side. I would have listened. Where did you go? I was so worried."

Raina looked away, out the window. "I'm sorry. I know I shouldn't have taken off. I know you needed me."

"It's okay. But . . . are *you* okay?"

"Maybe I should just . . . leave."

"Raina, you don't have to leave. You're not alone—"

"But I am, see? Aunt Liza will be furious with me, and besides her, I have no one. I certainly can't ask your family for help—"

"What are you talking about? Of course you can! You're a part of our family now."

Raina shook her head. "No, I'm not . . ."

"Yes, Raina, you are. With or without Casper—or Owen, for that matter." Grace couldn't stop herself from reaching out, pulling Raina to her in a tight hug.

Raina surrendered with a shudder.

"It's going to be okay." Grace smoothed her hair. "We'll figure it out." She put Raina away from her, met her eyes. "God is going to do something good, something more with this, I promise."

Raina tried a smile, but it fell.

"Are you still up to catering? Because I fear they're falling apart in there."

"I probably shouldn't tell you this, but I thought I saw smoke coming out through the double doors earlier."

Grace didn't wait for Raina to get out of the car.

"Perfect—191.3." Max pulled the thermometer out of the pig's hindquarters. The skin had roasted to crimson, the scent of the pork enough to reduce him to caveman. He could nearly taste the meat, juicy and succulent, dripping off the bone.

"Let's get it onto the platter and cover it with foil until the party gets here."

The sauce simmered on the stove. Max went into the kitchen, lifted the lid. The juices had soaked into the carrot and onion, the smell a mix of spice and sweetness. He stuck in a wooden spoon, tasted it. Tangy and sweet, but it lacked something. The flavors seemed too different, too unique to meld together.

He put the top on. Stared at the mess he'd created.

"Max?"

He turned, and for a second, his heart stopped. Grace stood in the doorway, her hair in waves, tied up with flowers and ribbon, beautiful strands cascading around her face. She wore a blue dress, short, V-necked, and from her fingers dangled a pair of gold high-heeled sandals.

"You look . . . beautiful."

She came into the kitchen. "What are you making? Did something burn in here?"

He stopped her with his hands on her shoulders. "Listen. I got this. I know I was gone, but I'm back now—"

"Gone. Max . . ." She shook her head. "You left me."

True. "I'm so sorry—I wanted to call, but my phone died and—"

"Shh." She held up her hand. "It's okay. I don't care."

She didn't?

He stood there like an idiot, hoping she couldn't hear his heart drumming in his chest. "Grace, I have to talk to you—"

The sauce bubbled over, out of the pan.

"Oh!" He turned and took off the lid while she cut the flame.

"What is that?"

"It's a red onion, carrot, and citrus glaze."

"For the . . . ?"

"Pork."

"What happened to the gingered-mango sauce?"

"It burned. And then we ran out of mangoes."

She stared at him, undone.

"But we found oranges and carrots and onions, and Max put it all together . . . ," Ty said.

Grace looked at Ty, and he slunk back into silence.

Raina appeared at the door, her face red, puffy.

Max wanted to ask but decided to keep his question to himself as Grace picked up a wooden spoon.

She tasted the sauce. Rolled it around her mouth. "It's good, Max."

He wanted to drop with relief.

"It just needs to be . . . hmm . . ." She turned to Raina. "Don't we have a blender somewhere?"

Raina fetched it from one of the racks, brought it to her, and plugged it in.

Grace ladled in some of the sizzling mixture from the pan. She put the top on. Glanced at Max with a smile. "Look at you, living dangerously, making mistakes."

"Nothing's a mistake with you, Grace." Oh, he wasn't sure what desperation drove him to say that, but he let his words hang there. "I'm so sorry I wasn't here."

"I forgive you," she said quietly. Then she hit Blend.

The sauce whirred together, the onions and carrots juicing into the mixture. She kept it going until it was blended. Then she turned it off and removed the top. Took a spoon and tasted it.

"You're not going to believe this," she said and handed him a fresh spoon.

Yes, he just might. Nothing bitter, just smooth and delicious, with a hint of ginger, garlic, the tangy sweetness of the carrots and oranges, blended so perfectly that they made an exquisite sauce.

"You amaze me," he said. "You need to know that."

"But you're the one who made the sauce."

"No, I just brought the ingredients. You added the magic." He took her hand. "Really, please, I need to talk to you."

"We have a pig to serve."

Oh, for . . .

"I got this," Raina said. "Ty—let's get this pig onto the serving table. Someone finish blending the sauce, and then, please, people, let's make sure we don't forget serving spoons."

She reached for her chef's coat as Max tried to pull Grace out of the kitchen.

"Max, I need to be here. We have so much left to do; we have to get the bread and salads on and—"

"Your team has this. You've trained them. Besides, Raina's here."

"Yeah," Raina said, putting on her coat. "I'm not going anywhere."

"See?" Max said. "It's time for you to get out of the kitchen and into the party."

Grace glanced back at Raina, but Max still had her hand, pulling her out into the reception area. He could hear voices, people starting to arrive. In the corner, the band was setting up.

He found her gaze, lost himself for a moment in it, then conjured up the words he had to say.

Courage. *Focus on life.* "You need to be here. With me. We never finished our conversation at the park, and there's something you need to know—"

"I already know, Max."

She did?

And then he saw it on her face, the truth in her smile, sad and edged with pity.

"Jace told you."

She nodded. "*You* should have told me."

He drew in a long, steadying breath. "I know. But I was . . . I was afraid." He took her by the shoulders. "And you should be too, frankly. It's not like cancer. This disease is going to take me from you slowly, like Alzheimer's and Parkinson's put together. I'll lose my mind and my body one agonizing step at a time. I'll start dropping things and forgetting things you say to me. I'll lose my balance, my ability to speak. Then I'll slowly lose my mind, even become irrational. I'll stop being able to care for myself. You'll have to feed me. And in my worst nightmares, I'll linger that way for years."

Her expression had become more solemn, as if finally the truth had sunk in. But there was more.

"Grace, the worst part is, you'll have to suffer through this alone. I can't give you children. I'm sterile—on purpose."

She nodded. "I understand."

He winced. "No—every time I look at you, I see family. A home. A long life with the one you love—this is what you want. And exactly what I can't give you."

Suddenly her expression changed again. She smiled, something so tender in her eyes, it could crumple him. She slid her hands up to cradle his face. "Oh, Max, don't you get it? You can give it to me—just not how I'd planned. We don't have to have a long life to be happy. The tragedy doesn't have to steal our joy. Has it occurred to you that maybe God brought you into my life not for your good, but for mine? That maybe it would be my *privilege* to walk through this with you? There are no guarantees in life, and we can't keep from living—or loving—just because it might be dangerous. Max, I—"

"Sharpe, you have about five seconds to get out of here before this gets ugly. And I promise you don't want that."

Max froze as he looked up and saw Owen

headed for him. His former teammate, despite being dressed in a suit, wore a patch over one eye, sick and clear evidence of Max's mistake.

"Owen . . . man, I'm sorry." He backed away from Grace. "Listen, we need to talk. I am so sorry about—"

"Owen, back off!" Grace's voice shrilled between them.

Owen stopped short, looking down at her.

She'd turned her back to Max, stepping between him and her brother. "You're going to listen to me whether you like it or not. You're a mess. You're angry and hurting; we all get that. And we love you. But Max is not to blame for your pain."

"Are you kidding me? He's totally to blame—"

"No, he's not. You are. It was a terrible accident; no one is denying that. And Max feels terrible about it. But guess what—your life isn't over. You're not dead. You have choices about the way you treat people and how you live."

Owen's face tightened into a frown. "You're seriously siding with Max? Over me?"

Grace seemed to hesitate for a second, and Max wanted to step in, to rescue her. *No, Grace—*

"Yeah, Owen. I choose Max. Because I love him. I love him more every day I'm with him. Max is amazing. He's kind and patient and frankly a thousand times braver than you've been lately. He's the kind of guy I was hoping to find someday. He gets me and makes me believe I can do more than I ever thought I could."

Max was trying to make sense of her words, but as he looked at her, the truth began to blossom inside him.

"Most importantly, Max is *God's choice* for me. Max is the gift, the *more* that God has for me, for as long as God will keep him on this earth. So you're going to figure out a way to forgive him or make the choice to walk away from both of us."

Owen's jaw tightened. "Awesome. That's just awesome." He strode away, but Max didn't care one more second about Owen and his anger, his issues.

Max is God's choice *for me.* Those words he grabbed ahold of.

Really, God? Even with . . . even with . . .

Grace turned. Vanished from her eyes was any trace of the pity, the sadness. "If he'll have me."

If he'll have . . .

That was it, wasn't it? Right now, right here, he could choose to share his life—the good, the bad, the ugly—with her, letting himself choose her too. Or he could walk away.

Courage.

"Oh yeah, I'll have you, Grace. For as long as I live. But are you sure? What about kids—?"

She put her hand to his mouth. "If God wants us to have kids, we'll have kids. We can adopt, and they will still be our own."

He touched his forehead to hers. "I'm God's choice?"

"I believe you've always been God's choice for me, even before I sat in 9B."

Max grinned. "Yeah." Then, with one quick movement, he swung her into his arms.

"Max!"

But he ignored her as he took the stairs all the way to the second floor, emerging onto a flat-roof deck that overlooked the Mississippi River. He set her down in an Adirondack chair.

The sunset spilled across the rooftop, gold and amber.

Max knelt in front of her.

"What are you doing?"

"Grace Christiansen, here's the deal. I need a swim buddy. Forever. And I'm pretty sure that I'm never going to have this kind of courage again. I know I'm going to wake up tomorrow convinced that you're making the biggest mistake of your life. But I promise to fight that fear, to stick around and not run away if you will agree to be my wife."

She leaned forward, her eyes shining. "That's the craziest proposal I've ever heard."

"Listen, I have to work with what I've got."

She took his face in her hands, capturing him with her beautiful blue eyes. "Then you have me. I'm only giving my heart away once, and it's to you, Maxwell Sharpe. Finally, completely. And forever. Yes, I'll marry you. It's time to live dangerously. It's time to live abundantly."

He pulled her into his arms, kissing her under the golden haze of the sunset. And he knew her words would be gloriously, deliciously true for the rest of his life.

Epilogue

"Grace, hurry up—It's almost on!" Eden's voice rose over the chatter of the commercials.

Grace opened the oven, pulled out the taco dip. "Has anyone seen the serving spoons? Mom gave me a bunch." She set the hot casserole dish on a cutting board, then began rooting through the boxes still lined up at the edge of the kitchen. She'd have the kitchen unpacked before Max returned from his road trip and conjure him up something tasty to help her and Raina christen their new apartment in Minneapolis.

"Try the box marked 'kitchen stuff,'" Eden said, getting up and grabbing a bag of chips. "Or we can double dip, Grace. It's just us."

"And me," Raina said, coming out of her room wearing an oversize Blue Ox fan shirt. Her belly protruded just enough to hint at the life inside her. "But I don't mind sharing."

She'd relaxed since the move to Minneapolis, even in the short time since they'd arrived, a sort of easiness, even hope descending over her. Of course, that probably came from the fact that she'd left town without telling her aunt anything about her condition—that would be an interesting conversation. But until Grace and Max's wedding, Raina planned on hiding out with Grace.

Grace had no doubt Casper lingered not far from her mind. But she hadn't spoken a word about either of Grace's brothers since the night of Eden's wedding. Not even to Eden, who'd discreetly noticed but hadn't commented.

Time. Raina just needed time and a friend. Family.

Grace found the box, opened it. "Yeah, here's my old apron and a bunch of plasticware. Mom gave me magnets off the fridge. And . . . a folder full of papers—weird."

"She was probably cleaning off her desk," Eden said, piling her plate with the cheesy dip. She went back to the game, where the announcer had begun his between-period commentary. "You know how she likes to pile stuff. Look through it; you might find your second-grade report card."

Grace tucked the folder under her arm, then grabbed a plate with dip, giving in to the use of a chip as a spoon. Building her new business—Signature Weddings—took up all her spare time. It helped that one of Eden's guests had signed on for her first event.

She settled on the sofa next to Eden. She might

have preferred to watch the game at Eden and Jace's place, on the huge flat-screen in their family room. But her tiny apartment had a charming homeyness with the hand-me-down furniture from her parents, the blankets and quilts from home.

On the television, the announcer showed highlights of Max's goal, the way he raced around the back of the net and fell into the arms of his teammates.

How she loved to watch him embrace life.

They segued into bench shots, and she spotted Jace in one clip, his eyes dark as he yelled at the refs.

"When did Max say it would be on?"

"After the second period sometime."

Raina joined them, sitting in an overstuffed chair covered with a blue quilt. "I still can't believe he agreed to do it."

"Why not? He's so good with kids, and it's a great opportunity to reach a huge audience." Still, she knew he'd had to dig deep, trust God, to find the courage. It only made her love him more.

Grace opened the folder, began to sort through it. Christmas cards from friends, a magazine offer in an unopened envelope. It looked like a smattering of old mail, lying on the counter for months. Oh, Mother.

"When is your trip to Hawaii?" Raina asked Grace.

"January. Max wants to scout locations for the golf tournament."

"Does he even play golf?" Eden asked.

"I don't know. Probably. He does everything." And why not? Embrace life while you can.

"You promise me you're not going to do something crazy like elope while you're there."

Raina looked up, her eyes wide.

"No promises," Grace said.

"Well, I suppose it might solve the problem of Owen and his hatred for Max."

At the mention of Owen, Grace glanced at Raina. She didn't look back.

"Oh, here it is!" Eden picked up the remote and turned up the volume.

A shot of Max scoring—one of last year's clips—came on the screen. It freeze-framed and Max walked into view in front of it. "Many of you know me as Maxwell Sharpe, right wing for the St. Paul Blue Ox."

He wore an apron that bore the Blue Ox logo over his team sweater. It only accentuated his wide shoulders, his hockey physique. His hair hung below his ears, and Grace saw herself in his arms, twirling it between her fingers. Then he smiled, that Maxwell Sharpe signature grin, and she recognized the man who'd charmed her into the wide ocean of life.

He stepped over to a kitchen, where a little girl about the age of six, with long blonde braids, wearing her own matching apron, sat at the counter. "But what you might not know is that someday, I won't be fighting for a puck. I'll be fighting for my life."

Max opened the oven, pulled out a tray of cookies, set it on the counter. "As the son of a father who died of Huntington's and a carrier of the faulty gene that causes the disease, my fate is a near surety." He scooped cookies onto a plate. Handed it to the little girl. "But hers isn't. Research for a cure has made great progress, and if we can figure out a cure for Huntington's, we may also be able to treat Parkinson's, ALS, and even Alzheimer's."

He picked up a cookie, leaned down, and smiled at the girl before taking a bite. Then he looked back at the camera. "Give the gift of a future. Donate to the Sharpe Foundation for Huntington's Disease Awareness and Cure Research."

The PSA ended on a screen shot of the foundation's website and a picture of Max in his hockey uniform, about age twelve, posing with his invalid father.

The room went quiet even as the TV flipped to the Blue Ox players piling back out on the ice.

"Wow," Eden said, reaching up to wipe her eye. "Yeah, that's—"

"Eden, Max doesn't want your pity. He wants your joy, your hope, your prayers. Okay?"

Eden nodded despite her wavering smile.

"Oh, my. I can't believe it." Grace pulled a crumpled envelope from the folder. "This is part two of the application for the Minneapolis Institute of Culinary Arts." She opened it. "When did I get this?"

"What are you talking about?"

"It's an invitation to send in a unique recipe." She looked at the postmark. "It came right during all the rush of mail from Darek and Ivy's wedding. It must have gotten mixed up with it and then set aside. But . . ." Grace set the application on the table.

"So are you going to create a unique recipe?"

The Blue Ox took the ice. A close-up of Max showed his game face. Determination. Fierceness.

The face of courage.

The face she loved.

"I think I already have," she said and reached for the dip. "Now it's time to eat."

A Note from the Author

For better or worse. Richer or poorer. In sickness and in health. . . . I'll be celebrating twenty-five years with my amazing husband this summer, and as I look back, it feels like time is but a blink. Just yesterday, I was walking down the aisle to his smile, wondering how I got so lucky. And life has been generous to me—four amazing children, a rich landscape of faith-building experiences.

It's not been without challenges, however. Many a day, as I lived in Siberia, I thought, *What did I get myself into?* And we've changed, become different people. Life and romance didn't always measure up to what I imagined. Thankfully, we've had a long-term view of the game. But what if I'd been promised only five years or less? Or what if my husband had a terrible disease that required me to care for him all our days? Would I have said yes to this adventure? It's one thing to pledge yourself to love and then endure through the unexpected challenges . . . completely another to look at life knowing that darkness is ahead.

I came upon the idea for this book a few ways. First, I had a friend who married her sweetheart, knowing he had incurable brain cancer. He died three years later, and she said it was the best three years of her life.

Then I had another friend who married young,

and just a few years into her marriage, her husband came down with early onset Alzheimer's. She nursed him until she couldn't care for him any longer, then fell in love with someone else and, although it was painful, divorced her first husband and married the other man. It haunted her.

I wonder if it was the perspective of knowing what lay ahead that helped the first woman rejoice, while the second felt robbed. Knowing her days might be few, my first friend feasted on every moment and ended well nourished, the taste of hope in her heart.

So often, in this Christian life, when things don't turn out as we hope or expect, we feel robbed. As if our promise to follow God, like our promise at the altar, guarantees happiness. Frankly, God promises us challenges, so we shouldn't be surprised when they happen. But how, then, do we cope?

Psalm 84:5-7 offers answers:

> Blessed are those whose strength is in you,
>> whose hearts are set on pilgrimage.
> As they pass through the Valley of Baka,
>> they make it a place of springs;
>> the autumn rains also cover it with pools.
> They go from strength to strength,
>> till each appears before God in Zion.

Pilgrimage. The journey . . . through life, toward heaven. God offers us refreshment in the desert and places of strength along the way. What if our happiness isn't only in what is ahead of us but in embracing the now? In enjoying the moments God has given us, even in the midst of suffering? What if we lived with a mind-set of rejoicing in the strength and the springs of today . . . in order to bear the desert of tomorrow? Perhaps the annoying vices of our loved ones might not be so frustrating. Perhaps our faith wouldn't seem so starved.

I wanted to write a cooking story because we love food around the Warren house. My husband is a fantastic cook—he loves to follow recipes and create gourmet food on the weekends. I'm more of an "open the fridge and see what I can create" kind of gal. We could drive each other crazy. Max and Grace's story shows me that perhaps we are, instead, a winning team, if we're willing to embrace the moment, the current ingredients before us, and enjoy the mess we make together.

Enjoy—no, feast—on the journey, one meal, one day at a time.

Thank you for reading Max and Grace's story. There are more Christiansen family adventures ahead! We still need to rescue poor Casper, and what about Raina? Then there's Owen . . . oh, frustrating, angry, broken Owen. And don't forget Amelia—she has a few surprises in store for her.

God bless you on the journey,
Susan May Warren

About the Author

Susan May Warren is the bestselling, Christy and RITA Award–winning author of more than forty novels whose compelling plots and unforgettable characters have won acclaim with readers and reviewers alike. She served with her husband and four children as a missionary in Russia for eight years before she and her family returned home to the States. She now writes full-time as her husband runs a resort on Lake Superior in northern Minnesota, where many of her books are set.

Susan holds a BA in mass communications from the University of Minnesota. Several of her critically acclaimed novels have been ECPA and CBA bestsellers, were chosen as Top Picks by *Romantic Times*, and have won the RWA's Inspirational Reader's Choice contest and the American Christian Fiction Writers' prestigious Carol Award. Her novel *You Don't Know Me* won the 2013 Christy Award, and five of her other books have also been finalists. In addition to her writing, Susan loves to teach and speak at women's events about God's amazing grace in our lives.

For exciting updates on her new releases, previous books, and more, visit her website at www.susanmaywarren.com.

Discussion Questions

1. In her letter, Ingrid describes Grace as her clone, both physically and in her personality, her fears. Who in your own family are you most like? How have those similarities helped you to better understand that person—or yourself?

2. Several of the Christiansens encourage, maybe even push, Grace to step outside her comfort zone. Did you see their encouragement as helpful or bordering on meddling? Have you ever had to similarly "encourage" a loved one? How did you decide how hard to push and when to let go?

3. Max and his brother, Brendon, face the same diagnosis but make different decisions about how to live in the face of their eventual illness. Whose approach did you most understand or relate to?

4. Even though Raina believes Owen is different from men she's known in the past, she finds herself falling into a familiar pattern of behavior with him—one she had sworn not to repeat. Do you think it's possible for a person to avoid making the same mistakes over and over? How? If Raina came to you for advice, what would you tell her?

5. Casper sees Owen leaving town and secretly envies him. Do you think Casper is doing the right thing by staying in Deep Haven? Have you ever felt torn between your responsibilities and your dreams? What did you choose?

6. Grace's fears of stepping outside her predictable life crop up in a number of ways, holding her back from chasing her dreams, traveling to Hawaii, even trying new foods. How do you see her courage growing throughout the story? Where does she still experience setbacks?

7. Max wants to make it to the hockey Hall of Fame to leave his mark on the world and let people know he was there. But Grace argues, "People know you were there because of the people you've loved." Whose perspective do you agree with? What would it mean for you to leave your mark on the world?

8. While Raina believes that a "good person" like her aunt Liza has earned the right to ask God for an abundant life, she knows "a girl like [her] had to make her own future." Do you believe some people are more worthy of God's help and blessing than others? Are you more inclined to ask God to direct your life or to make your own future?

9. John warns Casper that "[Raina's] been hurt and I don't want you to think you can fix her. . . .

That's Jesus' job." Casper agrees but secretly hopes that God will use him to help heal Raina. How did you react to John's advice? Do you think Casper was ultimately used for good in Raina's life?

10. When Max leaves her in Hawaii, Grace is devastated, believing that "she'd reached out— no, flung herself out—on this great adventure, and God had dropped her. Hard." Has there ever been a time when you felt "dropped" by God? How did you respond? Looking back, does the situation look the same to you, or has your perspective changed?

11. In this story, members of the Christiansen family begin to learn that Max was the one who accidentally injured Owen, ending his hockey career. Were you surprised by their response? If you found yourself in their position, would you be able to forgive Max?

12. Max finally shares about his Huntington's disease with Jace, who tells him that Grace has a right to know the truth. Would you have given the same advice if Max had come to you? Do you think Max was being selfless in sparing Grace or, as Jace suggests, trying to reject her before she could reject him?

13. Max's uncle Norm, who has watched a devastating disease ravage his family, gives his

nephews this perspective: "Without suffering, we don't need more; we have enough. But when we suffer, we can't help but reach out. It forces us into God's arms, and that's where we find not only what we need, but more than we can imagine. We find Him." Do you think that's true? What results have you seen from periods of suffering in your own life? How have these times affected your relationship with God?

14. What do you think the future holds for Raina? For Casper? For Owen?

15. Grace faces the difficult decision of whether to love Max when it means an uncertain future, one far different from what she imagined for herself. Do you think she makes the right choice?

Center Point Large Print
600 Brooks Road / PO Box 1
Thorndike ME 04986-0001 USA

(207) 568-3717

US & Canada:
1 800 929-9108
www.centerpointlargeprint.com